YOUR
EYES
ON
ME

Sam Blake is a pseudonym for Vanessa Fox O'Loughlin, the
founder of The Inkwell Group publishing consultancy and
the hugely popular national writing resources website
Writing.ie. She is Ireland's leading literary scout and has
assisted many award-winning and bestselling authors to
publication. Vanessa has been writing fiction since her
husband set sail across the Atlantic for eight weeks and she
had an idea for a book.

Also by Sam Blake

KEEP
YOUR
EYES
ON
ME

SAM BLAKE

CORVUS

First published in trade paperback in Great Britain in 2020 by Corvus, an imprint of Atlantic Books Ltd

This paperback edition published in 2020.

1 2 3 4 5 6 7 8 9

A CIP catalogue record for this book is available from the British Library.

Paperback ISBN: 978 1 78649 840 3
E-book ISBN: 978 1 78649 841 0

Printed in Great Britain

Corvus
An imprint of Atlantic Books Ltd
Ormond House
26–27 Boswell Street
London
WC1N 3JZ

www.atlantic-books.co.uk

For Sandra – without whose magic *nothing* would add up

And Emmet – the reader all writers would kill for
(and who was born to play Hamlet)

'People do not change, they are merely revealed'

– Anne Enright

Chapter 1

THE SUDDEN POUNDING on the front door was followed by repeated ringing of the doorbell. Lily Power pushed her tortoiseshell glasses up her nose and looked up from the newspaper she'd been reading. The ringing didn't stop. Or the thumping. She put her mug of tea down on the kitchen table with a crack. *What the—?*

She wasn't expecting anyone. And how had someone got through the street door and found their way up five floors to the tiny staircase that led to her attic flat? Fear crackled through her as the banging started again. Whoever it was, was clearly hitting a ten on their own panic scale.

This was central London, only a two-minute walk from the Euston Road, and Lily was alone. Both her flatmates had left first thing this morning; she'd heard them clattering in the kitchen, then the front door slamming. Twice.

She was all on her own and there was some lunatic at the front door.

Panic began to rise and Lily felt her mouth go dry. She'd literally just been reading about the increase in violent crime in London, about moped gangs and stabbings. About addicts who called to the door and mugged the householder before robbing the place. *Was that what was happening now?* It was already dusky outside, would be dark soon. Lily felt her chest tightening.

The banging stopped as suddenly as it had started, as if the person was exhausted. After all the noise, the silence gaped.

Lily slipped out of her chair, the sound of her own heartbeat drowning out any noises that might be coming from the other side of the door, along with the usually comforting distant roar of traffic and the creak of the old building.

She tiptoed across to the open kitchen door, the lino cold on her bare feet, her toenails painted a deep purple that matched the faded floral carpet in the narrow hallway. Her earrings tangled in her long auburn hair as she tipped her head to hear better.

Could she hear someone crying?

Suddenly there was another thump on the front door. Low down, near the floor. Lily felt herself jump what felt like a foot in the air. Who the hell was it?

If someone was really coming to rob the place, would they bang on the door? What if one of her flatmates or someone from one of the flats downstairs had been attacked and needed help? Lily couldn't just leave them out there if something was wrong. What if they'd collapsed and were lying bleeding on the doorstep?

She tried to curb her overactive imagination; it had a tendency to run off on its own and right now it was in overdrive.

Tiptoeing down the corridor to the front door, she peeked through the spyhole. She couldn't see anything, but she could definitely hear something. The snuffle of silent sobs?

Christ, she was going to have to open it. *What if someone was lying out there injured?* The last thump had sounded weaker, desperate, somehow.

Putting on the heavy safety chain as silently as she could, Lily held her breath and began to ease the door open, immediately feeling a heavy weight leaning against it, low down. The chain rattled taut.

'Thank God …' The voice was harsh and husky, but very familiar. She felt the weight lift from the door as the person on the other side moved away.

Jesus Christ.

Flicking off the safety chain Lily pulled the door open to find her brother Jack sitting slumped on the floor. His white dress shirt was open at the neck, and a black bow tie hung loose under the collar. His suit was filthy, and his fringe, always too long, fell into bloodshot eyes.

'Oh, Lily.' His voice was little more than a croak. *Perhaps that's why he hadn't just called to her through the door?* As he turned to face her, he burst into tears.

Lily's heart hit the floor. This was her gorgeous, good-looking, first-class-honours brother who never had to work for anything but who fought a constant battle with the storm clouds of depression. Brilliance had a flip side. When he shone it was dazzling, but when the weather changed … He'd been doing so well recently, making wonderful finds for the family shop and loving meeting new customers.

'What on earth's happened? Are you hurt?' The words came out of her mouth as they went through her head.

Lily bent down to haul him to his feet, manoeuvring to hold him up as she put his arm over her shoulders. The corridor was barely wide enough for them both but she half-dragged him into the kitchen, while also trying to see if he was bleeding. *Had he been stabbed?*

'Tell me what's happened to you?'

Collapsing into the chair she'd just vacated, Jack put his

elbows on the table and his face in his hands. She could barely hear when he spoke.

'Not me. The shop. I've lost the shop. It's gone. Everything's gone.'

Her arm resting across his shoulders, Lily looked at him hard. He wasn't making sense, and he smelled like an industrial distillery, which was obviously a contributing factor. How could he have lost the shop? You couldn't lose a shop: it was bricks and mortar. What sort of party had he been at to end up in this state? Was he hallucinating? Had he taken drugs?

Rubbing his back, she skirted the table and leaning to flick on the kettle, she reached for the instant coffee. She needed him to sober up and tell her exactly what was going on.

Turning back to him as she waited for the kettle to boil, Lily was hit by a deep feeling of dread. His face was buried in his arms on the table now, and from the creases, it looked like he'd slept in his suit. She glanced at the clock – it was after four in the afternoon. Where had he been since he'd woken up in this state?

The kettle clicked off behind her and Lily made the coffee, strong, putting it down in front of him. The dread was turning to panic, her stomach churning and a dull pain spreading across her forehead.

But she knew she needed to keep calm. Whatever had happened, Jack was falling apart. One of them needed to stay in control.

'Have some coffee and start at the beginning.'

Jack slowly raised his head, avoiding her eyes, his gaze firmly fixed on the mug. He put his hands around the thick earthenware like it was a lifebuoy.

'I lost the shop.' His voice was still little more than a croak. 'Edward Croxley invited me to a poker game and—'

'But you don't play poker?'

Jack cleared his throat. 'I do sometimes. With the guys from school. Usually the top stake's a hundred quid.'

'A hundred quid?' Lily couldn't keep the disbelief out of her voice.

Jack didn't answer, just rubbed his hand over his face and pushed his thick strawberry blond fringe out of his eyes. As if he hadn't heard her, he continued, 'I don't know how but I ended up putting the shop down in the game. I had a winning hand, I know I did, but then Croxley produced this running flush.' He grimaced as if he was back there in the room, looking at the cards spread out on the table.

'Croxley? You mean the Edward Croxley who used to organise those rave parties and got arrested?'

Jack nodded slowly. 'He only got a suspended sentence for possession in the end. He deals in art now.'

Lily looked at him. '*Only?*' Then it began to sink in. 'You bet Grandpa's shop? In a game of cards, and you lost it?'

'I wanted to die when I woke up and realised.' His voice dropped to a whisper. 'I've been standing on Waterloo Bridge for hours looking at the water, trying to work out how to tell you. It was so dark. Like it was waiting for me. It felt easier than— Oh, Christ.' He ran his hand across his eyes.

Lily adjusted her glasses and shook her head, hearing the words but not quite taking them in. 'How? I mean, how can he have the shop?'

'He made me write a promissory note. It was witnessed by the other guys in the game; one of them is a barrister. I had to give him the keys.' His voice was so low she could barely hear him.

'But all your stuff?'

'Will probably be in bin bags on the pavement by now.'

'And what about George?'

'Oh, Christ, I never thought of George. I haven't even fed him today.' Jack hid his face in his hands again, his shoulders heaving. 'I'm such a total fuck-up.'

Lily took off her glasses, laying them on the counter, and pushed her fingers into her hair, pulling it back off her face and holding it tightly at the back of her head, trying to steady herself. Her stomach was a tight ball of shock and fear, making her feel really sick. She looked at him, trying to find something positive to say. This wasn't the time for shouting or recriminations – yelling at him wouldn't help anything. She could see he felt as bad as he looked. He knew exactly what the consequence of this was. He'd lost his home, his job, the family business – a fourth-generation family business.

And he'd forgotten about Grandpa's cat.

It couldn't really get much worse.

Lily drew in a deep breath, fighting the nausea, trying to focus on what she could do to make this better. She needed time to think. But time was one thing she didn't have.

'Jack, I *have* to go to New York in the morning for this interview, but I'll change my ticket so I get home earlier and we'll sort this out.' She picked up her glasses and put them back on, gripping the back of the chair hard as if it was a life buoy. 'But first I need to find George and bring him here, and you need to eat. There's a pizza in the freezer – I'll stick it in the oven. You can sleep on the sofa here tonight and then have my room while I'm away. I'll call that solicitor that sorted out Grandpa's will and see what he says.'

Jack looked at his coffee cup again. 'He won't be able to do anything. Croxley got me pissed and cheated me out of the shop, and I was such a fucking idiot, I let him. I should have jumped. I couldn't even do that right.'

Chapter 2

VITTORIA DEVINE FLUNG her cabin case onto the cream jacquard duvet cover and reefed open the zip, catching her nail in the process.

'*Merda.*'

Reacting as much to her tone as to the unexpected arrival of the suitcase, Tchaikovsky, her huge black cat, dove off the bed, where he'd been sleeping, and disappeared under the dressing table. Vittoria barely noticed. White-hot rage was shooting through every vein, making her head pound. Marcus always joked that she exploded like Mount Etna at the slightest inconvenience, her Sicilian temper much too big to be contained in such a slight person. And right now that was exactly how she felt.

But this time it wasn't just about him not coming home for dinner.

How could this even be happening?

The moment Vittoria had ended her call to the detective in London, she'd known she needed to get out of the house and out of Dublin. She needed to think. To really think this time. The plans she'd made so far hadn't gone the way she'd wanted at all, and now this? This was a whole new level of treachery. She ran both her hands into her dark glossy hair and closed her eyes tightly.

After everything, how could Marcus have done this to her?

She'd known something was going on, something more serious than all the other times. She wasn't sure why – maybe it was the calls, the absences: he'd been spending longer than usual in London at 'meetings' between flights for months now. Like today – he was supposed to be coming home this afternoon but he'd suddenly been called into a meeting *apparently*, and it was someone's leaving do on Friday night so he wouldn't be back until late Saturday. Vittoria scowled, remembering their hurried conversation following his text this morning. Even when he was at home in Dublin, he was decidedly distracted. She'd had a quiet word with Aidan Kelly, his best friend – well, he was friends with them both – but he hadn't been able to tell her much. Then, a couple of months ago, it had suddenly hit her, the dual realisation this could be a serious affair and that she couldn't take any more.

And worse, she couldn't simply leave him.

Their prenup ring-fenced Marcus's family properties and money, regardless of the reason for the split. She hadn't looked at it in years but she knew it meant she'd have nothing. She should have known when she signed that she was being a total idiot. And now she was trapped like a bird in a jewelled cage, the bars legal documents weighted in favour of her husband, preventing her from taking her half of his family money, no matter why she left. She was only twenty-eight, for God's sake – she couldn't live like this.

Vittoria stared at her open suitcase, her mind whirling. Her first effort to find a solution had already been a total disaster. *Merda.*

Hiring the detective had seemed like her only option after that, but what he'd turned up was so much worse than she'd imagined.

How could Marcus get involved with someone who would trap him like this? Like *this*?

Now she had to come up with a proper plan. One that worked – one that would save her sanity. And she needed to get away, to get some headspace so she could concentrate on making it work; she couldn't afford another screw-up.

Vittoria picked up her phone from the bed and dialled the office. She hated to let down clients but she needed some time out. She couldn't help with anyone else's mental health unless she was in a sound place herself. And right now she felt like she was standing on the edge of a precipice, unknown waters churning below her. Her receptionist answered on the first ring.

'The Devine Practice.'

'Ruby, would you cancel my appointments for tomorrow and Friday, move them to Monday? I think there are only a couple, nothing serious.' Vittoria fought to keep her voice calm.

If her receptionist was surprised, she didn't show it. 'Of course, will do. Will you be on the phone?'

'Only for an emergency.'

'Yana was on just after you left – she said something about an article coming out this weekend? To remind you in case we got swamped in calls.'

'Oh, yes, I'd forgotten about that. It's about her anorexia almost ending her career. I'll call her. She was OK otherwise?'

'Yes, very chirpy. We were chatting for ages. She's absolutely loving being in Covent Garden. She's sending you tickets to the opening night of *Swan Lake* – it's next month, I think she said. She's so excited – she said rehearsals are gruelling but it's a wonderful interpretation.'

'That's good news at least, and thank you, Ruby. I'll be in on Monday.'

Vittoria ended the call and stared at her phone for a moment. She spent her days listening to people's problems, women like Yana, helping them through the minefield of body image, relationships and celebrity, and here she was, trapped and in trouble, and she didn't know where to begin. She still couldn't believe what she'd heard this evening. The absolute horror of it. The detective was so meticulous. Too meticulous.

Women didn't get pregnant by accident these days. That just didn't happen – had they planned it together? Maybe Marcus had finally found a bit of skirt that was more than mistress material. Maybe he'd been looking for a baby mama all these years and that's what all the affairs had been about.

Vittoria felt suddenly very, very sick. She couldn't let her head go there, couldn't think that that could be a possibility.

As if echoing her mood, she suddenly felt the muscles in her lower back twinge and begin to knot. She rubbed the spot and stretched, waiting to see if it would spasm. The trauma of the car accident was locked away deep inside, but her body wouldn't let her forget it. That or her shattered dreams that one day she would have children who would sail and ride and maybe dance, like she had. Memories began to bubble to the surface, and suddenly she was right back there as if it was happening all over again: *their argument over him chatting up some girl at the party, her storming to his open-topped sports car, so angry she couldn't get her seat belt buckled.*

They hadn't even been dating for long.

The scenes were like the stills from a horror film that played in black and white on the wall inside her head. Vittoria closed her eyes, breathing deeply, trying to fight the memories. *The moment of impact, the pain and the black fog that had enveloped her like a thick, suffocating cloud of volcanic ash. Hearing Aidan's voice as she emerged from the coma, the tears, hot on her face, as he told her what had happened.*

At times like this it was a battle to keep the memories from overwhelming her – there were reminders of that night and her lost career everywhere, from the moment she put on the radio in the morning to the twinges in her pelvis after her daily swim.

A part of her darkened as memories jostled for attention, like ghosts crowding in. She still yearned for that life, for what she'd thought her future held. She'd dreamed of being a prima ballerina – just like Yana – all her life, remembered the elation when she'd won the scholarship to the Royal Ballet School. She'd been fourteen, her idea of boarding school coloured by Harry Potter, the stunning White Lodge in Richmond that was to be her home for the next four years like a regal Hogwarts where the magic was the music. She'd missed the Sicilian sunshine and the beach, but not enough to make her homesick – she hadn't looked back from the moment she'd walked through the door.

And then she'd met Marcus, had literally bumped into him in Charles de Gaulle airport. She'd been on her way to an audition for a summer role in the chorus at the Paris Opera Ballet. Her plane had been delayed, and as she'd raced through the airport to find a taxi, she had literally run right into him, sending his coffee all over his uniform. He'd calmed her down and put her in a cab and, to her utter surprise, had been waiting outside the audition when she came out. He was older than her, but so charismatic. As they'd chatted over coffee, he told her how he'd skipped university, getting his commercial pilot's licence instead and taking his love for speed and freedom to a career that paid him to enjoy his hobby. Six months later she'd been totally in love. And in intensive care.

He'd stuck by her, though.

And she thought he'd loved her.

There were days that had followed when her loss was just too painful to bear, days when she wanted to curl up and hide in a dark place away from the world. Only Aidan really seemed to understand. He'd known Marcus at school; Marcus had been there the day his little brother was killed. He was the only one who had any concept of what loss on this scale felt like, of what had been going on inside her head, that some days it was just …

And now this.

After everything. This.

But she needed to pull herself back to the here and now, to the beautiful house that had become her safe haven – the place where she'd swum and danced her way back to fitness – and to her cream and gold bedroom and the sleek hard-shell suitcase in front of her. To her successes not her failures. Getting back into the present was the only way she could deal with the past.

Fighting the memories, Vittoria rubbed her back, stretching again, feeling the muscles relax a tiny bit. *Thank God.* She turned and opened the wardrobe door, pulling out a red dress, deliberately looking at it for a moment, forcing her thoughts back to when she'd last worn it. The pencil skirt was fitted with a narrow black belt; it always made her feel fabulous and attracted no end of compliments.

Right now she needed as much fabulous as she could get.

Where had she worn it last? To dinner at the yacht club? No, it had been that TransGlobal Airways crew benefit dinner in New York. In the palatial Calvert Vaux Hotel. Marcus had had a fit at the price of the rooms so they'd stayed at the Barbizon instead. He'd told everyone it was because *she'd* wanted to stay where Grace Kelly had stayed.

Vittoria felt her anger boiling again. He didn't scrimp when it came to his girlfriends. To one particular girlfriend. *The jewellery, the dinners, the handbags.* The detective had told her everything.

Yanking the dress off the hanger and tossing it in the case, Vittoria picked up her phone again and punched in her passcode with an impatient thumb. If Marcus could change his plans and stay in London at a moment's notice, she could change her plans too. She pulled up The Calvert Vaux Hotel website. She needed to get away and she knew exactly where she'd stay this time.

Chapter 3

As LILY SAT DOWN in the TransGlobal Airways business-class lounge in Heathrow, she still felt sick. All she could think about was Edward Croxley and Jack's face yesterday. Could you actually kill someone without getting caught? She'd never felt more like murdering anyone in her life.

It was all such a mess.

As she'd left the flat this morning, she'd stuck her head round the living-room door. Jack had been out cold, still in his suit, lying half-on and half-off the sofa, a blanket tucked over him, George curled up on the end. The ginger cat had looked up as she opened the door, glaring at her with his one eye. Well, it looked like a glare. George had loved their Grandpa and now loved Jack and didn't need anyone else in his life. He had made that perfectly clear from the moment he'd first arrived at Power's Fine Prints and Books – she couldn't remember how many years ago. Last night she'd found him easily, predictably lurking beside the bins behind the French restaurant a few doors down from the shop. He'd spat and scratched her as she'd closed the door on his cat box and then had run and hidden behind the TV as soon as she'd let him out. Her flatmates had been home by then and the explaining had started.

Lily took off her glasses and rubbed her eyes, yawning. None of them had got much sleep. She'd heard Jack moving around until about 3 a.m. and reckoned he'd passed out eventually from sheer emotional exhaustion.

This morning, the solicitor had confirmed what Jack had said. Worse, he'd pointed out that a highly respected member of the legal profession had witnessed the transaction in writing, and his insistence that a copy of the note was written out and witnessed for Jack's benefit made the whole thing even more binding. They could fight it, obviously, but he didn't think a judge would be very sympathetic.

The only saving grace was that the 'shop' reference, it could be argued, didn't include Jack's apartment on the top floor, so they still had that. But getting in without any keys was going to be a challenge. And if they did all end up in court, it would be expensive. Very expensive.

That was the biggest problem of all – they'd had to sell Grandpa's house to meet the death dues, and the shop was hardly a gold mine. It gave Jack a salary of sorts but most of the assets were tied up in the property itself and the stock. The place was crammed with antique prints and books that Power's had been acquiring for generations. Beautiful old prints that had been such an important part of their childhood and were now colouring Lily's future. At least, the future she'd been praying for until Jack had arrived yesterday.

Around her the hospitality lounge began to fill with TransGlobal transatlantic passengers. Thoughts of Edward Croxley and the whole mess whirled in Lily's head so much that she barely noticed a slightly overweight American sit down beside her. His dark suit was unremarkable in the sea of similar suits, his head bald, glasses poised on the end of his nose, but his nationality was somehow written all over him like a sign around his neck. Had she noticed him, Lily might have wondered why, with all the seats that were free, he had come to sit down right next to her.

The American opened his phone, switching it to camera mode.

But Lily was still busy with her thoughts. She could feel the pain that had been present behind her eyes since Jack had arrived in her flat beginning to grow again. The whole situation seemed more impossible the more she thought about it and now the tablets she'd taken were wearing off. She pushed her glasses up her nose and ran her hand across her forehead, smoothing her long hair into its thick ponytail. She had ibuprofen in her bag but it was a long flight. She needed to hold on until she got on board before she took more.

Edward Croxley's name pulsed with the throb in her head.

She'd only heard it vaguely before yesterday, and now he was thundering through their lives like a forty-tonne container truck with no brakes.

Bastard.

She still couldn't believe what he'd done, but it had happened, and she'd gone down every possible route in her head looking for a way to sort it out. There just wasn't one. Jack had lost the shop and, essentially, his home, his job. Everything generations of Powers had worked for. Everything he'd worked for and loved. In one evening.

Lily's stomach had been churning all the way to Heathrow and by the time the train doors had slid open she'd been feeling really sick. She wasn't sure if the migraine that was threatening had been brought on by the shock or by pure anxiety. *This was supposed to be the trip that changed her life, the chance of a lifetime.* This massive opportunity had come to find her, and the next thing she knew, Jack was banging on the door of the flat, his world in tatters.

She'd barely been able to sleep from the day the email had arrived from No. 42's human-resources director at their New York headquarters.

They wanted to offer her a job.

A proper job.

One that paid real money, doing the thing that she loved most in the world: designing jewellery. *That just didn't happen in real life.*

They'd seen her final-year show at Central Saint Martins and wanted her to go over to New York for a 'chat', to see what she thought of the place, to see whether she'd like to work with their team. Part of her just wanted to scream *yes*. In all honesty, she'd do it for free, but that wasn't very professional or businesslike. She really needed to start thinking like she was an award-winning graduate with a master's in jewellery design from one of the most prestigious colleges in the world, and not like a desperate, broke student.

She still couldn't really believe it. She'd spent those next few days after the email had arrived in a whirl, working out what to wear, thinking about what she needed to take with her, practising what she would say. It was New York, for God's sake. *No. 42* in *New York*.

And then Jack had arrived yesterday evening and told her what a swindling, despicable bastard dirt-bag Edward Croxley was. Lily didn't have enough adjectives in her vocabulary for her complete and utter hatred of Edward Croxley. And she wasn't even being dramatic.

Jack had literally wrung his hands as he'd sat at the kitchen table last night. He couldn't look at her. *He'd been about to jump off Waterloo Bridge.* Her big brother. Lily felt tears prick her eyes. The shop was only a shop at the end of the day – yes, it was history, their history, it was their last link with their grandpa, but if losing it had seriously made Jack think about ending his life? That made this whole thing a big step-up from just being a total disaster.

If he'd jumped and she'd found out why, she wouldn't even have bothered with the not-getting-caught bit of murder; she knew she'd have taken her sharpest pair of pliers and buried them in the middle of Edward Croxley's slimeball back.

Lily could feel herself getting angry again at the thought – seething, red-raw anger that *anyone* could push her brother to the point of ending his life. That anyone could take the family business from them, the shop that was like their second home – just like that, in a flurry of cards.

Memories of the shop and their childhood jumped into her head, memories of sitting on the high stool behind an old-fashioned till, copying Victorian engravings of curling fern leaves from antique prints into designs of her own; memories of her grandpa's hearty laughter, always there after their father had died. And a beautiful three-storey house in Islington and a one-eyed cat called George who hated her.

It was all gone now. Except George, of course. Jack's livelihood, his home. All gone.

God he was such an unbelievable idiot. *But Edward Croxley was an unbelievable shit.*

Beside her in the hospitality lounge, Lily didn't see the American lift his camera up high, taking a selfie that didn't include much of him but did include a whole lot of her cleavage.

Still absorbed in her own world, Lily became vaguely aware in her peripheral vision of a dark-haired woman striding across the lounge. Petite, dressed in a simple navy sweater and leggings, she was carrying a black handbag that almost dwarfed her, and she looked like she was coming to sit down beside Lily. But as she reached them, the corner of her bag knocked into the American's hand and his phone crashed onto the floor, the screen shattering on the tiled floor. Shocked, Lily tuned in, doing a double take.

'Oh my goodness, how clumsy of me.' The woman's tone was laced with sarcasm, her accent a strange blend of somewhere European, Italian maybe, and cultured English. Despite her slight frame, she had a presence that drew the eye. Lily pushed her glasses up her nose, and as she tried to take the scene in, she caught the glint of an enormous diamond on the woman's finger.

'Jesus Christ! What is it with you British women?' The American bent to pick up his phone. One of the lounge staff swept in from nowhere and, scooping it up, handed it to him.

The woman pursed her rosebud lips, slicked with a suggestion of gloss. Her heart-shaped face was elfin with a delicate pointed chin, but the fury in her eyes was unmistakable. Lily couldn't work out why *she'd* be cross when she was the one who had caused the accident. The woman interrupted her thoughts, her tone so insincere Lily took a hasty look at the American.

'I'm so sorry. I don't know how I didn't see you there. I'm sure you can get it repaired?' She scowled. 'But I'm afraid I am Sicilian.' She drew the word out and filled it with such venom Lily could feel her eyes widening in astonishment. 'So sorry to disappoint.'

The man glared at her and, scowling himself, stood up, picking up his briefcase. Lily was sure he would bark right back at her, but instead, he stalked off across the lounge. The attendant looked at the woman anxiously.

'Are you OK, Mrs Devine? Was he …?'

The woman raised her eyebrows, her dark eyes connecting knowingly with the lounge attendant's. 'I think so. Again. We have many words for men like that in Sicily, but in Ireland they say *sleeveen*. It's a good word, I think.'

The attendant rolled her eyes. 'Can I get you both a drink? Perhaps some Buck's Fizz?'

'Oh, I'm not—' Now completely confused by their exchange, Lily reached for her leather satchel, but the woman with the handbag patted the air as if to tell her not to worry and smiled at the attendant, her demeanour changing.

'That would be lovely.' She turned to Lily. 'Do you mind if I join you?'

'Please do, but I—'

'It's OK,' sitting down beside her, the woman lowered her voice, 'everything's complimentary.' She smiled. 'Enjoy it. I'm sorry to intrude on you like that but that man is ...' She rolled her eyes again, leaving the sentence unfinished. 'He was trying to take a photo of you. An inappropriate photo.'

Lily's mouth fell open. 'I didn't— Why?'

'I guess it's how he gets his fun.' She shrugged, her face full of concern. 'The air crew have constant trouble with him. He's been warned that he'll be banned from TransGlobal. That's stopped him groping them, so now he latches onto female passengers instead. Hopefully not today.'

Lily's eyes widened in horror, the full meaning of what had just happened suddenly registering. 'Yuck. Well, thank you for intruding – I had no idea, I was miles away. I didn't even know he'd sat down next to me.'

'I could see that.' The woman grimaced. 'We shouldn't have to deal with this sort of thing at all, but there are some very unpleasant people in this world. Are you a student?'

Unpleasant people? She had that right. Lily could think of one in particular.

Lily blushed hard. 'A recently graduated student, trying to look like she travels business class every day. How did you guess?'

The woman smiled warmly. 'You're grand – you look perfectly at home. It's nice to have someone to talk to who isn't wearing a Savile Row suit.'

Lily smiled, hesitating nervously for a moment. 'Do you fly a lot?'

'Quite often, mainly for business, but my husband's a pilot with TransGlobal, so I know all about Mr Hammerstein. Fortunately, I haven't had the pleasure of meeting him too often, thank goodness.'

'Thank you *so* much.' Lily shook her head. *How could she have missed that? Dear God, her Creepsville radar was usually very finely tuned.* The absolute last thing she needed right now was getting harassed in mid-air. 'I think I'm having one of those weeks.' Lily paused. 'It's been a total disaster and then I was supposed to be flying with Delta but there was some problem and my ticket was switched …'

Lily sighed inwardly. Really nothing else could go wrong this week. It just wasn't possible. Thank God this lady had intervened here. And, even better, it seemed she was able to help guide her through the complex world of business class air travel. Whatever about going to New York, she hadn't got the job yet, and she'd looked longingly at the pastries on the buffet table when she'd arrived, wondering if she could afford them. But then she'd started thinking about Croxley and the rage inside her had literally blotted out her hunger. She needed to calm down, if only so she could work out what to do about Croxley a bit more rationally. *There had to be something – some way of getting the shop back that she hadn't thought of yet.*

But this woman was a welcome distraction. She had that distinct European elegance, that Audrey Hepburn look that Lily had always admired but had never been able to work out how to pull off. Her dark hair was one length, thick, cut in a long bob, and she wore her sunglasses on the top of her head, casually holding it back. Lily took a discreet glance at her hand. The diamond was marquise cut, a really clear, pure colour, and had to be at least three carats.

'Did you say you were Italian?'

The woman smiled. 'Sicilian. But I've been living in Dublin for a long time and I went to school in England. Vittoria Devine – my husband's actually the Devine, or so he'd like to think.' She put out her hand, the diamond flashing again. Lily tried to stop herself from looking at it. Instead she put out her own hand.

'Lily Power. My mum's half-Irish. Well, she's from Boston so really she's American, but she thinks of herself as Irish – she lives near West Cork now.'

Vittoria smiled knowingly. 'Some Americans are more Irish than the Irish. But Power's an Irish name. We have Power's Irish Whiskey. You must have lots of Irish blood.'

'Way back my father's family were Irish too.'

'I can see it in your colouring, the red hair.' Lily pushed her glasses up her nose and blushed. 'You'd fit right in, in Dublin, much better than I do.' Vittoria laughed. 'I haven't even picked up the accent.'

'Oh, you have a bit. One of my friends in college is from Ireland and she says "grand" all the time. Whenever we meet I end up saying it too. I pick up accents too easily.' Lily grinned. 'You don't sound very Italian, though.'

Vittoria pulled her sunglasses off her head and slipped one of the arms into the neck of her sweater, making herself comfortable. 'I was very young when I left Sicily, and my dance teacher was English, so I've spoken both languages since I was able to walk. Sometimes I wished I sounded more like I was *from* somewhere.'

The attendant who had spoken to them earlier arrived with two tall slim glasses on a tray, her expression apologetic. 'I'm afraid the flight's been delayed by at least an hour. Can I get you something to eat?'

Chapter 4

'**G**OOD MORNING, Miss Power, can I take your jacket?'
Lily looked at the flight attendant in surprise. *How did she know her name?* 'Please, that would be great, where …?'

'Don't worry, I'll drop it back to you when we land. Come and sit down and make yourself comfortable.' She took Lily's denim jacket.

Lily glanced back at Vittoria, grinning. 'I'll see you in New York.' Her headache had lifted and they'd been chatting easily while they'd been waiting, the excitement of the trip finally bubbling through the horror of the previous twenty-four hours. Vittoria had been lovely, telling her all about New York, making her feel a lot less nervous.

As the flight attendant showed her to her seat, Lily could feel the champagne she'd drunk had gone to her head. *This was such a surreal experience.*

She was in business class.

She'd shrieked when she'd seen the tickets. Business class? She was working shifts in a coffee shop in St Pancras, had spent the last year living on baked beans and pasta. And now here she was in another world where everything was restful shades of grey, all sleek lines and complimentary champagne.

Each seat was in its own pod, with space to work or relax. And had its own TV screen. And a menu. And blankets.

24

Sitting down, Lily pulled out the thriller she knew she probably wouldn't be able to concentrate on enough to read and pushed her worn leather satchel under the seat, out of the way. She needed to look like she was doing something. Everyone else seemed to have Samsonite flight cases and leather carry-on luggage. They all looked busy and corporate and important.

Lily leaned forward to pick up the matt gold menu and surreptitiously looked over her glasses to the other side of the aircraft. Businessmen were settling into their seats, chatting to the flight attendants, obviously familiar with the routine and the pre-flight safety announcements. They all seemed so relaxed. Lily opened the menu, all complicated folds and lists of champagne and cocktails, and tried to focus on it.

She'd had such a lovely chat to Vittoria, had been distracted from the whole Croxley mess long enough for her to start enjoying the flight experience. But now that she was on her own again, it was all coming back like the cloud that had enveloped Jack, suffocating her and sucking her in. *How could she make this right?* The only way to get Jack back on track was to get the shop back. What would he do without a job, without a focus, if she was on the other side of the world? He'd gone through terrible depression when he'd been in school, just after their father had died, had lost so much weight with pure anxiety they'd thought he had anorexia. *There was no way she could let that happen again.*

She had to find a way to get the shop back.

She couldn't let Jack slip into that dark place he'd been in before. As Lily sat back in her seat, she suddenly felt overwhelmed. Perhaps it was the alcohol or lack of sleep, but unless she could get the shop back, *how* could she take this job and leave Jack behind on his own? It all suddenly felt impossible. Tears began to fall, hot on her cheeks. Lily reached down and wrestled a tissue out of her satchel, lifting her glasses so she could dab her eyes. She blew her nose.

The captain made an announcement but Lily didn't hear it. As Jack's face filled her mind, a deep pain began to form inside her chest.

She'd been devastated when their grandpa had died, a tragedy made so much worse by having to sell his home, their home, to pay the inheritance tax. The shop was all they had left. Jack was the fourth generation Power to trade in antique prints and books in Great Russell Street. That's why he'd studied art history, after all; he'd worked beside their grandpa, learning the trade every evening and weekend, since he was fourteen, and he had Rupert Power's instinct. He loved the shop as much as she did. She closed her eyes, her tears flowing freely.

And Edward Croxley had taken it and had pushed Jack to right to the edge.

'Oh, Lily, what's wrong?' A voice beside her interrupted her thoughts. Startled, Lily turned to find Vittoria sitting in the pod next to her, leaning across the divide, offering her a tissue. 'Please, take it. I've lots. Are you frightened of flying? You should have said.'

Lily was suddenly conscious of how awful she must look, of her red eyes. No doubt her nose was bright red too. She blushed, which made everything worse. 'Thank you, I'm sorry … It's not the flight.' Lily sniffed and dabbed her nose.

'Do you mind me sitting here? I asked the crew to move me, but if you'd rather have some peace?'

'No, no, please stay. I'm sorry.'

'Please don't apologise. Really, cry as much as you need to – it's good for you.'

26

Something about the way she said it surprised Lily, made her think that Vittoria had done quite a lot of crying herself and knew exactly what she was talking about. *But she looked so perfect. She was married to a pilot, had beautiful clothes – and diamonds – travelled to New York regularly. What could be wrong in her life?*

Leaning over, Vittoria squeezed her arm. 'If you'd like to talk we've got plenty of time.'

Lily took a deep breath; could she tell Vittoria? 'Something happened to my brother and I don't even know if I'm going to be able to take this job. It's such a huge move.'

'My God, is he OK?'

Lily grimaced. 'Physically, he's fine, but … he's had some issues in the past. And, well, he's in a really bad place right now.'

'But you've worked so hard. You're so talented. Could he not go to New York with you?'

Lily shrugged. She'd told Vittoria all about the job as they'd waited for the flight. She'd wanted to see her designs, had been fascinated by the piece that had won her an award in her final year, making Lily glow with embarrassment.

'Look, whatever's happened, there must be a solution. Tell me about it – I'm good with problems. I've got my fair share too.'

And a little piece of Lily's heart broke all over again. What did they say about the compassion of strangers? Vittoria had been so interested in hearing about Lily's life, about her jewellery and ideas, did she really want to hear her problems as well? *All of them?* She really didn't seem like the type of woman who had worries, and if she did, money certainly wasn't one of them. Lily was sure it was a very long time since she'd had to have beans on toast for dinner, if ever. But there was something about the way Vittoria had said she had problems too – Lily could hear a sadness in her voice.

Lily hesitated for a moment. Did she really want to talk about her brother's mental health, about the mess he was in? It was worse than any bad dream.

But Vittoria had been so nice to her and there was something cathartic about the thought of telling someone who wasn't involved. Being here in the totally improbable world of first class, she felt somehow insulated from real life, like it was a safe space to talk to someone she might never meet again, someone who until a few hours ago had been a total stranger.

But where did she start? Jack had finally come out with the full story last night, had told her about Croxley dropping into the shop looking for a gift and getting chatting to him, discovering they had more mutual friends than he'd realised.

Apparently.

Jack had been flattered to be asked to join the game with some of the boys he'd been at school with, boys who'd walked into their fathers' legal practices or got jobs in banking with their brothers' friends. Boys who were men now, but who had too much disposable income and no responsibilities; worse, no sense of responsibility.

'I'm sorry.' Lily stopped herself, wondering why she was apologising again. She blew her nose as the lights dimmed for take-off, the travellers on either side of them turning on their reading lights, deepening the darkness surrounding them. Lily was grateful for it, felt somehow cocooned, found it easier to speak. She kept her voice low so only Vittoria could hear. 'I found out yesterday that my brother lost the entire family business in a poker game. Actually, I think he was swindled out of it by— But, well, anyway, it's gone.' She took a deep breath. 'He loved it, the shop. He … he almost jumped off Waterloo Bridge. He couldn't tell me.'

There was a pause; then from across the half-partition, Vittoria's voice came, full of compassion. '*Mio Dio*, that's terrible. Is that even legal? How can you bet a business?'

'It's a shop. Antique books and prints. It's been in my family for generations – my dad only worked there for a bit: he was a jeweller and had his own shop in Hatton Garden – but my great-grandfather worked in Power's and first took on the shop. It was just books then and called something different – he was the messenger boy. The original owner had no children.' Lily took a shaky breath. 'My grandpa died the year after Jack left uni and Jack took over properly then. He loved it as much as I do.' Lily could feel the tears again. 'I just don't know what to do. I called the family solicitor but he said because Jack had written a promissory note for the shop and its contents, and it was witnessed, it's binding. The shop was left entirely to him so I didn't lose any of my student grants. It made sense at the time. The solicitor said we can fight it in court but it could take months and we haven't got that sort of money.'

Vittoria sighed, shaking her head, her forehead creased in a frown. 'That's just awful.'

'I've no idea what to do. Jack needs the shop. It's part of him.'

'But your parents?'

'My dad's dead,' Lily stopped for a moment, her voice a little strangled, 'and my mum's useless, to be perfectly honest. When my dad died my mum had a sort of breakdown. She went off to Cork to research her family history for a book and never came back. It'll never get published – it's about a thousand pages long at this stage and most of it is nonsense.

29

She's been doing it for years – we only hear from her every now and again.'

In the darkness, Lily felt Vittoria's hand on her arm, but she still couldn't focus. Losing the shop felt like losing the last piece of their grandfather. He'd been there for them through everything, with his wry sense of humour and incredible knowledge of, well, just everything. When she'd got her place at Central Saint Martins to study jewellery design he'd given her the most beautiful Bonhams catalogue from a 1930s sale – Fabergé and early Chanel. How could this have happened?

Jack had said it was an unlucky hand. But it wasn't. That was something Lily was sure of.

She was also certain Jack would never have even *thought* of putting the shop into the game unless someone else had suggested it. But what on earth would Edward Croxley want with a shop that was barely breaking even?

'And you're worried about taking this incredible job in New York?' Vittoria's words were soft but brought Lily back to the plane, to the dimmed lights.

Lily cleared her throat, her emotions swirling with the images in her head. 'I don't know if I'll be able to with Jack in this mess. He's got no family in London now apart from me, and no job, or anywhere to live. He won't be able to cope on his own.'

'But it's the chance of a lifetime. You can't turn it down. They've seen your work; they wouldn't be inviting you over for a chat if they didn't really want you.'

'I know. That's what makes it even worse. I need to find a way to get the shop back. I've just no idea how.' Lily sighed. 'But I've talked far too much, and I never even asked why you're going to New York.'

'I know this sounds ridiculous, but I need some space so I'm going shopping.' Vittoria smiled sadly. 'I had some bad news too. I need to cheer myself up a bit, and I need to get away to think about things, so I'm going to give my husband's credit card a full workout.'

'God, will he mind?'

'Well, he's the cause of the bad news, so I don't think he's got a leg to stand on, to be perfectly honest.' Vittoria hesitated as if she was choosing her words carefully. 'I've found out he's having an affair. I should say *another* affair.'

Lily winced. 'That's awful. Have you been married long?'

Vittoria stared ahead of her for a second. 'Too long, apparently.' Her voice was rich with sarcasm. 'You're, what, about twenty or twenty-two?'

'Twenty-three.'

'I met Marcus when I was eighteen. We were married by the time I was twenty-three. I was madly in love. He's older than me, quite a bit actually, but he swept me off my feet when we met.' She sighed, her face full of sadness. 'And I had the whole world in front of me.'

'But why would he do that? Have an affair, I mean. You're so beautiful.' It was out before Lily could think of a better way to put it, and she could feel herself blushing hard. People were always telling her she was too forthright.

'Thank you, you're lovely. But his current mistress is very beautiful. And she can give him something I can't.' Vittoria paused, her face strained as she said the word. 'Children.' Her voice was filled with so much emotion, Lily could almost feel it. She didn't quite know what to say. Vittoria didn't seem to notice, sighing as she continued. 'Which is rather ironic, really. I can't have children because of a car accident. I was in intensive care for months. Marcus was driving too fast …'

Lily reached over and touched her arm as Vittoria shook

31

her head. She put her finger under her eye, catching a tear 'Sorry. You've got me going now.'

Lily reached across the divide between the two pods and handed Vittoria her own tissues. 'Here, have one of these. And tell me what happened. You've listened to all my problems.'

'Thank you.' Vittoria smiled as the tears began to fall faster. 'I was a dancer, a ballet dancer. The school I was at in London was the Royal Ballet School. But after the accident … well, I couldn't dance any more. I had to rethink everything, all my plans, my career. I'd wanted to dance since I first heard music.' Her voice cracked. 'Part of me wished I'd died. That sounds terrible, I'm sorry …'

'Now *you're* apologising. I know the dedication it takes to get into a school like that. If something happened to me and I couldn't draw any more, I don't know how I'd cope. I understand completely.'

Vittoria smiled sadly. 'I thought my life was over, to be honest, but I had good A levels so I ended up going to university to study psychology, and Marcus proposed. We got married as soon as I left uni.' She cleared her throat. 'I've been lucky, I suppose. When I graduated we moved into his parents' house outside Dublin – his mother died just a few years ago. It's a wonderful house, and it overlooks the most gorgeous bay – some days it's like being in Sorrento. All the roads around it have Italian names.' Vittoria cleared her throat, a wistful look in her eye. 'I had everything – a handsome husband, an amazing house, and I set up my own business when we moved to Dublin. It's been hard work but it's doing really well …' The tears began to fall again. 'I've been ignoring his flings for years. He's away a lot but he always comes home to Dublin. This latest one is different, though – I think he's going to try and divorce me. His family solicitor made me sign a prenuptial agreement. His family is very wealthy and, well, my father has a restaurant but my parents always struggled. I got a scholarship to go to school in London – I worked so hard.' She faltered. 'Anyway, I didn't see anything wrong with signing when we got married – I thought we were going to be together forever.' She cleared her throat. 'If he divorces me I'll have nothing, only what I came into the marriage with.'

'Is there any way you can get out of it? The prenup I mean?'

Vittoria shrugged. 'I've checked, and unless he had assets that he failed to disclose prior to signing, there aren't really any grounds. I went into it with my eyes open. The reasons for a split aren't relevant.'

'It sounds like you'd be much better off without him.' Lily put her hand to her mouth. 'I'm sorry. That sounded rude. I'm too direct.'

Vittoria smiled. 'You're fine – directness is a very good quality. And to answer your question, I would, but I'd have to fight for a settlement. I have my own business but I don't draw a big salary from it; it's still growing. I run a clinic specialising in eating disorders and body image. I treat a lot of people from the dance and theatre world.' Vittoria let out a breath. 'A lot of my clients come to Dublin from London or LA to be treated because of the privacy I offer. They can't afford for the media or their management company to find out they might have an issue and my clinic is in a very discreet location. On top of everything else, Marcus's current girlfriend is an actress – she's in that world. It would be very easy for a few well-placed rumours to do serious damage to my business if I tried to fight him. I could end up with less than nothing.' Vittoria took in a ragged breath and the tears began to fall faster. 'I can't compete with her. She's carrying his baby.'

Lily could hear the distress and anguish in her voice. She

rubbed Vittoria's arm. The silence yawned between them, like a deep gorge with all their troubles swirling in the cold treacherous waters at the bottom. Vittoria shook her head, reaching for another tissue. 'I'm sorry, I guess I'm feeling a bit vulnerable at the moment,' she hesitated, 'very vulnerable, actually. Our house was broken into a few months ago too. I was there on my own. The man was armed. I really thought he was going to kill me.'

Lily's eyes opened wide with shock. 'My God, that's terrifying. But you don't think it had anything to do with your husband?'

Vittoria glanced at her quickly, her eyes full of fear. 'No, no, the police think he was trying to steal a painting. My father-in-law left quite a collection – we've been broken into before.'

Lily looked at her seriously, her voice low. 'But you think he could have been up to more than that?'

Vittoria shook her head again, as if she was trying to shake the idea away. 'I really don't know. Marcus got delayed that night so I was at home on my own.' She let out a long breath, staring blindly at the partition between them. 'It was horrible. I was asleep. He came into the bedroom.' Looking up at Lily, Vittoria's smile was weak as she continued. 'My self-defence lessons weren't much use at all. It's just … I'm one of these positive people who always finds a solution to things, but I feel like I'm totally trapped. And now, after everything that Marcus has done, everything he's taken from me, I can't just walk away with nothing, I can't. I'm not made like that.'

'I know exactly what you mean about feeling trapped, about not knowing what to do.' Lily paused. 'I've no idea how, but I have to find a way to get our shop back. Jack needs it.'

'It must be worth a lot, so close to the British Museum.' It was as if Vittoria needed to change the subject for a moment.

Her pain was so raw and hot Lily could almost feel it.

'The shop's beautiful. It's not very big but it's on three floors with an apartment in the attic. It's crammed full of things my grandpa bought at sales over the years. Even he didn't really know what's there. It's like a living piece of history.'

'Will this Croxley character sell it, do you think?'

Lily shrugged. 'I've no idea. I'd guess so – I can't see him getting into the antique print business. Jack said he deals in art a bit, but it's all much more modern stuff. Maybe he wants to open a gallery? I don't know why he'd want it. And we can't afford to buy it back. He'll probably sell it to some artisan coffee company who'll strip it out and paint it all pink.'

Vittoria let out a sharp breath, shaking her head. 'It's as well you're getting away. The distance will give you space to think and work out what to do.'

A smile fluttered at the corners of Lily's mouth. She liked Vittoria, and horrendous as her situation was, it was a reminder that she, Lily, wasn't the only one in the world with problems.

'It seems we're both in impossible situations.' Vittoria shook her head as she continued. 'Honestly, you just never know what's around the corner, do you? You dream and hope and you make plans and, look, we've both done so well. You're on the way to get the job of your dreams—'

Lily interrupted her, her tone ironic. 'We've both achieved so much but now we could both lose everything. It's just not fair is it?'

Vittoria shook her head sadly. Then she straightened in her seat as if she'd suddenly had a moment of revelation. 'But do you know something?' She stopped as if an idea was forming as she spoke. 'We've got six hours in the air and we're two intelligent women. It sounds like you need to sort out this

Croxley character and get your shop back, so you can accept this job—'

Lily interrupted her. 'And you *really* need to work out a way to get out from Marcus's shadow and get payback, but still hold on to everything you've built ...'

Vittoria nodded her agreement. She blew her nose. 'Why don't we see if we can come up with a plan?'

Chapter 5

As the door to her room in The Calvert Vaux Hotel closed silently behind her, Vittoria kicked off her boots and dumped her shopping on the gold Dralon sofa, heading straight for the mini bar. The decor was pure Marie Antoinette, every piece of furniture based on something French, period and ornate. Gold and burgundy fleur-de-lis, scrolled chair legs, an eighteenth-century canopy over the bed. It was beautiful but all faintly ridiculous. It wasn't quite the thirty-thousand-a-night legendary Calvert Vaux suite – she couldn't deny she'd been tempted when she booked, but even Marcus's sins didn't justify that type of insanity.

It wasn't cheap, though. She'd deliberately charged it to their joint card and he *really* wasn't going to be impressed when he got the bill. But Vittoria really didn't care. It was only two nights and she knew he didn't scrimp when he was travelling and taking his girlfriend out to dinner. He'd never had to worry about money. His father had been a high court judge, and as a senior TransGlobal Airways pilot he had a very healthy salary and he got to choose which routes he flew, which meant that he never went anywhere cold – his routes regularly involved weekly stopovers in far flung islands that were very warm indeed. He complained non-stop about how the job had changed, about how everyone was working longer and harder and how it felt like a glorified bus service these days, but Vittoria was quite sure that he used his buddy passes and company discount to make sure he wasn't stuck in paradise alone.

She mentally kicked herself. She was such a fucking idiot. '*Un fortutto idiota.*' She could hear her mother's voice in her head. Her mother been as passionate and hot headed as her father had been stubborn. He'd hated the idea of his only daughter going to London, but her mother had always dreamed big. Thank God she'd died before the accident; thank God she hadn't had to see Vittoria give up dancing.

Despite everything, though, Vittoria knew her mother would have loved Marcus – he charmed every woman he met. Which was half the problem. Vittoria had been so busy getting over the accident, getting her degree and then setting up her business, travelling to London and New York and Los Angeles to establish her client base, that she hadn't noticed how much time he was spending away. Although, when she thought about it afterwards, when she had finally realised that the non-stop texts to his phone weren't work related, quite a few things had fallen into place. And it was like a guillotine had fallen on her whole world, slicing it in half. And that had been long before she'd hired the detective.

Opening the tastefully disguised fridge, Vittoria selected a tiny bottle of gin and a can of tonic. The mini bar was limited, hardly enough to dull the day, but it was a start, and she could order more. She didn't normally drink but now she needed it. She took a sip, savouring the bite of the alcohol on her tongue. The ice was missing, but right now she wanted the hit more than the cold. It had been a long day and she had a lot to think about.

She'd landed, checked in and headed straight for Fifth Avenue, thinking that a bit of retail therapy was what she needed, but she hadn't been able to concentrate properly on shopping.

Her conversation with Lily had sent her head spinning.

Her glass in her hand, Vittoria walked across to the tall window overlooking Central Park. She was going to have a long hot bath in a minute but she needed some time first to process everything, to get her head straight so she could focus. Focus on how she could get out of her marriage financially secure, but also, as Lily had summarised so well, how she could get payback.

Marcus owed her everything.

Below her, yellow taxis vied for space with limousines outside the hotel, the lush green of the park stretching far into the distance. She couldn't hear the water from here, but sunlight sparkled off the jets from the fountains in the granite plaza, flashes of light dancing like nymphs high into the air.

Reminders of her old life were everywhere here in New York, in the Stravinsky that was playing in the lobby as she'd headed through, in the blue sky and the sunshine, in the babble of accents around her. She'd been so focused on her dancing career back then that she'd hardly noticed her surroundings, but now she could hear the echoes, feel the memories like they were something tangible. She'd come to New York several times while she was at school, to train with different troupes, to see the great ballerinas perform.

Ballet had taught her to be mentally tough, to focus, to strive for perfection. That same toughness and dedication had got her through the accident, got her a master's at university and opened the door to her own practice. She was young but she was working with people she understood like they were part of her own psyche, people who knew she had been through the same process. Dancers faced the same psychological issues that interfered with any athlete's performance – anxiety, injury, excessive competitiveness – but ballet had its special demons: a dancer's body was the instrument; it had to be finely tuned but it was incredibly visible. Every muscle, every sinew was on full view to a theatre of thousands at every performance, and body image was a huge issue.

A top dancer's performance was as much about the mind as it was about the body.

Right now, Vittoria knew she needed to summon the inner strength that had got her to London in the first place, the determination and drive that had seen her conquer her injuries and work out how she could get out of her marriage with her dignity and her bank balance intact.

She just hoped she hadn't used it all up.

She took another sip of her gin and felt tears pricking at her eyes. It was partly physical exhaustion, night after night of broken sleep. She hadn't felt properly in control since the night of the break-in. That had been less than a month ago, and then Phil, the detective, had told her about the baby. It felt like one thing after another piling on top of her.

Vittoria jumped as her phone began to ring. Putting her glass down, she went over to the chair where she'd dropped her shopping and started to root though her handbag. The phone went silent just as she reached it.

Aidan Kelly's number flashed up on the screen. Smiling, she tapped the screen to call him back. He answered immediately.

'Tori? Where are you?'

'I texted you. I needed a break. I'm in New York.'

'Your text said you needed some time out. What's that supposed to mean? I've been calling but your phone was

40

turned off. When I couldn't get an answer at the house I thought something had happened, that there'd been ...'

His voice faltered and Vittoria felt a flush of emotion for her husband's best friend who cared more about her than her husband did. Not for the first time, she wondered what would have happened if she hadn't been dating Marcus when she'd first met Aidan. And they'd become closer over the years. She couldn't count the number of times she'd ended up crying on his shoulder – about the accident, about Marcus's other women. She didn't know how she would have coped without him in her life.

'I'm fine. I'm sorry I didn't call. I knew you were in surgery all weekend. Marcus is in London – he's doing some training between flights apparently. Lots of meetings. I don't think he'll even notice I've gone.'

She heard him sigh. 'I was working but I was worried when I couldn't get you.' He paused. 'God, it's been mad. There's never enough beds and I was in theatre for twelve hours yesterday. I had about four hours' sleep and I was back on again.'

She could hear the exhaustion in his voice.

'I really don't know why you stay in public practice. Nobody can work like that – it's just mad.'

There was a pause, his response weary. 'You know why.'

She did. Late one night as she lay broken and bruised in a hospital bed, Aidan had told her about his wonderful nerdy little brother, about how he used to help Aidan with his maths homework and knew everything there was to know about black holes. About how he'd been bullied at school for, well, everything – for being too clever, for having freckles, for being rubbish at sport. About how, one day, those bullies had shoved Danny so hard he'd fallen down a steep flight of stone steps, and he'd never got up again. Vittoria had seen the whole picture in slow motion – Danny tumbling and Aidan running across the hall to try and break his fall, arriving a moment too late, Danny's neck broken, his young body damaged beyond repair. His voice had been little more than a whisper, but Aidan had told her then that as he had cradled him, helpless, tears hot on his face, he'd sworn to Danny and himself that he would never be so useless again.

And Aidan had honoured his promise, working his way through medical school to become one of Ireland's top orthopaedic surgeons.

Vittoria cleared her throat awkwardly. 'I'm sorry, you're right. And you're right to stay where people need you, where you can help the most.' She paused. 'I'm flying back to Dublin on Saturday morning – Marcus will probably want to do brunch on Sunday before he goes away next week. Can you join us? I might have to go to London myself next week.' Her voice caught.

'What's wrong?'

'What's usually wrong?' She paused. 'It's Marcus.' It took her a moment to find the words. 'His latest one is pregnant. Very pregnant, apparently.'

'Oh, Christ.'

'Those weren't exactly my words but they're close.'

'How do you know?'

'I had someone follow him. He's been spending a lot more time in London recently and I just got this feeling. It's not like there haven't been others, but this one felt different.'

'Have you told him you know?'

'Not yet. I found out and booked the ticket here. I'm still processing it, as we shrinks say.'

'You have to leave him. I keep telling you. He doesn't deserve you.'

42

'And lose everything? He could destroy my business – you know that. And after everything that's happened …'

'I know, I know, but … Who is she?'

'Some TV actress, that blonde who's in *Lies*. I need to work out the next move. I just needed a few days to think without seeing her face plastered on every bus. When I get back from New York I'll be clearer. Marcus is going to Sydney next week; he'll be away until the following weekend.'

'OK. Keep in touch, though, will you? If you disappear, I get worried. We don't need you adding to the victim statistics.' She could hear a noise in the background, his pager going off. 'Look, I've got to run, lovely. I'll see you Sunday.' He clicked off.

Vittoria sighed. She didn't want to be a statistic. And she certainly wasn't ready to become a victim of anyone – in particular, her husband's cut-throat lawyer.

Vittoria shook her head, a wave of emotion and exhaustion washing over her, making her limbs feel heavy. Between the break-in and the investigation and finding out about Marcus's latest woman, this Stephanie bloody Carson, she'd been running on adrenaline. She was physically shattered but it was emotional exhaustion too. At times like this that she wondered what she had done to deserve this level of bad karma in her life. From the outside it all looked so perfect, like a rosy red apple. But it was an apple that was rotten at the core.

And look at poor Lily – she was in an awful situation too, and she was such a talented, lovely person who was trying to look after her brother, to work hard and make a life for herself …

As she thought about Lily and this duplicitous Croxley character, Vittoria felt anger rising inside her. Lily was such an open, honest girl, obviously at the top of her field. She'd worked long hours to be the best, had been rewarded with this fantastic opportunity in New York, working for an elite brand – Vittoria knew exactly what that took, the personal sacrifice that being the best entailed.

And a game of cards had apparently wrecked it all.

And worse had almost lost her the brother whom she obviously adored.

Vittoria was an only child, had often wondered what it would have been like to have a sibling to share things with, to watch over her. She'd learned to be independent very young, resourceful and resilient; had learned that to get what she wanted, she needed to make things happen herself.

Vittoria pulled back the heavy brocade curtains to look out at the broader view for a moment, watching the tourists gathering around the fountains, looking at the traffic below. New York was always so frenetic. But despite the changing scene, Vittoria wasn't seeing it, she was completely absorbed in her thoughts. What amazed her most was, from Lily's description, how similar the men who had caused all this trouble seemed to be.

Edward Croxley and Marcus Devine.

A con man and an adulterer.

Two men who needed to find out how much damage they were doing and exactly how that felt.

Edward Croxley sounded like he came from a similar background to Marcus: he had well-off professional parents and had attended a top private school. What was it in that mix that gave these men such a sense of superiority, an assumption that they could do what they liked and get away with it, that there would be no consequences? Because the conversation she'd had with Lily had been all about the consequences.

44

Vittoria's mind drifted back to the plane. She'd suggested more champagne; Lily had looked like she needed it. Perhaps the bubbles had helped Vittoria relax, or perhaps it was finally having someone to talk freely to, someone who didn't know any of the players in the game, that had helped her focus. She hadn't dared tell anyone apart from Aidan that she'd had Marcus followed; it was like his having an affair was a sign of her weakness, *her* inadequacy, and that made her even more vulnerable. But talking about it seemed to crystallise something in her mind.

'I've really had enough now, but I'm not prepared to step back and give him a divorce, lose my home and perhaps my business. Too much has happened. That would be too easy.' Vittoria had paused, her voice low. 'I want him to feel the loss I've felt, the loss he's caused. It's his total arrogance that's the problem, like your Edward Croxley – he thinks the law doesn't apply to him either. They think they're untouchable.'

Lily had looked pensive for a minute, then said, 'You know, the rumours that you're worried about wrecking your business could be just as damaging for your husband. Being a pilot is a huge responsibility. If there was any doubt about his judgement, about his trustworthiness, he could wind up losing his job. And if he lost his job, wouldn't he lose memberships of his clubs? And he's used to a big income. That would be a bit of a shock too. I wonder what his girlfriend would think of him then.'

Lily had a point. A very good point.

And that had started a whole different conversation.

Which had given them both a lot to think about.

Chapter 6

THE SUN WAS STRONG on the back of Lily's neck as she left The Fenton Hotel and headed down Broadway for No. 42's new corporate headquarters in the Flatiron District.

Looking in the bathroom mirror that morning, bright lights reflecting off the antique marble washstand and utilitarian white tiles as she'd put on her make-up, Lily had shivered in anticipation at the thought of her interview. Interview seemed the wrong word, somehow – a 'chat' was how they'd phrased it. Reading between the lines, there didn't seem to be anyone else in the running for the job. Lily still couldn't believe it was happening. She'd put her hair up, winding it into a lacy silver clip she'd made as her very first project at Central Saint Martins. She felt it had always brought her luck. It had got her that first A grade and set her on an incredible path. She'd worn it for every exam and had been wearing it the day the email from No. 42 had arrived. Whatever happened with Jack and the shop, she needed to do her absolute best in this interview, and she wasn't taking any chances.

New York at the end of September was warmer than London and the heat was soothing after the tumult of the past twenty-four hours. The receptionist in The Fenton had said it was about a ten-minute walk to No. 42's headquarters and that the doorman would get her a cab. But Lily had shaken her head: it was a beautiful day and she'd enjoy the walk; she had a lot of thinking to do.

Nerves fluttered in her stomach as she headed south on Broadway. But as soon as she reached the intersection, Lily knew her grandpa was with her and that everything was going to go just fine. Around the bottom of the road sign was a flowerbed planted with ornamental cabbages. She'd almost laughed out loud. What were the chances?

Utterly ridiculous plants, somehow neither flowers nor vegetables, their beautiful frilled leaves always reminded Lily of the layers of Victorian petticoats. The colours were fading now, but one of her favourite botanical etchings was of ornamental kale – as her grandpa had always reminded her the cabbages were called. The artist had communicated the solidity and reliability of them, with the contrasting whimsy of so many frilled leaves but no flowers. She'd loved it from the moment she'd found it in a stack of auction odds and ends at the back of the shop, had discovered that in the language of flowers, cabbages represented profit and ambition. So what more fitting place for them than the cross sections of Manhattan?

She smiled as she turned the corner. Her final-year collection, the one that had brought her to the attention of No. 42, had been based on that print, on the glorious shapes and colours of cabbages. She'd created buttons and then a necklace of interlocking cabbage heads. Not that anyone saw them as cabbages now, in their abstract form, just their beautiful shapes. And her ambition.

*

The interview went past in a blur.

When can you start? The words rang in Lily's ears as she

signed out of the building and walked through the revolving door onto the street, the contrast between the silence of the office lobby and the roar of West 23rd a further shock.

Marianne Omotoso, the intimidatingly elegant ebony-skinned design director, had shown her into a palatial office with floor to ceiling windows on the twelfth floor. Lily guessed she was South African from her accent. Three men, one Latino and two Asian, all in dark perfectly tailored suits, were already seated on two pure white leather couches facing a low glass table. As Lily had stepped through the door she had an overwhelming feeling of light and glass and No. 42's signature lilac, and had felt for a moment like she'd been beamed up into an imperial spaceship.

They'd been full of questions but had loved all of her designs, had researched her to an almost intimidating degree. They'd asked her about her inspiration, about her father's Hatton Garden shop and about her grandfather's shop. That was what had tipped it, she'd quickly realised – very few students had her knowledge and experience of raw stones, her interest in antiques and her design skills. When she hadn't been hanging out minding her grandpa's shop, copying beautiful Victorian botanical etchings into her notebook, she'd spent her Saturdays and holidays upstairs in the tiny workshop in Hatton Garden. Her father had worked downstairs in the showroom, but his partner was a goldsmith with a passion for asscher cut stones who ran the repair and restoration side of the business. Lily still shared his workshop and had had her own bench and tools beside his for as long as she could remember.

Omotoso had been all smiles as she'd shown Lily back to the 'elevator', telling her to go to Fifth Avenue, to wander around their flagship shop. But Lily had been too distracted to do that right away; she was still in shock. The interview, chat, whatever it was, had been brilliant from start to finish; it was like they'd already decided to offer her the job before she'd even walked in the door. Well, she'd sort of guessed that from the email, from them inviting her over, but still …

Outside on the pavement, Lily was floating. So much seemed to be happening so fast. She wasn't sure if it was the warmth of the autumn sunshine or the good news or the jet lag, but a moment later she caught the scent of coffee and, tuning into her surroundings, found herself looking in the window of a coffee shop. Coffee was exactly what she needed right now. A bucket of it.

She pushed open the door and the delicious smell got stronger, helped bring her floaty head back to the here and now. There was a queue, but it moved fast, the banter between the staff and the obviously regular customers an entertainment all of its own. It was exactly how she imagined a coffee shop in New York would be. If her head hadn't already been full, Lily knew she would have spent ages just people-watching, looking at the fashion, listening to the chatter, absorbing the atmosphere.

Looking up at the blackboard over the counter, she ordered a latte. If Jack had been there he'd have ordered a 'nitro on draft' just to find out what the heck it was. For a moment a shadow passed across her heart. Jack's inability to resist temptation was at the root of his gambling, Lily was sure. He said it had only been one game, but she knew what he was like.

She'd left him the keys and told him not to leave the flat until she got back. She just needed to know that he was safe, that he wouldn't do anything stupid or get into a row with Croxley until she'd got back and had had a moment to work out what they should do next.

She'd got onto the plane with absolutely no clue how to get the shop back, how to salvage Jack's life from the mess he'd got into, but now, well, things had changed.

Her coffee in hand, Lily turned around to find a spot at the counter in the window had just become free. Setting her cardboard cup down on the polished brass shelf, she pulled out her phone, looking at the time. London was still six hours behind, and with all the problems Jack had had sleeping recently, she didn't want to risk waking him. And breaking the news that she'd got the job, now, after everything that had happened, would leave them both with mixed emotions. But she was absolutely bursting to tell someone. Bursting. Thank goodness she'd agreed to meet Vittoria for lunch.

Vittoria.

Now, in the broad light of day, their conversation seemed slightly fantastical, but that was the genius of the idea.

It was fantastical, and brilliant, and most of all safe.

And the only people who would get hurt were the people who were well overdue their comeuppance. Lily could hardly believe what Vittoria had told her about her husband. It sounded like Marcus Devine had a lot in common with Edward Croxley.

Lily knew she was normally Miss Sensible, the one who worked out exactly how everyone would get home before she even planned a night out with her girlfriends, but Croxley had changed the rules. He'd turned Jack's life on its head, he'd pushed him literally to the edge, and Lily couldn't stand by and watch Jack destroyed, not while she had breath in her. Jack might be older than her, but she'd looked after him as they grew up, making sure he changed his socks and that he ate properly; she'd been the one who had spotted his depression, who had persuaded him to go to the doctor. Their grandfather had been wonderful, but growing up without their parents they'd developed a bond that was stronger than blood. And if Edward Croxley picked a fight with Jack, he picked it with her too.

Lily sipped her coffee. It had been Vittoria's idea, really, but would she still be as keen when they met for lunch, after she'd slept on it? Lily hoped so. Right now, she really didn't have any other options, and she knew for sure she couldn't take on Edward Croxley on her own.

Lily's phone picked up the free Wi-Fi in the coffee shop, and she searched for Vittoria Devine's name.

The very first series of links that came up were about the break-in.

Lily felt the hairs standing up on the back of her neck as she read the Irish newspaper reports. Someone coming into your bedroom, into your private space, at night when you were in bed had to be terrifying. And if that man was armed? Vittoria had been half-frozen with shock but she'd had the presence of mind to hit the panic button on the alarm.

Lily went cold. What if he'd panicked and shot her there and then? It didn't say if it was a silent alarm. Lily was quite sure she would have been a basket case if it had happened to her.

Lily clicked through to another newspaper report. The Sunday tabloids had been full of speculation – a man from Northern Ireland had been seen in the area in previous days, a *well-known hitman*. Perhaps she was jumping to conclusions, but Lily couldn't help wondering if Vittoria's husband had had a hand in the man getting into the house. Was getting rid of her easier than a messy and public divorce that would have the tabloids hopping for weeks? If his girlfriend was a well-known actress, they'd just love the scandal. Had her husband hired him to kill her?

One article mentioned that it might have had something to do with a previous burglary when some valuable paintings had been stolen.

From the number of press stories, Lily could see that Vittoria and her husband were obviously a celebrity couple in Ireland, and his mother had been a well-known actress. Perhaps that's where he got his ability to string multiple women along – *his behaviour had to rely on a level of deception worthy of the stage*. Lily's heart ached for Vittoria – as if the break-in wasn't stressful enough, she'd found out about her husband's love child. It was the stuff of nightmares. Lily knew there were very few women who would come out of that experience mentally unscathed.

The Internet had thrown up pages of search results. One was a property piece in the *Irish Times* about Marcus, the pilot, and Vittoria, the former ballerina, developing his family home, adding a dance studio and a pool in the extensive gardens. The photo showed a magnificent house, Alcantara, overlooking the sea, its roof tiled a surprising bright green. How was that even news? Lily shook her head. She could see how Vittoria must feel totally exposed by her husband's affairs: the papers seemed to be happy to print anything about the two of them; what would happen if they got hold of something really juicy?

Lily pushed her glasses up her nose and clicked through to Vittoria's company website, The Devine Practice, all calming shades of cream and soft turquoise. Sipping her coffee, Lily did an image search, looking for a picture of Vittoria and her husband. It came up quickly and Lily could immediately see why Marcus Devine was popular with women. He had chiselled good looks, ice-blue eyes and greying, slightly curly hair in a trendy cut with just the right amount falling casually over his face. In the photo he was wearing a dark-grey roll-neck sweater and jacket at an event where everyone else seemed to be wearing a shirt and tie. Vittoria was standing just behind him in a figure-hugging red off-the-shoulder dress, her dark hair swept up. She looked stunning.

Scrolling on, Lily looked for more photographs of Marcus Devine. There were plenty. He seemed to be the poster boy for TransGlobal Airways. Lots of pictures of him in uniform, his hat under his arm, striding across the runway to a waiting plane, sitting in the cockpit. At film premieres and nightclubs. He was obviously a party animal. Many of the same faces appeared with him – a lot of blondes. The next photo was Marcus sailing, standing at the wheel of a large yacht.

Suddenly conscious that she could be sucked down an Internet rabbit hole, Lily checked the time. She needed to find out more about Marcus Devine, but that could wait; right now she had to get going. Lily was quite sure Vittoria was checking her out too. They'd had an instant connection, but one thing was for sure: they needed to be able to trust each other if this was going to work.

Their conversation had been a long and interesting one. Vittoria had listened to her and then, as they had got more comfortable, discovering how much they had in common, she had told her more about her own problems, about her husband's affairs. The first time Vittoria had realised what was really happening, she'd made it her business to find out exactly who he was seeing and when. Her words came back to Lily as a squad car roared past outside, sirens blaring.

'Knowing who the women were put me back in control. I found out everything about them. People are so careless online – they put out so much information, it's easy to build a picture.' Vittoria had shaken her head ruefully. 'It wasn't hard to check his personal email either – he's not very original with passwords.' Vittoria had smiled but her eyes were cold. 'He's been quite busy, but you know, he always came back to me at the end of the day. Part of me always knew they didn't mean anything.'

As Vittoria had sipped her champagne, Lily had waited with bated breath for her to continue. 'The women must get sucked in with his empty promises, the expensive gifts; he can be very convincing. This handsome man swoops into their lives with his jet-set lifestyle and lavishes attention on them. I can see how it happens. What they don't know is that, invariably, he loses interest. I'm sure they all think they're going to be the next Mrs Devine and are left devastated. I was pretty devastated after the first one, but now? Now I know it's about him, not them. About him wanting it all. He's like a child.' Lily could see how anxious Vittoria was. She kept playing with her glass, lining the foot of it up on the tray table and staring at the golden liquid inside, the bubbles rising to the surface in a constant stream. 'Soon after we were married we were out at some reception and Aidan, one of his best friends, joked that he was the most selfish man on the planet. I didn't realise it then, but he was right. So right ... I should have realised sooner.' She raised her eyebrows and did a half-eye-roll like she was joking, but Lily could see she was bleeding inside.

'But you stayed. After everything, you're still with him?'

Vittoria had shrugged. 'He's away a lot, I'm busy with my practice, so we don't have to see each other very often. I *love* my house ... I did love him. Once.'

On the way from JFK to her hotel, Lily had sat back in the cab watching the sparkling lights of Manhattan flash past, thinking about meeting Vittoria, about how strange life was. Vittoria could help her and she could help Vittoria.

And Lily needed all the help she could get.

Finishing her coffee Lily put the cardboard cup in the bin. She corrected herself mentally, smiling, pretty sure she'd need to get used to calling it a trashcan.

Everything Vittoria had told her was true – not that Lily had doubted her for a minute, but her grandpa had always said due diligence was vital in any partnership arrangement, and what Vittoria had suggested on the flight last night would change both their lives.

Back on the street, Lily hurried on. Around her New York continued to hum. The broad pavement wasn't too busy yet, although the traffic was constant. Across the road Lily could see a parking lot with cars stacked four high in some sort of fairground-esque contraption. Only in New York would they come up with a solution like that to a parking problem.

But New York seemed to be a city for solutions.

Lily put out her hand for a cab.

Chapter 7

*E*DWARD CROXLEY. Vittoria pushed her hair behind her ear and typed his name into her browser search bar. It was mid-morning but she'd only just woken up. After a long bath last night and several more gin and tonics, she had gone to bed and slept so deeply she'd completely forgotten where she was when she'd woken up. For the first time in weeks she felt really rested, and when she'd fully surfaced from sleep, and she'd worked out that she was in New York, in The Calvert Vaux Hotel, she'd remembered the flight and relief had swept over her.

When she'd got on the plane, part of her had been wondering if knowing the details of what Marcus had been up to this time had actually helped or was just eating her up inside. Hiring the detective had seemed such a good idea, but then it had turned out that he was incredibly good at his job.

A bit too good.

His notes on where Marcus had been during his last few trips to London had been detailed right down to the colour of his tie – and the flowing bohemian dresses and coat that *she* had worn.

What he'd ordered for lunch. And what she'd ordered.

And how on one occasion Marcus had gone from the hotel in Covent Garden, where they'd been at a secluded table for two, to Heathrow. And Stephanie Carson had gone in a different direction entirely. The detective had decided to follow her for a bit and wound up outside Queen Charlotte's and Chelsea Hospital. One of the oldest maternity hospitals in the city. But she hadn't been carrying flowers or picked up a gift on the way. She had had, in fact, a very small handbag. Chanel apparently. She'd been an hour inside, and then he'd followed her back to Notting Hill, to a house that on further checks had proven to be hers.

The detective, who had far too much hair for a man of his age, was actually a magician. Vittoria had smiled the first time she'd met him. He'd towered over her, although most people did, and had that solid, dependable air that came with the confidence of years of experience. He had only been retired from the Met a year or so, was still very much in contact with his police colleagues – but had obviously found his niche as a private detective. He'd done some more checks and found out Stephanie Carson's appointment at the hospital had been with a consultant. And it wasn't for Botox.

Still in bed, Vittoria reached for her glass, the freshly squeezed orange juice deliciously sweet. She'd slept through breakfast but had discovered room service offered all sorts of delights, including pancakes with piles of fruit and maple syrup, orange juice and English breakfast tea. She'd been sorely tempted by the pancakes. A million things were going wrong in her life and she knew the only way she was going to keep her head together was to make sure there were moments to enjoy in each and every day. But she was having lunch later, and even an extra session in the gym wouldn't cancel out that much food.

Perhaps it was being in New York, but she was feeling calmer today than she had in a long time. Perhaps it was because she had something to focus on that didn't repeatedly break her heart.

Pregnant. *How could Stephanie Carson be pregnant?* Marcus had always said he didn't want children, and let's face it, sleepless nights really wouldn't fit in with his social life, but had he been lying all along? For a long time, Vittoria had been so busy rebuilding her life and finding a new career, dealing with the loss of professional dance in her life, that she hadn't let herself think about that aspect of her injuries. It was only as she got older that it had started to weigh on her – she'd begun to think about all sorts of things, about legacy and age and ... and then the detective had told her about Stephanie.

If there was anything that made you want something so much you felt like it could kill you, it was someone else having it.

Jealousy wasn't a positive emotion but it had got her to the top of her class in London – she couldn't bear not being the best, and it was the same now. Stephanie had something Vittoria could never have. And that made her hate her even more. Almost as much as she hated Marcus for everything he'd done.

As well as jealousy, Vittoria had found that anger made her perform at her absolute best, on every level, whether it was on stage or at a dinner party. And, as well as her own problems, Vittoria was angry about Lily's situation.

Vittoria moved the pillow behind her up a bit and hit Enter on her phone. There was a full page of search results for Edward Croxley. The more Vittoria had thought about it, the more puzzled she was about why Croxley would want the shop at all. Lily had said it on the plane too. Vittoria had a feeling that if she could get to the bottom of *that* she'd be able to find a way to reverse the problem. She'd done some googling and then a lot of thinking about it in the bath. This morning she planned on some more research and then, if she didn't get far enough, she was going to call the detective and see what he could tell her.

Last night she'd gone online and established that Lily had been exactly right about Croxley's playboy status. He'd gone to a private boys' school and his social media was full of society events. Film premieres and parties. Beautiful women. He seemed like a younger, albeit less handsome, version of Marcus. Now Vittoria clicked back onto his Facebook page. She wanted to understand his world. She would need some sort of leverage to get the shop back – his friends might give her some pointers. Picking up the notepad and pen that the hotel had thoughtfully left on her bedside table, Vittoria started to work through his Facebook friends.

Edward Croxley certainly had a big network. From what Vittoria could see, he partied a lot but didn't seem to have any serious gainful employment. His LinkedIn profile suggested he was an event planner, but he didn't have a website, so what sort of business was that? He had almost model looks, his hair highlighted and swept back in what looked like a high maintenance cut, but wasn't quite attractive enough to get paid for it. Did these social types get paid to attend openings? Vittoria checked Twitter and Instagram. He didn't have a substantial following on any of the platforms, so perhaps not. He was, she clicked back to his Facebook page, thirty-two. That was a bit old to be living off your parents.

He had a flashy car and, Vittoria switched back to Instagram, a rather nice apartment, assuming it was his. As she went through the pictures, it certainly seemed like it was. He had a rather ridiculous looking dog, a fat pug that looked like it would roll if you tripped over it. She chewed the end of the pen. No visible means of support and plenty of money. Trust fund? Surely that would have been mentioned in one of the interviews he'd done? She opened a new search tab and scanned the results. There were several social items, one longer interview – she opened it and speed read. Nothing about trust funds. The emphasis seemed to be on his pushing his services as an event host, but she hadn't found a company that he was part of or owned.

So what did he do for money? Lily had said something about art. Perhaps that was it.

Vittoria felt her back twinge and shifted to sit up straighter, leaning over to take a sip of her orange juice, almost forgotten beside her. She opened another tab and tried a new search. It certainly seemed Edward Croxley had an interest in modern art. He dealt with both Beaufort Fine Art and Trafalgar's auction houses in London. That was *very* interesting. She'd been wondering how she might track him down but she was quite sure that the right enquiries there would give her what she needed.

Would his commission be enough for this type of lifestyle, though? Maybe. Some paintings sold for millions if you had the right contacts, so perhaps that was it.

She needed more information. Vittoria opened her email but hesitated for a moment. One thing she and Lily had agreed on was that, for any of their plans to work, not only did they need to distance themselves from each other, but also their circle of trust needed to be tiny, as small as possible. The minute that others started getting involved, things could go wrong.

The one person she felt sure could tell her about Croxley was Phil the detective. Vittoria bit her lip, thinking. She trusted Phil and he knew her well at this stage. And it would be completely logical for her to contact him to find out more about Croxley if she was going to do business with him – in fact, it would be remiss of her *not* to contact Phil to check him out. She fired off an email to him. *Let's see what he could tell her.*

A few minutes later her phone rang.

Vittoria looked at it in surprise, for a moment thinking it was Marcus checking up on her, but he'd hardly have realised she wasn't at home in Dublin yet. It was a London number. She let it go to voicemail. A few seconds later the message came through.

'Mrs Devine, Phil here. Sorry to call so late. I have some information on Edward Croxley. Could you call me as soon as you get this message?'

Vittoria's eyebrows shot up. Interesting. She rang Phil back on his mobile.

'Phil, it's Vittoria Devine. Thanks for your message – isn't it the middle of the night there? I'm in New York.'

'Oh, very nice. And, yes, almost morning, actually, but I'm on a job. I just got your email.'

'What can you tell me?'

Vittoria sat up again in bed, trying to stretch away the pain in her lower back, her curiosity piqued. This type of instantaneous reaction had to be significant. Either that or he was doing surveillance and was very, very bored.

'Several of my colleagues have been interested in Mr Croxley for some time. He was a small-time drug dealer for elite clients, but he seems to have expanded that network and is dealing in art now.'

'That's what I gathered online.'

'Have you met him, Mrs Devine?'

'No, no, not at all.' Vittoria thought fast. 'Marcus mentioned him in connection with his father's paintings. I wanted to make sure this Croxley wasn't some con man.' She kept her voice light. 'We both know my husband's judgement is a little flawed.'

'Indeed.'

Vittoria grimaced to herself. Only an ex-policeman could make a comment that sounded so loaded yet so non-committal.

Phil continued, 'I'm not sure he's someone your husband should be doing business with, to be honest. He's in the picture business alright, but Croxley was questioned over the death of a young lady called Arabella Smyth. She drowned in a swimming pool at a birthday party in Berkshire a few years ago.'

Vittoria frowned. That sounded familiar – he was right, it had been a few years ago she was sure, but the girl's family was Irish and the papers had covered the investigation for what felt like weeks. Arabella had been found naked at the bottom of the pool, everyone had taken cocaine and nobody could remember how she'd ended up there.

'Was Croxley there? At the party?'

'Yes, my colleagues reckoned he was a witness at the very least. He could have been involved directly, but they believe he knew exactly what happened and was covering up for his friends. He's one of these that thinks he knows the law better than we do. He rubbed a lot of people up the wrong way. If you come across anything that could help, I know the DCI on that job would be very interested in a chat.'

'Of course. I'll find out from Marcus what Croxley's doing now.'

'Appreciate that. If I hear anything this end about his interests in the art scene, I'll be in touch.'

'Thank you, thank you very much.'

Vittoria ended the call and pursed her lips, thinking hard. Edward Croxley had been questioned over a high-profile death. It sounded a lot like Phil thought Edward Croxley should be firmly behind bars right now. Vittoria could think of a couple of other people who would agree wholeheartedly with him on that.

The more Vittoria thought about it, the more she remembered of the case. That poor girl. You had to be so careful around water when people were drinking – Aidan was always saying it whenever he and Marcus had friends on their boat, and particularly when Marcus had insisted on throwing a party to celebrate the building of their pool at home. They'd had a huge row about that – it was her private space that she needed to train, to get her strength back, but of course he'd wanted to show it off. Vittoria sighed, putting her phone down on the bed. The last thing she'd needed when it was finished was a public reminder of why she'd had the pool house built in the first place.

But she didn't have time to dwell on the past now. This art angle was intriguing. That was something she could use to get to know Edward Croxley very easily. The Irish papers had been full of Marcus's father's collection and the stolen paintings after the burglary they'd had a few months ago. Croxley would only have to google her name to see she was genuine. Vittoria glanced at the time on her phone. She still had a lot more thinking to do but she needed to get out of bed and seize the day before she met Lily for lunch.

It was looking a lot like she really did need to spend a few days in London.

Chapter 8

'IT MUST HAVE been absolutely terrifying.' Stephanie Carson leaned across the scrubbed pine table in the centre of the open-plan kitchen in her Notting Hill home and topped up Marcus's coffee, pushing her thick blonde hair back over her shoulder as it fell forward. Her face was serious. 'Is she OK now?'

Marcus looked up from his phone for a moment and grimaced. 'Vittoria's pretty tough. She seems to be fine. Reckon she frightened him more than he did her – she can be pretty fierce when she loses her temper.'

Leaning back on the kitchen counter, shaking her head, Stephanie nursed her green tea, trying not to smile. It wasn't the slightest bit funny but he was always so irreverent. The rules just didn't apply to Marcus Devine and his world. She bit her lip. She needed to talk to him about Vittoria, about what they were going to do. She had been trying to move gently onto the subject but perhaps this wasn't the time or the best way to bring Vittoria up.

The whole thing was horrific. Stephanie knew Vittoria was still shaken by the intrusion – having someone walk into your bedroom in the middle of the night would, Stephanie knew, have left her paralysed with fear. But that didn't mean Marcus had to stay with Vittoria now. Stephanie's hand went unconsciously to massage her belly, straining against her white T-shirt, the silver stars across her chest catching the light as she moved. The whole break-in, so far removed from her bright, sunny kitchen, made her shiver with fear.

When she'd called Marcus that fated afternoon, his clipped, 'I'm in Dublin, can't talk, there's been an incident,' had had her literally pacing the floor with worry. She'd thought it had been a car accident – despite almost killing himself and writing off his car all those years ago, he still drove too fast. Thankfully, an hour or so later he'd called back, calmer, more in control, and although he'd only given her the briefest of outlines, she'd begun to relax.

It was a huge house, packed full of antiques, and had obviously attracted the wrong sort of interest. The one time Marcus had taken her there – Vittoria had been away on business somewhere – Stephanie had tried to hide her awe from the moment the high wrought-iron electric gates had started to slide back, revealing a sweeping drive and an uninterrupted view of the sea. She'd immediately understood why there were cameras on the drive and a state-of-the-art security system. He was only there a few days a week, when he wasn't flying, and managed to find enough reasons to stay in London regularly, but Dublin was his base. His friends were there, his home. His wife.

'The paper said she was lucky to be alive.'

Marcus shot her a blank look. He'd gone back to scrolling through his emails. Then, as if he'd suddenly caught up with what she was saying, he shrugged. 'There's been a lot of incidents like it around Dublin recently. Robberies. Tiger kidnappings as well. They've a big problem with gangs in the inner city. And after the last break-in … The guards reckoned he was a real professional – no fingerprints, and he had his face covered so the CCTV is useless. They think he came back for something specific – probably had a buyer all lined up. It was ironic, really. If you hadn't had that scare, I would have been there too. He could have shot us both.'

He went back to his phone. Stephanie could see from the concentration on his face, the focus in his blue eyes, that now wasn't the time to try and talk to him. She knew from experience that she needed to pick her moment. She felt her nerves flutter, anxiety opening a dark hole in her stomach. They had a lot to talk about, but timing was everything.

From the moment they'd met it had all been about timing. It hadn't taken her long to see that, while he might be almost twice her age, he absolutely lit up a room, had an inner confidence that was mesmerising. He'd seen her as Ophelia at the Old Vic and had sent the most enormous bouquet of flowers together with a handwritten card asking her to join him for a drink. As she had walked into the bar at Langham's, he'd been chatting to the barman about how to mix the best Martini cocktails, and she'd realised that, as well as being wealthy and successful, he was also very attractive. As it turned out, the whole evening had been a win–win – she could have listened to his cultured Irish lilt all night.

Even that first evening in the cocktail bar, he'd had his phone constantly next to him, keeping an eye on his stocks and shares. But she liked that. She understood drive and determination. She'd needed them both to get to RADA, and every time she went for an audition, even now, after the success of *Lies*, it was grit and focus that got her through. They had a lot in common.

But Stephanie couldn't help being curious about what had happened to Vittoria. Actually, about Vittoria in general. She was beautiful and successful but, from what Marcus had told her, very moody. One night he'd got a bit drunk and maudlin and told her he'd only married her because he felt so guilty about the car accident. What Stephanie couldn't understand was why he stayed with her at all, why he didn't just divorce her. He always ducked away from that question whenever she got close, but the more she thought about it, the more she was sure it was because of the guilt.

Things had to come to a head soon, when the baby came. Stephanie thought he'd have said something to Vittoria by now, but there seemed to be one drama after another since she'd discovered she was pregnant

She knew about the initial break-in. Nobody had been home then, but Marcus had been so upset – no amount of insurance money would replace his favourite paintings. Vittoria had been very unsympathetic, apparently, reminding him that she'd been saying for ages they should have the originals replaced with copies and keep the real paintings in the bank. It hadn't helped his mood in the slightest. And then the second break-in had happened. The Irish press had been full of it. It was almost like a real-life version of her hit series *Lies*.

'I'm amazed she didn't have the alarm on after the place had been broken into before.' Stephanie turned to refill the kettle.

Marcus looked up at her, the creases in his face making it slightly craggy, suiting the grey streaks in his carefully tousled hair, the nurtured stubble. 'Babe, do we have to talk about Vittoria?'

'Sorry, I'm just insatiably curious.' She put her tea down and walked around the table, running her hand along the back of his shoulder and kissing his ear. 'And I might write my own cop drama one day so I'll need loads of stories like that.' She frowned. 'The house is so beautiful – you can't risk anything happening when you're not there.'

Marcus looked up at her. 'You should definitely write your own show, sweet pea – I keep telling you.' He grinned. 'And don't worry, the house is very secure but getting someone to review the alarm and camera system is top of my to-do list.'

Stephanie smiled, feeling his eyes run over her. She knew from the look on his face that he wasn't thinking about his emails now, or alarm systems or Vittoria, and that was just how she liked it.

'But that's enough about my wife. What time are you due at the hairdresser's?'

She moved around the table and kissed him lightly on the lips. 'Eleven. What time do you have to be at the airport?'

Chapter 9

LILY COULDN'T UNDERSTAND a single word the cab driver said from the moment he picked her up. She'd smiled and made the appropriate noises and then looked busy with her phone, trying to avoid eye contact, cringing at the definite possibility that he'd think her lack of understanding was because she was wildly racist.

That was the last thing she wanted him to think.

His cab was spotless, smelling, rather incongruously in this cityscape of iconic buildings and constant traffic, of mountain pine. He was Eastern European, she guessed, had a broad, friendly smile and was, she was sure, quite lovely, but between his broken English, and the inflections and slang he'd obviously acquired living in New York, she was struggling to understand him. And there were only so many times you could ask someone to repeat themselves before they got really cross.

Was this what working in New York would be like? Panic fluttered in her chest as she looked out at the crowded pavements, the roads choked with yellow cabs. What if she couldn't understand people? What if she couldn't understand the people she worked with? How would she cope? Lily took a deep breath. She was being silly. There was nothing to worry about, not with the job anyway. She'd be fine with that. She had just been offered the job of her dreams – she'd be *fine*.

There were much bigger things to worry about right now.

She'd told Marianne Omotoso that she could start in four weeks. *Why had she said that?* It had made perfect sense at the time, and Marianne and her colleagues had smiled as if that worked for them – if she'd had to give in her notice in another job, it would have been four weeks before she could start, and they were expecting her to move halfway around the world.

Which meant she had four weeks to sort out Jack's mess, find somewhere to live in New York and get some clothes that looked a bit less Hackney vintage market and a bit more Rockefeller Center. She could feel the panic rising again. *Why had she said four weeks?* Lily shook her head to herself. She couldn't give up on her dreams, not after all the work it had taken to get her here. She just couldn't.

As the cab driver drew up outside The Calvert Vaux Hotel, Lily tried to make up for her inadequacy at conversation, handing him a twenty-dollar bill and waving away the change. Soon she'd have a salary and a proper job and she'd be able to take cabs whenever she wanted. He seemed genuinely pleased, which made her feel a little better, but as she stepped out onto the pavement, pushing the door to the yellow cab closed behind her, relief quickly turned to nervous anticipation.

The sort of anticipation that knotted your stomach and made you feel deep down sick. As if she wasn't feeling sick enough already.

Four weeks.

The interview had gone incredibly well, but now she was going to find out if Vittoria still felt the same as she had last night. Without the champagne, would their plan just sound totally mad? Was four weeks enough? It would have to be. Worst possible scenario, maybe Jack would be able to get a job in New York too and come and work out here?

But Lily knew that was highly unlikely. Whatever about her being a bag of nerves, he was a real home bird, needed his friends around him, his real friends. He'd been ready for the zombie apocalypse since he was eleven, but she couldn't see him leaving London. He even found country holidays a challenge.

So that meant she needed to make sure he had a job and a home before she left. That was all there was to it.

The Calvert Vaux Hotel was nothing if not impressive. Lily looked up at its soaring windows as she stood on the pavement. She could see why it was so iconic. Flags fluttered over the huge French glass canopy that covered the entrance from the elements. The pavement she was standing on was a chequerboard of black and white marble tiles, a hint at the opulence inside.

Pushing the rotating door, Lily was met by gilt and glittering lights, a deep pile cream-and-gold rug covering a marble floor, classical music filling every corner. The scent of flowers was strong from a magnificent arrangement on a round antique walnut table in the centre of the hallway. This was the type of place Lily loved to come to sketch, to sit and watch and feel.

'Lily, how did the interview go?' She spun around to see Vittoria, stunning in a fitted red dress and black patent court shoes, and any trepidation about meeting her again evaporated. Her smile was just as warm and genuine as it had been when they'd parted at the airport. Before Lily could answer, Vittoria guided her further into the hotel. 'I've booked a table in a nice private corner with a lovely view of the park. I want to hear everything.'

It didn't take Lily long to recount the excitement of the morning.

Vittoria flicked a white linen napkin onto her knee. 'If Marianne Omotoso is head of design, who were the men?'

Lily frowned. 'I'm not exactly sure, but I think one of them was finance, one an international sales manager or something and one definitely looked after their bespoke customers. They kept talking about Oli, about how he'd looked at all my designs, at my blog, at everything – he's the founder, Oli Lennon – I couldn't believe it.' Lily's hand went to her hair clip. 'They said he'd seen my clip in a photo and he wants me to do a suite of jewellery like this.'

'It's very pretty.'

Lily blushed. 'It started life as a silver tea strainer and a lace doily.' Her eyes opened wide. 'I couldn't tell them – they thought it was filigree.'

Vittoria's eyes sparkled as she laughed. 'They'll love your innovation. Why's it called No. 42? I've always wondered.'

Lily grinned. 'It's the answer to life, the universe and everything.' Vittoria frowned, not understanding. Lily laughed. 'From the book – and the film – *The Hitchhiker's Guide to the Galaxy*. The founder, Oli Lennon, knew Douglas Adams. Oli Lennon's family were South African diamond miners – actual miners not the mine owners. He said the jewellery world always saw him as an outsider – he was Arthur Dent hitchhiking through a galaxy of stars.'

Vittoria laughed. 'Well, he's certainly found his place now. No. 42's as famous as Tiffany's. I'm just so delighted that the interview went well.' She smiled. 'And you've got four weeks.' She corrected herself, her face suddenly serious. 'We've got four weeks.' She pursed her lips. 'And it sounds like this Edward Croxley needs to learn a lesson or two.'

One thing Lily had loved about Vittoria from the moment she had met her was that she got straight to the heart of an issue. Lily had apologised for being direct, but Vittoria was just like her – she didn't bother with unimportant small talk, was one hundred per cent focused.

'I need to find out more about him. I've only seen him once, and that was from a distance, at a reception for something. But he's got that look, that arrogant swagger.'

Vittoria leaned forward and patted her hand reassuringly. 'You don't need to do anything now – keep away from him. Let me have a think about what I can do to work out the balance. I'll do the finding out. I have someone in London who can help me and I already have some ideas.' She paused. 'The most important thing is that we don't know each other, have only met on the plane and for lunch now. That happens all the time.'

'Absolutely.'

'Do you have the notes for me?'

Lily leaned over and handed Vittoria a map of New York, folded so her biro ring around No. 42's flagship store on Fifth Avenue was clear. Lily grinned. 'The launch of their new collection is invitation only. I'll make sure you're on the guest list.'

'I'll look forward to it. So four weeks until you start.' Vittoria smiled warmly and bent down to open her handbag. 'This is the information about that lovely photo gallery I mentioned in the East Village, the 4th Street Gallery. You really should check it out while you're here – it's tiny but quite famous.'

Lily took the brightly coloured cardboard sleeve and flipped it open. Interleaved between the information about the 4th Street Gallery's forthcoming exhibitions was a page of Calvert Vaux Hotel notepaper with email addresses and passwords on it, plus Marcus's flight schedule for the next month. Vittoria was very efficient.

Lily smiled back. 'This is perfect.'

Lunch finished too quickly.

Now it was time to redress the balance.

Chapter 10

SQUATTING DOWN, his jeans tight at the knee, Edward Croxley looked at the bunch of keys in his hand impatiently and tried the third one on the ring. The lock on the roller shutter hadn't budged with the first two tries and he was starting to get impatient. After the lengths he'd gone to get this far, being locked out just wasn't an option.

This one had to work.

Behind him, further down the alley, he could hear the staff from the French restaurant chatting beside the bins. The scent of cigarette smoke wafted his way and he felt a deep pang for fags. He'd been off them six months but the stress of the last few weeks would have put anyone right back on them.

His hand trembling, Croxley jiggled the key in the lock and felt it move. *Thank God*. He glanced up and down the alley. It was only a few feet wide, snaking along the back of the shops on Great Russell Street like something out of secret London. He could just imagine Victorian cutpurses and pickpockets dipping down here, running as fast as they could to dodge the peelers, their bare feet silent on the damp cobbles.

He turned the key gently. That Power boy had said you had to do it carefully or the mechanism stuck, but if you got it right … He felt the lock on the heavy steel shutter give under his hand … and spring open. *Thank fucking God*. Now he just had to push it up.

How the fuck had the old man managed this every morning? Heaving up the roller shutter, he pushed it to head height, giving enough clearance to get in through the door. He flicked his fringe out of his eyes as he bent over to look at the huge bunch of keys again. The biggest key was for the front door – he'd worked that out. It was all the smaller modern keys that were confusing. All Chubb, all the same size and all silver, he had no idea how you were supposed to tell them apart. He should have got Jack Power to label them, but he'd been barely able to stand by the end of the game, had tossed the keys on the table and left.

Croxley didn't imagine when Power woke up the next morning with the hangover from hell and found the copy of his promissory note in his pocket that it would have been a good time to ask about keys.

It had seemed such an easy way to get into the shop and to give himself enough time to look around, to find the bloody box. Croxley smirked to himself. 'Winning' the shop had been a stroke of genius if he did say so himself. The moment he'd realised what had happened back at the sale, he'd thought about all the ways he could get the box back. He'd even considered just asking for it, but that would have been professional – and literal – suicide. Jack would undoubtedly have had a proper look at it and would have known exactly what was hidden in it. And then they would all be fucked.

He didn't know a whole lot about Jack Power, but Croxley knew that he'd got a first in art history, which meant he probably had a fair grasp of things old. Something seven thousand years old suddenly falling into his lap would stand out like a bitch on heat at a dog show.

This was far cleverer, and it gave him all the time in the world to search the place. But actually physically getting in was causing more of a problem than he'd expected.

Croxley chose another key at random and slipped it into the lock on the steel door. The old man must have been very security conscious. He held his breath as he twisted it. This time it opened perfectly and he felt a small jump of elation. Then he realised the door opened outwards. And the shutter wasn't high enough to allow that to happen.

Grunting, he pushed the roller shutter up. It still wasn't clear of the door. *Jesus fucking Christ – how hard was this supposed to be?* Then he saw the steel pole leaning against the wall, sandwiched between the shutter and the door. It had a flat plate soldered to one end, a hook on the other. Grabbing it, he used the flat end to push the shutter up. The other end was evidently to pull the shutter back down again. *Sorted. Now he was getting somewhere.*

Pulling the door open, Croxley fumbled for his phone in the pocket of his hoodie, switching on the flashlight so he could see inside. He almost jumped. The light danced back at him as if there were a circle of people lurking in the shadows, waiting for him. He took a breath, trying to still his heart – it was just the beam from his phone reflecting off panes of glass leaning against the walls.

Why was he being such a prat?

And where the fuck was the light switch?

He could hear the shop's alarm, his anxiety rising with every pip. Quickly he slipped into the darkened back room. The alarm panel was on the wall to his right, its bright readout counting down the seconds he had to put in the code. He punched in the number. Thank God he'd thought of asking Power to write *that* on the bottom of the note. The last thing he needed was the alarm going off and the cops arriving. The alarm disabled, he sighed with relief.

It took him a few minutes to find the light switch on the other side of the alarm panel, a few minutes in which he dented his shin on a box and sent a stack of pictures cascading onto the floorboards. He didn't care – he hadn't come for pictures.

Above him, a single light bulb struggled to light the room.

Just as Croxley's phone began to vibrate in his pocket.

Not again.

Pulling it out, he didn't need to look at the screen to see exactly who it was. He fought the urge to reject the call, then answered. Despite the acquired public-school inflection, the caller's accent was strong.

'What's happening?'

'I'm in.' Croxley didn't bother with pleasantries.

'You sure it's there?'

'Has to be. Your contact got it to the sale room – the only other person buying boxes of tat that day was Jack Power. He has to have it. As soon as I saw it wasn't in my box, I went back to check, and there was no sign of it anywhere.'

'So you keep telling me.' The voice was full of menace.

'It has to be here. There are loads of boxes from auctions in this place.' He scanned the room, full of cardboard boxes neatly stacked on floor to ceiling shelving. There were more on the floor, piled haphazardly. 'I can see their lot numbers.'

'I don't understand how it got moved from the box it was in.'

'He must have swapped some of the stuff around. I don't know, but by a process of elimination it has to be here.'

'Find it or—'

'I know, I'll find it.'

Croxley's mouth went dry. He didn't want to think about the 'or'. There was no 'or'. He needed to find the box and its precious contents. The moment he'd realised what had happened he'd been in a state of shock. He had literally stood there, the auction room musty with the smell of dust and old books, sweat trickling down his back under the tweed of his jacket. He'd searched the box he'd bought over and over again. It had been there when the sale had opened – he'd checked. But it wasn't there at the end.

It had all been going so smoothly until then. Auction after auction, the plan had been perfect. The artefacts were smuggled into the country, concealed in the random boxes that featured in every country house sale – boxes of books and miscellaneous china and oddments, all bought legitimately. Sergei always had buyers lined up, dealers or collectors – the country house sales were the last link in a very long and bloody chain, bringing plundered, smuggled or stolen goods into the legitimate market, creating an indisputable provenance. Who was to know what had been passed down for hundreds of years through families? And country house auctioneers were notoriously inept, had no clue of the value of anything that didn't have a foxhound on it. Artefacts from Iraq and Syria looked like old bits of glass or souvenir reproductions. It was a fool-proof system. Or had been until Jack Power had got in the way.

And of course, it had to be this fucking time that it went wrong. When the buyer was the boss and wanted something very particular – and wasn't the type of guy who messed about. He'd made it clear that in his part of the Soviet Union the delay there had already been in delivery would be taken very seriously.

Edward felt himself chill. The items in this particular consignment might be no bigger than his little finger, but they were virtually priceless.

As soon as he'd worked out what must have happened, before he'd dreamed up the card game as a solution to his problems, Croxley had tried everything.

Calling into the shop looking for a gift for his mother, he'd wandered around with Jack, picking stuff up, examining, asking about auctions and china and nineteenth-century Minton. He'd been there for hours and hadn't seen any of the items that had originally been in Lot 56 but had mysteriously moved. The main problem was that the box of stuff Jack had bought wasn't big, and this shop rambled over three floors, with every corner piled high with prints and dusty books and all sorts of fucking ancient crap. Croxley shook his head. He'd thought about organising a crew to break in, but how would they know what they were looking for? And if he told them, the chances of him ever seeing it again were minimal, to say nothing of how long it would take to find anyway.

That was the real problem.

Time.

Then he'd had a total stroke of inspiration. Some of the guys he hung out with had been at school with Jack Power, and they all liked a high stakes game. Popping into the shop again, he'd been having a friendly chat when he'd casually mentioned cards and the players. Power had been flattered to be asked, had jumped at the opportunity.

God, he, Edward Croxley, was good, but sometimes he was fucking great.

It was so easy and so, so obvious. Now the keys were his, he could search for the box in his own time, going through every floor, every shelf, every drawer if he had to. He'd decide what to do with the shop later – maybe it would be useful as a base for his art sales and the few antiques he dealt in. Although his gut told him that anywhere like this would be a bloody nightmare, things like insurance and actually opening at ten o'clock every morning weighed him down even contemplating them. But maybe he could get Power back in to run it? Now, there was an idea. And he was sure Sergei and his boss, Kaprizov, would be interested in selling some of their stuff through here too ... But that was for another day.

Now he needed to find the amulets.

They already had blood on them and would have a lot more if he didn't find them fast.

It was Sergei's fault in the first place – he was such a fucking idiot, and this time Sergei'd got it wrong and they both knew it. This time the goods should have gone straight to Kaprizov, not come through the UK at all, but Sergei had been full of how fool-proof their system was and wanted to show off and make sure that everything was totally clean by the time it got to Kaprizov. His idea was that, with the provenance they'd created with the country house sales, Kaprizov could offload the goods on the open market if he wanted to, neatly laundering whatever cash had been used to pay for them in the first place and making a tidy profit at the same time. Not that he was going to do that. These artefacts were meant as gifts.

Which made the whole fucking mess considerably fucking worse.

Croxley had to admit that finding all this stuff in country house auctions was genius in its own way, once he, Edward, did the finding. It created a paper trail that was hard to disprove.

When it worked.

He'd never forget the moment when he'd realised they weren't there, that instead of a collection of priceless almost seven-thousand-year-old Sumerian gold amulets, all that had been in the box were a few old books and a cigar box.

That would look good wrapped up with a gold ribbon for Kaprizov's nieces.

But now he was here.

And when he found the stuff, he was never going to do this again. There was too much stress involved – he was going to get back to what he was good at: organising parties and selling a few Picassos to make ends meet.

Croxley looked around him, unsure where to start. The auction had only been a week ago, so logically the box had to be near the top of all this crap in one of the rooms. Perhaps he should start on the top floor and work down? Croxley shook his head to himself. If Jack had come in with the box he'd have had a look through it, taken out the best pieces and put it down somewhere – Croxley didn't reckon he would have lugged it all the way up the stairs.

So he'd start down here.

He turned around and began to take in his surroundings properly. This back room looked like some sort of office, an old desk pushed up against the wall below a barred window. Piles of ledgers covered its surface and leaning against every wall were stacks and stacks of framed prints. Croxley turned, his Nikes silent on the fraying corded carpet.

In the very corner of the room was a huge metal safe painted a sludgy brown. It looked like a remnant from the Wild West.

Now that was interesting. But for another day.

Croxley turned around again, working out where to start. There was an internal door to his left. He'd better have a quick look around first to get a feel for the place – after all, the box he needed could be sitting on the floor staring at him in the next room. He pushed the door wide to find another storage room, this one full of books – ancient spines in muted shades lining the walls. The room smelled of old paper. On the floor, boxes were piled up under every shelf. Croxley took a step inside and leaned over to look in one. More books.

Across the room was another door. *It was like a fucking rabbit warren.* Striding across he pulled it open.

On the other side was the shop proper.

At the far end, the shutters were down – had been since Jack had pulled them and headed to that infamous card game. *One man's loss was another man's gain.*

Croxley's eyes began to adjust to the dimness and he headed for the front of the shop, skirting a huge antique globe plonked between the bookshelves and display cases. Heading down past a display table of books, Croxley could see a row of antique brass light switches beside the front door. Exactly what he was looking for.

Triumphantly he switched them on.

Now he was in business.

That box with the amulets had to be here somewhere and he was staying until he found it.

Chapter 11

L ILY YAWNED as she hauled her case up the stairs to her attic flat. A short walk down the Euston Road from Granary Square and the stunning warehouse transformation that was Central Saint Martins, the flat was at the top of a tall Georgian house that overlooked a leafy square with tennis courts, the birds loud in summer and squirrels dashing about in the autumn. The building had its own faded elegance, the ornate half-railings outside the sash windows, even this far up, thick with hundreds of years of paint. The rest of the crescent was divided into faded three-star hotels, the pavement constantly busy with bewildered-looking tourists dragging huge suitcases.

Turning up to the last flight, the narrowest of all, Lily stopped for a moment to look out of the landing window. She'd miss this when she was in New York. This building had such a sense of history – she could almost hear the maids' weary footsteps as they headed up here to their beds under the roof at the end of a long day, their room no doubt boiling in the summer and freezing in the winter.

Lily yawned again. She was desperate for bed but she had some things she needed to do before she could even try to sleep. Arriving on the top landing and opening the front door, she was greeted by the smell of stale, damp clothing and fried food. She groaned inwardly.

'Hello!' Lily called out to anyone who was in, to announce her arrival.

There was no response.

Perhaps everyone was out. But where was Jack? She glanced at the screen on her phone. The battery was low but there was no sign of a missed call or a message. She'd told him not to leave the apartment. But he was an adult now, could make his own decisions. He'd probably gone out for milk.

Lily dumped her bags in the hall and dipped into the kitchen. Checking the kettle was filled with water, she flicked it on and then headed for her room. Pushing open her bedroom door, she stopped abruptly, taking in the transformation and shaking her head. A sad smile crept out. Jack was such a dope, like fixing her room could fix the shop.

But he was trying.

Totally uncharacteristically, he had tidied up, straightening the bed and the patchwork blanket she'd knitted while she was revising for her A levels. It was a riot of colour, the squares all perfectly aligned, and he'd pulled it so the edges of the squares lined up with the edges of the bed. She might be slightly chaotic in some things, but balance and symmetry were very important to Lily and Jack knew it. On the dressing table he'd left a note leaning against the antique teapot he'd given her a week or so ago. She'd wiped it down when he presented it to her, delighted. It was designed for one, a pretty addition to her collection despite a hairline crack, but with the interview and everything, cleaning it up had slipped her mind. It was still stuffed with tissue paper and needed a proper wash, but No. 42 had sent her her flight details before she'd had time to look at it properly and date it. Looking at it now, would she really be able to take it with her? Packing up sounded easy, but was it?

In the back of Lily's mind, a voice wondered if she'd be able to go to New York at all, but she'd said she would – she had a month and now she had Vittoria.

Dumping her case beside the dressing table, Lily picked up the note Jack had left: 'Back at 6, will bring dinner. Hope you had fab trip.'

In the kitchen she heard the kettle boil. Before she did anything she needed a cup of tea.

*

Back in her bedroom, sipping her tea, Lily adjusted her glasses and worked out what she needed to do first. After her lunch with Vittoria, so much was swirling around in her mind.

She needed to unpack, but more importantly she needed to get things rolling on another idea. She picked up her phone and checked the time – it was still only two o'clock, although it felt like about six in the evening. She had enough time to send a few emails and have a nap before dinner – emails that included a particularly important message to an old school friend.

Unravelling her phone cable from the contents of her satchel, book, make-up bag and the TransGlobal business-class menu (she was putting that on her notice board), Lily plugged her phone in at the back of her dressing table and grabbed her MacBook. She'd unpack her case before she crashed out, but first … She pulled her pillows from under the duvet and stacked them against the wrought-iron bed head, sat down and opened her computer, powering it up.

She and Vittoria had agreed they would only correspond

if absolutely necessary by letter, mailed in the ordinary post, a message disguised as an invitation of some sort. There was to be no digital fingerprint, no digital trail.

Their goals were the same: payback; but, as they had quickly realised in both cases, it wasn't a matter of pointing the gun and firing it. They didn't need to do that. With both the men who were causing difficulties in their lives, they only needed to make sure that it was loaded and left within sight. With a bit of planning, Vittoria's husband, Marcus Devine, and that foul creature Edward Croxley – Lily could hardly bear to even think his name – could be relied upon to become the agents of their own downfall: it was just a matter of creating the circumstances.

As Lily opened her email there was a scratching at the window and she looked up to see George, her grandpa's ginger cat, glaring at her with his one eye. He pawed at the window again impatiently. Putting her MacBook down and kneeling on the bed, Lily slid up the stiff sash and he slipped inside, jumping off the sill, his coat almost the same colour as the polished boards. Lily closed the window and went back to the computer, conscious of him sitting regally in the middle of the floor as if waiting for an explanation of her absence.

A message from Marianne Omotoso pinged straight into Lily's inbox. Serendipity indeed. Lily clicked on it and, as if he'd realised she was doing something interesting, George jumped back up onto the bed beside her and took a look at her screen. She reached out to stroke his soft head.

'George, I've got some news for you. I've been offered a job.' She raised her eyebrows as she spoke and looked at him. He regarded her stoically. 'I'm going to need to move. I think you're going to have to stay with Jack.' George twitched his whiskers. 'But first we've got some jobs to do. There's this guy called

Marcus Devine who is trying to get rid of his very lovely and successful wife because he has a beautiful and needy mistress.'

George looked at her, unimpressed. It sounded like a fairy tale or a bad romance novel when she put it like that, and for Vittoria that's probably exactly how it felt. Lily remembered the pain in Vittoria's face as she'd explained everything. And a big part of the hurt was that Marcus was so barefaced about everything – even Lily had been surprised at that. Marcus Devine was so confident that no one was watching him in London, he didn't even try to hide his tracks.

Lily had googled Marcus's mistress, Stephanie Carson, from a terminal in the airport, careful to pepper her search history with other cast members from *Lies*. Even to the most suspicious of analysts she'd just look like a fan. Beautiful and young, Stephanie was a talented Shakespearean actress who was now the lead in a hit TV crime series. Getting to the airport early had given Lily time to look up some of the other names Vittoria had given her as well – the other women her husband had been linked to over the past few years.

Marcus Devine had certainly been busy.

Pushing her MacBook to one side, Lily leaned over the side of the bed and, careful not to disturb George, who had started purring and kneading her patchwork blanket, she reached for her satchel and Vittoria's file. Pulling out the handwritten sheets, she laid them side by side on the bed. Marcus Devine's email address was at the top, his mobile phone number, mother's maiden name, car registration numbers, his flying schedule for the next few weeks. And Stephanie Carson's home address. The only thing Lily seemed to be missing was Marcus Devine's passport number. They didn't know what information she'd need, so Vittoria had literally given her everything.

Lily leaned over George, picking up her tea from the bedside locker to take a sip. The afternoon was rolling on. But she'd given a lot of thought to her first move while she'd been on the plane, this time able to enjoy every moment of business class. She'd missed having someone to chat to, though. On this leg of the trip the man in the corresponding pod to hers had raised the partition between them before the seat-belt signs had even gone off. Not that she would have wanted to talk to him anyway, but it had given her hours to come up with a plan.

And it hadn't been that difficult.

Marcus Devine obviously had a very strong sense of his own self-worth; to him, his reputation was everything. You could see it in the way he posed for photographs, in how much he enjoyed the limelight. Being seen with beautiful women was all part of that.

So that was the place Lily needed to start.

And with a bit of help from her school friend Emma, who was desperate to break into celebrity features but was currently doing the horoscopes in the *Sunday Inquirer* and the *Daily Inquirer*, they'd be off.

Lily was sure Emma had said that the gossip columnist could file copy up to teatime on a Saturday for the next day's papers. They'd met for a coffee and a catch-up a few months ago and Lily had been marvelling about how fast a story could circulate. Emma had been full of how the different columnists worked, of who came into the office and who worked from home, how they found stories. It really was a world where anything was prey, but that didn't stop Em loving it. And she had her sights firmly set on the next rung on the ladder. Actually, any rung that got her writing properly instead of trying to make sense of the mystic ramblings of their astrologer and get her ideas condensed into fifty words.

Lily picked up a pen from her bedside cabinet and chewed the end. The trick was to make her email sound plausible but not create anything that could be litigious or get Emma into trouble. She smiled: this one was all about smoke and mirrors. She opened a fresh email. It took her a few attempts to compose it, flicking to her browser search page to be sure she had the right information. She read it over:

> Hi E, I overheard something when I was coming
> through passport control in Heathrow that I
> thought might be one for you ...

She finished the email and hit Send.
George regarded her suspiciously.
As well he might.

Chapter 12

DUBLIN'S ST STEPHEN'S Green was busy even at this time on a Sunday morning, buses, taxis and the famous horse drawn jarveys vying for space as they headed around Europe's largest garden square, a chill breeze rustling the remaining leaves of the towering trees. Despite the breeze, late autumn sunshine bathed the period entrance to one of Dublin's most famous hotels, brasses on the central rotating door polished to a mirrored shine.

Inside, the hotel's restaurant was busy too, a jazz quartet already warming up against the chink of china and whoosh of the coffee machines.

'Ciao, darling, how was New York?'

Smiling at his terrible Italian accent, Vittoria put down her phone and stood up to greet Aidan with an air kiss on the cheek, before he slipped off his jacket and slung it around the back of the chair. He looked good, his designer stubble a little out of control, a baseball cap pulled down over his military-style buzz-cut. He'd ditched his white coat for a casual T-shirt and hoodie, was obviously making the most of his weekend off.

'It was great, although jet lag leaves me so groggy, my brain seems to grind to a halt. I should have stayed in bed this morning.'

Aidan smiled. 'You know what Marcus is like – he likes an audience. He was only delighted when he texted me this morning.'

Vittoria rolled her eyes. 'I'm sure he can have his audience without me having to join him.'

'But he's not mentioned in a full-page spread, is he? You are. It's your photo in the paper. No one will know he's gloating unless you're here for people to recognise.'

Vittoria winced and passed Aidan the menu. She'd had a feeling that this article was a bad idea from the moment the journalist had called. But the Russian ballet didn't come to Dublin often, and the prima ballerina hailing a Dublin clinic for saving her from anorexia was a once in a lifetime story. Although, when they'd caught up on the phone, Yana had been worried that it stank of PR, was too obviously a way to raise the profile of the European tour. Vittoria had calmed her. She was sure, ultimately, it would be good for both of them. A dark-haired waitress arrived, interrupting Vittoria's thoughts, but Aidan was already waving the menu away.

'I'll have my usual.' He grinned at the girl, who responded with a faint blush.

Vittoria smiled inwardly; Aidan had no idea of his effect on women. He had an endless stream of girlfriends, each one thinking they'd be able to tie him down, but he never seemed to settle. It worried Vittoria – he was utterly adorable but he flitted inexplicably from relationship to relationship. And each time he introduced her to a new one, she wondered how long it would last. She took the menu herself.

'Thank you, and jasmine tea would be lovely,' she said, then, turning to Aidan, she shook her head. 'Honestly, you're worse than Marcus – don't you ever feel like branching out, trying something new?'

Aidan smirked at her suggestively. 'I've enough excitement in my life, thank you. I know exactly what I want.'

'Oh, stop. You are too bold.'

'So bold,' he corrected her, laughing and shaking his head. 'I love the way you manage to make Irish phrases sound Italian.'

She shot him a fiery look full of fun. 'Sicilian.'

'Ha, touché. Did Marcus tell you about the new sails we're looking at? Kevlar, the fastest and lightest available. I want *Danny Boy* to win *everything* next season.'

The waitress arrived with Vittoria's tea and a pot of coffee for Aidan as she answered.

'He hasn't told me anything. He only got back from London late last night. He went to the gym at some godforsaken hour this morning. I haven't seen him.'

'I think he was pretty glad you didn't stay in New York any longer – he got a call from the bank about your joint card being used.'

It was Vittoria's turn to smirk. 'I had my phone switched off. They really are very good at checking for fraud. Did he say anything?'

'He said a lot, none of it repeatable, and I'm guessing he's not going to say any of it to you.' He paused. 'You were OK on your own?' His voice was full of concern.

Vittoria smiled. 'Of course. You can't fault The Calvert Vaux Hotel.' Before she could say more there was a flurry of activity at the main door to the restaurant. From her seat beside the window, Vittoria watched as Marcus appeared in the doorway, greeting the staff like old friends.

Aidan had noticed the signs of his arrival too, threw Vittoria a look across the table.

The waitress had brought their order and just finished pouring Vittoria's tea as Marcus began heading towards them.

A moment later, the maître d' was pulling out a chair for him.

Wearing a black designer tracksuit, Marcus had his arms full of newspapers and bent forward to dump them into the middle of the table but Aidan caught them deftly and leaned across Marcus's empty chair to put them on the window sill. 'I'd rather not have coffee all over me at this time in the morning, thanks, mate.'

'I bought all the papers so we can see if anyone else picked up on Vittoria's moment.'

Her *moment*? Vittoria resisted the temptation to throw her tea all over him.

'We did guess.' She raised her eyebrows over the rim of her tea cup, but he didn't hear her, was greeting someone with a wave and a gestured conversation on the other side of the restaurant. From his hand movements it looked like it involved golf. 'For God's sake, sit down.'

He gave Vittoria a belligerent look more suited to a teenager and sat. 'Where's my green tea?'

A pretty blonde waitress appeared at his shoulder, carrying a tray laden with china. 'That's lovely, Sinéad – I hope you warmed the pot.'

'Of course, Mr Devine. I know just how you like it.'

Vittoria didn't look at the waitress but carefully put her cup down, trying to control her emotions, her temper. This was the first time she'd seen him since her conversation with the detective and it was taking all her self-control to stay calm.

Marcus reached for the papers, sorting through them. Without looking up, he waved the *Sunday Inquirer* in Vittoria's direction while he flipped open the news section of the *Sunday Times*, disappearing behind it.

'Did you get the *Business Post*?' Her tone was clipped but he didn't seem to notice.

'Of course, in the pile.' Marcus waved towards the window sill from behind the open broadsheet. He turned the pages as if he was looking to see if they had covered her 'moment'.

Aidan was about to lean across him to pass it over when, catching her eye, he raised an eyebrow, obviously picking up on her change in mood.

She rolled her eyes and shook her head. She could look later. 'Thank you.' Vittoria glanced at the *Inquirer* masthead. They had a picture of Yana pirouetting across the top. She leafed through to find the article. It was opposite the gossip column, *typical*, the main focus on Yana's love life. They'd used the picture of them both, though, taken outside the clinic and referenced her practice and Yana's near death from starvation. Vittoria read it quickly and then scanned the opposite page.

And a name caught her eye.

It took her a moment to absorb the few lines.

A few lines that rocked her to her core.

Pursing her lips, she glanced quickly at Aidan. He raised his dark eyebrows, sending her a *what's up?* look.

'It seems I'm not the only person in the papers today.' Catching the hard edge to Vittoria's tone, Marcus flipped down the corner of the *Sunday Times* and looked at her over the top of it.

'Huh?'

She threw him a steely look. 'I thought you were working hard in London all week – in meetings, training in the simulator?'

'I was. I've got to go back tomorrow to finalise the assessments before I go to Sydney.'

Vittoria pursed her lips, taking a moment to still the rage boiling inside her before she said, 'But the simulator is in Heathrow, not the West End?'

'It is.' Marcus frowned, obviously irritated. 'What are you talking about?'

Vittoria straightened the paper, glaring at him before she read out the piece she'd found. She fought to keep her voice low.

'Belle de Jour's Italian successor, reality TV star and rumoured high-class London call girl Bellissima Serata, has been busy ahead of the rumoured launch of her explosive tell-all book, *Stripped Back*. The *Sunday Inquirer* has been exclusively told that the party girl, a twenty-something double-D brunette beauty, who is a regular at society parties, was spotted with TransGlobal Airways top pilot –' Vittoria paused for emphasis '– *Marcus Devine's* doppelganger sipping champagne in The Velvet Club, London's famous strip venue, on Friday night. Bellissima's hunky silver fox companion was surrounded by blondes until she arrived for more champagne and a cosy chat in one of the club's private rooms.'

'What?' Marcus's reaction was explosive. Several other diners turned to look at him. 'What on earth's that about? I wasn't in The Velvet Club with anyone, never mind some tart …'

Vittoria didn't reply. Her face flaming, she folded the paper carefully and bent down to pick up her handbag. Slipping out of her seat, she stood up, her words hissed just loud enough for him to hear. 'How dare you.'

She threw the *Inquirer* at him, hitting the paper he still had in his hands with a satisfying thwack, and, without a backward glance, strode out of the restaurant. In the mirrors on the wall she could see people looking at her, could see there were copies of today's newspapers on almost every table. And the blonde waitress who had served them was smirking beside the bar.

She barrelled through the swing doors into the lobby, crossed the marble-tiled foyer and headed straight out through the rotating glass door, the uniformed doorman standing back to let her through. The late September sun was bright as she stopped on the broad granite step and took a breath, for a moment unsure what to do next. As if reading her mind, a second doorman took a step forward.

'Cab, madam?'

That was exactly what she needed.

His hand was already raised as she nodded curtly. A taxi materialised seconds later, and as the doorman crossed the broad pavement to open the rear door for her, she smiled gratefully. He knew her well; no doubt he'd seen the paper long before she had. The very thought made her cringe. Next time she was here, she'd make sure she tipped him well, but right now she just wanted to get home as fast as possible. As he pushed the car door closed behind her, Vittoria heard her phone ring in her bag. The doorman leaned in to the passenger window to give the driver her address. Hardly noticing the driver's backward glance at her, she pulled the phone out.

Marcus.

Well, he could go to hell.

As if Stephanie fucking Carson wasn't enough for him?

She rejected the call and it rang again.

Aidan this time.

She really wasn't ready to speak to him either.

How could Marcus be so *public*? Her emotions swirled, shock and humiliation blending to make her feel positively sick.

Until now, Marcus had always kept his dalliances impeccably discreet, understood the respect she was held in professionally. *Valued her.* Or so she'd thought. That had obviously all changed with Stephanie Carson's arrival on the scene.

Was this some sort of mid-life crisis? How could he be so blatant with, of *all* people, a celebrity escort? In a strip club of *all* places? Anger flared inside her as she found herself actually lost for words, her thoughts careering into each other so violently she felt like they were creating some sort of black hole in her head. A painful one that was spreading across her forehead with each pulse of her heartbeat. Jet lag always made her groggy, and right now she really wasn't up to dealing with this. Vittoria felt tears pricking at her eyes.

How had she not seen this coming? She'd given Marcus Devine her whole life; their relationship had cost her the dance career she'd worked so hard for, children, almost her mental health. And now this?

The lights changed and the cab swung over Leeson Street Bridge and around the bend but Vittoria was hardly aware of it. It was all too much. She listened to people's problems every day, but who could she tell her problems to? Aidan knew most of it but she held back even from him. Lily Power was the only person she had voiced her most personal concerns to, and now this ...

There was something inherently reckless about being seen in a club like that, with a woman like that. It didn't exactly make you look sensible and dependable. How would TransGlobal feel about one of their top pilots acting like an irresponsible *idiota*? What would this do for their business, for his reputation, let alone his marriage? *What on earth had he been thinking?*

His reputation.

Vittoria's whole thought process stopped for a moment. Stopped and recalibrated. And the feelings of humiliation and rage flowed away to be replaced by deep, quiet laughter.

Lily Power.

Why hadn't she realised sooner? Fighting a smile, Vittoria pulled out her phone and searched for the report online. She read it again. 'Have been told … exclusively … rumoured … doppelganger.'

My God, Lily was good.

It was all supposition and not one word was litigious, no matter how furious it made Marcus. Every word was carefully chosen to mislead. And if he tried to sue for defamation, he'd look even more guilty: *the lady doth protest too much*. Vittoria smiled. She switched her phone off and chuckled to herself, shaking her head, relief washing over her. She hadn't expected anything this fast, but this was exactly the type of thing they'd discussed.

Strike one.

This put Marcus completely on the back foot and made her, Vittoria, look like a victim.

Now it was her turn to do something for Lily.

Chapter 13

VITTORIA PUT HER elbows on her office desk and opened the file in front of her, the map of New York with No. 42's headquarters ringed in blue still at the front. As she scanned the page her desk phone lit up with another incoming call. Thank goodness Ruby was on the ball downstairs. The article about Yana in Sunday's paper had had an amazing effect on business: on top of her deferred clients from last week – she hadn't stopped all day yesterday – people were literally queuing up for appointments. She'd finally left the office at ten last night, exhausted. She was going to need extra staff if the enquiries kept coming in like this. And thank God not one person had mentioned Marcus. She was sure they had made the connection, but they were all struggling with something in their own lives, so perhaps they understood.

Today had been just as busy so far, but the ink-blue velvet couch behind her was now finally empty, for an hour at least. She'd made up her case notes, plumped the deep rose-coloured cushions and changed the tissue box ready for her next appointment, and now she had some time to breathe. Lily's notes had been pulling her back since the whole debacle with Marcus on Sunday.

The sun was streaming onto the desk and Vittoria leaned over to open the office window. Sunday felt like a long time ago now. She didn't feel any less sick about it but, *grazie Dio*, Marcus had stayed out after they'd seen the paper, though God only knew where he'd gone – perhaps to *Danny Boy*, to the marina in Dun Laoghaire. Wherever he'd ended up, Vittoria had spent the afternoon working out in the studio, the stereo turned up as high as it could go as she spun across the boards.

When she was dancing she could lose herself, it was the only time when she didn't need to think. She became completely absorbed in the music, became part of it. Music was in her soul; dance was in her bones.

But so was justice.

She could have stayed in the studio all evening, but she knew Monday would be busy, so instead she'd finished up with a swim, star-like lights shining up through the water, deliciously warm. It had been almost six by the time she'd showered and had gone up to her bedroom. Marcus still wasn't home. Which was probably a good thing. As she swam she'd been thinking about a way to make her position really clear. It wasn't hard.

Gathering his things from the bedroom, his clean uniform and meticulously polished shoes, she piled everything outside on the landing, dumping his jacket on top. Going back to the en suite, she added his black leather wash-bag to the pile, and then she'd gone down to the kitchen to grab salad and cold chicken from the fridge and brought it upstairs with her. And locked herself into the bedroom.

He was sleeping in the guest room for the foreseeable future, no question.

When he *had* finally got home late Sunday evening and had realised that the bedroom door was actually locked he'd got really mad. She'd smiled to herself. She could feel the heat of his fury coming through the closed door like a wildfire.

'Vittoria? Are you in there? What the fuck are you playing at? Open this fucking door!'

In her bedroom she'd plumped up the pillows behind her and texted Aidan:

M back. Have locked him out of
bedroom è molto arrabbiato.

Very angry was an understatement. She couldn't resist a smile as Aidan's reply came straight back:

Be careful xx

Marcus had thumped the door so hard, the sound had echoed around the house. 'Let me in, Vittoria. I know you're in there. I can hear your phone. Who are you texting? You know that was all nonsense – it's a tabloid, for Christ's sake, they make it all up. I've no idea who that woman was. I wasn't even there.'

She'd been tempted to ask where he had been – *curled up with Stephanie Carson, maybe, in their love nest in Notting Hill?* But she knew silence was more powerful. And it made him even madder.

'Will you open this fucking door? You're totally overreacting. Typical bloody Italian, I should have known when I first met you!'

Then she'd heard his footsteps as he stamped back across the hall and the texts had started.

So she'd switched her phone off.

Yesterday morning she'd woken up at five, had heard him accelerating down the drive, the engine of his Jaguar XK1 roaring. He was flying all this week, would have taken off from Heathrow for Singapore last night, heading for Sydney.

With stop-overs, he wouldn't be back until next Tuesday, and as she'd trotted down the winding staircase to the kitchen yesterday morning, she'd felt a lightness in her step she hadn't felt for ages.

He was obviously furious, although how any of this could be her fault she had no idea. She had no regrets about locking him out. It was about time he started to feel the real impact of his actions.

In her office, Vittoria turned her face to the sunshine and listened to the surf breaking on the beach across the road. The sounds of the traffic on Strand Road blended with the call of seagulls. One thing she loved about Ireland was never being far from the sea. Much as she'd adored living in London, literally breathing dance, feeding off the energy of the city, she'd been brought up a stone's throw from the sea and it always calmed her.

After the accident, when she'd finally got out of hospital, Marcus had brought her home to his parents' house to recuperate, his mother and the housekeeper fussing over her. But she'd realised it was the ocean that she needed to help her heal. Walks on the beach were an essential part of her physio, morning and evening, but also part of her mental healing.

The housekeeper had had hot milk and nutmeg ready for her every night when she'd come in from her walk. As she'd held the mug in her cupped hands, warm, safe, healing, she'd decided going back to London, to university, was the next step. And from then on, Vittoria's focus had been singular. She knew what she wanted, but it had taken every particle of her being to achieve it. Had she realised she was leaving Marcus behind? It didn't matter; he hadn't tried to keep up. Now she knew that, even then, he had been totally focused on his own career, on his friends. On the other women.

After the accident she'd been in a bad place, had felt like she was in a dark tunnel, like everything she knew was being shaken and turned around her. She hadn't expected to feel like that again, but then she'd got the news about Stephanie Carson and all those feelings had come right back.

She'd always succeeded before, had worked hard, had had to overcome all sorts of obstacles – she'd always coped. But the Stephanie Carson thing had rocked her to her core, and until she'd got on that plane and spoken to Lily, she'd felt like things were slipping away from her, like her points of reference were changing. Too fast.

Now, not only had Lily given her something to distract her, but their chat had relieved Vittoria of that crushing feeling that she was utterly powerless, that life was happening to her, rather than her taking part in controlling it. The relief that she finally had a way to fight back, that Marcus was getting what he deserved, at least in a small way, made her feel literally a thousand pounds lighter, even made the constant nagging pain in her back a mere irritant.

What did they say about a problem shared?

But Lily's problems were just as overwhelming as Vittoria's, and now they needed her full attention. From the moment they'd parted, her mind had been whirring, exploring ideas and possibilities.

Pulling her keyboard towards her across the desk, Vittoria pursed her lips and opened a search window. She was going to find out everything she could about Edward Croxley. There had to be something that would give her leverage to get the shop back – she just needed to find out what it was and come up with a plan.

On Sunday night, as she'd curled up in bed, Marcus's fury still hanging in the air, she'd started thinking about Croxley and the Arabella Smyth story, about the poor girl's death.

About how easy it was for something like that to happen and how dangerous swimming pools could be. Croxley might not have been arrested, but the articles she'd read had all hinted at the shared responsibility of the other partygoers to look after their friends. Drugs and drink were a lethal cocktail, even when there wasn't a risk of drowning. This Edward Croxley was a very intriguing individual.

But it was still puzzling her why he wanted the shop in the first place.

Why had he targeted Jack, when presumably there had been other people in that same card game who had assets? More easily disposable assets.

Lily had said that he'd invited Jack to the game. She'd told Vittoria that Croxley had wandered into the shop a couple of times, that he and Jack had got talking, discovering they knew people in common; and then, the very first time they'd played cards, he'd got Jack drunk and the shop had ended up on the table.

It sounded to Vittoria like he'd deliberately gone after Jack with one thing in mind. But why? Vittoria knew that if she could get to the bottom of that, she'd find some answers. She really needed to meet Croxley face to face, to read his body language, to get the measure of him. All the photos of him at art galleries only told her so much.

But his interest in art had to be her way in.

Vittoria picked up a pen from her desk and twirled it through her fingers, thinking. Marcus had quite an art collection, even with the pieces lost during the burglary. Most of the paintings had belonged to his father, but others he'd bought himself for investment over the years. It was a mixed ensemble of styles and periods, an extensive and much admired collection.

Vittoria did a search for the Beaufort Fine Art website and picked up the phone. It was answered quickly.

'I wonder if you can help me. My husband has some paintings he wants to sell, and someone said that Edward Croxley might be able to help but I've managed to lose his contact details. I know he's worked with you – would you have them?'

Vittoria's face twitched as the lady who had answered made helpful noises and then said, 'What sort of paintings are they?'

'European, mainly, a mixture, some Renaissance, some more modern. I'm really not sure. We live in Dublin and his family has been collecting for years – it's the Devine Collection. A lot of them are very dark and religious and, quite honestly, they aren't to my taste at all and I really need to redecorate.'

As if the receptionist could completely understand the problem, she said, 'I'm sure we can help – we do a lot of work with Edward. Will I introduce you by email?'

'That would be great, thanks so much. I can send him some images and see what he thinks.'

'If you don't hear from him, do come back to me – sometimes people's spam filters are a nightmare.'

Vittoria gave the lady her email address. A moment later an email from Beaufort Fine Arts pinged into her inbox. Perfect.

Vittoria quickly typed an email.

        Dear Edward,

        Lovely to e-meet you. My husband has some
        paintings to sell from a family collection.
        I'll be in London in a few days and wondered if
        we could meet to discuss.

        Kind regards,

        Vittoria Devine

She hit Send. If Croxley was a party animal, he might not be checking his email too early, which gave her more time to investigate his background. As she flashed through the search results, she saw another *Irish Times* article about Arabella Smyth that she'd missed.

Vittoria found the page link and clicked through. The article was a few years old now, grim in its reading. As she sat thinking, an email pinged into her inbox.

> Dear Vittoria,
>
> Lovely to hear from you, I'd love to hear more about your paintings. Could you send pictures of them so that I can see who might be interested? My terms are 30 per cent in a private sale. If you prefer to auction, I can work with Beaufort, although often the best prices are paid by private collectors. I look forward to hearing from you.
>
> Best,
>
> Edward Croxley

Bingo.

Chapter 14

SITTING IN HER OFFICE, Vittoria checked her watch. She still had thirty minutes until her next client. She knew she should eat, but she had more pressing things to do right now.

As soon as Lily had mentioned that Edward Croxley dealt in art, an idea had started to form in Vittoria's head. An idea that was a natural step from something she had already laid the groundwork for.

With everything going on recently, finding a way out of their prenuptial agreement had become her top priority. Finding a lawyer to advise her in Ireland where everyone knew everyone else was the first problem, so she'd ended up with one in London. Ridiculously, the *reason* for a divorce wasn't a factor. And it had quickly become clear that discovering some undisclosed assets seemed to be the only chance she had – if Marcus had hidden anything from his initial signed declaration then the document would be null and void. It had taken her a long time to work out how on earth she could suddenly discover something big enough to be effective, but then one evening she'd come home early and switched on the TV to a programme about proving the provenance of lost old masters. And *that* had reminded her of a conversation she'd had at the art auctioneers Rahilly's.

Quickly opening an incognito window on her computer, Vittoria accessed a Yahoo email account. She rarely used it, but there were times when she didn't want people knowing her business. Or, more importantly knowing they were dealing with her. This was definitely one of them. To be really sure, she'd set up a virtual private network so her IP address was hidden. She found the email contact address she wanted.

> Dear Eileen,
>
> So sorry this is short notice. The quality of the previous delivery was superb — all three paintings arrived safely. Would you be able to deliver the last one this Thursday? I know that's a little sooner than discussed. My wife is redecorating and the interior designer is only available to meet on Friday.
>
> Kind regards,
>
> Marcus Devine

Vittoria smiled. Her original plan for these pictures would dovetail nicely with what she needed to do now for Lily. The timing couldn't be better. She'd told Marcus she was ordering some rugs from Scotland when he'd queried the charge on the household account. Eileen thought she was dealing with him directly, and being based in Scotland, if anything was mentioned in the Irish press about their matrimonial difficulties, she'd be very unlikely to see it. Vittoria had thought about every detail.

It was the TV programme that had made everything connect. She smiled. Marcus had dragged her into town that Saturday morning; she hadn't even wanted to go to look at more paintings. It had been a glorious spring day, the morning sunshine bathing the pavement, and she'd wanted to go shopping in Grafton Street rather than spend hours in the museum-like auction house viewing lots stored deep inside. While Marcus had gone ahead with one of the directors, Vittoria had hung back, enjoying the sunshine coming in through the glass door, and started chatting to the young man looking after the reception desk.

He had a slight stutter; Vittoria hated to see people struggle and had made a point of listening. He'd explained that he was in his final year of a master's, his thesis all about the Nazis rumoured to have holed up in Ireland after the Second World War, about the incredible works of art that had been looted by the Third Reich and, apparently, lost. She'd been delighted to hear his hesitation go as he warmed to his subject, reaching for an iPad to show her some of the paintings he had been researching. His words came back to her now.

'Currency was hard to move – its value is constantly fluctuating – but art retains its value.' He'd shaken his head. 'So much disappeared, apparently without trace. Every now and again something comes to light, like that huge collection that was found in 2012 in Munich.' Vittoria had become really interested then. And as he'd explained about a dealer called Cornelius Gurlitt, his eyes had lit up. He made it sound like the plot of a James Bond movie.

'It was like Gurlitt was invisible: he didn't have a job, wasn't registered for tax, he wasn't even in the phone book, but he was living in an apartment worth over a million euro. It was rumoured in the art community that he was living off the proceeds of looted art, but you'd wonder how nobody said anything before then – his father had been one of the Hitler's key art dealers. Eventually a judge ordered a warrant for his

110

apartment to be searched and they found this incredible haul, pieces by Picasso, Matisse, Renoir and Chagall, more even than that. The collection was thought to be worth more than a *billion* dollars.'

It was really quite incredible.

And what was more incredible was that many refugees from the Third Reich had ended up in Ireland. What she *hadn't* realised was that these 'refugees' had brought art with them. It was perfectly logical really, she just hadn't thought about it before. Vittoria could just imagine the plundered antiquities and gems that had wound up in Ireland after the Second World War.

Where there were secrets, there was always profit.

And she badly needed a high-value secret to suddenly appear in Marcus's life. A high-value secret that meant the prenup was worthless so she could divorce him and keep half his assets and, with a bit of luck, the house, and he could go and shack up with Stephanie Carson, poorer and – this was the twist she really loved – terrified if it got out, that he'd be savaged by the tabloids for his family's Nazi sympathies. A painting had been so obvious; she couldn't understand why she hadn't thought of it before. And a painting that had been hidden because it had a murky past was perfect.

Vittoria's desktop pinged to tell her that her email to Eileen had been answered. The last painting would be delivered on time. Perfect.

Vittoria searched for a high-resolution image of the picture she'd ordered and, closing the incognito window, opened her own email to reply to Edward Croxley.

Dear Edward,

Thank you for coming back to me so quickly. I'm attaching an image of one of the paintings we

are hoping to sell. It's imperative that the
sale is discreet. I will explain more when we
meet. I'll be in London on Friday — I'm staying
at The Hogarth Hotel on Great Russell Street.
Perhaps we could meet in The Lighthouse Bar at
5 p.m.?

Kind regards,

Vittoria Devine

It had also been the receptionist in Rahilly's who had told her that many collectors these days had their most valuable paintings copied so they could enjoy them at home, knowing that the originals were safely in a bank vault. And he'd mentioned Eileen, a copyist – a legal forger – who he'd heard was excellent. She could reproduce anything to look precisely like the original, right down to the artist's brush-strokes. Vittoria had loved his phrase 'legal forger'. It had stuck in her head.

He'd been a positive mine of information.

Chapter 15

EDWARD CROXLEY almost dropped his phone when he opened the image Vittoria Devine had emailed him. He pushed his fringe out of his face with the palm of his hand, his fingers black from what felt like about a hundred years of dust and dirt accumulated in Power's Fine Prints. He'd taken a break to check his email and there had been Vittoria Devine's reply. Waiting for him.

Perhaps his luck was turning.

After the day he'd had, it was about bloody time.

He was sitting on the bare floorboards of the top floor of Power's Fine Prints. This was the third time he'd been back in as many days and he still couldn't find what he was looking for. Logically, he knew that the bloody box had to be somewhere fairly obvious, but unfortunately Jack Power didn't seem to have read the same memo on logic that he was working off. And when your life depended on finding something, the search needed be fairly thorough.

He'd been through the shop area the first time he'd come in; it had taken another visit to do the second floor; and now here he was, covered in crap up on the third floor, where, in all honesty, he didn't think anyone had been since about 1840.

He looked again at the image this Vittoria Devine had sent. It looked very familiar, although he couldn't remember the name of the artist or the picture – but he did remember it was one that he'd come across before. It had been in an article in *Vanity Fair* – he was sure of it. Which meant that it definitely wasn't a load of old tat. Far from it. He saved it and did an image search.

Christ what would he do without Google?

A moment later the image appeared.

Edward was unable to resist a grin. He *knew* it had looked familiar – it had been painted by Camille Pissarro, was part of a series. And this one, *The Boulevard Montmartre at Twilight*, was part of a collection looted during the Second World War and sold through a Swiss art dealer in 1941. According to the expert quoted in the article, its current location was a mystery.

The smile curled across Edward's face. No mystery. It was in a private collection in Ireland. But how the fuck had it got there?

It only took Edward another few minutes and another search to connect Vittoria Devine to Marcus Devine and the Devine Collection.

Curiouser and curiouser.

And what was even more interesting was that they wanted a very discreet private sale. And this was exactly the type of painting that a very discreet private collector would be very happy to pay a *lot* of money for.

Edward could already think of a few people who would be interested, collectors living in France and New York who weren't too interested in exactly how a painting had ended up on the market but would be very keen for it to end up in their personal collection.

Edward glanced back at the image Vittoria had sent. Pissarro had painted the same sweeping street scene of Montmartre many times – in the winter, in the rain, at night. Edward smiled to himself. Most of the others were in museum collections. The commission on this would be very sweet. Very sweet indeed.

But then he returned to his current problem with a bump. If he didn't find these fucking amulets he wouldn't be around to enjoy the commission. Christ, why was this happening? If it had been anything else, something normal, something that wasn't thousands of years old, he could have found another one – although finding four would be a challenge, even if that was an option, but … He shook his head and, putting the phone down on the dusty boards beside him, rubbed his face with his hands.

After all his efforts to get into the shop it was looking like the box wasn't here after all. So where the fuck was it? This morning, before he started on this last storeroom, Edward had meticulously searched Jack Power's attic apartment at the very top of the building. No sign of it. Why would he have carried it all the way upstairs anyway?

On the second floor he'd found a box with a battered copy of *Rebecca* in it, had felt his heart pumping. At this stage, one cardboard box looked like another one, but he was pretty sure there had been a copy of *Rebecca* in the one he was looking for. Someone had torn the lot docket off the outside, so Edward couldn't be totally sure, but it was as close as he'd come so far. The only problem was that the copy of Du Maurier's classic, foxed and water-stained, was the only thing in the box.

Edward let out a breath, sweat breaking out down his back. Sergei was getting impatient. More to the point, Igor Kaprizov was too, and he wasn't someone Croxley wanted to upset. The amulets were for his four nieces, one of whom was getting married – perhaps they were the 'something old'. Six and a half thousand years was fucking old alright. And their age added to their rarity, that and the fact that the ones Croxley was currently looking for were one of the few examples outside of the British Museum.

What the fuck was he going to do? He'd thought of every possible option. Jack Power was hardly going to be pleased to see him, never mind willing to talk to him, if he turned up asking questions about a cardboard box. And if Power realised what was in it, what he was looking for, he'd be well and truly fucked.

Croxley knew, assuming Power had them, that he could swap the shop back for the amulets – that was a no-brainer. But Jack Power wasn't stupid. Not only would he understand the value of the amulets when he saw them, he'd have a good idea of where they came from as well. And he'd make Edward pay. Pay big time. Although parting with a couple of million in cash was looking like an increasingly attractive option compared to being offed by the Russian mafia. He'd been looking over his shoulder since the auction and the moment he'd realised the crucial items he was supposed to be collecting were missing. He'd hardly slept since then.

Edward could feel a headache starting behind his eyes. Maybe this painting was the answer? Maybe he could do some sort of deal and use it as a sweetener to buy him more time with Kaprizov? His niece was getting married in Paris after all. Serendipity, perhaps?

Croxley shook his head. What on earth had Power done with the box? He didn't drive so it wasn't in the boot of his car. *It had to be somewhere.*

Croxley opened an email to reply to Vittoria Devine.

Whatever he was going to do about these amulets, he needed to come up with a solution damn quick. He really didn't know how much longer he could stall Sergei for. Maybe this painting really was a currency he could use.

He might be bargaining for his life.

Chapter 16

'LILY POWER, you're a magician.' Lily spoke out loud, smiling to herself as she leaned in closer to the pair of 4K monitors on the desk in front of her, scanning the image she'd been working on. Marcus Devine smiled back at her. Beside him, apparently in the cockpit of a Boeing 787, was an Italian escort by the name of Bellissima Serata. She wasn't Italian at all – she was Romanian – and she had achieved her fame via a dubious track of dating the right people and winding up on a reality TV show about a select London borough that Lily doubted she'd ever visited in daylight. But she *was* writing a tell-all memoir – *Stripped Back: Sex, Scandal and Secrets* – purporting to be a 'true account' of her many tabloid relationships. It was amazing what you could find on the Internet when you started to look. Lily had to give it to her, though: she was a beautiful girl. A beautiful girl who undoubtedly loved publicity.

Her eyes locked on the screen, Lily moved her mouse and made a fractional change to the image. She needed to get the shadows just right, so that Bellisima's hand rested casually a little too far up Marcus's thigh. Convinced that it looked like the real thing, Lily sat back in her chair with satisfaction.

Behind her the door opened, and her friend Nathan stuck his head into the tiny editing suite. She hurriedly closed the image, leaving a photo of one of her designs, a ruby-encrusted bird-shaped brooch, on the screen instead.

Coming into the room, twisting his diamante stud earring, Nathan glanced at the screen. He was wearing a red plaid shirt loose over a Superman T-shirt, the short sleeves of the shirt revealing tats covering his arms.

'You're a star for letting me use your kit. My MacBook is just too small for anything ultra-high-definition. These monitors are great.'

He shrugged. 'No problem. So when do you go to New York?'

Lily grinned. 'Soon, only a few weeks now. I'm so excited.'

'Better than painting fur.'

She arched her eyebrows in question.

'That's where I started off in animation, painting fur.'

'Are you serious? I never knew. Is that even a thing?'

'I'm afraid so.' Nathan laughed. He rubbed his ginger beard philosophically, shaking his head. 'You go to the top art school in the world and end up painting the hairs on a rabbit's arse. What can I say?' She laughed as he continued, 'So do I get the brownies now or do I have to wait even longer?' Nathan eyed the Tupperware box beside the keyboard that Lily had brought with her. 'It's almost coffee time. You know I run on caffeine and chocolate.'

'You have to wait. There's one more thing to do. Give me ten minutes.' She made a sweeping motion with her hands.

He laughed. 'Right, but be quick. I'm dying here.' Slipping out, he closed the door behind him.

She'd met Nathan on her first day at Central Saint Martins. She'd been totally lost and absolutely soaked to the skin. The rain had been biblical and she'd been practically drowned alive, her hair straggling down the back of her very wet mac.

He'd spotted her at the entrance to the college, and must have been going somewhere much more interesting, but he'd taken one look at her and wordlessly steered her to the ladies so she could get dried off. When she'd come out, she'd been amazed to see he was still there, leaning against the wall, silently tapping his Converse to the beat of whatever was playing though his earbuds. A bright-red messenger bag slung over his shoulder, jeans held tight against his ankles with old-fashioned bicycle clips, he'd had the beard even then. He was in his last year, about to graduate and head into animation, had literally taken her under his wing because the exact same thing had happened to him on his first day.

And she was a fellow ginger.

They were a dying breed – as he'd explained the next time she'd bumped into him, heading across Granary Square, his aviator shades reflecting the dancing water fountains – they had to stick together. They'd high-fived and stayed friends ever since.

And few people could manipulate an image like Nathan. He'd taught her how to use Photoshop to start with, and he'd been delighted to hear from her when she'd texted the previous night asking if she could use his equipment for a project. He'd suggested she come down to his office at Red Fox Films the next morning on the condition that she brought her homemade brownies. Smiling, Lily had texted back and gone straight to the kitchen and switched on the oven.

Lily turned back to the screen. She had one more image to work on. Opening her Dropbox, she extracted the second photo she'd chosen.

Vittoria had given her the password to Marcus's Google account. She'd been very careful to pick her moment when she'd first logged in – she knew that Gmail flagged up log-ins from new devices, sending the user an email to alert them. It was a protection against getting hacked – a pretty useless one if the hacker happened to be in your account at the time and could delete it. Which was exactly what she had done the first time she'd logged in. She'd had a good look around, checking the photographs backed up to Google Drive, including a whole range of selfies that had given her lots to work with.

She just needed to change the date stamp on this one and she was all finished.

*

'Did you see the paper?' Lily's school friend Emma arrived in the café on Great Russell Street in a flurry of shopping bags, her white blonde hair pulled back in a ponytail. 'My God, why did I wear boots and a coat? It's almost October and it feels like August. Must be global warming.'

Dumping her handbag and purchases onto the bench seat opposite Lily, she leaned down to give her a quick peck on the cheek before pulling off her padded jacket and collapsing into the booth. Lily had chosen a table inside the café well away from the huge glass window, where they could speak in private without being ogled by everyone who passed by on the street.

Before Lily had a chance to give her thoughts on the weather, Emma sat up, her eyes wide. 'So, how was New York? Did you shop?' Lily shook her head in amusement at Emma's flushed face. Emma opened her eyes wide. 'I *need* to know.'

Lily laughed. 'I didn't do much shopping, but I got a job.'

Emma's shriek made everyone in the restaurant look at them. She grabbed Lily's shoulders across the table. 'Seriously? At No. 42?'

Lily suddenly felt a huge full-body blush hitting her. She was partially saved by the waitress coming over to them to take their lunch order.

'Good news, ladies?'

Emma grinned at her. 'The best. What are you having, Lils? We need to celebrate. Bellinis? Say yes! You have to – I've got to live the life I want or it will never happen!'

'Go on, you're bonkers, you know that?'

Emma grinned at her slyly. 'I am but I've got a friend who's going to design jewellery for No. 42 in *New York*. So there.'

Smiling, the waitress took their orders, and the moment she turned her back, Emma said, 'Oh. My. God. I can't believe it. No. 42. They do *all* the stars.' She was almost breathless with excitement. 'That's just so fantastic. Do you get a staff discount?'

Lily shook her head, laughing. 'I've really no idea – I forgot to ask. But they want me to design their private bespoke pieces, so I should have some fantastic celeb exclusives for you with a bit of luck.' She paused. 'So tell me, how's work going?'

'Brilliant. Absolutely brilliant. They loved that thing about Bellissima Serata. Loved it. Thanks so much. A few more scoops like that and I might never have to write another horoscope.'

'Actually, I think I might have a few more bits for you,' Lily said, pausing suggestively to make Emma squirm for the gossip. 'It seems that pilot's doppelganger has been busy again.' Lily grimaced. 'I just feel so sorry for his wife.'

Emma bit her lip. Lily could see she was trying to seem casual but was failing badly. She was a real reporter at heart – even in school Em had always had that killer instinct that you needed for news. She was tough and she was a worker – Lily admired that in anyone. You had to fight to get what you wanted in this world, and Emma had had to win her place on the staff at the *Inquirer* and she was going to make sure she worked her way up.

As if to confirm Lily's thoughts, Emma's phone pipped. 'Sorry, just need to …' She quickly flicked it open to check her messages. 'It's alright, nothing earth-shattering.' She put it down beside her on the table, completely missing Lily's swiftly hidden smile. Being in news meant being in touch twenty-four seven, and Em was all over it.

Unaware of Lily's thoughts, Emma leaned in and lowered her voice. 'The lovely Bellissima has been on social media non-stop since Sunday denying she was ever at The Velvet Club with Marcus Devine … But she would, wouldn't she?' Emma chuckled. 'And a story like this is one way to sell a book …'

Lily raised her eyebrows. *Maybe someone else was going to benefit from all of this as well as Vittoria Devine.* 'Would she be that cynical?'

Emma did a double take. 'Would she what? That type of coverage doesn't do her profile any harm – she's probably put her prices up.'

Lily shook her head, her eyes wide. But before she could comment, Emma said, 'So how do you know her – Bellissima, I mean?' She tried to make the question sound off-hand but Lily knew she was fishing. Thankfully the waitress arrived with their order, giving Lily a few moments to think. She'd worked it all out, but she needed to be so careful.

'Enjoy ladies.'

As the waitress left, Lily picked up her glass and grinned at Emma as she did the same. A Bellini at lunch-time was completely ridiculous but she did have something to celebrate. Taking a sip, Lily put her glass down and shook out her serviette, keeping her voice low as she answered. 'I don't know her at all. I told you, I overheard it in Heathrow.' Even to Lily that sounded a bit weak.

Emma wasn't giving up. 'But how did you know who she was – she could have been anyone?'

Lily pursed her lips. 'OK, you've got me. Listen, this can't go *anywhere*, but I know this hostie who works for TransGlobal. She had a bit of a fling with Marcus Devine, and she was really pissed off when he dumped her. He promised her the earth to get her into bed and then totally ghosted her.'

Emma scowled. 'That's really not very nice. Sounds like Captain Devine needs to be taken down a few pegs. And his poor wife! Not nice at all …'

'Exactly. Then my friend heard he'd been hanging out with this Bellissima. He flew to Milan with her in the cockpit, apparently. I don't know if that's just pure gossip, but my friend was really upset.'

Emma's mouth fell open, her fork poised above her salad. 'But isn't that all sorts of illegal these days? What if she'd been blackmailed by ISIS or something?'

Lily shrugged. 'I've no idea, but I suppose when you're the captain, you're in charge.'

'That could be a huge story, you know.' Emma looked at her hard. 'Could I talk to your friend?'

Lily grimaced. 'She can't have any part in it or she'll lose her job, and you didn't hear it from me either, or someone will find out it came from her.' Lily paused. 'But she did send me some photos.'

'You serious?'

Lily pulled out her phone, glancing up to make sure no one could see or hear them. 'Listen, this is really important. I have no idea if these are real, so if they go anywhere you *have* to make sure you're covered, make sure someone else makes the decisions on them. My friend is so bitter, he was such a total bastard to her, that I'm really not sure if any of this is true.'

'Got it.' Emma grinned. 'But there's no smoke without fire.'

Chapter 17

BY THE TIME VITTORIA got home from work on Wednesday evening the pain in her back was nagging at her and she had even more texts and missed calls from Marcus. Thank goodness he'd be in the air somewhere between Singapore and Sydney tonight and she'd get a bit of peace. She really didn't need any more messages clogging her phone or her inbox. She'd been flat out trying to fit in as many clients as she could so she could clear her diary for the next few days.

Coming into the kitchen and dumping her handbag on the polished kitchen table, she pulled open the kitchen drawer to look for her pain killers. The ones she'd taken earlier were starting to wear off and she needed something stronger. She popped two out of a blister pack and took them quickly with a glass of water before slipping a pod into the coffee machine. Turning to lean on the counter while it percolated, she looked out of the French windows, past the green-tiled pool house and on out to sea, the evening sun glinting off azure water. Vittoria fought a Cheshire Cat grin. She wasn't going to answer any of Marcus's messages claiming he'd never met this woman or been in The Velvet Club.

Sometimes silence was the most powerful tool.

Tchaikovsky slipped off a pine chair and began to wind around her legs purring, standing up on his hind legs to attract

126

her attention. She reached down to stroke his velvet ears absentmindedly, her head full of her meeting with Edward Croxley on Friday.

This painting was really going to work for her. She knew how good Eileen was. And it would arrive tomorrow, in time for her to take it to London. She would leave the others securely in the attic, hidden away from prying eyes. They were all very high value but not nearly as commercial as this one. It was the most accessible and recognisable, would be attractive to a wider market.

Everything was going to plan.

There was little chance that Edward Croxley would detect it as a forgery. Eileen was a world-recognised copyist who supplied museums as well as private collectors with copies of priceless paintings – she was the absolute best.

But Vittoria knew, no matter how convincing the painting was, in the art world it was all about provenance. Marcus's father's collection and the legacy of the Nazis hiding out in Ireland made anything turning up in Dublin all the more plausible. Plus, Vittoria had had an idea that would make the provenance rock solid. She would be taking a letter to London with her, one that just needed a postscript added to allay any doubts Croxley or his buyer might have. She just had to call in to a gentleman who lived in Mile End to have it brought completely up to date. Eileen had explained how she needed to contact him. It was complicated to say the least, but Vittoria could completely understand why.

The key was that the painting gave her the perfect opportunity to talk to Croxley and get to know him better. If he could find a buyer, the money would be very useful in the grand scheme of things but, more importantly, it gave her power. Vittoria was quite sure it wouldn't do Croxley's reputation any good if the truth came out, and if the buyer discovered it wasn't the real thing, it could get quite messy.

It was leverage, and that's what she needed to persuade him to destroy the promissory note and return the keys to Lily's shop.

The coffee machine bubbled and whirred behind her and she picked up her cup. Once she was in London she'd get a better feel for the best route forward. She planned to stay for the weekend at least. Marcus wouldn't be back from Sydney until Tuesday and then he had a week off. A week she had a feeling he'd end up spending in London – no doubt at vague 'meetings'.

Vittoria sipped her coffee, smiling to herself. It was quite possible that Stephanie Carson had seen the article in the paper too, and that would give Marcus even more problems. At least he was away all week on this trip so he'd have some time to get his story straight.

But no matter how much he denied it, this was the type of thing that clung to you. Lily was so sharp. That was exactly the quality Vittoria had recognised in her the first time they'd met. International corporations only hired the very, very best. No. 42 had done their research, and from the moment Lily had explained why she was going to New York, Vittoria had been very sure Lily was someone who would go places. But one of the things Vittoria really loved about Lily Power was how humble she was – she really had no idea of her talent. There was something incredibly charming about the fact that Lily had been blown away that an American company wanted to fly her business class to New York. Vittoria could still hear the excitement in her voice.

Vittoria hoped Lily held onto some of that wonderful naivety when she became immersed in corporate America.

She had a feeling she would. Lily had won all sorts of awards at college – a college that was one of the top in the world – yet she really had no idea how special she was. Vittoria wanted to do everything she could to help her shine.

And getting her grandpa's shop back was vital to Lily's success.

Vittoria sighed. When somebody crossed one of her friends, they crossed her too, and this Edward Croxley's behaviour to Lily and Jack had been despicable. He had a lot to answer for.

And he wasn't the only one.

Vittoria tucked her hair behind her ear as she thought about Marcus – and Lily's stroke of genius with the newspaper story.

Marcus making a statement denying any entanglement with this Bellissima was a waste of time. The only thing he could do to straighten things was to make it public that he was briefing his lawyer to take a libel suit, but that would all be hot air. Anyone with half a brain could see there were no grounds for libel – which made the whole thing sweeter still.

Vittoria smiled to herself as she poured her coffee and glanced at the clock. She wanted to pack and then get her workout done and have a swim before dinner.

Following her upstairs to her bedroom, Tchaikovsky shot ahead as she opened the door and plumped himself down in the middle of her snow-white duvet, pretending he was invisible, a puddle of darkness, unmoving. Vittoria shook her head. Marcus didn't allow him in the bedroom, but they had their own secret code. When Marcus was away, Tchaikovsky stretched out beside her like he owned the whole house, his purring impossibly loud.

It only took her a few minutes to pull her suitcase out of the wardrobe and throw her clothes onto the bed. The last time she'd done this she'd been in the grip of an all-consuming rage; now she was a whole lot calmer. She smiled to herself. Last time she'd just thrown her favourite outfits into the case; this time she needed to be more considered. Smart business was the look she needed. Expertly folding everything, she slipped off the navy pencil skirt she was wearing and padded into the bathroom to put on her dance gear and grab a swimsuit.

Researching Edward Croxley had given her an idea that needed some thinking about. She needed to do some proper research to clarify a few details, but she did her best thinking in the studio and the pool.

Chapter 18

THE LIGHTHOUSE BAR in The Hogarth Hotel was already getting busy. It was only five o'clock but it was Friday and London was obviously winding down into the weekend.

As the lift doors closed silently behind her, Vittoria headed down the dark wood corridor, candles already flickering in the recesses. Through the open glazed doors at the end, she could see the bar with its brass rails, soft lighting and row of high-backed leather stools. The room was beautiful, looked more like a salon on a luxury 1930s liner than a lighthouse, pale-grey velvet sofas clustered in gossiping groups, the staff hovering in period uniforms, making Vittoria feel like she'd stepped back decades. There was something utterly decadent about this hotel that captured the Bright Young Things and the Bloomsbury set perfectly. Behind the bar, mood lighting backlit colourful bottles that picked up the warm paintwork. Soft jazz filled the room, and the barman began vigorously rattling a cocktail shaker full of ice, adding to the feeling that she'd slipped back in time.

Vittoria glanced around trying to decide where to sit. First impressions were so important. She'd changed as soon as she'd checked in, was now wearing wide-legged silky black trousers and a casual black shirt with a loose tie neck and black lace panels on the shoulders. She'd pulled her hair up in a clip that matched her diamond ear studs. She was quite sure Croxley appreciated good jewellery and would be assessing her from the moment they met. She was also sure he would have checked her out online, but the small details were what contributed to creating an overall impression. She needed Croxley to trust her and believe *everything*.

'Good evening, madam, would you like to sit?' Meeting her as she stepped through the doors, a dark-suited man Vittoria knew to be the manager bowed slightly as he spoke, taking in the room in a wide gesture. Vittoria smiled. Fabulous, incredibly courteous service was another hallmark of this hotel, and who didn't love being treated like royalty?

'Thank you. The bar, perhaps?' Crossing the parquet floor ahead of her, he pulled out a stool in the middle of the bar and Vittoria hopped up onto it.

'And for madam, a drink?'

'I'm waiting for someone, but can I have a glass of champagne, please?' It was early but Vittoria wanted to make sure that she looked like part of the place when Croxley arrived.

Vittoria watched as the barman poured her drink, delivering it ceremoniously in a beautiful glass set on a thick paper coaster with a silver partner dish of nuts and olives.

Vittoria glanced over her shoulder at the huge nautical brass clock above the door. The hand clicked around to 5 p.m., and a man she recognised from his Facebook profile picture appeared through the street door to her right. She focused on her glass, picking up the elegant stem and taking a sip, pretending not to have seen him. He was every bit the art dealer in a long tweed coat that enveloped his angular frame, narrow pea-green trousers and a paisley silk cravat tied at his neck. Looking younger than his thirty-two years, he pushed his blond fringe out of his eyes as he caught sight of her.

Smiling, he approached. 'Vittoria Devine, I presume?' Vittoria turned in her chair and returned the smile as he continued, 'Edward Croxley at your service.' He inclined his head as she put out her hand to shake his. Very gallant.

'Thank you for agreeing to meet me at such short notice.'

'Not at all. You have a very interesting –' he paused pointedly '– collection.'

'Thank you.' Vittoria smiled warmly. 'Will you join me?'

Edward caught the eye of the barman and ordered a scotch. Pulling out the stool beside her, he slipped off his coat, throwing it over the back before he climbed onto it. 'Now, tell me a little about your painting. How did you come by it?'

Vittoria took a sip of her drink. The ambient music in the bar was just loud enough for them to speak comfortably without anyone being able to overhear them except the bartender, who she was quite sure was listening. 'It's part of my husband's father's collection. We actually didn't realise we had it until we were broken into recently. Several paintings were stolen – not many, thankfully – but when I went into the attic to fill the gaps on the walls, I found a stack of canvases in a corner.'

'In the attic?'

Vittoria took another sip. 'I know, it's ridiculous – people talk about "hidden assets".' She rolled her eyes. 'The house belonged to my husband's parents. His mother was an actress and very flamboyant. Her taste in art and mine were quite different, so when she passed away, I changed a few things around. Everywhere needed a lick of paint. I put a lot of paintings in the attic. Marcus must have forgotten about these, and I hadn't realised there were more up there.'

'There are more like this one?' Vittoria could see Croxley was fighting to keep the surprise out of his voice. The barman delivered Croxley's drink and, apparently using the interruption to digest what she was saying, he sipped it.

Watching him, Vittoria shrugged. 'There are so many, really, I've no idea why his father bought them. The one I sent you a picture of was at the back of the attic behind Marcus's school trunk. It was wrapped up in hessian with a couple of others.'

'Others like this one?' He was pushing the point, trying to sound nonchalant and failing badly.

'Not like it – all different but there were four of them together. They're all old if that's any clue. I've no idea why they weren't on show in the house, although some of them are rather hideous. From the dust they looked like they'd been in the attic forever. There are a couple of cubist-type oils, black and white, that are just grim.'

Edward smiled like he had a far greater knowledge. 'They sound interesting. But I think I might know why they weren't on show. I'd have to see the other paintings, but I believe your father-in-law was a colleague of Eamon de Valera's? There are photographs of them together online.'

Vittoria shrugged. 'Of course. They were members of the same club. Irish society is very small.'

'Did you check up on the artist of the painting you showed me?'

Vittoria shook her head. 'I'm sorry, we've had rather a lot happening recently. To be honest, I'd forgotten about it. I thought you could tell me?'

'It's by Camille Pissarro. Part of a series. Quite an extensive series but the majority of the others are in museums around the world.'

'Really? You surprise me. It's a nice enough painting but it's not very exciting, is it? It's so grey. Who wants a painting of a wet evening?' She shrugged. 'But I'm sure someone will like it more than me.'

Edward laughed. 'I think we can safely say there are a few people who might like it. I have a contact who adores French art. He's originally Chechen, I think; but he travels a lot and his niece is getting married in Paris.' He took another sip. 'I think I need to see it before I can discuss it with him, though.'

'Of course, it's in my room. Will I get it?'

Vittoria made to move off the stool. Croxley put his hands up. 'It may be a little too public here. Could you bring it to my shop in the morning?'

His shop? That was an interesting interpretation.

'Of course, where is it?'

'Just a few doors down the road, Power's Fine Prints. I'm closed at the moment ... stocktaking ... but I could meet you there in the morning? Just bang on the shutter, around ten o'clock?'

'*Perfetto*.' Vittoria smiled and lined the broad foot of her glass up with its coaster. 'So tell me a bit about you, Edward Croxley.'

Chapter 19

V ITTORIA HADN'T learned anything she didn't already
know about Edward Croxley the previous night, but
they'd had a very pleasant chat during which he'd flirted
mildly and made much of his connections in the trade.

And he'd been very interested in the other paintings Vittoria
had 'found' in the attic.

They'd chatted about Irish politics and the effects of Brexit
and about Sicily for about an hour, an hour during which
she'd fed him all sorts of information about Marcus and his
family, about the collection and just how extensive it was.

By the time they'd parted, Edward Croxley had been very
firmly on her hook.

Now, as she stood at the top of the hotel's grand steps
looking out at Great Russell Street with the painting, well
wrapped in several layers of plastic as well as its hessian
shroud, under her arm, it was starting to rain.

Vittoria pulled up the collar of her coat and hurried in the
direction of the shop.

She'd looked it up on Google Street View last night and
discovered it was literally just a few minutes away across
the junction, 'Power's Fine Prints and Books' written in
gold antique lettering, clearly visible against its bottle-green
exterior.

After weaving between tourists and students on the broad pavement, Vittoria waited at the pedestrian lights. Bloomsbury was such a beautiful area, the buildings elegant, many, she was sure, passed on from generation to generation.

Like Lily's shop.

The lights changed and Vittoria crossed the road and hurried along until she reached the shop. As Croxley had said, it was closed, dark-green steel roller shutters pulled down on the window and street door. Which seemed rather illogical to Vittoria and confirmed in her mind her earlier suspicion that Croxley didn't want to run the shop as a gallery at all.

If he did, why close? Why not open at least for a few hours each day and sell some stock? The Powers had obviously been making enough money in this location for many years, so why stop?

It just underlined her theory that he had a different agenda. And she intended to find out exactly what that was.

Despite her black leather gloves, Vittoria had no intention of banging on the steel shutter. Rooting in her handbag, she pulled out her house key and used it to knock on it.

Croxley was obviously waiting for her. She'd hardly taken her hand away when she heard movement inside and the shutter began to roll up.

'Good morning. Bit of a damp one.' Croxley ducked out and glanced up and down the road as she slipped under the shutter. She hadn't noticed last night because she'd been sitting on that high stool, but he was shorter than Marcus, maybe five ten. Everyone was taller than her, of course – unless she was en pointe, when she gained about six inches in height – but he was short for a man.

'It is. London has a special kind of damp.' She paused. 'This is a lovely location.'

Holding open the inner shop door, Croxley smiled. 'I adore Bloomsbury. Now let's have a look at this painting.'

Vittoria smiled back at him. *He was keen*. Heading to the shop's glass counter, she put down her package and pulled off her gloves before beginning to unwrap it. 'I hope getting X-rayed in security didn't do any damage. *Mio Dio*, I've only just thought of that.'

'I'm sure it's fine.'

Vittoria could almost feel Croxley's impatience crackling through the air in the stillness of the shop. As she lifted the painting to take off the layers of bubble wrap and grey tissue paper, she took a quick look around.

She could see why Lily loved this place, from the handwritten cards under the prints cramming the walls, to the faded spines of the rare books displayed in the glass case beside the counter; it felt like an old friend.

'There, that's the last layer.' Vittoria pulled back the hessian to reveal the canvas. Under the shop lights, the yellows in the street scene lifted, sparkling through the grey twilight that gave the painting its title. It was a mysterious view of the traffic in Montmartre, of windows lit to the night, of carriages driving through the rain. Vittoria suddenly had the feeling that this image held many secrets.

Vittoria heard Croxley exhale beside her like he was trying not to show his enthusiasm.

'Can I look a little more closely?'

'Of course.' She stepped backwards as he pulled an eye glass out of his jacket pocket and picked up the painting, examining the back of the canvas. A moment later he turned it over, studying the brush-strokes in the painting itself.

Vittoria smiled to herself. One thing she knew for sure was that it would pass his examination. Eileen had explained when Vittoria first got in touch, pretending to be Marcus's PA, that she used period canvases sourced from the location each painting was originally created in. Attention to detail was everything, right down to using the same tools individual artists had used, replicating the same brushes, even the type of animal hair the artist favoured. The types of people she worked for didn't accept anything less than perfection. She was at the top of her game and expensive with very good reason. Like many things, it was all about detail.

The only way Eileen's paintings could be identified as fakes, apart from analysing the paint itself, was if she wanted them to be – sometimes her collectors needed tiny changes in the new pictures so that they could tell the difference between the real ones and the reproductions. And sometimes they wanted perfect reproductions so that even an expert eye would be fooled.

Croxley's voice brought Vittoria back to the shop. 'Mm, very nice. I think you can get a good price for this.'

'Really? I do hope so.' Vittoria bit her lip. 'But it needs to be very discreet.' She took a deep breath before continuing. 'I'm sure I can talk to you in confidence, but my husband needs to raise some cash to fight someone who thinks they have some dirt on him.' She pushed her hair behind her ear. 'There's a woman. She's *molto* dangerous. She's causing some problems for us. It seems to be the only solution, and there can be no paper trail.'

Edward nodded slowly, his eyes on the painting. 'I think that can be arranged. But obviously—'

She cut in. 'Obviously we're prepared to increase your commission for a discreet sale. That goes for all transactions, not just this one.'

Vittoria could have sworn that if Edward Croxley had been a dog he would have started to wag his tail and pant. She could see a slight flush in his cheeks as he nodded again.

'I think we can keep this all extremely quiet. The buyer I have in mind isn't a man for publicity. He has an extensive but very private collection.'

'*Perfetto—*'

As Vittoria began to speak, Croxley's phone rang, loud in the empty shop. It was lying on the counter beside the wrapping that Vittoria had removed. He glanced at it and paled. A name had flashed up on the screen.

Now who was Sergei?

Vittoria smiled. 'Take it, I'll be a few minutes.' She picked up the wrapping as if she was busying herself. Croxley hesitated, glancing at her, then picked it up. As if it was his mother calling, he pulled a face to her as he answered it.

'Excuse me.'

She smiled knowingly as he turned around and took the call.

Glancing at his back, as she pretended to gather up the tissue paper, Vittoria pulled her own phone from her pocket and slipped it onto the counter. Punching in the password, she deftly began recording.

'Really, I'm on it. They have to be here somewhere … Look, I've searched but I can't get into the safe. They could be there. I need to ask him.'

There was a pause. Vittoria didn't catch the next bit, but Croxley began pacing, listening to the caller. She didn't need her master's in psychology to see the stress he was under, to see that he was bluffing heavily to whomever he was speaking to. It was very obvious that his Russian friend, assuming Sergei was Russian, was putting him under a lot of pressure.

'I know. I told you I'd sort it. I'm here, aren't I?' Croxley paused. 'I know about the timing. I'm hardly going to forget, am I? Look, I'll find all of them – they are just so small. If they're not here, the next move is to ask discreetly. We can't be too obvious – you know as well as I do what could happen if it gets out. I know they *said* they didn't come from the museum but anything from that area has blood all over it.'

Croxley stopped pacing, his back to her, he put his hand out to lean on a bookshelf. Vittoria could see his knuckles whiten as he gripped it.

'I know. I'm on it.'

He finished the call and looked at the phone for a second, as if he'd forgotten that she was there. Vittoria tapped her own phone to stop it recording and slipped it back into her coat pocket. Swiftly wrapping the painting, she made a fuss of pushing it into its original protective plastic. She leaned over it, frowning. In the reflection in the glass case behind the till she could see Croxley still had his back to her.

'Ooops.' Deliberately interrupting his reverie, she jiggled the painting into its covering as if she was concentrating solely on what she was doing, as if she hadn't heard any of his conversation. 'There, all done.' She glanced at him. 'I'm so sorry – I hope I didn't interrupt?'

Turning around slowly, Croxley shook his head. As if she was completely unaware of any underlying tension, she continued innocently, 'So do I need to leave this with you to show your buyer?'

It took a moment for Croxley to register what she was saying, then his public smile was back in place. 'Yes, yes, that would be great. I'll give you a receipt, obviously.'

She laughed. 'That seems a little ridiculous, honestly, but I'm sure Marcus will be furious if I don't get one.'

Croxley was a very good actor. He smiled conspiratorially, as if he hadn't just had a very heavy conversation with an aggressive Russian. Vittoria grinned back. She needed to process what she'd heard but she was getting a much clearer picture of why Croxley had wanted the shop.

There was something here.

Something very small and very valuable that this Sergei wanted.

And wanted badly.

Something Croxley couldn't find.

What on earth could that be?

Chapter 20

AS VITTORIA LEFT Power's Fine Prints in Bloomsbury, over in Notting Hill Lily dipped into the door of an artisan coffee shop and looked around for a table. It was a patisserie as well as a coffee shop and obviously very popular on a Saturday morning, the scents of freshly baked cakes luring passers-by in from the pavement. When Vittoria had given her Stephanie Carson's address, she'd looked it up and seen that this coffee shop was almost opposite her house. The perfect location to get a feel for the neighbourhood. And a feel for Stephanie Carson.

Queuing up, she ordered a latte just as a table in the broad window became available. Lily indicated to the girls behind the counter that she'd sit down.

It was a tiny table, covered in a cheerful red chequered cloth, and it had a perfect view. Settling in to her chair, Lily looked out across the wide road, trees dotted down both sides, their leaves turning shades of russet.

The houses looked Victorian and, although terraced, many had three floors, the brickwork a pale yellow, windowsills crowded with planters and flowerboxes. Several had ornate stained-glass panels above the front doors. Lily could see Number 121 easily, with its low white-capped brick wall and an elegant ball-cut bay tree in a pot beside the front door-step.

It looked like something out of a magazine. As she watched, a tortoiseshell cat popped up from the paved front garden and sat on the wall washing itself.

Lily wasn't an expert on property but she wondered how Stephanie Carson could afford such a lovely house on an actor's salary. She knew Stephanie was the lead in that crime drama *Lies*, but even with a top ITV salary – she'd checked out some of the actors on *Coronation Street* to give her a guideline – it seemed a tall order. When Lily had looked up the address, she'd found that it had been bought three years ago for almost a million pounds.

Perhaps Stephanie Carson had invested in property incredibly wisely and sold on her previous home for a massive profit?

Lily rather doubted it. She was twenty-three, the same age as Lily, and she'd only had theatrical parts until her TV break on *Lies*.

But perhaps she had wealthy parents.

Or a wealthy boyfriend.

As Lily nursed her coffee, she watched the world go by. She wasn't entirely sure why she was here – the chances of actually seeing Stephanie were very slim, and she didn't have any of Vittoria's detective's capabilities in following people if she did appear. But Lily wanted to get a sense of the area, of Stephanie's life, and although she had a million things to do to get ready for New York, her time was her own now. With everything happening at No. 42, she'd decided to hand in her notice at the coffee shop in St Pancras station – she really had too much on her mind to focus on which customer wanted a skinny latte and who wanted a flat white. She had enough savings to last until her first No. 42 pay cheque arrived, and, incredibly, they were going to look after her relocation and rental costs for the first three months until she got settled in New York. Marianne Omotoso had mentioned

144

it in her interview but Lily hadn't quite taken it in – the whole experience had been so overwhelming. When she'd formally accepted and Marianne's delighted email had arrived, she'd laid everything out in black and white.

And one thing was for sure, they really wanted her.

Which was an idea that Lily was still having problems adjusting to. She'd talked about it to Nathan over brownies in the Red Fox Films kitchen and he'd smiled at her in complete understanding, shaking his head. 'That's called imposter syndrome. Wait till you get to New York and people start fawning all over you, then you'll really feel like you're in some sort of giant reality experiment …'

Nathan had no idea how close he was to the truth. Her life was starting to feel like a TV drama, and she hadn't even left London yet.

But key to getting to New York at all was getting the shop back – and the clock was ticking. So rather than sitting in the kitchen of her flat worrying, here she was sitting opposite Stephanie Carson's rather lovely house.

At least working towards Vittoria's goal made her feel like she was doing something to sort out her own problems. She was on Stephanie's case and she prayed that Vittoria was being as diligent with Edward Croxley.

Lily had absolutely no idea how Vittoria was going to manage to get the shop back, but she had absolute faith that she would. There was something about her that inspired confidence and gave the impression that she didn't take any prisoners. Vittoria had said on the plane that they were two intelligent women, but Lily had the distinct impression that Vittoria was a lot more intelligent than she was, that she was one of those super-bright all-round super-successful types that was just brilliant at everything they did. The type that was head girl in school, got four As and played tennis for England. She sure hoped so. Lily reckoned she had a plan that could, literally, bring down Marcus Devine, but she was quite sure Vittoria would need to use all her skills to find out what was going on with Edward Croxley.

Lily felt the dark hole of despair opening up in her stomach. She'd sent Jack off to an auction today. If they couldn't trade from the shop, they could trade from home for a bit once they had some stock. Jack had lots of contacts. He might not make much but if he had something to sell he would have something to keep him in the game, and to keep him busy.

And the last thing Lily needed was Jack getting depressed. She corrected herself. *More depressed.* Ever since he'd turned up on the doorstep, she felt as if he'd retreated into himself, that a part of him was distant, lost. And she needed to find it again before she could head to New York.

At least work was distracting him a bit.

He loved country house auctions; you just never knew what might turn up.

As Lily nursed her latte, across the road the front door of Number 121 opened. Lily's eyes widened as a woman who was undoubtedly Stephanie Carson stepped out. She wasn't wearing a coat, had her handbag under her arm and her mobile phone to her ear as she turned to pull the door closed behind her. Lily took a quick swig of her coffee as Stephanie walked to her front gate and out onto the pavement, pausing to check the traffic so she could cross the road. Lily watched in amazement: she was heading directly for the coffee shop.

Casual in jeans and running shoes, Stephanie Carson was wearing an A-line navy T-shirt that stretched over her pronounced bump. She had her thick blonde hair pulled back in a ponytail. A moment later the bell on the café door tinkled and Stephanie came in, still speaking into her phone. From where she was sitting Lily could just hear her conversation.

'Of course, I'll see you on Tuesday. And I'm fine, really. I love you, darling … I know, I'm missing you too.'

Stephanie clicked off the phone and smiled at the girl behind the counter, who obviously knew her well. The girl grinned at her. 'Almond croissants?'

Stephanie laughed. 'Please. My God, I don't know what it is about them but I just can't stop eating them. I wake up thinking about them.'

The girl leaned into the display case to bag the pastries. 'At least it's not coal – could you imagine craving that?'

Stephanie laughed and began opening her bag to look for her purse. Behind her Lily stood up, her phone in her hand as if she was texting. Heading for the counter, Lily caught the eye of the girl behind the till. 'Can I get another latte, please?'

'Of course, I'll bring it over.'

Stephanie glanced up at her and Lily made an exaggerated look of surprise. 'I don't believe it. You're not Stephanie Carson?' Lily shook her head in disbelief. 'My goodness, I was only talking to my colleagues in New York about you the other day.'

Stephanie's face was cold, her grin polite. She was obviously used to being spotted and not a fan of having to talk to people who thought they knew her.

'Really? That sounds interesting.'

Pretending she hadn't noticed Stephanie's reaction, Lily continued, 'I work for No. 42 – we're looking to make a splash with our new collection in the UK. I was telling Marianne, the design director, about your TV show. We're looking for rising stars for a new range launching in January.'

It was Stephanie's turn to look surprised. 'Oh.' Her whole attitude changed. 'That sounds *very* interesting.'

Lily shook her head again, glancing back at her phone like her text was far more important than the conversation. 'How mad to bump into you.' She smiled absentmindedly. 'Lovely to meet you.'

Lily turned to go back to her table, as if the conversation was over. Behind her Stephanie said loudly, 'Do you know, I think I might have something too – have you got green tea? And I might have one of those croissants now?'

Lily turned back, her brow furrowed, deep in thought, apparently only half-concentrating on what was going on in the coffee shop. 'Would you like to join me? I was supposed to be meeting my brother but he's going to be ages, apparently.'

Stephanie smiled, her whole face lighting up. 'That would be lovely, thank you. I'd love to hear more about No. 42 – I haven't heard anything from my agent.'

Pulling out a chair, Stephanie sat down, putting her phone next to her on the table. As she bent sideways to slide her handbag under the chair, struggling with her bump, Lily glanced at her screensaver just before it went to sleep. Marcus Devine smiled back at her.

She was utterly shameless.

As Stephanie straightened up, Lily switched off her own phone, dropping it into her satchel. 'We're looking at lots of different people – the PR team might not have got to the agent stage yet. Obviously, it's a very important position for a brand like ours. They have to do lots of background checks.'

'OK, right.' Stephanie's colour heightened very slightly. 'So tell me what you do. Do you work in New York?'

The girl arrived with her coffee and Stephanie's pot of tea as Lily said, 'I'm starting officially at the end of the month. I'm a jewellery designer – I'm going to be working on their bespoke ranges. I was with them last week and we're looking at campaigns for the launch of a new high street range.' Lily sipped her coffee. 'They want to make the fact that I'm English into a story for the press and we were working out how that could tie into their marketing strategy for the retail lines.'

Stephanie thought for a moment, then said, 'That's so interesting – how can I help?'

'Well, I'll be working on one-off commissions, suites of jewellery for their top-level clients, but we're going to develop retail lines around the themes of the commissioned pieces. So if Beyoncé is wearing one of our star tiaras to the Grammys, there will be a range of star products to match it in high street shops. We want people who will be well-photographed to be wearing those ranges too. I adored your show *Lies* and I thought you'd be perfect; you've picked up a huge following.'

A smile flicked across Stephanie's face. 'That sounds great. So you're looking for brand ambassadors, really?'

Lily took another sip of her coffee. 'Exactly. We'll supply you with jewellery and obviously pay you a retainer to make sure you mention No. 42 whenever you can. I'm sure you've done it for other brands?'

'No, actually, I haven't, but I adore No. 42. I've already got some of their pieces – a friend brought me the Asteroid cuff and earrings for my birthday.'

'Wow, you have a very nice friend – that's a gorgeous collection. In silver?'

'Rose gold.' Stephanie blushed faintly.

As well she might. Lily knew that the cuff alone in that collection cost over seven thousand dollars. Marcus Devine must have spent the best part of ten thousand on his lady love's birthday gift.

It had probably cost him about the same to hire a hitman to try to murder his wife.

Chapter 21

VITTORIA SHIVERED as the taxi dropped her off outside Mile End tube station. It was starting to rain and a stiff breeze was sending rubbish tumbling up the broad pavement. She had an overwhelming feeling of greyness as she pulled her coat around her and pushed the cab door closed. She wasn't sure if it was the overcast sky or the expanses of concrete, but for a moment she was sure the driver had brought her to the wrong address; this area felt like it was a long way from anywhere called Paradise Gardens.

Anxiety made her stomach hollow, nerves fluttering like trapped birds. She couldn't afford for this part of the plan to go wrong. Looking around her, Vittoria got her bearings before making a beeline for the route that she had carefully memorised. The apartment she needed was apparently only a two-minute walk away.

She headed down a side street into a warren of multi-storey flats, netted windows rising above her like watchful eyes in blank faces. Reaching what appeared to be the entrance of the building she needed, she spotted a sign on the wall to her right indicating floor and apartment numbers. This was it.

On the outside the building looked smart enough, but as she took a step inside the lobby area, it was a different matter. The lifts were covered in graffiti, 'out of order' signs stuck on the steel doors, the darkened corners of the concrete hallway littered with syringes and McDonald's wrappers.

Vittoria started up the stairs, the heels of her boots echoing with every step. She kept to the shadows, praying she wouldn't meet anyone, her mouth dry, her heart careering. On the sixth floor she found another sign with the apartment number she needed. The flat was at the very end of an open landing, children's toys strewn along the walkway. Looking out over the balcony, she could see dark clouds gathering, promising more rain.

She reached the door and knocked, waiting a few moments. There was no reply. *Merda*.

She knocked again.

Vittoria's stomach fell. Whatever about Croxley getting excited about a missing Pissarro turning up for private sale, proving its provenance was vital to his actually selling it. And that was why she was here. She had no idea how long this would take but it was vital that she got it organised today.

Before she'd left Dublin, Vittoria had thought long and hard about provenance. She didn't need a bill of sale – it wasn't that sort of picture. What she needed was a way of demonstrating how it might have come into the collection.

It had been so obvious when she'd finally come up with an answer. Marcus's father's dinner parties had been legendary and were precisely where this type of thing would have been discussed. They provided the perfect solution.

Years ago, Vittoria had been amazed to read that, at the end of the war, then Taoiseach Eamon de Valera had visited the German Embassy in Dublin to offer his personal condolences over the death of Adolf Hitler, his political allegiances fuelled by anti-British sentiments. It had all been in a review of a thriller set in post-war Ireland – the

'Emergency', as the Irish referred to the Second World War – the author capturing the hostility towards the UK perfectly. As a neutral English-speaking country, Ireland had become a very attractive stopping off point for anyone who needed to vanish from the victorious allied forces.

Marcus's father was a judge; he mixed in political circles. It didn't require a huge leap of logic to make the connection: it was just 'proving' it that was vital.

But there were reams of Judge Devine's letters and papers in Marcus's winter study, in the drawers of the huge leather-topped desk his father had used. Pulling it open, pushing aside the spare pairs of spectacles and old fountain pens in the central drawer, Vittoria had started going through everything, looking for something that she could make work. His mother had kept diaries, mainly about the weather and her hair appointments, but occasionally who was coming to dinner, often detailing the menus themselves. Which had made quite incredible reading as she'd flicked through; Vittoria knew her diet was restrictive but the very thought of the amount of food that was served made her feel quite queasy.

The diaries gave her fabulous context and a way for others to verify the document Vittoria planned to create. Eileen the copyist had given her – well, had given Marcus, whom she thought she was corresponding with – the name of a man who was a wizard with all sorts of documents. 'Marcus' had emailed in a panic saying he needed someone to write a letter in his father's hand – he'd spilled coffee all over a pile of documents heading for an exhibition at the Law Library and needed them replaced as discreetly as possible. It had sounded a bit odd even to Vittoria, but it was the only thing she could think of on the spur of the moment. And it had worked.

Sifting through the papers in the drawers, old play programmes, articles torn from newspapers, the stubs of cheque books, eventually Vittoria had found what she needed: a letter from Marcus's father to his mother, one that said very little except that he'd be back in Killiney soon. Which didn't help anyone, but the fact that it was one line and the rest of the page was blank, and it had been dated 17 July but with no year, made it the perfect vehicle to substantiate the supposed origin of this particular painting – and several more, should they be needed. He hadn't even signed it. It looked like it might have been wrapped around something, Vittoria had no idea what.

It had taken Vittoria a while to get the wording right, but the letter just needed another paragraph in which Marcus's father mentioned that he had invited some acquaintances to dinner, including a wealthy Dutch businessman and prominent art collector. In the letter, Marcus's father wanted to make sure that a vintage port was well aired and that they used the crystal decanters with the family crest.

It needed to be dated 1964.

Vittoria had done her homework.

It wouldn't take Croxley a moment to discover that the Dutch businessman, Pieter Menten, had later been convicted of being a member of the SS. There were several newspaper reports about how the house he'd bought in Waterford had been looted and set on fire, how the local gardaí had suspected Mossad.

Raymond Bahnschrift, the man who had been recommended to write the letter, had been hard to contact. But perhaps that was a good thing in his line of work.

He didn't have email or a mobile phone, preferring to communicate by post, and with time tight Vittoria hadn't been sure she would hear back from him. But a message had been waiting for her when she arrived at the hotel. Short and cryptic, it had directed her to a postcard in a nearby newsagent's small ads noticeboard. On the reverse, she'd found the time of her appointment written in a spidery hand: *Saturday 3 p.m.*

Mr Bahnschrift obviously didn't take any risks.

Or answer his front door very quickly, come to that.

Vittoria could feel eyes on her back as she waited on the landing outside. She glanced across at the walkway in the opposite block. There was no one there that she could see, but the feeling of being watched didn't go away.

How long should she wait? She'd been told to call in at three; he was expecting her. Vittoria knocked again. Perhaps he was just a little deaf?

Her hands thrust into her coat pockets, her fingers cold despite her leather gloves, Vittoria glanced over her shoulder again. And almost jumped as she heard the safety chain on the door jangling. It opened a crack. At the bottom a small dog's nose poked out of the gap and she was hit by the stench of tobacco. As the door opened to the limit of the chain, a tiny man wearing a cardigan and a silk cravat looked her up and down. Then, as if satisfied, he unhooked the chain and left the door ajar as he headed off down the corridor, apparently expecting her to follow him. Stiflingly hot, the flat smelled so strongly of cigarettes as she stepped inside that Vittoria began to feel her head swim.

In the living room at the back of the flat, a single armchair sat in front of a TV, the sound turned down. The whole room was meticulously clean, the magazines lined up on a low coffee table in front of the chair with military precision.

'Now, young lady, what do you need?' He didn't introduce himself. His voice was raspy, his accent cockney but with a hint of something – Austrian, she thought. His manner didn't exactly invite conversation so she wasn't going to ask.

Pulling a plastic file out of her bag, Vittoria showed him the various notes and letters she had found that demonstrated Judge Devine's handwriting, the original letter in its clear plastic bag and her notes for the additions. He took them and shuffled over to a table beside the window, spreading them out, nodding, as he bent over them to look closely. His hands were tiny but soft, like a woman's hands, his fingers stained with ink

Reading over the notes, he raised a bushy eyebrow at Menten's name, looked at her hard, as if he recognised it.

'Come back at five. I'll have everything done by then.'

Vittoria pulled the envelope of cash from her handbag and put down it on the table. Then he nodded to himself and, as if he'd forgotten she was there, moved over to a polished bureau and, flipping down a central fold-out desk with a flourish, pulled out an untidy box of pens and bottles of ink. The bureau was crammed with papers, a pile of passports neatly stacked on one side. Vittoria hid her surprise. The covers were different colours – green, blue, burgundy. Beside them, under a bottle of ink, was a pile of pink papers that she recognised as the old-style British driving-licence documents. It was small wonder governments had switched to plastic cards. Ruby, her receptionist at the office, was English, still had her British passport and driver's licence. They'd laughed over them one day, comparing photographs.

Bahnschrift was obviously a master forger.

And had no need to be polite to his clients.

His back to her, Vittoria took it that she was dismissed and headed back down the hall, the dog, some sort of elderly terrier, watching her from the armchair with bright eyes.

Pulling the door behind her, Vittoria hurried down the stairs. She didn't know quite what to do with herself for the two hours she needed to wait. Outside, turning to her left, she walked back up towards the roar of traffic on the Mile End Road, spotting a Starbucks on the opposite side. She headed for it.

Nursing her coffee, sitting in a corner as far away from the window as she could get, she pulled her phone out and tried to look busy.

Thank God nobody spoke to her.

Time ticked slowly by. She read the local paper from cover to cover. Then the *Metro*. Then the *Evening Standard*.

At five o'clock she made her way back. It was beginning to get dark.

Her palms were sweating by the time she got to the sixth floor. This time, Bahnschrift didn't even open the door, instead wordlessly passed her a brown envelope with everything in it. She had a moment of panic wondering if he'd even been able to do it, but heading back to the top of the stairs, she stopped to quickly open the envelope. Checking over her shoulder, she unfolded the letter, and almost laughed. Despite the dim light, she could see Bahnschrift was a true artist. The new section of the letter blended perfectly with the original line and was signed, as if in haste, with Marcus's father's initials.

Now she had everything she needed to authenticate, not just this painting, but also the others that she had 'found' in the attic.

Chapter 22

LILY WAS A MORNING PERSON, and even on a Sunday she was up early. Looking out of her bedroom window, she could see that it had rained during the night and the world looked washed clean. The tennis courts and park were still quiet, the normally busy streets somehow hushed like they were taking a few moments to contemplate before the city fully woke up.

Lily had been doing a lot of contemplating herself last night. Contemplating life and a bottle of white wine. Both her flatmates were away for the weekend and she and Jack had the place to themselves. She could hear him snoring on the sofa as, still in her pyjamas, she headed for the kitchen and the kettle.

Meeting Stephanie Carson yesterday had given her a lot to think about. Although she hadn't said it in so many words, it was very clear that Vittoria's husband Marcus was lavishing a lot of attention on his latest mistress. Hopefully Vittoria would never know how much money her husband was spending on Stephanie, but it seemed likely to Lily that he'd helped her buy her house and was helping her financially. He obviously had the money. But that wasn't really the point.

As Lily reached for the kettle, very pleased to have the kitchen to herself, she reached over to turn her phone on –

she'd left it plugged in on the kitchen counter last night – and it immediately pipped with a text. She glanced at it as she turned on the tap. The first cup of tea of the day was better than any glass of white wine.

Lily paused, the kettle in her hand. The text was from Em.

Have you seen the paper??!! Got
my promotion, I'm on features,
baby!!!!!

Lily's eyes widened. Boy, Emma must have been out partying last night. A slow smile grew on Lily's face – the pictures had landed. She looked at the kettle. She was desperate to see the paper, but it was only 6.30 a.m. and the newsagent's wasn't open yet. The dew was hardly dry and she needed tea first. It took her a moment to realise she could check the story online. She'd get the proper copy later.

The kettle boiling behind her, Lily sat down at the kitchen table and opened her MacBook. She found the story straight away: 'Caught in the Cock Pit'. Lily winced. Em was chancing her arm, but then it was exactly what her bosses loved. Plenty of controversy, lots of people talking. Lily checked the sharing buttons – the article had already been shared thousands of times across Facebook and Twitter. It looked like it might go viral.

Lily scanned the copy, barely there beside the huge photos, but Emma had the by-line. Lily couldn't help but grin, delighted for her friend. And Em had listened to her – in the exposé piece below the pictures, Em had explained who the main players were, speculating on their relationship but also asking if the pictures were indeed real or purely a publicity stunt generated by Bellissima. Lily felt like punching the air. Emma was just the best.

There was no way Bellissima was going to sue – she'd love the publicity. And Marcus Devine? There was enough in Em's 'do-we-believe-this-or-is-it-a-con tone to make it impossible for him to sue. To say nothing of the fact that private individuals taking on a corporation the size of Media Holdings Inc., with its turnover of almost £2 billion, needed to be very sure of their ground. The photo looked like a selfie, so only Bellissima and Devine knew for sure if it was real or faked, and any protests he made would make it look like he was as guilty as hell. Not only of cavorting with a woman of dubious reputation who wasn't his wife, but, *much* more importantly in Lily's masterplan, in the process clearly breaking a ton of aviation security regulations. Who was to know she hadn't smuggled an explosive device on board?

The kettle boiled and Lily got up to make her tea, her smile wide. It was time for her next move.

Chapter 23

VITTORIA AWOKE with a jerk, sweating, her back in spasm, her heart beating hard. Her eyes fixed on the milky white ceiling, she pushed her hand into her hair and focused on breathing deeply, fighting the pain and trying to work out where she was. Images jumbled in her head, the moment of the accident, more pain. Then memories of waking in hospital, the shock, merged with her lying in her bed at home, waking suddenly, conscious she'd heard something.

Glancing around the room, she began to surface from the nightmare, to register the elegance and neutral colours of the room, remembering that she was in The Hogarth Hotel in London. The door to the en suite was ajar, just as she'd left it, her leather jeans lying over the back of the padded corner chair. She'd closed the heavy curtains tightly but the huge round mirror above the desk-come-dressing table picked up a sliver of light, reflecting it in a fluid pool on the slate grey carpet.

Relief began to flood through her.

She wasn't in hospital or at home.

Thank God.

Lying in the crisp cotton sheets, memories of the break-in were closest to the surface, feelings of terror stirring up everything she had buried about the accident. Vittoria caught her breath. She'd woken suddenly the night of the break-in too, like now. Listening hard, she had tried to filter out the sounds of the old house, the distant suck of the sea on the beach, the swish of the trees on the avenue moving in the wind. The huge curved glass sash windows in her bedroom were impossible to double glaze and let in every sound.

Vittoria had fallen in love with Alcantara the moment she'd seen the house with its sea views and stunning gardens. It reminded her so much of home with the constant sound of the surf. She pulled the duvet around her and, easing into a more comfortable position, took a deep breath, her heart only beginning to calm. The fear was still real, too real. There were cameras all over the grounds at Alcantara – it was a huge property, had a top of the range security system that was connected directly to the gardaí.

But that night she'd been expecting Marcus to come home and had left the alarm turned off.

Vittoria gripped the sheets, trying to control her breathing. She closed her eyes tightly, willing the picture of the door slowly opening to leave her. But it was imprinted on her memory. The dark shape slipping into the room. The silhouette of the gun. She'd shouted at him, and after a moment that was frozen in her memory, the man had disappeared as quickly as he'd appeared, the sound of his feet pounding the stairs echoing through the house. She'd hit the panic button but the shock of what could have happened wouldn't leave her.

Vittoria turned over slowly towards the window, burrowing into the bed-clothes. Where *had* Marcus been that night? He'd said he was coming home for dinner when she'd spoken to him earlier that day. And everything had been confirmed. But as time had ticked on, and the food had started to congeal, she'd realised he wasn't coming home. And he wasn't answering his phone – it was going straight to voicemail. Furious her careful plans for the evening would have to be abandoned, she'd sent a text to reorganise everything and had decided go up to bed with a book.

She hadn't bothered putting the alarm on. Marcus wasn't flying for a few days so it was more than likely he'd arrived in Dublin and had met Aidan for a few drinks in the yacht club or somewhere. He never remembered to turn the alarm off when he'd been drinking, and the last thing she wanted was to be woken up by the siren going off – she'd had wall-to-wall meetings scheduled for the next day after an intensive session with Yana, the Russian ballerina, first thing.

That night, waiting for him, Vittoria had dozed off, her book beside her. Then she'd woken with a start, sure she'd heard something. Half-asleep, she'd assumed it was Marcus coming in, but he usually made a lot of noise, banging doors on his way up. And as she'd surfaced from sleep, she'd realised that the house was quiet. Too quiet. She'd strained her ears, listened hard. Then she heard it again. The sound of a door gently opening, a board creaking on the landing.

And she'd known someone was in the house.

And that it wasn't Marcus.

Vittoria pulled The Hogarth's feather pillow under her head. She wasn't sure if she would ever be able to forget that night. *Thank God the panic alarm worked independently from the main security system.*

He should have been there. Everything would have been different if he'd been there.

Vittoria shivered. She'd been so shocked when the guards had finally arrived that she'd hardly been able to speak. They'd tried to call Marcus but his phone must have been off. Then they'd tried Aidan, who had been in the car and on the way over before the garda had even finished the phone call. He'd wrapped his arms around her and stayed with her until Marcus had finally turned up after lunch the next day. He'd been held up in London and hadn't thought to call, apparently. That was Marcus all over.

If he'd let her know that he wasn't coming home, so many things would have been different. She'd have put the alarm on for one thing.

Vittoria turned over again to face the bedroom door, the stiffness in her back easing. She had no idea what time it was, but it felt early. And now she was wide awake. Sitting up, she reached for her phone and, out of the corner of her eye, immediately saw what had woken her. She'd asked for the Sunday papers, quite a few of them, and the staff had slipped a magazine under the door. She could see a piece of notepaper folded into it – probably telling her that rest of the papers were hanging on the doorknob of her room. Vittoria rolled her eyes. It must have been the sound of the magazine on the carpet that had disturbed her sleep, the door rattling as the heavy bag of papers was hung up.

Opening her phone, Vittoria saw that it was only 7.30. She'd ordered breakfast for 9.30 and knew she really should go back to sleep for a few hours. She could go through all the papers over breakfast in bed.

She had a feeling Edward Croxley would be in touch this morning too. Vittoria pursed her lips, thinking. What exactly had he said on the phone?

The thought made Vittoria begin to relax. She was back in control now. Sitting up in bed, she pulled the pillow straight behind her, her mind more alert. She wanted to get to the bottom of Croxley's phone call yesterday. The more she thought about it, the more it seemed to explain the whole drama with the card game.

If Croxley was looking for something small, something hidden in the shop, he'd need time to find it. And short of getting a job working for Lily's brother Jack, 'winning' the shop had actually been quite an inspired move. It sounded like these small items were of very significant value and Jack would be just as interested in them as Croxley was, if he knew what they were.

Vittoria found the recording on her phone and played it back. There was a lot of background noise, the rustle of tissue paper, cars passing on the road outside, but Croxley's voice was clear enough – she knew she could get it cleaned up when she got home, but right now if she played it again … It took a few more goes and then she caught it, the words she'd been sure that she'd heard when he was speaking to the mysterious Sergei: 'museum' and 'blood'.

So whatever was in the shop was small, extremely valuable, and from the sarcasm she'd heard in his voice, sounded like it came from a museum located somewhere there had been bloodshed. Which suggested a warzone or occupied area? That suggested the Middle East to Vittoria. Hadn't the museum in Baghdad been looted a few years ago? She couldn't remember who by, but she'd seen it on the news: the building had been ransacked, thousands of priceless antiquities destroyed or stolen. Her curiosity piqued, Vittoria opened Google on her phone. What could be very small and portable but very valuable, have come from a museum like that and be of interest to a Russian collector?

For the amount of trouble Croxley was going to, whatever he was looking for had to be very rare, but it could be anything. The more she searched, the more Vittoria felt she was right about the museum. It had to be Baghdad. Although what on earth the item could be, she had no idea. There seemed to be endless possibilities.

But it must have had ended up in the shop relatively recently, Vittoria guessed. Had Jack bought something unwittingly that the item was being smuggled inside? Vittoria frowned and screwed up her face. She needed to talk to Lily to see if any of this sounded familiar, and she needed to do it before she left London.

Over lunch at the Calvert Vaux Hotel in New York, they'd decided that if they needed to meet they would contact each other by post. Vittoria just needed to send Lily a note inviting her to … Vittoria thought for a moment – it needed to be somewhere very public and busy where they could talk but without anyone noticing them – the National Gallery? They could very easily stand in front of a painting and appear to be discussing it. But the British Museum was closer and always packed. And, Vittoria's mind worked fast, if whatever Croxley was looking for was from the Middle East, perhaps that was the floor they needed to meet on – Lily might see something that jogged her memory. Yawning, Vittoria leaned over to put her phone on the locker next to the bed. The British postal system was very reliable. If she posted a card on Monday it should be with Lily on Tuesday morning. Vittoria's flight wasn't until eight o'clock that evening from London City airport. If she met Lily in the afternoon, they would only need a few minutes for Vittoria to explain her suspicions.

*

At 9 a.m. Vittoria's phone alarm went off. She'd gone back to sleep after waking so early, and now she stretched stiffly and slipped out of bed, heading to get the shower running before her breakfast arrived. The Hogarth's plumbing always took her a few moments to work out; two shower heads and mysterious dials with indecipherable markings made it a bit of a challenge no matter how many times she stayed there. Vittoria had stayed in a lot of hotels on her travels and the guest information on how to operate the TV and Wi-Fi and the location of the gym never seemed to include basics like how to get the shower working. She still reckoned that the most impressive thing about James Bond was that he could walk into his hotel bathroom in *Casino Royale* and switch the shower on at the right temperature first go.

Her shower finished, wrapped in one of the hotel's thick white robes, Vittoria bent down to pick up the magazine and quickly opened the door to unhook the bag of newspapers, bringing everything over to the bed to leaf through.

The *Sunday Inquirer* was on the top.

And a picture of Bellissima Serata was on the masthead.

Vittoria suddenly felt a hideous blast of déjà vu. Last time it had been Yana – what was she going to find now? Opening the paper, Vittoria recoiled at her husband's smiling face, the photo blown up to almost the full size of the page. Beside him – *in the cockpit? Dio Mio!* – her hand clearly snaking up Marcus's thigh, was Bellissima Serata in a low-cut black dress, all her assets on view.

Vittoria's heart dropped. *What had he been doing this time?*

And in the cockpit? Surely that was against *all* the security regulations? It certainly didn't look like he was concentrating on his job. Even if they were on the ground and the plane was empty there were incredibly strict rules about the public having access.

Vittoria's mind flew as she picked up the other papers and hurriedly flicked through them. There was no mention anywhere else – it looked like an *Inquirer* exclusive. Vittoria closed her eyes, trying to centre herself, to control her panic. The *Inquirer* must have a vendetta against Marcus – it was just like … last time.

Perhaps the shock had made her stupid.

This was exactly like the last time.

Vittoria relaxed, smiling as a knock on the door announced the arrival of her breakfast.

Chapter 24

I**N NOTTING HILL** Stephanie Carson was finding it increasingly hard to sleep at night as her bump grew. And with Marcus in Singapore, in a completely different time zone, texting her what felt like every two minutes to see how she was feeling, she'd really not had enough sleep. As her clock clicked around to nine thirty, she decided to get up, stiffly rolling on her side and swinging her legs out of the bed. It was Sunday – she could have a nap later if needs be.

A few minutes later, leaving the kettle to boil in the kitchen, she ran back upstairs to have her shower, luxuriating in the relaxing warmth of the water. Filming yesterday had been brutal; she didn't know if she'd ever get rid of the soreness in her muscles. Letting the hot water wash over her back, Stephanie decided she'd throw on her jeans and collect some almond croissants and the papers across the road, and then she'd come home and settle in for a relaxing morning.

*

The sun was shining in through her large bay window as Stephanie pulled out the kitchen chair and sat down to look at the papers. She loved mornings like this, fresh and bright with the ground still wet last from last night's rain.

She yawned and stretched. She had spent all yesterday afternoon on set chained up in a shipping container, curled up with her back to the camera. The director was trying to get as much in the can as he could before she had the baby. So far clever angles had concealed her bump from the viewers and the writers had managed to get around her projected absence with a twist in the script. They were in the middle of a complex storyline about a Mexican Don blackmailing a banker – it was all organised crime and drugs and their ratings had never been so good, so it needed to be right. Although any of the other five storylines that she'd discussed with the director would have been less arduous than the one they'd gone for, she was sure.

They'd had so many script meetings to nail it down. The director had been really keen on one treatment where her character, Lola Dalloway, undercover at an embassy reception, had her champagne poisoned with ricin. The idea was that Lola would collapse and be rushed into intensive care. Which meant they could cut in lots of shots of her in hospital while the rest of the cast tried to work out if her cover had been blown, if the drug had really been intended for her or if something even more sinister was going on. It would have the tabloids hopping with speculation about her survival, and then, when she'd had the baby, she could recover dramatically.

Which was completely ridiculous, as she'd quickly found out. She'd needed the loo and, slipping out of the script meeting, she'd googled ricin to find out what on earth they were all talking about. It came from castor oil beans, apparently – and was super deadly, if that was a thing. As she'd sat on the loo she'd realised it would be just as easy *not* to bring her back into the show, and she wasn't about to risk *that*.

She'd marched back into the room and told them exactly what she thought of *that* plan. She *might* have shouted a bit and burst into tears, but they'd all hurriedly decided that Lola surviving a poisoning attempt was stretching things a bit, so now she had been kidnapped and was being held in a shipping container somewhere near Canary Wharf.

Which was where Stephanie had spent yesterday. Wondering if a champagne reception, with or without ricin, might have been a better option after all.

There was so much secrecy around these storylines that she wasn't even sure where the shipping container had been exactly, just that it was bloody uncomfortable and the silly cow who was covering the lead camera kept getting the lighting wrong.

She still had no idea either how she was supposed to get away, but if the cast had no idea which way the storyline would go, the acting was better, more heartfelt and genuine. Apparently. Nobody knew for sure if she'd live or die.

Stephanie took a sip of her tea and opened the magazines that came with the *Sunday Times*, flicking to her horoscope at the back of *Style* magazine. According to her stars she was going to have a surprise this week. *She just hoped it was a nice one and very expensive.*

Pushing the rest of the *Sunday Times* to one side, Stephanie scanned the *Sunday Inquirer*'s front page, picking up a croissant and taking a bite as she opened the paper.

She froze, the pastry suspended halfway between her mouth and the plate.

Marcus smiled back at her, filling almost the entire page. Beside him was some tart with pneumatic tits, sitting far too close to him.

Frowning, Stephanie began reading the article. The tart had

been in that terrible TV show Stephanie couldn't remember the name of, but she did remember the tabloids getting very excited about her experience with poles, and not the ones with a capital P. *Christ almighty, what had Marcus been doing?* Stephanie felt her temper boiling. It was bad enough she had to share him with that cow Vittoria …

Stephanie reached for her phone. She had no idea what time it was in whatever part of the world Marcus was in, but he had some explaining to do. Stephanie hit Marcus's number. It was engaged.

He was probably talking to the tart.

Impatiently, she hit Call again, knowing her number would show on his phone as incoming.

He still didn't pick up.

Staring at the pictures in the paper, she realised there was an inset of Marcus in one corner of the bigger image. He was in a nightclub, a cocktail in his hand. He'd obviously taken this woman out for the night and then taken her up in the cockpit. Or perhaps he'd met her on a flight.

She tried him again. Still engaged.

Furious, Stephanie stood up and turned around to find her iPad on the counter. She needed to see if this was online too.

Of course it was.

Bellissima Serata looked back at her smugly, pouting, her breasts pressed into Marcus's chest. That had to be a stage name. Stephanie did an Internet search for her, masses of links appearing. Instagram, Facebook. Stephanie typed 'translation' into Google. Bellissima Serata meant 'beautiful night' in Italian. She bet it had been a beautiful night, an expensive one too.

Stephanie reached for her phone just as it started to ring.

'Have you seen the paper? I can only see it online.' Marcus sounded breathless.

'I think half of London has seen it by now.'

'It's bad.' It was more of a statement than a question.

'It certainly is. What the fuck's going on?'

'I don't know, honestly, I've no idea. There was a stupid gossip piece in the paper about me being in The Velvet Club with her last week. It's all nonsense – I've never met her.'

'Why didn't you tell me? For God's sake.' Stephanie scanned her iPad and checked Twitter. 'She doesn't seem to be denying knowing you.'

'Well, she's hardly going to do that if she can get this sort of coverage is she?' Marcus snapped back at her. 'I'm sorry. It's not a real photo but no one will believe me. Work has been on; I have to go to a meeting on Tuesday as soon as I land. I don't think I'm going to be getting a promotion.'

'But what can they do?'

'Suspend me?' His voice cracked. 'That photo was supposedly taken in the cockpit. That's against about fifty major regulations.'

'Jesus. But you can't lose your job – what will you do?'

His voice was low and angry. 'God knows. I'll probably end up flying for some spurious African crop sprayer.'

Stephanie's mind whirred. How was she going to afford the house, the baby, without Marcus working?

'But you need to prove it's photoshopped. There must be a way. Where were you that night? There's a date stamp on the corner of the little photograph.'

Marcus breathed in sharply. 'According to the date and time stamp I was flying the next day, which,' he stopped, as if he was trying to control his voice, 'on top of everything else, breaks the eight-hour bottle-to-throttle rule. But it's nonsense. I wasn't drinking. That night I was with you.'

'So you can't have been there, in that bar, with her?'

'Obviously.'

'So—'

He cut her off. 'If I tell them I was with you, Vittoria will find out …' He said it slowly, like he was speaking to a child.

'Well, what's wrong with that?'

'Christ, Steph, we've been over this. She could do anything. She'll fight the prenup and try and take me to the cleaners, for one thing. She'll want the house. My father's house. If we end up in court, *everything* will be out there. The press will love every bloody minute of it.'

Stephanie exhaled loudly, trying to keep her voice level. 'Well, if you want to keep your job, it doesn't look like you've got much choice.'

'I can't … I'll think about it. I've got forty-eight hours before the meeting to work something out.'

'She's going to go nuts anyway, you know. You're all over the bloody papers with some sleazy ex-stripper. Someone's going to tell her.'

'That's not as bad as her finding out about you, about the baby – you can be sure of that.'

She heard his phone pip with an incoming message. 'Look, that's another call coming in – I'd better go. I'll call you later, sweet pea, when I've more idea what's going on.'

And with that he clicked off.

Stephanie looked at the phone, anger bubbling inside her. This gave him the perfect reason to tell Vittoria that he wanted a divorce. And he didn't seem to have realised it. If Stephanie was married to him, being plastered all over the news with a tart would be enough reason for her to throw him out, and she was quite sure Vittoria wasn't that different from her.

But she really needed him to keep his job. She knew his family had loads of paintings and antiques and stuff but she needed support. She loved this house and private schools were expensive. If the price he had to pay for keeping his job was losing half his assets to Vittoria, was that really that bad? Whatever way you looked at it, there didn't seem to be a good way out of this one.

Stephanie knew she should have pressed him to tell Vittoria sooner, but he'd always had some sort of excuse – all the stuff going on at home, the burglaries. She should have told him to choose, to make up his mind, but part of her couldn't face that, couldn't face the chance that he might leave, that his home and lifestyle might mean more to him than she did.

Stephanie massaged her bump. The last thing she wanted was to have to fight a huge paternity suit, but if it came to it, there was no way her son was going to lose his birthright. If Marcus thought Vittoria could be difficult, he hadn't seen anything yet.

Chapter 25

SERGEI WAS WAITING for Edward Croxley when he arrived upstairs in The Nest Restaurant at The Rookery in Covent Garden. It was busy even though it was only Monday. A private club, it was an ideal place to meet – the noisy chatter of diners and the sounds from the open kitchen made it hard for people to overhear them. And it was very busy – the least likely place they might be accused of meeting to discuss sensitive business.

Croxley had left his coat downstairs and made his way up the broad unvarnished wooden stairs slowly, his suede shoes silent on the treads. Generously proportioned rooms opened off every landing of the Georgian townhouse, giving a variety of restaurant experiences, some more formal than others. Looking in as he passed, Croxley recognised a lot of faces from the TV and stage, beautiful women and men in deliberately casual, yet obviously expensive jackets.

But he wasn't thinking about who he might bump into.

He needed to come up with a convincing story to buy him a bit more time with Sergei and, more importantly, with Igor Kaprizov. He wished he had never even met them at this point.

Why had he got involved with the Russians in the first place? He knew why. And it wasn't like he hadn't realised how dangerous they were, but he'd been lulled by the knowledge that they looked after their own and they paid well. Very well.

It had all been so easy, too easy. Meeting Igor Kaprizov at a private view at a gallery in Mayfair, they'd got chatting beside a rather ridiculous monochrome print of something with feathers. Kaprizov had invited him to a reception in Kensington, and then there had been an invite to his stunning home overlooking the sea in Cannes, lemons growing on the trees shading the patio, fabulous wine, beautiful women …

Croxley should have guessed they were checking him out, that they'd identified him as an ideal go-between for their black-market art business.

Bringing antiquities into the UK through country house auctions created a path to the buyer that had been wiped clean of Middle Eastern dust and made everything very respectable. British aristocratic families were notorious collectors, had travelled the empire acquiring all sorts of items, and anything could turn up in the hidden drawer of a games box or a bureau.

Croxley had to admit the country house sale route was genius. Even if they did find them, local auctioneers didn't always recognise or have the experience to date these types of items – indeed, he'd discovered London dealers didn't always get it right either. And the Russians banked on that ignorance. They knew what they were doing and often had a group of hungry buyers organised for a very private auction before the items even left Iran or Syria. They had just needed a pair of trusted hands, hands with a reputation that would give buyers confidence, to pick up the items legitimately and bring them to them.

And he'd walked right into their plan. He'd been wowed by Kaprizov. By the money and the lifestyle. Then he'd met Sergei, Kaprizov's number-one operative in London. He was charming, knew people Edward had been to school with, had flattered Edward with his knowledge of the big deals he'd done.

They'd expected Edward to join them in Cannes, had mentioned it at that party in London. Kaprizov's plane would be available; a car would collect him. Kaprizov's secretary had called him with the travel arrangements as if it was the most normal thing in the world. The first day they'd gone out on his yacht, had eaten lunch on the deck, the sun strong. The girls had all been Russian, he'd assumed – they certainly didn't have any English, but then they hadn't needed it. He'd got back to the villa that night drunk and exhausted, had fallen into the bathroom and then into the huge bed.

It was only in the morning that he'd found the newspaper, casually left on the dresser – the *Irish Times* from July 2008, his name listed as one of the partygoers at a twenty-first birthday party in Berkshire that had ended in tragedy.

And he'd known they were closing in.

And then over dinner, the men had spoken English, laughing at the tale of what exactly had happened to one of Igor Kaprizov's business partners, one who had double crossed him, and how much he'd screamed to die. Edward really hadn't needed to hear the whole story to be reminded of how they dealt with their opponents.

Later in the evening Sergei had taken him to one side, handing him a cigar as they leaned over the ornate wall separating the patio from the cliffs below, the sea lapping as the tide changed, the scent of roses drifting on the evening breeze. And he'd explained what they needed and how good Kaprizov was to work for, and how he looked after his own.

Croxley had known he was snared then, that if he was in, he needed to get as much out of them as he could.

And everything had been going so smoothly.

Sergei looked after him well; he'd become more involved in the art business, had sold several pieces for them, appearing to be the front man on some big deals that publicly had done him no harm at all. They had helped get his name out there, which was obviously how Vittoria Devine had heard of him. Which was looking like it could be a very good thing.

By the time he reached the top floor of The Rookery, Edward Croxley could see Sergei busy with his phone, waiting for him. His white blond hair cropped military short, he was at least a head taller than anyone standing close to him and was wearing a navy linen blazer and white open-necked shirt, dressed down with jeans and handmade shoes.

Sergei looked up and acknowledged him, indicating two stools at the end of the counter. They sat down, and on the other side a chef began preparing sushi, an enormous cleaver in his hand.

Sergei frowned as he spoke. 'So do you have news for me?'

Before Croxley could answer, the waiter materialised behind them, handing them menus. To his right, Croxley was vaguely aware of another man sitting down beside him on the next stool, discussing football with his companion. Croxley groaned inwardly – the last thing he needed now was an update on the Premier League. The man's friend left him for a minute and the man spun around on his stool, playing with his phone.

At least he'd shut up.

Croxley needed to concentrate on his conversation with Sergei and make sure he didn't accidentally promise something he couldn't deliver, while at the same time buying himself some time.

He didn't want to be distracted by anything.

They ordered and a moment later the waiter was gone. Croxley picked up the glass of water that had appeared beside him and, turning to Sergei, kept his voice low. 'I've searched the shop. They aren't there. Which means Jack Power must have them.'

'So we need to talk to him and get them back.'

Sergei made it sound so perfectly simple.

'The *only* problem with *that* is he'll realise they're valuable and will start to wonder why the fuck they were hidden in an old box of books that was for sale at an open auction in the home counties.' Croxley paused, trying to hide his annoyance at the obvious stupidity of revealing the whole operation to Jack Power. 'We'll have to think of a reason why they were in there, something plausible, otherwise he could suss the whole thing and then we'll be blown.'

Sergei shook out his napkin and shrugged. 'I don't think discussing it with him will compromise the operation. It's worked very well. We might just have to go out further into the country to different auctions, find other ways of adding lots. I don't think that's an issue.'

Shaking his head, Edward kept his voice low. 'But he'll realise that I knew there was something hidden in the box and he'll start wondering how and what's going on. He might not realise exactly, but he'll smell a rat and after losing the shop he'll come after me.'

Sergei curled his lip. 'Give him back the shop. Trade it for the goods. Tell him you feel bad about taking it.'

As if he hadn't already thought of that. 'You think that won't raise his suspicions?'

Sergei shrugged. 'I don't really care. Igor is getting impatient. He's paid good money for those amulets – they are a special gift for the bridesmaids. We do not have time

179

for any more messing about. The wedding is very soon.'

'I know, I know. Look, leave it with me. I'll work it out.'

'I would love to leave it with you, Edward, but there is no more time. I can only give you forty-eight hours and then we will have to send some people to talk to Jack Power.'

'But he'll realise. He knows too much.'

Sergei shrugged. 'Not a problem. We will make sure he doesn't get a chance to speak to anyone.'

Edward felt his mouth go suddenly dry. Had Sergei just suggested killing Jack Power?

And if he killed Jack, what was to stop Igor Kaprizov's people coming after him?

'I'll get them for you. I'll get them as soon as I can. Give me till Thursday.'

The waiter arrived with their plates. Edward had never felt less like eating in his life. He picked up his fork and stabbed a piece of broccoli as if he was totally in control. *Now it was time to reveal his hand.*

'I have something else I want to show Igor. It's very special, a missing masterpiece by Camille Pissarro, an oil of Montmartre. It's called *Twilight*. I think Igor's niece will love it. It was painted in 1897.' Sergei raised his eyebrows as Edward said hurriedly, 'It's a private sale, part of a very well-known Dublin collection, but there seem to be some pictures that aren't on the public record.'

Sergei shrugged like he didn't really care. Croxley continued, trying not to sound too desperate, 'The original owner of the collection was a judge – he had some strong links to the Third Reich.'

'Igor may be interested. I will tell him. But first you will get the amulets back.'

'Of course.' Edward shrugged like it was a given. 'I'll email you a photograph of this painting. Show it to Igor, I know he's going to love it. For his niece. She's getting married in Paris, isn't she?'

Sergei shrugged again and, picking up his burger in his huge hands, bit into it hard. Edward turned back to his plate.

What the fuck was he going to do?

Chapter 26

THE BRITISH MUSEUM was busy when Lily got there, a bus load of French school students snaking their way through the barriers to the bag check, excited and jostling. Lily tagged onto the end of their group.

Nerves had been fluttering in her stomach since she'd picked up Vittoria's card that morning – at least she hoped it was from Vittoria. The postcard just had a picture of the British Museum on the front and *There's a fascinating talk on in the Egyptian Room 3 p.m. Tuesday* written on the back, unsigned.

Acutely aware of the days slipping past – it wasn't long until she started with No. 42 – Lily had no idea if Vittoria could fulfil her end of their deal. She'd seemed completely confident she could when they'd last parted, but how on earth was Vittoria going to engage with Croxley and get the shop back? Lily was trying hard not to worry.

Her job was to sort out Marcus Devine, and that seemed to be going very well. Emma had been keeping her abreast of the effects of the *Sunday Inquirer* story. From what she could gather, Devine wasn't answering his email or his phone, had got off a Sydney flight that morning to go straight into a meeting with his superiors.

Lily smiled to herself. She had no idea where Emma got

her information but she imagined the paper had no end of moles in Heathrow airport listening to celebrity conversations and tipping off the paparazzi when stars arrived. Emma had found out that Marcus had been suspended from duties pending a more formal meeting this coming Friday. Whatever the outcome of that, he had a lot of explaining to do to his employers, his wife and his mistress.

That ball was rolling nicely. And it was time to think about setting some more in motion.

Even with the shop gone, Lily had plenty to do before she left for New York, people to catch up with and say goodbye to. She had no idea when she'd get time off to come back home. American companies weren't overly generous with holiday allowances and, anyway, she wanted to get really stuck in and make her mark. And to do that she needed to work very hard. Going the extra mile to make a good impression held you in good stead in the long run.

She'd spoken to her flatmates and they were happy for Jack to take over her room at the flat for the time being, so he wouldn't be homeless, thank goodness – it wasn't ideal but it would be preferable to him sleeping on friends' sofas.

With her mind so busy, Lily wasn't concentrating on the queue to the bag check until one of the French students stepped backwards and bumped into her, bringing her out of her cloud of thoughts.

Lily glanced at the time on her phone. She was early but the bag check was slow. The French teenagers didn't seem to mind; school trips were all about having fun. When Lily had been at school or coming on trips here, her grandpa would have been working just a short walk away, looking out the window for a glimpse of her passing on the way to the museum. The memory opened a dark hole in her chest.

It had started to spit rain again by the time Lily emerged from the other side of the tent that housed the bag check. Her head down, buckling up her satchel, she crossed the broad paving stones to the steps heading up to the grand main entrance of the British Museum. A Japanese couple were sitting next to a sign that said 'Please don't sit on these steps' taking selfies.

Skipping past them, Lily crossed the black and white tiled hallway into the bright main atrium, immediately calmed by the light reflected off the white stone walls and the incredible sweeping lines of the building. She knew exactly where the Egyptian room was and headed up the staircase to her right, looking down at the open coffee shop far below as she climbed the steps. A bridge connected the landing to the doorway of the Egyptian room. It was already filled with crowds of British school children, smart in their uniforms, sheets of paper and pencils in their hands.

Lily headed through the Sumerian room and into the Egyptian section, spotting Vittoria immediately, her dark glossy hair catching the light from the display. Her back to Lily, Vittoria was looking into a glass case of artefacts, apparently intently reading the signs beside them. She was dressed like a tourist in skintight jeans and boots, a dark grey poncho with black braiding hiding a cream silk shirt. Even in jeans she had style. Lily stopped beside her, greeting Vittoria's reflection in the glass case with a quick smile. Her eyes fixed on the exhibits, Vittoria spoke very quietly.

'He's looking for something that was bought at a sale. Something *he* should have bought but which Jack must have bought accidentally. It's small, something very ancient and incredibly valuable that might have been looted from the museum in Baghdad or somewhere like it. It's definitely from somewhere there has been fighting in the past.'

Lily felt her eyebrows raise in surprise. *What on earth? How did Vittoria know?* Questions jostled for attention but she knew this wasn't the time to ask. Croxley had wanted the shop so he could find something? That seemed mad, but somehow made sense. Whatever it was Croxley wanted, it must be very valuable indeed that he couldn't just ask Jack for it. Lily nodded slowly.

'Can you check with Jack? If you can work out what it is, I can use it to get the shop back. If you can't I've something else lined up that might work, but Croxley's in trouble, he's frightened. Whoever wants it is very powerful indeed.'

'I'll talk to Jack.'

'Good, I've decided to change my ticket so I'll be here for a few more days. I've rented a mail box through a virtual office company.' Vittoria reached into the back pocket of her jeans. 'I've written the address on the back of this flier. I'll leave it on the top of one of the display cases in a few minutes for you to pick up. If you need to talk to me, get someone to drop a note in. If you find what Croxley's looking for, have it couriered to me there. Make sure you don't come yourself. The staff will text me if anything is delivered in business hours. Try and be a quick as you can. ' As Vittoria turned to move to the next exhibit, she smiled reassuringly. 'Don't worry, I'll have this sorted out before you leave for New York.'

Chapter 27

'THAT'S EXACTLY what she said – you need to *think*.'

Jack looked back blankly at Lily and then stood up abruptly, disturbing George who was curled up asleep on Lily's bed in a pool of evening sunlight, his whiskers flicking as if he was dreaming. Lily was sitting in the chair beside her dressing table. The room was barely big enough for both of them but Jack began to pace, his hands in his pockets.

'Don't you think I'd know if I'd bought some early Middle Eastern artefact by accident? The last sale I was at was that one in Hertfordshire, the country house with the ridiculous name.' Jack screwed up his face, thinking. 'I went to look at the sporting prints but they weren't in nearly as good condition as the catalogue had suggested. There was a walnut desk I looked at, with a roll top and a secret drawer, that was nice. And the box of books. There were a couple of copies of *Rebecca*, about four different Virginia Woolfs and a book called *The Essential Art of the Gentleman Printer* by Gloria Harrington. That's a little gem, and I knew I had the perfect collector for that.' He shrugged. 'So that's all I bought.'

Lily turned around to her dressing table and put her head in her hands. 'Could it have been a different auction? Where did you go before that?'

'I haven't been to a house auction for ages. It's not like

we need stock. My mission for the last two months has been cataloguing everything and grouping it so I can contact interior designers and give them themed collections. I really want – wanted,' he paused, 'to get to the back of the storerooms and shift all the stuff that's been there for yonks.'

'OK, so just think back – St Albans, do you remember seeing Croxley there?'

Jack screwed up his face and thought hard then shook his head. 'But I was down the front. If he'd been bidding from the back of the room I wouldn't have seen him. And, really, I'd be surprised if he was there. From what I've heard, he deals in proper modern art. Your friend has to have taken him up wrong. Perhaps she misheard him?'

Lily shook her head. 'How on earth could she have come up with something as odd as this? She doesn't know that you go to country house sales. And she's a psychologist – she's used to listening to people and understanding what they're not saying. She has to be right.'

'But something looted from a museum in the Middle East? How would something even remotely that valuable end up in a country house sale in St Albans, Lil?'

'I think that's the point. Whatever it is was smuggled into the country. If it gets bought "legitimately" in a sale, it's suddenly kosher. All sorts of things turn up in house sales.'

'I'm not seeing it.' His hands in his jeans pockets, Jack put on his stubborn face.

Lily turned to look at him, her eyebrows raised. 'Well, we need you to start seeing it, because right now it's the only option we've got.' She cleared her throat, trying to control her temper. 'Think back to when Croxley came into the shop, before he asked you to the card game – did he say much? Just think, will you?'

'OK, OK, keep your hair on. I'm thinking.' Jack rubbed his face with his hands and went to sit back down on the bed. 'So he came in a couple of times. Maybe three. Yes, definitely three. The first time he asked what type of things we stocked—'

'Like it's not written over the door?' Lily's voice was full of sarcasm.

'Well, there is that. He seemed very interested in smaller items; we just chatted. He was really interested in the books. He asked when I went for lunch, I think, asked if I closed up when I went out. That struck me as a bit odd at the time.'

'Good, what else?'

'So he wanted to see around the shop the first time. Said he was decorating a new apartment. He was really looking about, checking out stuff stacked in the corners, having a good nose.'

'And ...?'

'And that was it.'

'OK, so the next time?' Lily said it slowly, trying to hold onto her patience. If this was Jack's idea of trying to remember something, she'd hate to see what forgetting was like.

Jack stared at a spot on Lily's rag rug, pursing his lips. Lily was about to speak when he said, 'So that time he said he was looking for something for his mum. He said she loved *Rebecca* and did we have any copies. So I said I didn't – I'd already sold that early edition. So then ...' Jack screwed up his face.

'Hang on, the box from St Albans had a copy of *Rebecca* in it, didn't you just say?'

'Yes, two. One was really foxed. Like I said, I sold the other one.'

'So isn't that a bit of a coincidence? Of all the books that were ever published he asks about that one?'

Jack shrugged. 'Well, yeah, I suppose so … But then he started talking about china. I mean, we don't even stock china so I'd no idea what that was about. He said his mother collected one of the Stoke factories – I can't remember which one.'

'Royal Doulton? Wedgwood, Moorcroft?' Lily looked at him, her mind racing – how did that connect with a copy of *Rebecca*?

Jack frowned and ran his hand into his hair, rocking slightly like he was willing his memory to work.

'Minton. It was Minton. He said she collected Minton.' His tone was triumphant. 'But how does that help?'

Lily sighed. 'I don't know but it must be related to all this somehow. Did he say anything else?'

Jack shook his head. 'When I said we didn't stock china, he sort of got a bit impatient. That's when he asked me to the card game. It was like it suddenly occurred to him.'

Lily turned back to her dressing table, biting her lip. There had to be something they were missing. But Jack didn't know anything about antique china – it just wasn't his thing. It was more her area. As the thought arrived in her head, she looked at the little teapot on her dressing table, at the delicate hand-painted pattern of forget-me-nots, yellow pansies and pale pink roses, and almost slapped her forehead. It was the classic Minton pattern.

Glancing quickly at him, she picked it up to look at the maker's mark on the bottom. It *was* Minton.

'Where did you get this?'

'What?' Jack looked up, puzzled. 'Oh, from that sale in St Albans. It wasn't—' He suddenly stopped then began to speak slowly as it dawned on him. 'It wasn't in my box of books. It was in another one. I saw it and thought you'd like it. I sort of swapped it into mine right before the auction started.' Lily looked at him incredulously, 'Ah, don't look like that. It's not that bad. It's not like I was pulling a fast one … well, not really. And I said it to the auctioneer afterwards, that somehow the teapot had got into my box. He wasn't bothered at all – it's cracked and the rest of the set is missing. He was only interested in selling the furniture.'

'But this must have been in the box Croxley wanted. He must have gone nuts when he collected his box afterwards and found it wasn't there … How did he know you'd bought it?'

'I was the only person bidding on books. The others were all furniture dealers – they weren't interested. The whole lot only cost me twenty quid, and he had to drop to that.'

Lily shook her head. 'The teapot's worth more than that.'

Jack shrugged like he really didn't know.

Lily picked it up again and lifted off the lid. The inside was stuffed with greying tissue paper. She'd glanced at it when Jack had dropped it over to her, had given it a wipe, meaning to check out the maker's mark and date later. Then the email had arrived from No. 42 and, as if a tornado had hit the house, one that would lift her right of Kansas, her world had gone into a spin.

Now Lily carefully pulled out the paper. It was all screwed up, as if it had been stuffed in to protect the china from impact. Pulling the bundle of tissue free, Lily put it carefully on the dressing table and opened it up.

In the middle lay four gold charms. At least, they looked like charms. Lily picked them up carefully. They were a dull gold, obviously a high carat value, and they were articulated, hanging from loops.

'What the hell are they?'

'I've no idea but I think these are what Edward Croxley was looking for.' Lily turned them over. 'They're containers. Look – they're in parts, like they were designed to hold something.' Lily screwed up her face. 'We had a lecture on …' It took her a few moments. 'They're amulets. Do a search, these must be what he was looking for.'

She smoothed the tissue paper while Jack went to get his phone, charging on the floor. The screen was smashed but his iPhone was faster than her Android, its memory choked with photographs.

'Now let's see what Google says.' It only took a moment. He stared at the phone.

'Well, come on!' Lily looked over his shoulder impatiently. She had no idea how he coped with that phone, the smashed screen would drive her insane.

'Do these look the same? Apparently there are some in the British Museum. They're Sumerian, seventh to sixth century BC.'

'And very likely looted from the museum in Baghdad. Small, easily portable. How much are they worth?'

Jack did another search. 'This result says up to $6,000 each. But that's assuming you've got them to sell. I'd imagine the majority of them are in museums around the world. I mean how long ago was the seventh century BC? They have to be incredibly rare.'

'And highly collectible – you could wear these now.'

Jack looked at her quizzically. 'They are thousands of years old.'

'I know, but someone Croxley knows wants them for something.'

'Something old, something new … I'm reading this thriller where someone put a baby's bones in the hem of a wedding dress and this detective finds them.'

Lily grimaced. 'That's horrible. Were they the something old or the something new?'

'No idea, haven't got to the end yet. So what do we do now?'

'We give them to my friend.'

'Whoa, is that a good idea? Why can't we just go to Croxley and tell him we've got them and we want the shop back?'

Lily raised her eyebrows. 'Because if these were smuggled out of the Middle East and Edward Croxley is a link in the chain to get them to the buyer, a buyer who is happy to buy goods looted on the black market, I don't think Croxley is going to be very happy that we know he's involved. We don't know who this buyer is but my friend said Croxley was frightened – she said the name on Croxley's phone was Sergei.'

'So Croxley's selling these to some Russian dude? That's playing with fire.'

'Exactly. So much as we need to get the shop back, it's not much good to us if we're both at the bottom of the Thames with concrete blocks around our ankles.'

'I don't think they do that any more. It's all nerve agents these days.' He hesitated. 'Except that dude that hung himself ...'

Lily turned around to him, her face paralysed with fear. 'What's to say he won't have my friend killed?' Lily closed her eyes. What on earth had she got Vittoria into?

Chapter 28

WHEN STEPHANIE CARSON slowly surfaced from sleep on Wednesday morning, the autumn sunshine was pouring in through the gap in her curtains, but rather than enjoying its warm glow, she felt chilled to her core. Marcus had been tossing and turning beside her all night and sometime in the early hours had gone downstairs, enabling her finally to sleep. As the memory of the previous night began to hit her, she woke up fully, shocked and mentally broken into so many pieces she wasn't sure she'd ever be able to reassemble them.

Marcus had finally come home yesterday in a taxi, his face grey. From where she was sitting in the living room, she'd seen him come up the tiled path, heard his key in the door but stayed where she was. She was having a glass of wine – the first of her pregnancy, but tonight she really needed it. On the granite breakfast counter she'd spread out the papers, Marcus's face staring back at her from the double-page spread with Bellissima Serata, the dark-haired tart, flashing her tits at the camera. What the hell had he been doing?

Dropping his flight case in the hall with a clatter, he'd come straight through the kitchen to the lounge where she'd been sitting on the sofa, failing to watch TV. He'd paused at the double doors, his uniform tie pulled loose. He'd just stood there not saying anything. She didn't stand up.

'How did your meeting go?' She couldn't look at him.

'Well, they saw the pictures.'

'Them and half the world. They realised it was the same woman that the papers said you were in The Velvet Club with?'

'Yes. No. I mean, it's not real – I've never met her.' He came into the living room and sat in the armchair, his face in his hands. 'Why won't anybody believe me?'

'Because there's a photo, maybe?' Stephanie's tone was full of sarcasm. They'd been over this, but she couldn't resist the dig.

'But it's not real. Someone's photoshopped me in. I don't understand this, any of this.'

'Why would anyone do that, exactly? How could the paper print a fake picture?'

'I've no idea.' He rubbed his face with his hands again. 'I've just no idea. I have to go to a disciplinary hearing on Friday.'

Stephanie had looked at him, the hand holding her wine glass frozen in the air. 'I thought you said you could sort it out today?'

'I thought I could. But because the picture shows her in the cockpit, and that's against regulations, it takes it to a whole new level.' His voice was strained. 'And the other one shows me having a few jars,' he shook his head, 'when I was flying the next day.'

And she, Stephanie, was the only person who could say that he wasn't out that night, that he was tucked up at home with her.

'You're going to have to tell them you were here.'

Marcus didn't answer for a moment, like he'd already given it some thought. 'I don't know if they'll believe me. Quite apart from the fallout with Vittoria, they're going to think you'd be inclined to support me. If we pretend that I'd just dropped in for an innocent dinner, they're bound to find out it's more than that.'

'I don't see why they wouldn't believe me.' Her tone was stubborn.

'Well, for one thing, you're an actress, so you're paid to pretend. And you're carrying my child. That gives you a bit of an agenda.'

Stephanie tried to get comfortable. It was all so much to take in, and she couldn't get the image of that well-endowed olive-skinned bitch out of her head. She didn't know if the woman in the picture taken in the bar was Bellissima as well – she had her back to the camera. Maybe he had another one on the go. Whoever it was, it looked like they were all having a great time.

But for all his flaws, Marcus was fastidiously professional about not drinking before he was flying – was he telling the truth? Had the picture been faked? Or had he got carried away and had a drink that night? She knew the penalty for that was immediate dismissal. The implications hit her again, as if someone was stabbing her already broken heart with a knife. If he lost his job how would she cope?

Thoughts swirled in Stephanie's head, anxiety making her feel suddenly extremely sick.

She wasn't sure what was worse. Had he been seeing this Italian whore? He was married after all, and she, Stephanie, was the other woman. Perhaps he had other other women in other places, places he flew to every week. Who knew what life he led when he wasn't with her? He'd told her he loved her, that he wanted their baby, wanted it more than anything, but he'd said from the start that leaving Vittoria was going to be complicated.

Remembering their conversation of the previous evening, Stephanie turned over in bed trying again to make herself more comfortable, waves of emotion washing over her, her eyes hot with tears. She should have been stronger about him divorcing Vittoria in the first place – it wasn't like they had any children. But he seemed weighed down by guilt about the car accident, like it was his duty now to stay with her. He'd poured it all out one night.

'We were at a party, it was late, I was tired. But it was my fault. We were having a row about this girl. How stupid is that? I was angry; I was driving too fast.' They'd been cuddled up on the sofa when he'd told her. He was just back after a different Sydney trip and had seven days off so she'd cooked an amazing dinner and opened a bottle of his favourite brandy. He'd sipped it as he'd continued, his eyes full of pain, his voice husky. 'She was in intensive care for months – her pelvis was crushed. She couldn't dance any more. She'd got a scholarship to the Royal Ballet School – she'd been there for *four* years, and I ended her career in one moment. And I can't even remember what happened.' He'd sighed. 'I must have blacked out. I remember Vittoria screaming and the next thing I woke up in hospital. The car flipped and she was thrown out, apparently. It was a 1972 MG, red, beautiful car. I had the roof down – it had been such a bloody cold wet summer, it was the first time I'd been able to use it that year.' He'd shaken his head and, turning to her, kissed the top of her head. 'I'm so sorry. I love you so much but it's so complicated.' He'd sighed. 'The thing is, her injuries mean that she can't have children now either. I did that to her.'

He hardly needed to say that if Vittoria found out he was having an affair she'd feel like the crash was happening all over again, would feel that he'd taken her best years as well as her career from her. Stephanie had felt him shudder.

Somehow she'd always hoped Marcus would come up with a solution, but he seemed almost afraid of her, of what she might do if she found out about everything, which seemed a bit ridiculous.

Last night, Stephanie had watched him get up and pour himself a drink, the golden liquid splashing into the cut glass. He hadn't bothered with ice.

'Was that you in that picture?'

Standing beside the drinks cabinet, his back to her, he'd said, 'Of course it was me. It just wasn't taken on that day. And certainly not with her. I've never even met this woman. I just have to prove it.' He sighed deeply.

Stephanie took a sip of her wine. 'So what happens next?'

He turned around and looked at her, taking a large swig of his brandy. 'At this disciplinary hearing? I think they're going to sack me.'

'Can they do that?' Her hand went unconsciously to her belly, smoothing the soft grey fabric of her sweater over it.

'TransGlobal Airways are a multimillion-pound corporation and at the moment I'm seriously embarrassing them in the tabloid press. They need to be seen to be acting.'

'Can't you fight it? I mean, it'll be unfair dismissal, won't it?'

Marcus sighed. 'I don't know if I can afford to take on TransGlobal. We'd have to go to court and, whatever happens, even if a court found in my favour, I couldn't ever work for them again …'

'But there are other airlines?'

Marcus grunted. 'There are, whether they'd want to take me on after I've been tainted by taking a case against my employer is a different matter.'

'But if it wasn't you, if you weren't there, you must be able to prove it?'

'In the picture in the bar I'm wearing that T-shirt you bought me, the one that came in the wrong size and you had to get it replaced. Have you got the receipt? It'll have the date on it and show it was bought after the photo was supposedly taken.'

Stephanie frowned, thinking. 'I ordered it online – I'll have the emails.'

'So that's one thing. It just means you might have to be brought into court to testify.'

Stephanie shrugged. 'What's the problem with that?'

Marcus looked at her. 'Vittoria, mainly. Obviously.' He shook his head. 'I've been thinking about it and I think I'm going to need to take an action against the *Sunday Inquirer* in the first instance – if I've any hope of TransGlobal believing me, they'll expect that.'

Stephanie pursed her lips. 'They must have been pretty sure to publish those pictures. Their lawyers must have looked at them.'

'Exactly. And the captions are really cleverly phrased – they imply it's me and a real photo but there's enough ambiguity in the article for them to say they knew they were faked all the time. I'd have to sue them for libel, for bringing my reputation into disrepute, but their lawyers will dig through every detail of my life and find out about you. You could have the paparazzi camped on the doorstep.'

Stephanie put her glass down, a feeling of utter desolation washing over her. She hadn't had alcohol for over eight months and now it tasted horrible, as horrible as this whole mess was.

This wasn't how her life was supposed to go. She was regularly in the press, used the papers as much as they used her, but with something like this, the paparazzi would be everywhere – they could rip her career to shreds. How could she afford childcare and get back to work if Marcus had no job? Would they even be able to stay together if Vittoria found out?

It was all *such* a mess. Stephanie turned over again, still not comfortable, and winced as the baby kicked her, objecting to all the movement. Stephanie rubbed her stomach. That brand ambassador job with No. 42 was starting to look very attractive from a financial perspective, but would they be interested if she was in the middle of a sex scandal? One thing was for sure, she needed to get that moving and get the paperwork signed before anyone found out anything about this. It would be a solid income for the next twelve months. That girl she'd met, Lily, had been talking about after Christmas, but she needed things to happen faster than that.

A moment later she heard Marcus's tread on the stairs and he put his head around the bedroom door. 'I brought you tea, and there was an almond croissant in the fridge. I've warmed it up.'

She turned over to look at him. His face was pale with exhaustion. He looked about ten years older than he had when he'd left for Sydney.

He came around to her side of the bed and put the tea and croissant down on her bedside locker, then sat down beside her on the bed.

'I've been thinking. I do have to contest this. I have to go into the meeting on Friday saying I'm suing the *Sunday Inquirer*.'

'But that could cost thousands.'

'It will. I've got savings, quite a lot in bonds and stuff, and money from my parents too, but I want to transfer them into your name or into a trust for the baby. That way, whatever happens I'll know you've got something to fall back on, and Vittoria won't be able to touch it.'

Stephanie put her hand on his and squeezed it. She really couldn't bear to lose him, to lose this life they'd built. When he was in Dublin with Vittoria it was just like he was flying, and she looked forward to the next time she'd see him. She'd got used to that, could share him quite happily when she knew he was thinking about her and she would see him soon. And the time they had apart made the time they had together all the better and more precious. She picked up her tea. So much was changing so fast. And she hated being so out of control of events that she had no idea what might happen next. 'Thank you.'

'I need to talk to a lawyer, but I'm not planning on losing. It's not going to be easy.' He shook his head. 'It'll be a risk but I can't lose the house. My parents worked so hard for that – it was their dream.'

'I'm sure Vittoria wouldn't let you risk it either – it's technically half-hers while you're still married.'

He didn't seem to be listening. 'I need to move those assets pretty quickly. It'll mean me going back to Dublin today. I need to get to the bank and do the transfers in person.'

Stephanie frowned. 'When will you be back?'

'Thursday evening latest, earlier if I can manage it.'

'You've really thought about this?'

He nodded. 'I don't have any choice.'

Chapter 29

VITTORIA'S PHONE rang just as she had found a quiet corner in The Hogarth's Lighthouse Bar. The velvet sofa was a little soft but it was cosy, and with the morning sun streaming in it was bright and cheerful. She'd already been out this morning, had just ordered a smoothie and was about to check her email when Marcus's name flashed up on the screen.

She paused for a moment, wondering whether to answer the call. But he rarely called her unless there was an issue of some sort. She swiped to answer, pretending she didn't know it was him.

'Hello, Vittoria Devine.'

'It's me.' At the other end he hesitated. 'Did you see the Sunday papers?'

'Which papers?' She deliberately sounded surprised.

'The *Sunday Inquirer*.'

'Why would I be looking at the *Sunday Inquirer*?' Pausing, Vittoria lowered her voice, as if Yana's problems were the biggest issue on her radar right now. 'I'm busy – I'm in London, remember? Yana is rehearsing in Covent Garden and needed some support. There's a lot going on. I can't discuss it.' Then, as if realising something was wrong, 'What was in the paper this time?'

Marcus cleared his throat. She could almost hear him fidgeting on the end of the phone. 'They have some pictures. There was that ridiculous thing about that Italian woman?'

'The pole dancer turned TV star?' Vittoria said it in a voice that made it sound like she wasn't seeing the ridiculous side. 'People will think you've got a thing for Italians.'

Ignoring her comment, he paused like he was summoning the words. 'So on Sunday they published some pictures. Of me and her. But they were photoshopped – I've never met her.'

Vittoria cleared her throat. 'Why would anyone be interested in photos of you – or her – with anyone? And why are you only telling me now?'

'I was in the bloody air. I only got back late yesterday.' Vittoria could feel her temper rising. He couldn't tell the truth if he tried. She knew exactly when he'd landed and where he'd been. 'Apparently she's got a book coming out. I think she's looking for PR, to attract attention. I think I could be one of many with this. I'm just first.'

She kept her voice calm as she answered, as if she was talking to a patient: 'But how do they have pictures if you've never met her? What sort of pictures are they?'

'They were photoshopped – they have to have been. There are pictures of me all over the place. I've never met her, but these photos put us together in the cockpit on a flight to Milan, apparently. She's never been in the fucking cockpit with me – it's a total fucking nightmare.'

'Is that it? Pictures of you together in the cockpit?'

He cleared his throat again. 'There's a picture of me having a few jars. Someone's interfered with the date stamp. It looks like I was having a brandy a few hours before I was due to take off. I wasn't, obviously – it must have been taken on a totally different day – but TransGlobal have gone through the roof. I had to go straight into a meeting when I landed yesterday. There's a disciplinary hearing on Friday.'

'*Dio*, that's serious. Do you think they'll sack you?'

Marcus's voice was husky. 'I've no idea but if I don't fight this *Sunday Inquirer* story it'll make it look like I'm guilty as hell. I can't go in on Friday like a pussycat waiting to be kicked.'

Vittoria thought of Tchaikovsky at home, being spoilt rotten by their housekeeper. She didn't know any cat that was waiting to be kicked.

'So what can you do?'

'I'm going to need to act against the *Inquirer*. Unless I take a case, I look as guilty as sin.' In The Hogarth Hotel, Vittoria raised her eyebrows. *That was one way to put it*. He continued, 'When I go into the meeting with TransGlobal I need to show them that it's all slander, it wasn't me.'

'OK, I get that, but—'

'I know, it could cost thousands, but it's my reputation. Even if I never work for TransGlobal again, I need my reputation – without it I may never work for anyone.'

That would be a problem …

'So what are you going to do?'

'I'm going to sell some of my father's paintings. I should be able to raise enough cash to cover an action. I need a bit of capital behind me.'

Sell his father's pictures? Vittoria's mind reacted as if she was spinning across a stage: fast and with total precision. But this time she wasn't falling into the protagonist's arms – he was falling into hers. And the music was like poetry.

'Are you sure? Your dad's pictures?' Vittoria injected just the right amount of horror into her voice.

'I know, I know, but it's the only way I can raise capital.'

'But how? You can't go public, to an auction house, or everyone will know – the press … *Mio Dio*, they have enough to talk about.' Vittoria paused as if she was thinking. 'There is someone … I met a guy here, a guy called Edward Croxley. I think he might be able to help. He's a broker – he sells high end art. He's freelance, can find private buyers so there's no need for anyone to know what's going on. If you put any of them into a sale in Rahilly's there'll be questions, and it's so slow.'

'That's what I need: discreet and fast.'

'I'll get him to contact you. Where are you now?'

'Heading back home – I've got some stuff to do before this hearing. I'll come back to London on Friday.'

Vittoria found herself nodding. 'Maybe you should see Croxley on Saturday in Dublin? He'll need to see the pictures to value them. You could get the Friday-night flight back home? But absolutely don't breathe a word of it to anyone.'

'I'm not going to. I need to get the papers filed for a libel action against the *Inquirer* as soon as possible. The best that can happen on Friday is that I'm suspended pending a full enquiry. They'll have to wait for the outcome of my action, I presume, before they fire me, or I could sue them for wrongful dismissal.' Vittoria took an audible intake of breath as he continued. 'I know, it's a total fucking mess. Can you see if this guy will meet me at the house on Saturday? Then at least things will be moving. I'll need a quick sale or two.'

'Of course, I'm sure he'll be *very* keen to see the collection.'

'How long are you in London for?'

'I'm not sure – it depends on Yana.'

'OK, it looks like I'll be home for the weekend but I'll probably need to be back in London on Monday.'

'Call me if you need anything. I'm sure it will all work out.' Then, almost as an after-thought, 'Where will you stay?

Presumably you can't use the crew hotel if you're suspended?'

He answered quickly. 'Oh, I'm sure I'll find somewhere.'

She bet he would.

*

There were some things in her life that Vittoria would have dearly loved to have changed, but her ability to plan under pressure wasn't one of them. Dance required rapid decision-making: if a lift went wrong your reaction speed was crucial to avoiding injury, injury that could end your career.

Ever since she had been a little girl, sitting on the stairs listening to the stories of the men drinking late at night in her father's bar, she'd understood that some people were winners and some were losers. Passion and focus were vital to success. She'd learned then what she needed to do to get what she wanted, to achieve her goals. And being able to adapt to changing circumstances was crucial; survival was about flexibility. It was a mind-set that had helped get her into the Royal Ballet School in the first place. And she knew she'd only kept her sanity after the accident because she was able to adapt. She'd adapted to life in London, to being so far away from home, and then she'd adapted when her dreams, and her bones, had been shattered.

Now, as she sat in The Lighthouse Bar musing over her conversation with Marcus, her mind was exploring possibilities, looking at every option, every nuance, building a picture. She'd often thought of the ballet as a fine painting, but a painting made up of many moving parts. Understanding how all those parts connected and intersected to create the picture was as vital as learning her own part in the play.

She smiled to herself. The play was the thing.

205

Chapter 30

A SOFT RAIN was beginning to fall as Lily stood on the pavement across the road from Power's Fine Prints, but she hardly noticed. She leaned back into the shelter of the Thai restaurant Jack always called Noodles Galore in some sort of funny-to-him James Bond-esque reference she'd never understood. It was too early for it to be open and here she felt invisible, shielded by the ornate half-pillars on either side of the lacquered front door.

She had been heading to Oxford Street to try and improve her business wardrobe, hoping beyond hope that they didn't have Primark in New York – it was all she could afford until she got paid – but instead of getting the Victoria Line into Oxford Circus, in St Pancras her feet had guided her to the Piccadilly Line, and before she'd realised it she'd arrived at Tottenham Court Road. Minutes from Great Russell Street.

And now here she was, and opposite her the dark-green roller shutters were still firmly pulled down over the door and window of her grandfather's shop. It felt all wrong in the busy street. The shop looked blind, as if it had turned its back on its friends. Around her people were rushing about, businessmen with their collars pulled up; students with laptop bags and determined looks on their faces; lost-looking tourists pulling trolley cases, their phones in their hands.

Had they noticed? She saw a few passers-by glancing at the closed shutters, but they hurried on, focused on their own business, on their own dramas.

Lily felt a dark hole open in her stomach – did any of them have worries like hers? As if losing the shop wasn't bad enough, what had she got Vittoria into? If Jack was right and there was some sort of Russian mafia involvement in this business with Edward Croxley, what had she done? The minute Jack had made the connection, Lily's mind had skipped back to one of the *Guardian* long reads about the mysterious deaths by 'suicide' of a list of men who had all had links to Russia through their business interests. It had made shocking reading. One of them had been impaled on a railing after apparently jumping from a window – who committed suicide like that? It had made her shiver then and it was making her shiver remembering it now.

Lily pushed her hands deeper into the pockets of her parka and heaved a sigh, tears pricking at her eyes. Looking up, she could see the tiny attic window of Jack's apartment on the top floor, normally brightly lit because he never remembered to turn the light off. He was as bad in the flat, leaving the loo light on like electricity was free. For someone so intelligent he really wasn't the most practical person in the world, which was something else that was worrying her: he was utterly adorable but he needed to be organised, to have someone checking up on him. And if he was out of his environment, how would he cope then? He had his routines established in the shop, understood the business like he knew how to breathe.

Was he the type of person who could work for someone else? Who could adapt to new systems and people? She was sure he would, he'd find a way – he was terrifically bright, after all – but would he be *happy*?

Happiness was more important in Lily's personal handbook for life than anything else. And Jack's happiness had been something she'd nurtured and cherished for as long as she could remember. She'd always protected him.

But perhaps that was where she'd gone wrong. If he'd made more mistakes, been exposed to the tougher side of life a bit more, would he have been taken in by slimeball Croxley's charm? Lily let out a sharp breath. She'd never know. And a bit further on in her personal handbook for life was a whole chapter about not having regrets, not focusing on what had already happened but dealing with the here and now, with the things you could control.

Would they get the shop back? Would Vittoria manage it? Lily had packed the amulets into a padded envelope and organised a courier to deliver them to the address that Vittoria had given her, exactly as she'd been told. But that wasn't an end to the problem – now Vittoria would have to negotiate with Croxley.

Lily took a deep breath, trying to calm her nerves. There was no question that Vittoria was a clever woman, as sharp and switched on as anyone Lily had ever met; Lily just hoped she was being sensible, hoped that being so scarred by her husband's latest revelation didn't make her reckless.

Lily really didn't know how Vittoria had put up with him so long; from everything Vittoria had told her, and from what she'd discovered online, Marcus Devine was just like Edward Croxley – entirely self-centred and never once taking a moment to think about how his actions would affect the people around him. And Vittoria's pain was so very personal, had to run even deeper than Lily's own, and that was a pretty awful place to be.

Marcus Devine really deserved everything he got.

Lily knew she should probably feel a tiny bit guilty about the series of events she'd created to destroy him, but actually, honestly, she didn't. The part of her that had hardened when Jack had stumbled onto her doorstep the day after he lost the shop was the part of her that was dealing with Marcus Devine. In another life Lily was quite sure she'd never have got involved, would never have even entertained Vittoria's suggestions. But the day he'd turned up on the doorstep, broken, she'd seen the pain in Jack's face, had heard the tremor in his voice, had been utterly paralysed when he'd said he'd almost jumped off Waterloo Bridge. It felt like her heart had actually stopped beating for a moment, and when it had restarted, she'd been someone different.

Thoughts of Jack snapped Lily back to the present. She'd heard him talking to George again last night and had been woken herself at 5.30 a.m. by the calls of scavenging seagulls. Didn't they say that seagulls came inland ahead of a storm? It never ceased to surprise her when she heard them in London, but with the river running through the heart of the city, it was perfectly logical. And they were scavengers, after all, looking for easy rich pickings in the busy city.

Like Edward Croxley. A natural scavenger always looking for a quick solution, for easy money. Except nothing was going to be easy for him now that he had Vittoria Devine to deal with.

She glanced across the road at the shop again. It was like an old friend who had lost its way, and Lily intended with every particle of her being that everything would be back on track before she left for New York.

It had to be, or how could she go?

Chapter 31

VITTORIA'S SMOOTHIE arrived just as Edward Croxley walked through the main door of The Lighthouse Bar. She picked up the squat glass and twirled her straw through the pale pink froth, pretending she hadn't noticed him. In her peripheral vision she saw him scan the bar looking for her. Then he was heading her way.

'Good morning.'

She looked up, as if she'd been deep in thought and hadn't noticed him. *Well, at least half of that is true.* 'Oh, Edward, lovely to see you. How are you getting on with my painting?'

Croxley sat down opposite her in a tub armchair, smiling. He was wearing the same dark overcoat with a Liberty-patterned shirt and ink-blue narrow-legged chinos. 'Great, actually. I've got a buyer.'

'Really, so quickly? That's fantastic.' Vittoria raised her dark eyebrows and opened her eyes wide. 'Can you tell me who it is?'

'He's a Russian collector. I do a lot of business with him.'

'Super, tell me all about him. Why don't you have a cup of tea, or would you prefer a smoothie?'

'Oh, coffee for me.'

Vittoria signalled to the waiter hovering beside the door, then turned to Croxley. 'How do you like it?'

'Cappuccino, please.'

The waiter materialised beside them, catching his reply to her. 'Any pastries, sir?'

'Go on, while you're here you might as well – they have lovely Danish.' Vittoria smiled warmly. She could see Croxley was desperate to talk about the painting, and she was deliberately slowing him down with the coffee-ordering nonsense. After Marcus's phone call things were slotting into place in her head, but she needed time to process them.

'Lovely, that sounds perfect.'

The waiter disappeared, and Vittoria turned back to Croxley. 'So you were saying you've done business with this Russian person before? What does he collect?'

'Oh, all sorts of European art and antiquities, some Middle Eastern. One of his nieces is getting married in Paris in a few weeks so your painting was particularly appropriate. He's starting a collection for her as a wedding gift.'

'That sounds wonderful. Is he based in London?'

Croxley nodded. 'He has a place here but he's in and out. He runs several companies.'

'And he's a cash buyer?'

Croxley leaned in to reply just as his coffee arrived. He sat back impatiently as the waiter laid a paper placemat on the table and put the coffee cup meticulously onto it, then placed a crisp white napkin and silverware beside it and, ceremoniously, the icing-sugar-sprinkled pastry.

'Thank you.'

Vittoria almost laughed at Croxley's impatience, the thanks coming through gritted teeth. As soon as the waiter disappeared, Croxley leaned towards her. 'He's offering two million dollars.' He paused as if for effect. 'He needs to see something indicating the provenance of the painting first, though.'

'Of course.' Vittoria bent down to her handbag, hiding a smirk. Croxley was some chancer, to use one of Aidan's favourite phrases – she knew Pissarro's work sold for between three and five million.

But two million was good.

Under the circumstances.

'I don't have a bill of sale but I have a note written by my husband's father mentioning a dinner party that he was planning, hosting a very well-known art dealer of the period, a Pieter Menten. He was Dutch, very involved with the Third Reich – the SS, as it turned out – which was to be his ultimate undoing. After the war he moved to Waterford. As you know, the Irish government were quite sympathetic to any enemies of the English; they'd fought a bloody civil war only a few years before to gain their independence. It seems Menten sold several paintings to my father-in-law for his personal collection. Paintings that, I'm beginning to wonder, perhaps weren't his to sell in the first place.'

Vittoria passed over the note, the envelope obviously old but crisp. Croxley looked at it closely, noting the postmark, Dublin 1964, and opened the letter, nodding as he read the postscript.

'Amazing how the scent of cigarettes lingers after all these years, isn't it?'

'Indeed. My father-in-law was a very heavy smoker. I think everyone was back in the fifties and sixties. How times change.'

'The buyer will want to check this.'

'Of course. There's a lot online about Menten. He was arrested by the Dutch and his house in Waterford rather badly vandalised. It was rumoured he'd come to Ireland with some significant artworks but, fortunately, it appears they'd already been secured in Dublin.' Vittoria smiled, leaning back for a moment. 'Can you tell me your buyer's name?'

'It's probably simpler if I don't, if that's OK.'

'It's not your friend Sergei then?'

Edward paled a shade and looked surprised. 'Sergei?'

'You know who I mean, Edward – let's not play games here. I know a lot about you.'

'Sorry?'

'Well, it's very important to me that I know who I'm doing business with. It's purely due diligence.'

'You want to sell the painting?' There was a hard edge to Croxley's voice.

'Of course, and I'm very pleased you've found a buyer. But I have some other issues that I need looked at too, issues that I'm hoping you'll be able to help me with.'

'More paintings?'

'Well, yes, my husband has decided to put more of the collection up for sale. He'd like you to go to Dublin to see them on Saturday. He'll be at home then.'

'Oh.' Surprised, it took Croxley a minute to take this in. 'Similar paintings?'

Vittoria nodded. 'A mixture, really. We seem to have quite a few old masters. It's an eclectic mix. I can send you pictures of them.'

'Great, that sounds good. I'm free on Saturday.'

'I'll organise your flights and hotel, and obviously I'll pay you an additional fee. I'd rather our initial transaction wasn't mentioned, so I was thinking, perhaps, a thousand pounds for your day would help? Would that be sufficient? Cash obviously.'

'That sounds very acceptable.'

'*Perfezionare.*' Vittoria leaned forward and put her glass down. As she did so, her gold charm bracelet slid down her arm, three dull gold charms clattering on the table. His attention drawn by the sound, Croxley looked at the bracelet and his face froze. Vittoria withdrew her hand and pulled the bracelet from the sleeve of her jacket so the charms were clearly visible.

'That's an interesting bracelet …'

'Thank you, isn't it?' Vittoria looked at it deliberately and smiled at him. 'But now, Edward, tell me about Arabella Smyth and how the poor girl came to drown at her best friend's twenty-first birthday party. That was very unfortunate. Her poor parents. It must have been a comfort for them to have you so close to her when it happened …'

Chapter 32

MARCUS GLANCED BACK up the stairs as he opened the front door. Stephanie had gone to sleep after he'd taken up her tea and croissant. She'd been tossing and turning all night. He had too, pretending he was asleep whenever she turned over. Jet lag was really hitting him this time, but his head had been churning all night, looking for solutions, wondering how on earth all this had happened.

It was warm and sunny outside, the morning rush hour replaced with a steady flow of traffic along the broad road. He waited for a gap and crossed to the coffee shop. He needed to make a phone call where there was no danger of him being overheard, and he was sure the patisserie would have something for lunch to save Steph cooking before he went to the airport. She adored cooking, was always grinding things up and creating new blends of spices, but he was quite sure that this morning she wouldn't be in the mood. With a bit of luck, they might have a few more almond croissants left as well.

With all this going on, Steph needed cheering up.

She was being very understanding about this Bellissima bitch, but, let's face it, he was cheating on his wife with her – it wouldn't be outside the bounds of possibility that he'd had a fling with Bellissima as well. He could hardly tell Steph that he'd got in a mess a few times before when he'd been trying to keep multiple relationships going, had learned his lesson then and sworn never to repeat it.

Pausing outside the shop, Marcus leaned on the Victorian railings that separated the front garden of the house next door from the pavement. He glanced over at Stephanie's house – the curtains were still pulled upstairs on the big bow window of her bedroom.

He pulled out his mobile. He'd been expecting to leave a message so was surprised when it was answered.

'Marcus, how are you doing?' Aidan's voice was raised slightly, as if he was somewhere noisy. 'Give me a minute.' Marcus heard a door open and suck closed as Aidan continued, 'That's better. A&E's like the Mad Cow roundabout this morning – Piccadilly Circus has nothing on us – it's a bloody nightmare. You know, sometimes private practice looks damn attractive. There are days when I don't know what the fuck I'm doing here. I've got my finger in the dam but there are so many fucking leaks we're all going to drown anyway. You'd think I was the only orthopaedic surgeon in Dublin with a specialisation in spinal surgery. Reckon I'm just the only one stupid enough to answer my phone.' He sighed heavily. 'So what are you doing?'

'I'm just back from Sydney – yesterday, actually. Did you hear about this press thing?'

'The photos? Yes, a few people have mentioned them.'

'Vittoria?'

'Let's just say a lot of people have seen them. What's the story?'

'They're fakes. I've never met that woman. But whoever decided to create them has got it in for me. I've got to face the music at TransGlobal on Friday.'

216

'Can you prove that they're not real? I mean, where were you when they were supposed to be taken?'

'Well, that's where it gets complicated. I was with Stephanie on the date the one where I'm supposedly out drinking was taken. It looks like it was the day before I flew to Milan – whoever created these certainly did their homework on my roster.'

'So why can't Stephanie say you were with her? That seems like a no-brainer – you've got a witness who can put you somewhere else, mate. I'd go for it.'

'I wish. The thing is Stephanie is pregnant. Very pregnant. She's due in a few weeks.'

'Pregnant by you?' Marcus winced at Aidan's tone, the hard edge in his voice.

'Eh, yes.'

'And you're only telling me now? Holy fuck. What about Vittoria?'

'Look, mate, I'm sorry. I wanted to tell you before but … it's a bit tricky.'

Aidan interrupted him. 'You can say that again. Marcus, you're such a wanker.' His voice was full of contempt. And he was right. Marcus knew he should have trusted him. They'd put the past behind them now – Aidan was his partner in their thirty-six-foot yacht and trust was vital if you were out at sea in the middle of a storm. It could mean life or death.

'Look, mate, I'm sorry, but as soon as one other person knows a secret, well, it's not a secret any more. I couldn't tell anyone. Not about the baby, not till I've worked out what to do anyway.'

'You're cutting it a bit fine with a few weeks to go. Are you going to tell Vittoria?'

Marcus cleared his throat. 'Well, I'm away a lot and Steph

doesn't mind that I have to go to Dublin a bit. She knows Vittoria and I aren't exactly close. I know you get on with her, but she's quite highly strung – she can be very moody, you know.'

'All women are moody, Marcus. It's their prerogative – they have to deal with men every day.'

Marcus could almost hear him saying, *men like you*. Marcus cleared his throat. 'She changed, Aid, after the accident. It's probably post-traumatic stress or something but—'

'Marcus, she had to give up her dancing career. Have you any idea how hard that is for a girl from her background? The Royal Ballet School only takes the best. It's all she ever wanted to do. And,' he lowered his voice, 'don't forget her internal injuries. I think I'd be pretty moody carrying that around with me, the constant pain.'

'I know, I know, which is what makes Steph being pregnant even more of a problem – and not exactly a perfect character witness. If I've been lying to my wife, TransGlobal are hardly going to trust what she says, are they?'

Aidan grunted in response. 'Are you going to ask Vittoria for a divorce?'

There was a pause. 'That's where it gets a bit more complicated. We've a prenup that protects me, but she'll do everything to drag me through the dirt with Steph and the baby on the scene. She'll take it to court and the press will have a field day. I can't risk some sympathetic judge throwing the prenup out. I need to make sure the baby's secure.' Aidan didn't reply. Conscious of the silence between them, Marcus filled it. 'So listen, mate, the reason I'm ringing is that I'm going to go legal on this. I have to clear my name but it's going to be expensive.'

'That's for sure.'

'It's just, the boat …'

'You're worried about the boat? In the middle of this meteoric fuck-up *Danny Boy* is finally your biggest problem?' Aidan's voice was filled with contempt.

Not catching on to his implication, Marcus backtracked hastily. 'No, no. I mean, I think I'll be grand. I'm going to sell some pictures to raise the capital but I need to make sure Steph's looked after too. The marina fees are paid for this year – it's just that new set of racing sails that we were talking about …'

'You'd rather keep that 15K in your back pocket?'

'Right now it seems sensible.'

'No problem, we can wait until the spring. The boat's going to be up on the hard for the winter so we won't be needing fancy new sails. See how it goes. What happens if you lose?'

'That won't happen. All this stuff is fake news; I just need to prove it. Worst possible scenario, I'll be bankrupt.'

Aidan paused like he was thinking. 'That's not a good position to be in. Do you think you should transfer everything over to Vittoria? If it's in her name, then at least some of your assets would be safe from the banks. Whatever about the divorce court, you've no chance against the *Inquirer*'s lawyers if you lose.'

Marcus thought fast for a moment. There was so much going on right now he could hardly concentrate but maybe Aidan had a point. Vittoria could be volatile but at least he had some chance of negotiating with her. The *Inquirer*'s lawyers wouldn't take any prisoners – if he lost, it would be everything. Maybe moving cash to Stephanie wasn't the only thing he should be doing tomorrow. He needed to think about the house and should definitely sell his share in the boat to Aidan while he was at it.

'Fuck, you're right, and you should buy me out of the boat – only for a euro or something, but we should get it signed over so nothing can happen to it. I've an appointment booked to talk to my lawyers. I'll get that drawn up and signed and courier it over to you. And I'll see what they think about Vittoria and the house, putting it in her name to protect it from the *Inquirer*'s thieving lawyers makes a lot of sense. Christ, I need to talk to them. It's just if something happened to me, like I had a heart attack in the middle of it all, who'd look after Stephanie?'

Aidan sighed and then said slowly, as if he was trying to get his head around it, 'Are you going to change your will to include Stephanie?'

'The baby, definitely. I can look after Stephanie alright once I can keep everything quiet and Vittoria onside, but this is my son we're talking about. We're going to call him Lochlan: it means Viking – well, of Viking descent.'

'And *lachain* means a crowd of ducks,' Aidan muttered. He cleared his throat. 'If Vittoria finds out, she's not going to be impressed.'

'Only if she finds out. I'm hoping I can keep it all nice and quiet and tidy.'

'Marcus,' Aidan said it like he was about five years old, 'if you go up against a tabloid newspaper you can be sure they will find every piece of dirt. I'd get the house transferred before you even start. It'll make Vittoria feel secure when it *does* all come out – it'll be like you're supporting her. You need to tell her that you think they're going to try and discredit you and to be ready for it. There's quite a lot of dirt for them to find, let's face it.'

'Christ, I never thought of that. You're right.' Marcus turned around and looked back at Stephanie's house. The curtains in the upstairs window twitched. 'Look, I've got to go. I'll keep you posted.'

Chapter 33

STEPHANIE TURNED on the hot tap and pulled up the sleeves of her baby blue sweatshirt to wash their plates as Marcus came up behind her. He put his arms around her and kissed her neck.

'I promise I'll sort all of this out. For you and junior.' He ran his hand across her belly, resting it there, waiting to see if the baby kicked. As if he heard him, Stephanie felt a movement. Marcus kissed her again and unwrapped himself so he could pick up his hat from the kitchen table.

'I'll be back Friday as soon as the hearing's over.'

Stephanie smiled over her shoulder at him, her hands wet with suds. He kissed her quickly and headed for the front door. As soon as she heard it close, she grabbed a tea towel and, drying her hands, went to the front window and watched as Marcus got into a waiting taxi. In the living room, her handbag was resting on the end of the sofa. It only took her a moment to find the piece of paper she'd scribbled Lily Power's telephone number on.

Taking a step back to look at it dispassionately, this whole situation suddenly seemed utterly bizarre. How had any of this happened? She knew women who would do anything for publicity but this Bellissima was just incredible. Everyone knew full well Marcus was married to an eminent psychologist –

you only had to search for his name on the Internet to discover that. It was pretty obvious that he'd immediately deny the woolly allegation that he'd been with her, this Bellisima, in The Velvet Club – but the photographs? She was shameless, looking for every scrap of publicity. She was the type who loved being hounded by the paparazzi and Marcus was an easy target. He was a society creature, loved to go to gallery openings and charity events, was often photographed by the society press. Stephanie had managed to keep out of photos with him, but they'd had to be so careful, taking separate taxis, her leaving ahead of him.

Biting her lip, Stephanie hesitated for a moment, her mobile phone in her hand. Would she look too keen if she rang now? It was Wednesday and she had only met Lily on Saturday. She'd been hoping Lily would call her.

Stephanie took a deep breath. The last series of *Lies* would air in the spring, by which time she'd have had the baby and hopefully would have slimmed down again and be out of these awful maternity jeans and into real clothes that didn't make her look like a beached whale. Which meant that she could get back on the PR circuit. But the next series hadn't been commissioned yet and Lily had been in the business long enough to know that anything could happen in TV. Just because a show was popular didn't mean it was getting the advertising ratings it needed. Numbers gave her a headache so she didn't even want to know, but she couldn't just assume Marcus was going to look after her. Especially not now.

Stephanie pulled at her ponytail and mentally shook her head. If this whole thing went to court and it came out that the night when they were suggesting he'd been out drinking with Bellisima, he'd actually been with her here in Notting Hill, then she'd *have* to give evidence. And if Bellisima's lawyers wanted to shoot holes in his credibility, showing the judge that he had a long-term mistress would be the perfect way to do it. If he could lie to his wife, wasn't it just as easy to lie to his employer, to lie about his drinking and who he was socialising with?

And if the court didn't tear him apart after that, Vittoria surely would.

Stephanie knew how the press worked – if this came to court, she'd have photographers with long lenses practically hanging out of the trees along the road. The very thought of it made her cringe. And it was almost the end of September now – she was due in three weeks. She could be quite sure that if Marcus brought a case against the *Inquirer* they'd be looking for dirt on him from the second it was filed – he'd be followed and they'd both be papped. Going backwards and forwards to Dublin to keep up appearances wouldn't fool them. It would be impossible to keep their relationship quiet with his name on Lochlan's birth certificate.

Stephanie went back through to the kitchen and sat down heavily at the table, her head in her hands.

The real question, the one she'd been avoiding, was when all this came out would Marcus choose to stay with her or go back to Vittoria? Because they wouldn't be able to return to how they were now, with him sharing his time between London and Dublin. And if he lost his job and Vittoria took everything, how would they manage?

They hadn't talked about what would happen after Lochlan was born, but she had assumed that he'd move in with her. He had been so overjoyed when she'd told him she was pregnant – well, shocked at first, but then just so happy – she didn't think he was going to leave her.

She could give him something Vittoria couldn't.

At least he was transferring money to her tomorrow as soon as the banks opened. It sounded like a lot of money but she hadn't wanted to push for an exact figure – would it be enough for everything she needed, for a proper education for their baby? Stephanie had grown up on a council estate – she didn't want that for her Lochlan, but she didn't know if she could afford the repayments for this house on her own. In fact, she knew for sure she couldn't.

Stephanie felt a kick and massaged her stomach. Lochlan must be able to read her thoughts.

She'd always managed before, had found a way that didn't mean relying on anyone else. When she'd got her first part she'd been totally out of her depth, had worked so hard to make sure she did the best possible job. And hard work always paid off.

Right now she just needed a back-up plan. One that enabled her to earn enough money to cover childcare and pay for a flat – she adored this house but she wasn't about to go bankrupt to keep it. And being a brand ambassador for a luxury store like No. 42 would open up other doors, she was sure. The very fact that she had been approached by No. 42, however informally, meant her agent could get in touch with others. All she needed was a regular stipend from a few places, plus the few bits of voiceover work she did, and *then* if they recommissioned *Lies* she'd be laughing, and if they didn't she'd be OK too.

She picked up her phone and dialled Lily Power's number.

Chapter 34

EDWARD CROXLEY didn't look back at Vittoria as he left The Hogarth Hotel. Watching him go, she picked up her glass to finish the end of her smoothie. He seemed slightly shell-shocked, she had to admit. Which was precisely how she wanted him.

Sucking up the last of the pink froth in her glass, she glanced behind her out of the huge paned window. It was a beautiful day and she had a lot to think about. She needed some headspace to work out the next move. An idea that had already been forming in her head had crystallised with Marcus's call.

'Everything alright for you, Ms Devine?'

Vittoria smiled up at the waiter; he was always so welcoming and attentive. 'Thank you, Joel – everything is wonderful as always. I'll sign for this and then I'm going to go for a walk, I think.'

With the sun on her face and autumn leaves tumbling around her feet, Vittoria was so deep in thought she hardly noticed where she was walking. Wandering into a charity second-hand bookshop, she found herself scanning the spines, finding a wonderful compendium of Hitchcock's films. She opened the cover and, running through the index, discovered many she had never heard of: *Number 13*, *Always Tell Your Wife*, *Woman to*

225

Woman, *The White Shadow*, *A Passionate Adventure*. They felt like the story of her life … *The Pleasure Garden*, *Dangerous Virtue*. It was like the book was waiting for her.

With her purchase firmly under her arm, and her head full of Edward Croxley and Stephanie Carson, she headed towards Gower Street and London University's Senate House Library. The iconic Art Deco building always made her think of MI6 and, for some reason, the women of the Special Operations Executive who had operated behind enemy lines during the Second World War. It towered with such authority, its pale grey façade stark against the sky.

Vittoria felt like she was behind enemy lines now. Marcus had declared war and she was going to have to fight for everything she believed in to survive.

Taking a moment to pause in the sunshine, she leaned on the wall at the corner of Mallet Street and looked up at Senate House across the road, lost in thought. Then, from behind her, she heard the strangest clanking noise. Startled, she turned to see what it could be. The old wall she was leaning on bordered the edge of some gardens, the foliage lush, but the railings along the top of the wall had all been cut off, leaving a row of iron stumps behind.

Adjusting the weight of the book under her arm, she looked properly, puzzled, quickly spotting a sign that explained it. It was a sound installation – the iron railings that had once run along the wall had been removed during the Second World War and had been replaced with a sound projection. That was the noise she'd heard. She put out her hand to run it along the ghost railings and heard the clanking noise again – it sounded exactly as if she was running a stick along them. Vittoria took a step back. How strange and wonderful. It was if they were there, but not there.

Looking at the invisible railings, their ghostly presence still there to hear, a few things fell into place in Vittoria's head.

She knew exactly what she was going to do next. It was complicated, but the railings had given her the idea. She just needed to arrange an appointment to pop back over to Mile End to see Mr Bahnschrift.

Vittoria pulled her phone out of her coat pocket and glanced at the time, checking for any missed calls. Nothing from Croxley yet. Hardly surprising; he had a lot to think about.

The day Edward Croxley had thought it was OK to swindle Lily and Jack out of their livelihood had been a very bad day indeed. Granted, he'd had other considerations – he was playing a very dangerous game with some very dangerous players – but whatever his problems were, his solution was despicable.

And one he would live to regret.

Croxley's face had been a picture when he'd seen the amulets. She'd collected them the minute the mail-box company had texted her to say a parcel had been delivered, and on the way back she had popped into a jeweller's to have three gold hook catches fixed onto her bracelet so she could clip the three amulets onto the chain. The fourth had been lodged in the hotel's master safe.

His mouth had literally fallen open. He'd been so shocked that he'd hardly taken in what she'd said about Arabella Smyth, about how easy it would be to get the case reopened. His eyes had been fixed on her wrist as she held it up to show the amulets off. 'Pretty, aren't they? I believe they are quite sought after.'

'Only three?'

'No, I have a fourth too.'

'What do you need?'

'Apart from the keys to a shop in Bloomsbury and a certain promissory note?'

He'd raised his eyebrows. 'Apart from? How much do you want for the amulets?'

'Oh, they're not for sale.' She'd paused. 'Rather, I have a proposition for you. It's a little delicate. It concerns my husband ...'

As she'd explained, his colour had drained.

'And what if I won't?'

'Well, it's not really a case of won't, to be honest. When you agree I'll give you these three little treasures. When the job's done you get the fourth. I'm going to leave it at Power's in the safe – it can be collected there.'

'But what you're asking—'

'I'm asking you to be a witness, Edward, a witness to a set of circumstances – that is all. My husband is in trouble at the moment, Edward. He's about to lose his job and have what's left of his good name dragged through the mud. I'm quite sure he's not in a good place mentally. I will ensure that everything runs like clockwork. I assure you, you can trust me.'

Croxley had started shaking his head as Vittoria continued, 'You'll be paid well, too. I don't expect people to do things for free. An extra five thousand pounds on top of the thousand we agreed previously.'

Croxley's eyes had nearly come out on stalks. Vittoria had taken a sip of her smoothie. One thing about *bastardi* like Edward Croxley was that their greed would always win over common sense and caution. It was a common human condition.

There was a good reason it was one of the deadly sins.

Leaning back against the wall, the sound installation behind her, Vittoria glanced at the time again, running through everything that had to be done in her head. She needed to go back to her hotel now and get a message to Mr Bahnschrift in Mile End as soon as possible, but then she'd go to the theatre this evening. The stage door of The Dominion Theatre was right opposite the entrance to The Bloomsbury Hotel, just a short walk from The Hogarth Hotel where she was staying, and they had just opened with Hitchcock's *Rear Window*. She switched the heavy book to her other arm. Now she'd be able to read up on the making of the film before she went to see the stage production. She smiled to herself – serendipity was a strange and wonderful thing.

As she turned to head back, Vittoria's phone pipped with a series of texts. She took at cursory look at the first from Marcus and then saw there was one from Croxley. *Perfect timing*. As per her instructions, it was vague, but she knew exactly what it meant.

Your terms agreed. Will need full
details of delivery.

She texted him back.

Lighthouse Bar 2moro at 10 and
will give you the particulars.

It was starting.

Chapter 35

A S THE FRONT DOOR closed behind Jack, Lily put down her mug of tea and waited for a moment, listening to his feet on the wooden stairs, making sure he hadn't forgotten anything and was doubling back for it. *Had he remembered the shopping bags?* She'd sent him to Sainsbury's with a list, insisting that just because he wasn't opening up the shop didn't mean he could spend half the morning asleep on the couch and the rest of the day moping about.

And they needed milk.

She'd heard him again last night, muttering to George and moving around as quietly as he could so he didn't wake anyone, but very much awake himself. Depression gave him insomnia – she'd felt cruel waking him up this morning but she needed him to get into a normal sleep pattern and perhaps being exhausted would help him get at least one decent night's sleep. But right now she had something she wanted to do that she couldn't risk him walking in on.

A moment later, she heard the ground-floor street door clang closed and hurried to her room to get the notes Vittoria had given her and her MacBook.

Back at the kitchen table she powered it up.

She'd already logged into Marcus's Gmail: she'd looked at Marcus's schedule, double-checking it with a flight-tracking website that allowed her to follow the route of individual planes by their flight number. It was incredible to see just how many aircraft were on the move across the world at any moment in time. But she was only interested in one, and she'd needed to make sure that it *was* in the air and hadn't been delayed so she could log in undetected and delete the alerts that the account had been logged in to from a new device.

But he was off this week, so this time she just had to keep her fingers crossed. Lily logged in. She'd been keeping an eye on his email traffic, checking his location and travel history and looking at his appointments. If she had a bit longer she'd have been able to check what he was watching on YouTube, but one step at a time. And she needed to be fast just in case he was checking his email at the same time.

It had to be said, his mail wasn't very exciting – he had his work emails going into his Gmail account but there didn't seem to be anything very personal arriving separately to that. Lily had signed him up for a couple of porn websites via his TransGlobal email address, and one for sexually transmitted diseases, to spice it up a bit. The opt-in emails for their mailing lists had gone into spam, so finding them quickly, she clicked to confirm she wanted *all* their marketing communications and any from anyone else they thought he might be interested in. She opened another window and found a weapons manufacturer and signed him up for their mailing list too, just for good measure. She was sure his TransGlobal address could be accessed by his employers, who would be likely to check it for evidence in light of the recent revelations in the press. She'd make sure they had a few surprises.

Scrolling through, Lily had been surprised the first time she'd looked at it that Marcus's own email was so bland, but perhaps she shouldn't have been. No doubt he suspected that Vittoria might check up on him, so maybe he was being careful to keep his communication with his mistress to WhatsApp or text or to delete anything vaguely compromising. Lily checked the trash just to be sure. There were only a few emails there, taxi receipts mainly. All pick-ups or drop-offs to a certain address in Notting Hill. Interesting. The fact that there wasn't much else in there suggested to Lily that Marcus checked and cleaned up his email quite regularly. Perhaps she just needed to check more often to find something she could work with. Or *perhaps* he had a private email account just for Stephanie Carson? That would make more sense. She needed to do some more digging, see if he'd used this address as a recovery email – perhaps there was an email linking this to another, more secret account.

Lily pushed her glasses up her nose thoughtfully and glanced back through Marcus's inbox – there were several email newsletters from boat manufacturers, an email about sails. She knew she could look at them and then mark them as unread, but she really didn't have time, and she could get a lot from the subject line, or where someone had left that line blank – like his friend Aidan, who rarely seemed to put a subject in his emails – Lily could see the first line. Seeing an email from him, she smiled to herself. Vittoria had told her Aidan had been a huge support to her, that his patience with his friend's behaviour was wearing thin. The email was one line:

> Mate, what the fuck have you done this time? Do
> you ever think of V?

At least Vittoria had someone she could turn to, someone who understood.

Lily scrolled down a bit further, but it wasn't the emails she was interested in today. Moving her mouse, she opened Marcus's calendar.

Vittoria had told her that he always nagged her about her gold leather-backed appointments diary, how out-of-date it was not to store everything on the cloud. So everything he was doing should be noted here and Lily had plans for his diary. She'd waited until Emma had texted her to confirm that he was meeting his bosses on Friday before she started rearranging his appointments. He needed to have other things on his mind or he might realise things had been moved.

Lily played with the end of her ponytail as she scanned Marcus Devine's week ahead.

Tomorrow morning, Thursday, he'd made an appointment with what appeared to be – Lily frowned as she read the entry and opened another tab, checking the company name – a firm of solicitors based in some very swanky offices in Dublin city centre, according to the photos on their website. She'd thought for a minute it might be a firm of accountants – it had one of those generic partners-type names that only lawyers or accountants with little imagination could come up with.

But a lawyer's office? What was he going to discuss? Lily smiled. She didn't need to be a genius to work out that he needed advice on his legal position after the newspaper article. Let's hope that was it. She flicked back to the company website. It was a big firm, big enough to have specialist litigation lawyers as well as the sort that did your will and sold your house.

Jeepers, was he thinking of selling the house? Lily had seen from the look in her eyes just how much Vittoria loved that house, that somehow she felt it had taken an active part in her recovery. For a moment Lily wondered if Vittoria felt, perhaps subconsciously, that if she left the house she'd lose all the progress she'd made physically, that being there was keeping her going. Perhaps it was. The human mind was a complex thing, that was for sure, and Vittoria was better qualified than Lily to understand it.

Lily heard a car pull up outside, doors slamming before it drove off. She glanced out of the kitchen window. She couldn't see the road below properly without standing up, but it was a sure sign she needed to get a move on. Jack could come back any minute.

Clicking on the calendar, Lily changed the appointment with the law firm from 10.30 a.m. to 11.30. Being an hour late would mean he *might* miss his slot entirely – it would certainly mess up his day. From the look of the firm, Lily was sure that he wasn't their only important client – they probably had a pretty busy schedule.

She just hoped they weren't the type of company that sent you a text reminder of your appointment the day before, but that would be a bit crass for a company like this. It wasn't like he was booking in to get his hair cut or have a massage.

Lily scanned the next few days. Marcus had a meeting marked for Friday morning – *11.00 a.m. TG HR Adelphi House.*

Adelphi House was TransGlobal Airways Corporate Headquarters. Em had said Marcus had been suspended and had texted to say he was due in to discuss the situation on Friday. The meeting had to be about that. Lily felt her heart rate increase, her palms suddenly sweaty. Was he going to get the sack? She truly hoped so. He certainly had a lot of explaining to do, which was going to be quite a challenge under the circumstances.

There'd be no harm in making that meeting a bit later. She changed the 11.00 a.m. to 12.00 noon.

It was definitely the type of meeting you'd turn up early to, but even if he went in half an hour early, he'd still be technically half an hour late, which would smack of arrogance, unreliability and *very* bad manners. All qualities that would make him even more unpopular with his bosses.

It was possible he had the time etched on his mind, but if that was the case, then he'd probably think the incorrect time was just a typo. Lily was being very careful not to leave any indication that anyone had been snooping about. She closed out of Marcus's email, a twinge of something spiralling in the pit of her stomach. Was it guilt? Or maybe worry? Lily sighed. She knew she was playing havoc with Marcus Devine's life, but really he'd brought all this down on himself: she was only settling the balance. A balance that had a very important shop on the other side. She heard the street door bang closed downstairs. This was about Jack and getting his life back on track and, really, she'd do pretty much anything to ensure his happiness.

With so much happening in his life right now, messing with Marcus Devine's head was going to be easy and, Lily was sure, quite effective. And she was only getting started.

Chapter 36

MARCUS HAD TO put the kitchen lights on when he came downstairs on Thursday morning. Dublin Bay was dark and overcast, a storm out to sea turning the water a strange green, a colour he always thought of as Beachy green. His father had given a painting to the yacht club they were both members of – it had already been gifted its twin, a view of Kingston Harbour by Beachy, and the water was the exact shade of the water today. It didn't bode well. It was as if the sea here was mirroring the storm brewing in London.

To make it worse he felt hung over, still groggy from trying to adapt back to European time. It was always the same with the Sydney trip. He loved Singapore but it always left his body clock completely upside down. Maybe he was getting too old for this job. When he'd first got his licence, almost twenty-five years ago, the world had been a different place – air travel had just started to change, low-cost carriers coming in, Ryanair and easyJet bringing the costs way down. But TransGlobal had still been one of the world's greatest airlines then, glamorous and exciting; the air crew had been gorgeous and there had been none of this #metoo crap. Now every second person flew, the industry was swamped with Eastern European pilots who all looked about fifteen and *everyone* was working longer hours and had faster turnaround times.

It was all going to shit. Marcus sighed. If things were different he'd be looking at early retirement, but that wasn't even a viable thought right now, never mind an option.

Marcus shook his head, fighting a yawn. Normally the seven days he had off after the Sydney run was spent trying to get back into European time, but right now he had too much to do. With everything happening, the last thing he had time for was to catch up with his sleep and get back into a normal routine. Christ, he needed caffeine, and plenty of it.

Waiting for the coffee machine to do its thing, he leafed through the post that the housekeeper had left on the kitchen counter. How long had Vittoria been away? There seemed to be tons of it. Mainly junk, needless to say – he tossed another envelope addressed to Vittoria on her pile and shuffled to the next letter, one for him. From the insurance company.

Marcus looked at it, stunned. Why hadn't he thought of that? He'd totally forgotten that they were due to pay up on the stolen paintings from the first break-in anytime soon.

He grimaced. Vittoria had said something about getting more cameras in the grounds after the second break-in, to make sure they covered the whole garden too. He rubbed his hand over his face. He couldn't remember if she was doing something about that or if he was supposed to. Christ, with everything going on, she wouldn't be very impressed if he asked her – it would be obvious he'd forgotten. But he could ring the security company and check.

The espresso machine clicked, the light changing, the sound of coffee trickling into his cup somehow triggering a memory. She'd said something about the pool house, making sure there were cameras active inside as well as outside. He focused on the cup, willing the conversation to return. Jesus, he was getting old. He had no idea why she wanted them there, but he wasn't about to ask. Hadn't she said something about wanting to see the whole property before she went to bed? That was it, she was worried someone could hide in there. Perhaps she thought the guy who had broken in had been hiding somewhere before he got into the house?

Whatever had happened, it hadn't been helped by the fact that he'd been with Stephanie that night – she'd had a late scare, unexpected spotting, and had gone into hospital and he'd stayed with her. By the time he'd realised he hadn't called Vittoria to say he wasn't coming home, it was far too late. He was sure she'd be asleep in bed.

They'd kept Steph in for the night and he'd slept in the chair beside her, holding her hand, waking in a panic every time she moved in her sleep. He'd turned his phone off so it didn't disturb her.

And the next morning, when he'd switched his phone back on again, there had been a stream of texts and missed calls from Aidan saying Vittoria was fine but an intruder had got into her bedroom. Going back through the messages he'd discovered Vittoria had made dinner, which was a diary event in itself, and had been pretty annoyed that he hadn't turned up.

Christ, he felt sick just thinking about it. What were the chances of it happening that night, of all nights? He'd thought about telling her about Stephanie then, and almost been ready for it, except when he'd got back to Dublin he'd found that she was at the police station looking at photofits and there were guards crawling all over the house.

He couldn't exactly tell her he was leaving her at that point. And what if she found out Steph was pregnant? That would break her. He knew how much she wanted children. Right before the first break-in she'd started talking about adopting, had brought it up first at a dinner party in Ballsbridge, chatting to the wife of one of his pilot buddies. He hadn't even wanted to go and somehow they'd all ended up talking about children and she'd said how much she wanted them and he'd felt like a murderer all over again, the murderer of his own children.

Marcus shook his head. It was all so complicated. He wasn't even sure that he'd ever loved her – he'd played the part, of course, and he had to admit his friends had been insanely jealous. Vittoria was the most beautiful girl he'd ever seen, with the most amazing body, and he'd wanted her, wanted all of her from the moment she'd sent his coffee all over him in Charles de Gaulle. He'd done everything it took to win her.

And then the accident had happened and it had turned both their lives upside down. He couldn't leave her then. He still had no idea what had happened that night. He had definitely blacked out, not that he would ever admit that or he'd never have been able to keep his commercial licence, but something had always niggled him, he wasn't sure what, something to do with a girl. But he couldn't even remember the party, never mind getting in the car.

Marcus shook himself as a shiver ran up his spine. He'd been the one to walk away like nothing had happened. He'd had his seatbelt on, had a fairly sizeable bruise on his shoulder where he'd hit the car door when it rolled, and nettle stings. And that had been it.

Marcus looked at the envelope from the insurance company in his hand and tore it open. He'd given everything to Vittoria; now he needed to focus on himself and making sure Stephanie and his son were well looked after, and this payout, he was sure, would help.

He scanned the letter. They had taken a commercial rate on the missing paintings rather than an auction price, basically undervaluing them by about thirty per cent. Great. And they were insisting on increased security. But they would be sending a cheque as soon as everything was to their satisfaction. Marcus heaved a sigh of relief. Four paintings had been taken, worth around a million euro. After the excess, they were paying six hundred thousand. It was all bollocks and normally he would have been straight onto his solicitor, but right now a cheque for 600K could do a lot for the mortgage in Notting Hill.

Realising his coffee was going cold, he sipped it black. To secure the money, he needed to show he had the security stuff underway. Those cameras Vittoria wanted were suddenly urgent.

He picked up his phone as it pipped with a text. From Vittoria.

Check the attic. I think there are
some pictures your dad never hung
up there.

Marcus looked at the text, his brow furrowed. More paintings?

Thank fucking God, but what had his dad put in the attic that he hadn't shown in the house? Every wall was crammed with original paintings. There had been moments recently when he'd wondered if his father had been trying to sink undocumented cash, to make investments that would pay off in years to come. Like the marble statue of an angel that had been at the bottom of the stairs for as long as he could remember. Who had spare cash for museum-standard sculpture like that to stick at the bottom of the stairs?

When he'd had the paintings valued originally for the insurance, the expert from Rahilly's auctioneers had whistled at that bust, his eyes wide. Marcus had meant to get it itemised, but it was marble, too heavy to lift and it would survive a fire, so it would only add to his premiums. Vittoria had never liked it – the minute the assessor had left she'd had it moved to the cupboard under the stairs with the hoovers and cleaning materials. There was little chance of a burglar finding it in there.

So the attic was his next stop, right after he'd called the security-camera people. And then he'd get straight over to the solicitor's. He opened his calendar; he was due at 11.30. Still plenty of time. It was just as well he'd got up early. He yawned and scanned the insurance letter again. They were sending someone – tomorrow – to look at the improved security arrangements.

Tomorrow? Christ. There would be nobody here. He had to get back to London early tomorrow so he was fresh for this hearing. He needed to move the appointment to next week, and he needed to get the cameras organised before their man arrived. Abandoning his coffee, Marcus checked the time again: 9.30 a.m. The security company's offices would be open by now. He fired the insurance company an email to change the appointment and scrolled through the numbers in his phone. Thankfully, the security company answered quickly

'Marcus Devine in Alcantara, Killiney. I think my wife might have been in touch with you already about increasing the number of cameras we have linked into our CCTV system?' He listened to the reply. 'No? Christ, perhaps I was supposed to call you. She's going to murder me.' Marcus warmed to the sympathetic laughter from the man who had answered. 'I don't know if you can do anything but the insurance assessors are coming next week and obviously I was supposed to call you weeks ago … Yes, I know. Feckin' women, you know yourself. She says we need two new cameras, one in the pool house and one on the drive?'

The guy on the end made a comment about skinny-dipping and Marcus chortled. 'I don't think you'll get to see, mate, the video's all recorded here – sorry about that.'

Marcus listened for a moment, then burst out laughing. 'That too, mate. But, look, I have to go back to London tomorrow. I need the cameras in today for this insurance guy. What can you do? It'll be worth your while ...'

Marcus hung up, smirking to himself. Money talked, end of. He just needed to make sure the technicians took an envelope for Tadgh O'Sullivan back to the office with them. Looking for a pen at the back of the kitchen counter, he wrote the guy's name down on the insurance company letter. It was only fair; he'd been very helpful.

Tadgh had said he'd call him back, but Marcus reckoned the camera team would be there mid-afternoon, which gave him time to get to the bank before he did anything else and transfer his bonds and savings over to Stephanie. Then he'd be able to see about these other paintings Vittoria had texted about.

Chapter 37

THE ATTIC LADDER was one of those extending ones that was hidden in the ceiling. As Marcus used the pole he'd found in the utility room to hook the catch he smiled to himself. He hadn't done this since he was fourteen and had sneaked up into the attic to have a covert fag.

Now, as he pushed back the hatch the ladder slid down easily like it had been used recently, was well oiled. Trying the steps for steadiness, Marcus began to climb, his phone in his hand. As he cleared the trapdoor, his head in the darkness of the attic, he switched on the flashlight on his phone, swinging it around the space. The house was two storey, but it hugged the hillside and the roof space was relatively low. He certainly wouldn't ever be looking at a loft conversion to create a games room in this house. Stooping, Marcus climbed over the top of the ladder and looked around. The attic had been floored at some stage, but it had been a repository for suitcases and old sets of curtains and china and God knew what ever since he could remember.

What had Vittoria been doing up here to find a pile of paintings? Perhaps, like his mother, she'd been storing china – the point was that she'd seen some canvases that Marcus didn't know anything about. Which meant if they were sold, they wouldn't be missed. Swinging his phone torch around, he took in the trunks and suitcases, the housekeeper's old sewing machine. It smelled strange up here, almost too dry. He'd only been to Ayres Rock once, but it was like that, a still, eerie feeling, like time was frozen.

Ignoring the feeling in the back of his neck, Marcus looked around, leaning forward to reach the furthest edges of the attic with his flashlight. It was a big house, had a big footprint, and the attic was huge.

But Marcus didn't have to look far. Leaning up against the chimney breast, right in front of him, he could see three different-sized canvases stacked facing the red brick. Even without seeing the frames and the paintings themselves, he could see they were old from the charcoal and chalk numbers scrawled on the back – sales lot numbers, maybe?

He climbed closer and bobbed down beside them to get a better look, glad he was in his jeans. Pulling the first one back, he looked at it, using the light from the phone to help. It looked incredibly old – Renaissance, perhaps.

Puzzled, Marcus pulled back the second one. It was totally different, a cubist oil in black and white – something from the 1930s, maybe. Strange they were so different, and so different from the paintings in the rest of the house. And they didn't have much dust on them, not that it was terribly dusty up here. It looked like Vittoria must have found them, moved them closer to the trapdoor and forgotten to tell him about them. He turned off his flashlight and let his eyes adjust to the low light coming through the trapdoor. Marcus picked up two of the paintings and moved them closer to the hatch, then went back to have another look at the first one. It looked very old – he couldn't be sure – was it a girl in a field, maybe? It was hard to tell. He'd have a proper look at them in the light.

Downstairs, arranging the paintings across the kitchen table, the spotlights on full above him, Marcus could see these were something special. And he could see why his mother would have insisted they stay in the attic. None of them were to her taste at all – she had favoured the impressionists, loved soft colours and pastoral scenes.

Guessing at an appropriate description, Marcus did a search for similar images. The first one was the 1930s cubist monochrome.

There it was. The exact picture.

It took him a few minutes to absorb the information. He pulled out the kitchen chair and sat down heavily. *What on earth?* He checked the second one. Then the third. A pattern was emerging.

The caption that appeared with the first one said it had been missing from Hanover since 1937. It had been painted in 1912 by an artist called Albert Gleizes. Another one, a portrait he'd thought was of a girl before he looked closely, was *Portrait of a Young Man* by Raphael, which had been looted by the Germans from a museum in Poland in 1939.

Raphael. Holy fuck.

He leaned over it, looking closely at the brush work. It was definitely real.

Marcus sat for a few minutes, shocked, absorbing the information, his mind unable to process it.

Then things began to fall into place.

His father had known De Valera. Had he introduced him to Nazis who were hiding in Ireland after the Second World War, Nazis who had brought art with them to sell on the black market, to keep themselves in the lifestyle they had grown accustomed to? Marcus remembered sneaking out of bed in his pyjamas, listening through the banisters as people arrived at his parents' dinner parties. People with foreign accents.

His father was a well-known art collector in Ireland. Had he bought the paintings but been unable to show them in the house because of their rarity and provenance? Or had he been given them as payment to help with something else?

Marcus had no idea what that could have been, but his father had been a powerful man with a public profile. If he'd met a known war criminal, he'd have been obliged, surely, not only professionally but also morally, to report their presence in Ireland? But what if he hadn't? What if he had looked for them to buy his silence?

It was a long time ago; Marcus knew he could only speculate. But however they had got here, these paintings were worth thousands, maybe millions. And Vittoria obviously had no idea of their value. But Marcus was quite sure her art dealer friend would, and, as she'd suggested, if he was happy to find buyers away from auction rooms, then he was definitely the man to sell these.

Marcus felt a huge surge of relief. With the money from these pictures perhaps he'd be able to divorce Vittoria after all, to buy her out of the house, and he'd definitely be able to make sure Stephanie was well looked after *and* he'd be able to fight this bloody *Inquirer* thing.

With this sort of money, he could hire someone to find out exactly who was behind the photographs, find out who would want to damage him like this. He knew papers always protected their sources, but knowing who was doing this and, more importantly, why was starting to eat him up.

The only problem he had was time, or lack of it. He needed to get this guy of Vittoria's over here fast and get all the pictures sold. He was sure it would take time to find buyers for paintings of this level of worth.

Marcus smiled to himself. Perhaps his luck was changing at last.

Chapter 38

'HAVE YOU heard from her?'

Lily turned away from the kettle and leaned on the kitchen counter, keeping her fingers crossed behind her. She was wearing her baggy work dungarees and a skinny T-shirt – there was no way Jack would see her hands behind the folds of soft paint-splattered denim. 'No, not yet. She'll be in touch in due course.'

Sitting at the kitchen table nursing his tea, Jack grimaced. 'Do you really trust her? I mean, how do you know her?'

Lily put on what she hoped was an innocent face with a good dose of sincere and worried mixed in. 'I told you, through college. I was checking out Edward Croxley and she came up on his Facebook page as a friend of a friend. I'd met her at a party and we'd got on well. I only got in touch to find out more about him.'

'But you said she'd been swindled by him too?'

The kettle boiled and she turned around to pick it up. Thank God she didn't have to look at him; she hated lying to him. He was right to be suspicious, but this time she just needed him to trust her and do what he was told.

They'd talked about it on the plane, their voices low although no one could hear them in their little first-class pod. There was no way anyone could know of their connection.

That's what made the whole plan work. Lily would have loved to have told him all about it, but it was crucial that Jack wasn't involved. Lily felt grateful all over again that she'd been flying business class – if they'd met in economy they'd never have been able to talk without a whole load of people hearing and none of this could have happened. Their whole meeting had been so utterly random – her ticket had been changed to TransGlobal at the last minute, and Vittoria had been flying out of Heathrow rather than Dublin because she was using an employee family pass. *Perhaps the Universe knew that a few things needed rebalancing.*

But obviously Jack was curious – he'd been asking all sorts of leading questions since they'd found the amulets. Lily's silver bangles jangled down her arm as she reached up to the cupboard for the mugs. *She just needed to keep to her story.* She kept her back to him as she answered, taking out the teabags.

'Well, sort of, I don't know the details but I think she was dating Croxley or something and he walked out on her really abruptly. That was before they realised that a bunch of jewellery was missing. She couldn't prove anything, obviously.'

'But she wants to get one over on him too.'

'Exactly.' She poured the water into his mug and turned around to hand it to him, the teabag still in it.

He looked at it and looked up at her, rolling his eyes. 'I did give you a teapot you know …'

Lily suddenly realised what she'd done and opened the drawer beside her to give him a spoon to fish the teabag out. 'Sorry. And I'm not using an antique Minton teapot for your tea, Jack Power.' She gave him a wide-eyed look.

Jack grinned back at her cheekily. Then his face became more serious. 'I'm still not sure it was a good idea to give her those amulets. Does she have any idea what they're worth? If we sold those we could probably buy another shop.'

Lily shook her head impatiently, her long silver earrings tangling with the wisps of hair that had come out of her ponytail. 'No, Jack. We don't want *any* shop. We want our own shop and everything that goes with that.'

He grimaced again, rubbed his face with his hand. 'You're right. Of course you're right.'

'Women are always right; I keep telling you.' She leaned across the table and ruffled his hair. 'It'll be fine – we just have to sit tight. Now, beans on toast for lunch or scrambled egg?'

Turning back to the counter to prepare their lunch, Lily pushed her glasses up her nose and sighed quietly. She couldn't tell Jack anything about Vittoria. She really did hate lying to him, but it was vital nobody ever knew about their deal.

They had to remain strangers. That was the beauty of the whole thing. She'd been deliberately vague, hadn't even told Jack Vittoria's name. Particularly hadn't told him her name.

Now she had the amulets, Lily was quite sure Vittoria would be able to sort out Croxley, to get the keys back and destroy that note Jack had signed, and then they'd all be able to get on with their lives. Like Jack said, the amulets had to be worth a fortune – they had some in the British Museum. She could see why Croxley had gone to such incredible lengths to get them back, but that also meant that the people he was getting them for wanted them very badly and weren't the sort to take no for an answer. Which was worrying Lily a lot. Did Vittoria know what she was doing? Was she playing with fire?

Perhaps they both were.

Lily knew she'd find out soon enough. There had been a postcard on the doormat when she'd come back in from the workshop earlier, a London tourist card with pigeons on the front. On the reverse it had just said *Hello, Lily! Having a fabulous time. Russell Square Friday 4 p.m.?* There was no postmark over the stamp.

Russell Square had a beautiful little park in the middle. Surrounded by high railings, it was presided over by a statue of Lord Bedford and was one of the many little oases of calm in the city.

Lily guessed that Vittoria meant to meet her there.

She glanced over at Jack as she opened the fridge to look for eggs. He was sitting, staring morosely at his phone, but she could see from his face and the speed he was scrolling that he wasn't reading anything or taking it in. She knew how sick he felt about the whole card-game thing, and finding the amulets wasn't actually making it any easier. Croxley's involvement with something that was so obviously stolen or being traded on the black market made this even more scary.

Lily just hoped Vittoria had some news for her this afternoon. She wondered if Croxley would give up the keys to the shop even if she *did* give him back the amulets, but Lily was sure Vittoria could be persuasive. She was a psychologist, after all, understood how people's minds worked, how to press their buttons.

And so far everything had gone smoothly. Lots of things were actually working out quite well. Perhaps there was a karma rebalancing thing going on?

Emma had got her promotion at the *Inquirer* after landing the photos, and today she was meeting Bellissima Serata to do a multi-page exposé on her life. After the publicity the pictures had generated, Bellissima had been snapped up in a huge publishing deal by a publisher who had paid the earth for some pop star's memoir. Lily had even had a proper chat to Jack about playing cards, but he'd got such a fright the last time, she didn't think he'd ever be tempted to play for more than half matchsticks ever again. It was the adrenaline he loved in a card game, using his skills to outwit the other players. And now she and Vittoria were using all *their* skills to outwit the other players in their own game.

She'd persuaded Jack to try chess for a bit instead.

Marcus Devine was the only one really suffering now, and Lily knew he was well overdue payback after everything he'd done. His recklessness had ruined Vittoria's life when he crashed his car. But driving a vintage open-topped sports car too fast was pretty typical for a man like that. She could see why he'd become a pilot: it was the perfect job for him. Vittoria had told her that he'd learned to fly a private plane before he'd learned to drive; getting his commercial licence had been way easier than doing any real work in university. So while his school friends slogged through their degrees, he'd very quickly been on a very comfortable salary, living the film-star lifestyle. Flying had been more glamorous then, although Marcus Devine certainly made the most of it even now. From the press she'd read on him, Lily could see his arrogance shining through. How many other women did he have around the world? Stephanie Carson would be much better off without him. Women managed as single mothers, and Lily knew she'd be fine. The sooner she saw Marcus for what he really was, the better.

Stephanie had left a message on Lily's phone about being a No. 42 ambassador. It had been a spur of the moment idea on Lily's part, but actually, when she thought about it later, she realised that it might give Stephanie a bit of independence from Marcus Devine, and that couldn't be a bad thing.

She just needed to make it into a real thing.

She'd emailed Marianne Omotoso about the idea of a British focus for the collection she'd be designing and she'd loved it, thank God, asking to see any designs she already had in progress. Getting Stephanie involved would be a natural extension. No. 42 had no end of top models and actresses wearing their jewellery. Lily just needed to work out how Stephanie could bring extra value to the brand and everything would fall into place. Their marketing budget had sounded incredible. When she'd been to New York for her chat they'd been talking about launching a new line in October, the conversation peppered with names she'd only seen in *Vogue*. She'd sat in awe listening. No. 42 obviously didn't do anything quietly and they were talking about painting the whole Fifth Avenue store lilac and wrapping it in a giant crystal bow, releasing white homing pigeons to symbolise their message that women should have freedom to be themselves. Lily didn't even know where you'd find five hundred white homing pigeons in New York City, and then one of the men in suits had suggested putting jewelled identity rings on them. She'd been speechless.

The toast popped and Lily tuned back into the kitchen. She needed to change the subject. 'Marianne's assistant has sent me a load of information about apartments in New York. They look amazing. Thank God they're furnished.'

Jack glanced up from his phone. 'I hope you'll have room for guests. I'm happy to sleep on the sofa.' He half-smiled, his hair flopping into his face. Lily looked at him. God, she'd miss him so much, and she could tell he'd miss her. With everything happening with the shop it was easy to put his dark mood down to that, but she knew he was worried about her going. It wasn't like he didn't have friends, but they'd become so close after their dad had died. Their mum had been practically useless since the day she'd given birth. If it hadn't been for their grandpa they would probably have ended up in care. Lily hadn't even told her what had happened with the shop; she was sure they'd have it back before anyone needed to know.

Lily smiled at him. 'How are you doing selling those books?'

'What books? Oh, the ones that were in the box with the teapot? Good, actually. The guy who I thought would like *The Essential Art of the Gentleman Printer* loved the Virginia Woolf. He wants me to find a pile of first-edition Bloomsbury-set novels. They sell at over a thousand pounds each so there should be a nice profit if I can get them at the right price. He's got some printing press that Woolf used or one like it – I think he's going to start a museum or something. His office is stuffed full of metal type. I've never seen so much.'

'That's great news.'

Jack nodded. 'Gives me something to do. When will you hear from your friend?'

'Soon, I hope, soon.'

Chapter 39

SITTING ON THE EDGE of her bed in The Hogarth Hotel, Vittoria ran through everything in her mind. Thursdays were always busy in The Lighthouse Bar so she'd reserved a table for lunch in The Orlando Brasserie, with its black and white tiled floor and glazed roof. She'd meet Croxley at the bar and then they could sit down and discuss business.

Marcus had found the paintings and needed Croxley to see them as soon as possible. He was flying into London for the day tomorrow and would be back in Dublin on Friday night. He'd sounded very upbeat on the phone, not at all worried now by the disciplinary hearing in the morning. 'I really don't think these paintings are worth much but they'll certainly help. How did you find them?'

Vittoria had been in The Lighthouse Bar when the phone had rung. 'I needed a vase for that massive bunch of flowers the office sent after the break-in. I suddenly remembered your mother had had a huge one. It seemed silly to buy one, so I went up to have a look. I found the vase right in the back corner of the attic, and when I turned around I saw the corners of the pictures sticking out from behind a pile of suitcases. They were filthy – goodness only knows how long they'd been there. I moved them to nearer the hatch and was going to bring them down when I'd sorted out the flowers but then the phone rang – Yana was having a crisis – and I forgot about them.' She paused. 'We've never had a proper look in that attic – there could be all sorts of stuff up there.'

'I reckon my mother must have stuck them up there.'

'That's what I thought. I only glanced at them but that black and white one is hideous. Not her taste at all.'

'I've dug out some of the others that Mum wasn't keen on, so we've quite a collection for your art man. With a bit of luck, he'll be able to raise enough to fight this case and then we can all get on with our lives.'

'Great, I'm seeing him today – I'll make the arrangements. Did you hear from the insurance company yet?'

Marcus grunted. 'There was a letter here when I got home, and I've got the camera people coming. I don't know why you want them inside the pool house – it's not a requirement for the insurance.'

Vittoria cleared her throat. 'I told you, I just want to be able to check everywhere before I go to bed. After the last time, I realised he could have been hiding down there the whole day and I wouldn't have known.' She hesitated. 'Actually, you should put those new paintings down in the pool house, just to be on the safe side. If we did get broken into again nobody is going to look there for art. With the extra cameras it will be easy to keep an eye on it, and it's very secure.'

'Good point. I'll do that. The camera people reckon they'll have everything wired up in a few hours. When are you back?'

'I'm not sure. There's a lecture at the Royal Academy I'd love to go to on Saturday while I'm here. I've been so tied up with Yana I haven't even done any shopping.'

'She seems very demanding these days.'

'She's one of my key clients, Marcus. Her position brings me in no end of business and she pays very well – she seems to have limitless cash. I need to be available for her or she could go elsewhere.'

His response was grudging. 'Grand, I'll call you on Friday after the hearing.'

Vittoria pursed her lips. Everything was falling into place.

After her conversation with Marcus she'd come upstairs to get changed for lunch and to switch on her laptop: she had lots to check. Years ago she'd read an article by an eminent historian who felt that one of the major causes of the First World War had been railway timetables. It had sounded so odd that it had stuck in her head, but in fact, when she'd researched it, the historian had demonstrated that the timetabling had to do with the mobilisation of arms. And the increased threat from the change in timetabling had resulted in the German invasion of Belgium.

Attention to detail was everything.

On the bedside locker, a postcard was lying beside the hotel phone – she'd found it slipped into the pages of the Hitchcock book. The illustration was from *Alice in Wonderland*, with a quotation below it: 'Sometimes I've believed as many as six impossible things before breakfast.' She smiled to herself.

Today was all about making the impossible happen, perfectly.

*

As the lift doors closed behind her and Vittoria headed down the corridor to the bar, she could see Croxley was already waiting for her. He was sitting on one of the stools, one leg folded over the other, apparently nonchalantly, but she could see from the way his foot was tapping in the air that he was nervous. She smiled. She held all the cards now.

'Edward, lovely to see you. Why don't we go through? I've a table booked for lunch.' Vittoria's voice was slightly louder than normal and several people turned to look at them.

'Of course.' Then as they were walking towards the doors of the restaurant Croxley leaned in to her. 'Is it a little public?'

Vittoria smiled reassuringly. 'It'll be fine, and they do the most wonderful risotto. I don't normally let myself but Marcus called earlier with some news, so I think we can celebrate a little.'

Their orders placed, Vittoria sat forward in her chair, nursing a glass of white wine. The restaurant was filling up, the noise level rising.

'Marcus is very much looking forward to seeing you. He's got several paintings that came from the same source as the one you're already handling. I'm keeping that as a surprise, so don't mention it when you meet him.' She paused. 'He's had a bit of bother with the press recently – the *Sunday Inquirer* ran some photos last weekend with him and some Italian escort ...' On the table beside them, the woman's eyebrows shot up. That was the thing about this restaurant – the tables were all so close together that if you were a tiny bit too loud the next table could hear everything. And Vittoria wanted them to. 'The photos have caused an issue with TransGlobal Airways. He's one of their lead pilots – sorry, I can't remember if I told you that? So anyway, he has to sort it all out and it's very likely everyone's going to end up in court.'

Croxley raised his eyebrows. 'That sounds expensive.'

'Exactly, which is why he wants to sell some of these paintings. The Devine Collection really is extensive. The ones we discovered recently seem to be a very random bunch. Some Art Deco and one that looks Renaissance. But I'm not an expert at all.'

'You don't have to worry about that – I am.'

Vittoria smiled. 'Precisely.' The waiter arrived with their orders as she continued. 'And while you're there I'd love you to look at the pool house – there's a huge wall down by the changing rooms that really needs something on it – maybe a mosaic? I'm hoping you can source something but you'll need to take measurements.' She bent down to her handbag and pulled out a pen and paper to draw a diagram for him. It only took her a second to sketch it.

'See, this is the house and this is the pool?' She glanced at him to see if he was paying attention as she went on. 'The changing rooms are at the back. There's a phone here.' She tapped the paper with the point of her biro. 'That's the wall I want the mosaic on. Or maybe a huge painting? I'm not sure. Once you've seen it you can give me some ideas.'

Edward's face creased in a frown. He glanced anxiously across to the women on the next table as he flipped open his napkin, his voice lowered as he spoke. 'That sounds fine. And on the other matter?'

'I'll give you very precise instructions. Get a taxi from the airport. But I'm sure it will all go very smoothly.' Vittoria picked up her fork. 'The new pictures are very sought after from what I can gather. Presumably you'll need to bring them back to London with you?'

Croxley nodded. 'I'll need to get them checked here but that letter you showed me speaks volumes in terms of provenance. I don't imagine there will be any difficulty at all with the buyers I have in mind.'

'That's perfect. Now, I need to give you this.' Vittoria reached down to her handbag and produced a tiny antique jewellery box. It was navy leather and had a brass button to flip open the lid. She passed it to Croxley. Nestled on a blue velvet base, their intense yellow colour reflected by the white satin, were three amulets. He raised his eyebrows.

'You'll have the fourth when you get back from Dublin as we discussed. Now do you have anything for me?'

Reaching inside his jacket pocket, Croxley handed her a scruffy piece of notepaper. Scrawled across it in fountain pen was Jack's note, the witnesses' signatures below his. Croxley slipped his hand into his side pocket and produce a heavy bunch of keys.

Vittoria smiled at him. '*Perfetto*. Marcus is very much looking forward to meeting you.'

Edward Croxley was going to help her in more ways than Marcus could possibly imagine.

Chapter 40

A LOUD BUZZ made Marcus Devine look up sharply. Very few people called to the house except by prior appointment. He'd been so busy researching the paintings he'd found after his conversation with Vittoria, he'd totally forgotten about the CCTV camera installation people. He reached to depress the gate button and glanced at the clock – it was already 2 p.m. He had no idea where time was going today. He'd been late getting to the solicitor's, apparently – their stupid girl must have written his appointment down for the wrong time – so the meeting had been very rushed. He'd signed all the documents to transfer the house into Vittoria's name – there was no need for her to know anything about that just yet – and got the papers for the boat organised for Aidan. He still wasn't completely sure about signing the house over to Vittoria, but Aidan had made a good point. It felt a bit rash when it was unlikely that their marriage would survive everything the *Sunday Inquirer* was likely to throw at him, but whatever chance he had of negotiating with her, he'd definitely lose the house if he lost the case and ended up bankrupt. Being prepared was half the battle.

He hadn't had time to change his will in favour of Stephanie – the solicitor had insisted that that needed more planning –

but his heirs were already included in the standard wording, so that was one less thing to worry about.

Then he'd got to the bank and it had taken an hour to get everything sorted out, the bonds cashed and balances of various accounts transferred. It had amounted to more than he had expected, a lot more, but thank God, whatever happened, that was safe now in Stephanie's name.

Glancing at the CCTV camera screen in the kitchen, he saw the gates closing and a van nosing up the drive. He needed to be quick. Picking up the paintings, he opened the pantry door and slipped them inside, leaning them, front facing, against the wall. The housekeeper would be in later but they'd be safe there while he sorted out the camera people, then he could take them down to the pool house. That was a very good idea of Vittoria's. He'd get the security guys to check the whole system while they were there. They'd had two break-ins and, even with the extra cameras they were insisting on, the insurance premiums were likely to skyrocket unless the house was like Fort Knox.

Thinking about it now, he'd better get someone out to check all the locks and maybe look at more secure fencing as well. Vittoria had always felt that the end of the garden behind the pool house was a bit weak. She was always saying there was no point having an eight-foot wall around three-quarters of the property and a shaggy hedge on the last side. And there was a public footpath on the other side of the hedge, one that ran between two public car parks. It was constantly busy with people coming to the beach, joggers and dog walkers. The front gates were electric, controlled from the house, but if the opposite end of the garden was wide open to attack it seemed all a bit pointless. Like having a locked front door but leaving the garden door open.

He had enough on his mind right now, though. Once he'd got the camera people organised down at the pool house, he'd come back and finish his research on these pictures. He really wanted to get back up into the attic and see if there was anything else up there, but he needed to do that when he had a bit of time, to go through all the trunks and boxes systematically. It was starting to look like his father had known some very influential visitors to Ireland and they'd obviously understood that art was one of those things, that, like jewellery, held its value. When he thought about the dinner parties, there had been a lot of people he didn't know and strange chocolates, his mother getting dressed for dinner and arriving downstairs in a cloud of Chanel No. 5, the dining room glittering with the best china, candlelight sparkling off the crystal.

Vittoria had never understood his parents' life. He'd always thought they'd host dinner parties like that but she hated to cook, which had surprised him, bearing in mind her father owned a restaurant, but perhaps that was why. She associated the kitchen with being forced to help out when she was exhausted from her dance practice. His mind drifted for a moment, back to the day they'd met. She'd had an inner glow even then, a magnetism he couldn't describe. Every guy in the airport had had his eyes on her. And he'd been captivated. He'd waited for her outside the audition and taken her to lunch. She'd hardly eaten anything, had seemed amused by his attention. He'd just moved to TransGlobal then and was flying out of Heathrow; she'd got a permanent position with the Royal Ballet and Paris had been forgotten. She hadn't looked back. They'd seen a lot of each other, and then that summer he'd brought her to Dublin, to the house, the bay glittering beyond the garden with reflected stars, and she'd been smitten.

He'd taken time off and they'd spent every minute of her holiday together that they could, although she practised for hours every day. Until the night of the accident.

But he didn't want to think about that now. He'd seen hints of Vittoria's turbulent personality before but afterwards she'd been even more dramatic. Perhaps that was the nature of being an artist – as a ballerina she was like a finely tuned machine, one that was prone to the wheels falling off every now and again. Thank God Stephanie wasn't like that. She had her moments, but she was just much, much more normal than Vittoria had ever been.

The front doorbell rang, interrupting Marcus's thoughts, and he went to answer it. The CCTV guys were smart in navy and orange boiler suits that matched their van, tool boxes ready in their hands. Marcus had no idea how Vittoria always managed to find the most expensive tradesmen in the country to work on the house, but right now he hoped their ability and, more importantly, speed, matched their branding. He couldn't afford any more break-ins with paintings like the ones he'd just found casually left in the attic.

'Thanks for coming so promptly, lads. My wife wants a new camera put in the pool house and we need an extra one on the drive – there's a bit of a blind spot on the bend. I think we might need one to cover the rear hedge too. Can you have a look at what we've got and make sure there are no other hidden corners?'

'No problem. It was your wife who was here when the guy broke in, wasn't it? She's the ballerina?'

Marcus grimaced – the press had reported on the whole debacle.

'Brave lady. A lot of people would have just panicked.'

'Vittoria doesn't do panic. She's very controlled.'

264

'Just as well. We'll check everything, make sure all the footage is being recorded properly.'

'Excellent. The guards thought the guy might have been in the house for some time, that he was looking for a particular painting. We didn't tell Vittoria that, obviously – it's bad enough that he was here at all, never mind that he might have been creeping around all day looking for something specific. He's on the CCTV but he's got a mask over his face. The only place that hadn't been touched in the first break-in was our room. There's a landscape up there that I think he must have been after.'

The first of the technicians shivered. 'Christ, rather you than me, mate. Don't get that in a three-bed semi in Ballybrack.'

Marcus laughed. 'Bet you're a damn sight closer to the pub there too.' He stood back to show them into the hall. 'Here, it's this way. We've a CCTV room next to the kitchen – all the recording equipment's in there.'

Leaving the technicians to start work, Marcus went back to his iPad in the kitchen. And looked long and hard at the images of the paintings. They were all lost, had been looted by the Nazi regime. Marcus closed his eyes. He'd never have expected his father to have actually consorted with these types of people, to have drunk and dined with the Nazi party. But part of Marcus wasn't surprised: his father was as right wing as they came, and he was a man's man – he'd never allowed Marcus's mother to learn to drive. It was as well they'd died so close together or she would have been forced to get the bus into town, leaving two very fine Mercedes parked in the double garage. They were collectors' items now, a sports car and a saloon, both fire-engine red. When his father went out he liked to be noticed. Perhaps that's why he had married one of Ireland's most celebrated actresses. Perhaps it was his mother's legacy that had drawn Marcus to Vittoria and then Stephanie. Who knew.

His strongest memories of his mother were clouds of perfume, cigarette smoke and gin cocktails. She'd slept almost all day and had shone in the evenings at their celebrated dinner parties, while Marcus had been brought up by a nanny. Several, actually, all young and very pretty. It was only as he'd reached university that he'd finally realised the reason for that, had become aware of his father's string of mistresses that included several of his friends' wives. But Richard Devine was one of those men that everyone wanted to know. Charismatic and charming, as well as very, very wealthy, he'd had it all.

It was strange, but Marcus realised he hadn't thought this much about his father since his funeral, the enormous church in Foxrock crammed full. He'd been sent off to boarding school in Blackrock, even though they only lived down the road, so he really hadn't seen much of his parents during term time, and in the summer his mother had vanished to Antibes, and his father had sailed. Quite often, he'd just played tennis and swam the whole summer, hanging out at the yacht club, occasionally helping with the junior sail training.

But none of that mattered now: what mattered was looking after his unborn son and how he was going to get through this meeting tomorrow.

Perhaps this was his father finally stepping up and helping his own son when he was against the wall? The money these paintings would generate would take the pressure off completely. Marcus smiled – he could almost buy his own airline with the profits from the sale of these paintings if the estimates online were anything to go by.

Perhaps that was something he should seriously consider.

He was going to win this case – there was no question in his mind – and he was going to make sure he destroyed the rag journalist who had run the story in the process, to say nothing of this Bellissima tart. Marcus shook his head. He had no idea why she'd picked him – maybe it was because the tabloids were already interested in him. Whatever the reason, he was quite sure she was behind it, looking for publicity for her book. The stupid bitch was going to get some shock when they all ended up in court.

Chapter 41

VITTORIA WAS ALREADY sitting on a bench in Russell Square when Lily got there. It was only a five-minute walk from the tube station and busy even in the late afternoon, the gated park attracting students from the nearby University of London, businessmen taking time out, as well as mums bringing their children home from school or the shops. Winter was on the way, the leaves on the lime trees floating lethargically to the ground.

Lily headed for the middle of the square where a fountain sent up jets of water from a paved circle, pigeons bathing in the puddles and bubbles. One was pure white and making a very thorough job of staying that way. All his feathers were fluffed out as he dipped into the water, evidently enjoying his ablutions. Lily smiled. She was sure he wasn't a homing pigeon but she wondered what he'd think of a huge flock of his relatives being released amid a flash of crystals in the New York sunshine.

The sound of bubbling water and birdsong, together with the rustle of the surrounding trees, made the circle of benches that surrounded the middle of the square a popular place. But busy was good. The more people who saw an accidental meeting between strangers, the better. From the moment the postcard had arrived that morning, Lily's stomach had been churning with a potent blend of nervousness and excitement. What did Vittoria need to speak to her about? Did she have news?

Spotting Vittoria's crisp bobbed haircut from behind, Lily went and sat down on the opposite end of the bench she was sitting on, glancing at her politely as she did so. Pulling out the popcorn she had in her satchel, she scattered some on the ground around her feet, immediately attracting a huge number of hungry pigeons. It was like they communicated by telepathy, calling their friends to join them.

Like the other people seated around the fountain, Vittoria appeared to be watching the pigeons, taking a few moments out from a busy life. She was wearing a boxy black jacket and a red and black scarf tied cleverly at the neck. Perhaps it was that or her high-heeled ankle boots that made her look so elegant. Lily wasn't sure, but everything she wore was a complete contrast to Lily's layered sweaters and scarfs, her floral dresses or denim dungarees.

They couldn't be more different. Or, as Lily had realised during their first meeting, more similar.

As Lily threw down another handful of popcorn, Vittoria looked at the birds flocking around her feet. 'They're amazing, aren't they? I've been wondering how the white ones manage to stay white in this city. I always seem to have a fine layer of grime all over me whenever I've been walking around for the day.'

A woman with a pushchair stopped beside them, her toddler delighted with the scrambling birds. Lily smiled at her, turning to Vittoria. 'I love this square – it's so peaceful, even with all the traffic and madness outside.'

'We've a few similar at home.' Vittoria smiled. 'I'm from Dublin. There are some grand Georgian squares like this, and we've got a fabulous park called St Stephen's Green right in the middle of the city.'

'I've never been to Dublin – is it lovely?'

'Very.'

Acknowledging the two women on the bench, the woman with the pushchair moved off.

Vittoria leaned over to open her handbag, resting on the wooden seat between them, her voice low. 'We need to be quick but I've got something for you.'

Lily glanced at her as Vittoria slipped a stiff paper bag out of her black leather handbag and absentmindedly put it down between them, continuing to search in her bag as if she was looking for something.

Lily moved her satchel onto the bench in front of the bag. 'What is it?'

'Take a look.'

Lily slid the paper bag towards her, behind her satchel, and made a show of flipping back the soft leather flap, at the same time slipping her hand inside the small paper carrier. She caught her breath. She could feel a set of keys and tucked in beside them, a thick envelope. Her eyes open wide, Lily sat stock still and stared at the pigeons pecking at her feet. She knew how important it was that this looked like a casual conversation, two strangers meeting and chatting about the weather, but she suddenly had a massive urge to throw her arms around Vittoria. She kept her voice low, little more than a whisper.

'How? I mean … how?'

'The amulets. I gave him back three of them. He has a fairly heavy Russian friend, a business associate, who needs all of them rather urgently. I think he might call into the shop on Monday to get the last one. It's in the bag as well. His problem is with Croxley so you've nothing to worry about – just have it ready for him.'

Lily glanced at her quickly, anxiously. 'You're sure?'

'Absolutely.' Vittoria paused. 'I gave Croxley a painting that he was going to show the Russian – his name's Sergei. I suggested he leave it in the shop. It's quite valuable and that's the most secure place he has access to.'

'But he won't be able to get it if we've got the keys?'

'Don't worry, I'm sure the Russian will ask for it when he collects the amulets.'

'I'll have a look for it as soon as we get back in.'

Vittoria nodded. 'Croxley thought this guy Sergei's boss would be very interested in it.' She smiled. 'Now, to make everything run smoothly, I need you to do something for me. It's not complicated at all, but it needs to be done precisely as I tell you. Precisely.' She glanced at Lily and tucked her hair behind her ear. 'On Friday night at six I need you to go to The Hogarth Hotel and book in to room 520. It will have suddenly become available. There's cash in the envelope in the bag.'

Lily pursed her lips for a moment and, without looking at Vittoria, reached inside her satchel for her sketchbook and a soft B pencil. Out of the corner of her eye, she could see Vittoria's brow cloud for a moment, but Lily hummed as she began to sketch the strutting white pigeon and the scene around them.

With everything going on at the moment, to get what Vittoria needed her to do absolutely right, Lily knew she needed to write it down. There was already so much swirling in her head – but discretion was an absolute priority and a list floating about that Jack might find could take a lot of explaining. Lily needed to hide the information, and what better way than in a drawing of the park. She drew in the child's buggy, viewed from behind, a badge on the back embossed with the number 520.

'That's really very good. I wish I could draw. It's a gift to be able to record a moment like this so accurately.' Vittoria's voice was full of admiration.

Lily glanced at her, smiling. 'I like to get the detail right. It makes such a difference.'

'So true. Can I watch?'

Lily grinned. 'Of course.' She put her satchel – and the paper carrier bag containing the money and the shop keys – on the paving stones at her feet, as if it was the most natural thing in the world. Vittoria shifted in more closely as Lily deftly drew in some more pigeons.

Lily desperately wanted to ask why that particular room, why 520 was so important, but Vittoria continued, her voice low. 'The Hogarth Hotel, don't forget.'

Balancing the sketchbook on her knee, Lily sketched an open book in the top corner of her page. The Hogarth Hotel had been named after Virginia Woolf's publishing company.

'Take a bag with some clothes and wash things so it looks like you're going to stay. You'll be given two room key cards – both operate the door and the lights.'

Lily nodded curtly as if to herself as Vittoria explained. 'Leave one key in your room, with your coat and bag – unpack so your things are in the bathroom – take the other key and go home.'

Lily drew a bag underneath the child's buggy in her picture, a toothbrush sticking out of the flap, a bunch of toy keys lying beside it.

'On Saturday morning I'm going to drop an envelope in to your shop. Inside will be my mobile phone.' Vittoria looked at her hard, then looked at the picture. Lily drew a phone in the buggy pannier. Beside her, Lily heard Vittoria take a breath. 'This is the important bit. On Saturday I need you to go back to your room. At 3.15 p.m. use the connecting door to go into 521, the room next door. It'll be open.'

'How?'

Vittoria smiled, 'Let me worry about that.'

Lily drew a clock on the apex of a building in the background, marking in the time.

It only took Vittoria a few more moments to explain, Lily's pencil moving swiftly across the page.

And then they were finished.

Lily put the pad on the bench beside her and leaned down to her satchel for another handful of popcorn. She threw it out to the pigeons, her voice low. 'You're sure that's it? That's all you need me to do?'

Vittoria nodded. 'It's the timing that is absolutely crucial.'

'No problem. I'll be there. Where will you be?'

'I've got a few things to do.' Vittoria smiled at her enigmatically. 'I'll be keeping busy.'

Chapter 42

EDWARD CROXLEY sat on the chaise longue in his studio apartment and put his head in his hands. Matilda snuffled around his feet with her pug nose, her corkscrew tail moving in what, for Matilda, was a wag. She was almost round, like a little barrel on legs; he needed to stop his neighbour feeding her scraps when she minded her or he'd have to start carrying her soon. She looked at him with her liquid brown eyes. She was gorgeous and Edward needed gorgeous right now.

Christ, how had he got himself into this mess? Perhaps it was his own fault – he'd been showing off that night at the gallery, had made more of his art trading than it really was, but when a Russian oligarch turns up on your skyline you don't tell him you've been selling chocolate-box prints for old ladies in Kent. It was Croxley's nature to big things up, always had been. But perhaps it was time to stop.

The small balding man with the slightly alarming black eyebrows had been so interested in what he did, he'd told him too much. He, Edward Croxley, was a total fucking idiot. He should have realised that he was being sized up for something. Kaprizov's English was heavily accented, like he'd never been bothered to learn it properly. But who needed to worry about learning another language when they had beautiful women fawning all over them and an entourage who looked after their every need. He'd invited Edward to another party, and it hadn't been long before the five-star Mayfair lifestyle and fringe benefits had sucked him right in.

Going to the sales and buying what he was told was so easy. Well, it had been until the fuck-up with the amulets, and the message had come through loud and clear that it was his job to sort it out.

He'd been convinced they had to be in the shop. At least he'd been right about Jack Power buying the box. Who put six-thousand-year-old amulets into a fucking teapot anyway? Someone somewhere should get roasted for *that*.

Croxley flicked his fringe out of his eyes and pushed his glasses up his nose. They were a fashion statement, didn't help him see at all, but he'd got used to them now, and they made him look clever. He was good with that.

Matilda rolled over beside his foot with a loud sigh and then farted. She looked up at him, expecting her stomach to be rubbed. He reached down to oblige. He had his iPad on the pouffe in front of him – he'd been in the middle of googling Vittoria's husband, Marcus Devine, when a wave of despair had hit him.

Now he had Vittoria on one side and Sergei on the other. How bad could it be?

At least he had three of the amulets. When he'd dropped them off earlier, Sergei had looked at him and shaken his head. Edward had actually wanted to punch him, but instead he'd said, 'I'll have the fourth this weekend, plus more paintings. If Igor liked the look of the last one he's going to be very happy. I have it safely stored at Power's Fine Arts. You can collect it there at any time.'

'He does not want paintings. He wants these gold charms for his niece's wedding and for her three bridesmaids.

Something old the British saying goes. Igor wants the groom and his parents to know that he will stop at nothing to ensure Anastasia's happiness.'

Croxley was quite sure Igor Kaprizov would manage that.

Now he tried to bring himself into the moment. He needed to find out as much as he could about Marcus Devine to make sure he wasn't taken unawares on Saturday. Vittoria had been very precise about what he needed to do.

Edward had cringed, his stomach rolling over, the minute Vittoria had mentioned the pool. He hadn't been near a swimming pool since that party, since Arabella; the image of her lying there face down at the bottom of the crystal clear water would never leave him. She'd been so pale, her blonde hair waving like a plant in the movement of the water.

Even now it made him feel sick to his stomach.

He'd gone upstairs to look for an empty loo, had seen her stumble into a bedroom followed by about six jocks. It was her friend's birthday and she was a virgin, so it was high time to put an end to that, apparently. But then she'd started screaming. He'd seen a scuffle through the open door, heard the bang as the French windows were slammed open, then a splash. She'd jumped off the balcony right into the pool. She'd been drinking, doing lines. Whatever had happened, she'd never surfaced and no one had jumped in after her. And the water had washed away any DNA.

Edward bit his lip. Pools just weren't his thing.

His heart lurched. He'd thought for a moment Vittoria was trying to frame him, but she needed to sell the pictures and only he could do that. No one threw away two million quid – more if you took the other pictures into account. And it was pretty obvious Marcus Devine had to be right on the edge.

Riffling through the newspapers in the basket beside the

chaise longue, he found the *Sunday Inquirer* and shook it open. The photos of Bellissima and Marcus Devine were pretty big. *Devastatingly big.* Edward could see why Vittoria was upset. He'd crossed paths with Bellissima a few times and she was a total bitch, always looking for anything that would get her picture in the paper.

Could he do what Vittoria wanted? Did he have any choice? He needed that fourth amulet or there was a very good chance he'd wake up dead one day next week, and if his neighbour was left to look after Matilda, she'd pop.

Croxley had thought the painting would help smooth things, but it was the amulets that Kaprizov wanted – he'd get to the paintings later. He was interested in those, for sure, but he had a one-track mind, and right now that was focused on his niece and making sure she was totally and blissfully happy on her wedding day, and if that meant giving her amulets that had been covered in blood from the moment the first looter had run up to smash open the museum doors, then so be it. Edward didn't see how they could possibly bring her luck, but that wasn't his problem. Making sure Sergei got them was, and right now Vittoria Devine had the last one.

She'd booked him on a flight at lunch-time from Heathrow. He'd be in Dublin by 1.30 p.m. and needed to get a taxi to the house in Killiney. There were gates and a long drive but Marcus was very friendly and he needed some good news. That's what he'd be delivering.

All he had to do was have a brandy with Marcus and then go down to the pool house to see the paintings and give him an idea of what they were worth. What could be simpler?

Chapter 43

I T WAS EARLY evening when Vittoria's phone rang. She'd been lying back with her eyes closed, and the sound made her jump. Reaching for her mobile on the bedside table she could see Aidan's name on the screen. He spoke before she could say even hello.

'You've been very quiet – how are you doing?' His voice was full of concern.

Vittoria stretched and sat up in her bed, pulling the pillow straight behind her and hooking her hair behind her ear out of the way of the phone. The curtains were open and she had a lovely view of the grand buildings on the opposite side of Great Russell Street. She knew she had a busy day tomorrow, had been resting, working through everything in her mind, mentally checking and double checking. In the background at Aidan's end she could hear the sounds of a busy hospital, voices and the clattering of trolleys. Aidan must have just finished his rounds. She could see him standing in his white coat, the pocket bristling with pens, his stethoscope around his neck and a face mask pulled down around his neck. He always wore a black T-shirt to work with black denims and a chunky brown leather belt. He was going grey now, like Marcus, but wore his hair shaved, and started the week clean shaven but by Friday had very sexy stubble. That and his sparkling blue eyes had the nurses fawning over him. With good reason.

'I'm sorry, I've been busy.'

'But Marcus—'

'Needs to keep his trousers on a bit more often.'

'Vittoria …' His tone was warning.

'There's no point getting "thick" with me, as you say. He's the one with the pregnant mistress and spread all over the tabloids.'

She mentally kicked herself. Lashing out at Aidan, the one person who was a constant in her life, who was lovely and reliable and everything Marcus wasn't, was the last thing she wanted to do. Sometimes she said things she really didn't mean. It was some sort of weird defence mechanism. At this stage, after all these years, she was pretty sure he understood her, but she didn't want to hurt him.

'I just wanted to make sure you were OK, lovely.'

'I'm doing good now the shock has worn off.'

'Have you spoken to him about it?'

Vittoria tried to keep the irritation out of her voice. 'Which part exactly? He's denied being with this Bellissima but he can hardly deny paternity, now, can he?' She drew a ragged breath. 'And I'm not going to tell him I hired a private detective to find out what he's been up to. It's not as if she's the first – or the only one, come to that. I think he's had more than one on the go at a time. Poor bitches, they've no idea.'

'I know you're hurt, but—'

'Aidan, *mio piccolo amore*, I'm sorry, but I'm all out of sympathy. He's brought everything that is happening on himself. And it's gone too far this time. He's gone too far.' She left the sentence hanging. 'He hasn't changed since he was at school, you know. But it ends here.'

Of everyone she knew, Aidan was probably the only person who truly understood what Marcus was really like, what she'd been through and the extent of her injuries after the accident. He'd monitored her case closely. He'd been called to A&E when she'd originally been brought in, had been part of the team that had wired her back together, and then he'd stayed beside her through every step of her recovery. He'd been friends with Marcus in school – they'd fallen out at the time Aidan's brother had died and then lost contact. But ironically, on the night of the crash, he'd dropped into the same party she and Marcus had been at on his way in to work.

With Marcus visiting the hospital most days, and Aidan keeping a close eye on her, the two of them had reconnected, had gone on to buy a boat together, naming it after Aidan's younger brother, Danny, who had died so tragically and so young. And Aidan had become a permanent fixture in both their lives. A very welcome fixture. There were times when, without him, Vittoria had been sure she'd have gone quite mad.

'You know I'd told him I wanted to start thinking about adoption? I'm heading for thirty. If I'm going to be a mother, I want to be a young mother.'

'You'll always be young, Vittoria – as long as you can hear music, you'll dance and that will keep you young forever.'

Her voice softened. 'If it wasn't for you I'd be in a wheelchair, and I would probably be quite deranged.'

'You know you're a fighter. I've never seen you give in to anything; you'd have found a way.' Behind him she heard a voice and the phone clattered like he was putting his hand over it. A moment later he was back, his voice a little louder. 'I need to be quick, they're waiting for me.' She could hear a woman's voice in the background as he continued. 'How long are you staying in London?'

'I'll be back officially on Sunday.'

'Sunday? That's good. Did the card arrive OK? You've got it?'

'I have, thank you. It came this afternoon. Thanks so much. I suddenly realised I couldn't buy anything without Marcus seeing exactly where I've been and what I've been spending. I need some privacy and this *is* London.'

Aidan laughed. 'What have you done with your own cards? Maxed them out already?' Fortunately, he continued, saving her from having to come up with an answer. 'I could have just sent you mine, you know.'

'You're lovely but I think someone would have noticed that I'm not Dr Aidan Kelly, don't you? This card doesn't have a name on it so I won't need to pretend I'm you. Your text with the PIN number arrived, so I'm good to go now.'

'Make sure you buy something gorgeous – treat yourself.'

A wave of emotion filled her eyes with tears. Aidan was such a gem – she'd told him she needed a prepaid Visa currency card from the post office, and he hadn't even queried it or asked when she'd pay him back. 'Oh, Aidan, what would I do without you?' She caught a tear with her finger.

He laughed. 'Most people want to get rid of me – apparently my jokes are terrible. What time are you back? I'm racing all day Saturday. Marcus said he's busy but I've got a full crew for *Danny Boy* and it's almost the end of the season.'

'That sounds like a lot of fun. I land about 4.30 on Sunday, I think, should be back at the house by 5.30. Why don't you come over for supper?'

'Sounds good. Marcus will probably want to talk about his legal thing, about suing the *Inquirer*. He said he has to be in London again on Monday.' Before she could answer he dropped his voice. 'You sure you're going to be OK?'

'I'll be grand, honestly.'

'I hope so.' His tone said it all. 'I'll see you Sunday.'

She clicked the phone off, the sincerity with which he had spoken hanging between them like a kiss.

Chapter 44

THE ICE CHINKED in the glass as Stephanie put it down on her kitchen table beside Marcus. His uniform jacket was slung around the back of the chair, his tie loose.

'Thanks, sweet pea.'

He rubbed his eyes. He didn't think he'd ever felt this tired, but it wasn't just the jet lag from the Sydney trip: the disciplinary meeting had left him emotionally exhausted, utterly drained. Maybe he was getting too old for this job. But now, with the baby, with school fees, running two households ...

'So tell me, how did it go?' Stephanie interrupted his thoughts.

Marcus took a deep breath. 'Probably as I should have expected.' He paused. 'About as badly as it could have done, really.' He sipped his brandy. 'Didn't help that I was late. I don't know how the fuck that happened.'

She didn't say anything. Marcus glanced at the kitchen clock. He'd been in the house over half an hour and hadn't been able to speak yet, had come in and sat down and stared into space, trying to sort out his thoughts.

He was starting to understand what shellshock was all about.

He looked at the clock again. He didn't have long, needed to get a flight back to Dublin to be ready for Vittoria's art dealer tomorrow so he could start turning this fucking mess around. At least the brandy was helping. Taking a sip, he lined the glass up with the grain in the table, looking for the right words. He needed to explain to Stephanie: she deserved that.

'I didn't expect it to be easy but I wasn't expecting that level of hostility. They were waiting for me in one of the conference rooms. Christ, their faces when I walked in. I checked and double checked the time – I thought I was at least forty-five minutes early, but … Jesus, I was late. I must have put the time down wrong or something. I don't know how I did that.'

'You've had a lot on your mind.'

He hardly heard her, took another sip of brandy. 'There were three of them sat in a row on the opposite side of this huge table. They'd taken away all the chairs – there was just one pulled out on my side of the table.' He closed his eyes, remembering the set-up. Highly polished, the table top reflected the men's stark white shirts and dark suits, their ties the only variation in their corporate uniform; the one woman, the human resources director, was wearing a dark dress with a white collar. It was like they'd coordinated deliberately to intimidate.

The room was small, dominated by the table, decorated to look like a Victorian dining room, with thick brocade curtains and panelled walls, hunting paintings in heavy gold frames hanging on the walls. Ridiculous in the context of a modern building but reeking of empire and British authority.

'It was like the fucking Spanish inquisition. The bitch from human resources was like a machine gun with her questions. Who was this Bellissima, what had she been doing in the cockpit, why had I been in a strip club with her? I mean, it was so fucking stupid. Everyone knows tabloids make stuff up all the time.'

He rubbed his hand over his face. He'd shaved so carefully this morning, made sure he had knife-edge creases in his uniform, but none of it had helped. Across the table, Stephanie was sitting slightly sideways to allow space for her bump. With her blonde hair tied back and very little make-up on she looked lost and vulnerable.

'What did they say about the suspension?'

He shrugged. 'That it's still in place. I think I've bought some time telling them I'm suing the paper for defamation. I'm not sure how long. They said for me to keep them informed at every stage and to talk to them after I've seen my lawyers. I didn't tell them I'd spent yesterday morning with them.'

'And the photos, did they believe you that they were fake?'

'I don't know.' He rubbed his face again and took another swig of his brandy. 'I think they were planning to sack me there and then, but I explained about the photoshopping, that I had witnesses who had seen me the night that one of me drinking had supposedly been taken. They want it all in writing.'

Stephanie winced slightly as the baby moved. She rubbed her belly. 'So what's next?'

'I've transferred funds over to your bank account. I did that yesterday; it might take till Monday to show. About a half a million euro.' He was looking into his glass, didn't notice Stephanie's eyebrows shoot up. 'You'll need to talk to your accountant about putting it into trust for the baby so you don't lose half of it in tax.' He spoke slowly. 'I cashed in a load of bonds and moved the bulk of my savings. If it all goes wrong, I could end up bankrupt. I don't want the lawyers getting their hands on money that should be yours.'

'But it won't come to that?'

'I hope not. I'm going to need to find forensic experts to look at those photos, hire a detective to get evidence of my movements on the days the pictures relate to. If I can get CCTV of me somewhere else, then it'll prove that the pictures are faked and I won't need to bring you into it at all.'

'That's going to be expensive.'

'With that and the lawyers, it's going to cost thousands. But I'm going to sell some paintings, some Vittoria found in the attic. I didn't even know they were there. They're very valuable. I've got a dealer coming from London to look at them tomorrow. He can organise a private sale and keep it out of the media.' Marcus glanced at the kitchen clock. 'I'm going to have to go, sweet pea. I want to get back tonight to get ready for this guy.'

Stephanie nodded. Their time together always felt too short. Sometimes she felt like they never finished a conversation. 'When will you be back?'

'Monday lunch-time – I'm seeing the lawyers again first thing. I'll come straight over when I land. I'm hoping this guy will sell the pictures fast and then we can get the ball rolling.'

'Why don't you bring them here?'

'I don't want anyone seeing me with them or him. The bloody paparazzi seem to know everything these days, and someone is using photos of me in the press. I don't want to take any risks. He can bring the pictures back with him tomorrow and then there's no association to me. They've had a bit of a chequered history, from what I can gather, and I've enough to deal with. Vittoria will have checked him out – if she thinks he can be trusted, that's good enough for me.' He stood up.

'Let me call you a cab.' Stephanie reached for her phone.

*

In the back of the taxi on the way to Heathrow Marcus pulled out his phone and dialled Vittoria's number. He couldn't put off telling her about the meeting any longer. She answered on the third ring.

'What happened? I've been waiting for you to call.'

There was an edge to her voice. He let out a sigh through clenched teeth and recapped the events of the day.

'So you're briefing the lawyers on Monday?'

'That's about it. I'm hoping this guy of yours can give me an idea of the value of the paintings tomorrow so I know where we are.'

'That makes sense. Turn your phone off when you get to Dublin – if the press gets wind of your meeting with HR from anyone in TransGlobal they'll be trying to get in touch for a comment. You don't want to say anything they can misquote. I'll call you on the landline to see how you get on with Croxley. You'll know it's me – very few people have that number.'

'I think only Aidan does at this point. No one uses landlines any more.'

'Just as well, honestly. Keep the gates closed too. Don't let anyone in at all. You don't want some guy pretending he's coming to clean the windows getting pictures of the house.' Vittoria had a hard tone to her voice but Marcus knew she was right. She was usually right. It was one of the problems of being married to such a high achiever. After everything, she'd aced her exams, getting a distinction in her master's. She didn't mess about.

'Christ, this is such a nightmare.' Marcus let out a sigh, anguish raw in his voice.

'It's your worst nightmare. But hopefully it'll all be resolved quickly.'

Vittoria ended the call and Marcus looked at the phone in his hand. It was going to be expensive whichever way he looked at it, but like always, she was right.

He was the victim here and the lawyers would prove it. He just need to hold onto that thought.

Chapter 45

'I REALLY NEED to get this oiled.' Jack looked over his shoulder at Lily and grinned, his fringe flopping in his eyes. The steel protested as he heaved up the shutter on the back door of Power's Fine Prints. Jack pulled it to waist height using the handles on the bottom edge and then shoved it up far enough to get the pole their grandpa had made from its corner. Slotting it underneath, he pushed the shutter up to its full height and laid the pole gently back against the wall, pulling the bunch of keys out of his jeans pocket.

'You won't believe the mess he made. I was tidying up all last night.'

Lily smiled to herself. The moment she'd handed him the keys, he'd shot off to check out the shop, had been gone for hours. She'd been desperate to look herself but he needed time alone there, to get his head straight, and he was going to have to get used to doing things on his own when she moved. Before she could answer, Jack had the door open and the alarm had begun to pip. He disappeared inside and Lily could hear him punching in the code. A moment later he hit the light switch. The single light bulb struggled to light the room but it was pretty clear there was stuff everywhere.

The back room was always dark, the narrow alley running behind the shops letting little light in through the wired glass, the iron bars on the window blocking out more. Lily stuck her head inside and looked around. Loose prints were scattered over the floor, the paper yellowed and foxed, books thrown on top of them, many open as if someone had flicked through the pages to look inside and then discarded them.

Edward Croxley had *really* searched the place. Lily felt her temper rising at his total disrespect for the past, for the leather-bound volumes that had survived pestilence, flood and literal bombs to be flung like rubbish on the floor. But then the amulets were just as valuable – more so, bearing in mind his circumstances and what might have happened if they hadn't found them. And they were *very* small.

'Come through. I cleared up the shop yesterday – it's not perfect but it's straight enough for us to open. I can do the store rooms and upstairs gradually. You never know, I might find some other hidden gems we didn't know we had.'

Following him through to the main shop, Lily stuck her hands in her dungaree pockets and grinned, her heart bursting at Jack's complete change in outlook, at his positivity. She'd always loved opening up the shop in the morning with their grandpa, loved the smell of old books that accumulated there overnight, as if they had all been busy visiting each other and chatting while she'd been away, but for Jack, this shop was part of him. And its loss had been a black hole that had literally sucked in everything good about his life from the moment it had gone to the moment she'd handed him the keys.

As he reached the front of the shop ahead of her, Jack flicked on the main lights, turning and throwing a grin to her over his shoulder. She could immediately see where things had been moved: the globe was over to one side; some of the pictures on the walls were still slightly crooked. She felt an urge to check the first editions in the display case to make sure Croxley hadn't damaged them, but Jack was already rolling up the front-door shutter, the sunlight streaming in, dust dancing in the beams of light as if they were magic. A moment later Jack was outside, pushing up the shutter on the window, letting in even more light.

Lily felt tears welling up, but she turned and brushed them away before Jack could see them. He didn't seem to notice, but came back inside and stood with his hands on his hips looking at the window display and out onto the street.

'I reckon instead of having a mishmash of everything in the window, we need to theme it each week or every two weeks – we could do botanticals one week and maps the next, maybe animal etchings the next. We want people to stop and see what's new. And you know that shop opposite the museum, the one that has all those hilariously titled books? Let's look for some crazy ones – *How to Groom Your Moustache* or *Climbing the Pennines with Yaks*, I don't know, but there have to be some here like that. I think it'll get people talking. And maybe –' he paused like he'd had a sudden revelation '– maybe sharing the display on social media. We need an Instagram account. Why didn't I think of that before? And a hashtag, something quirky people will follow.'

'*Climbing the Pennines with Yaks*?' Lucy laughed out loud. 'Well, while you're looking for that, I'm going to find those bird of paradise prints – I need to check out the colours. The photos didn't come out very well on my phone.'

'That's exactly the type of thing I mean. If you do a collection of birds – or remember the cabbages you did for your final show? If you do anything like that for No. 42, we can do a window, add in pictures of the collection or, even better, a video screen showing the pieces in 3-D. Could you film some on your phone?'

'I think you're getting a bit ahead of yourself there, J, but it all needs freshening up – that I agree with one hundred per cent. Is upstairs a total mess?'

Lily wasn't sure if she was ready to see what Croxley had done to the store rooms. *Christ, she hoped he hadn't damaged anything.*

'Yes, but, look, it all needed a spring clean, has done for years. I've been wanting to catalogue everything and reorganise, so let's use the opportunity …'

Lily grinned. The difference in Jack was incredible. Personally, she'd always found that anger made her focus, gave her direction. She could imagine Jack's reaction when he'd first come in, but he was channelling all the negative emotion now and looking at the shop with new eyes: that could only be a good thing.

He continued, interrupting her thoughts. 'Oh, and I found that picture you said to look for – it was under the counter. I put it in the safe in a Selfridges bag.'

Lily fingered the leather jewellery box in her pocket and made a beeline for the safe.

Chapter 46

IT WAS STILL DARK when Vittoria slipped out of the door of room 520 in The Hogarth Hotel and headed for the lift wearing Lily's coat, a pair of imitation tortoiseshell glasses and an auburn wig, a small padded envelope concealed deep inside the coat pocket. She'd never really thought that the lock-picking skills she'd been taught by her eldest cousin when she was nine would ever come in useful, but had been pleasantly surprised to discover that she hadn't lost her touch. With the right tools, opening the connecting door between 520 and 521 had been as simple as slicing butter.

In 521, she'd set her alarm for 3 a.m. but she'd hardly slept, adrenaline coursing through her as she'd tossed and turned. She'd already been wide awake when her phone had finally pipped. Today was going to be the longest day of her life but Vittoria knew she had reserves of stamina that few people possessed.

For the next twenty-four hours she would be running on the very same adrenaline that had kept her awake, and her nerves.

When it was all done, then she could rest. *It was all about mind over matter*. After the accident the doctors hadn't expected her ever to walk again, let alone dance, but she couldn't live without that connection between her mind and her body, the sound of music stimulating her muscles to react, to create. It was the way she was made.

Downstairs, she'd hovered around the corner from reception, waiting for her moment. Despite the early hour, there were still people in The Lighthouse Bar, the stragglers from a wedding perhaps – they certainly looked as if they'd started the evening dressed smartly, but now seemed to be draped along the bar, empty champagne bottles littering its length. Vittoria felt sorry for the staff, who were no doubt dead on their feet but had to keep the guests happy. But from the amount they'd obviously drunk, she was sure the takings were worth the overtime.

Vittoria had only had to wait a few moments for the doorman to be distracted from his post by the girl on reception. She could hear them laughing in the alcove that hid the reception desk. She'd been watching him for the last few days and prayed that he'd be leaning over the desk now, his back to the corridor, in what seemed to be his customary position during the quiet moments of the day.

It was important nobody saw her or at least, if they did see her, that they didn't recognise her. She'd be picked up on the hotel's CCTV cameras, but she'd had a good look at the bank of screens behind the reception desk, and with the coat and wig and glasses she knew she could pass for Lily.

The nylon Pacsafe cross-body bag she wore under Lily's coat contained everything she needed for the next twenty-six hours. She couldn't carry a bulky hold-all or her trolley case so had reduced the contents to the absolute essentials: latex gloves; the Irish passport and a pink paper driver's licence she'd collected from Mr Bahnschrift in Mile End; the Visa Debit card that Aidan had sent; and a cheap unlocked phone she'd picked up in Tottenham Court Road. She'd been practising opening the back of it wearing the gloves – she just needed to fit the SIM card and it should work just fine. It was a back-up in case something went wrong and she couldn't send the texts she needed to from the correct phone. She'd run through this a million times in her head, had checked and double checked the travel connection times, had memorised the schedule. It was going to work. For her and for Lily.

This was it.

Deep down, Vittoria knew that the irony in all of this was that if Marcus had kept his eyes on her and not been distracted by every passing piece of skirt, the outcome of today could be so different.

But he hadn't. And he'd lied and lied again.

And the reason for the accident, the accident that had almost ended her life, had been his wandering eye as well. Vittoria could still feel her anger rising whenever she thought about it.

Croxley's eye had wandered too: to the dazzling riches that could come his way if he pushed things just a little bit, not doing anything overtly illegal but at the same time facilitating the importation of antiquities from war-torn areas. Antiquities that people had died trying to protect.

Edward Croxley obviously didn't give a damn for truth or history or the preservation of ancient civilisations. He was purely interested in profit. And it was time Croxley paid the full price for his part in a chain that got people killed and sold irreplaceable objects to the highest bidder.

Vittoria glanced around the corner towards the front door again and, satisfied she wouldn't be seen, slid past the reception desk, her Nikes silent on the polished wooden floor.

Outside the air was crisp with the promise of a new day and a hint of autumn. The main entrance to the hotel opened straight onto Great Russell Street, and Vittoria slipped down the broad granite steps like a shadow. Behind her on Tottenham Court Road she could hear police sirens, the clatter of a bin lorry starting its rounds, but here the streets were empty, shopfronts closed, the streetlamps throwing pools of yellow light onto the paving stones and the piles of black sacks clustered, knotted tight, waiting for collection.

Vittoria hurried along the pavement, not waiting for the pedestrian lights at the junction. There seemed to be a lull at this time in the morning, like the city was caught between night and day, like it was resting and waking at the same time. Like everything was about to happen.

Crossing the road, the sound of her runners was hollow in the stillness. Outside Power's Fine Prints, Vittoria pulled the padded envelope out of her pocket and slid it through the letter slot in the roller shutter. Lily had told her the mail was captured in a wire cage on the other side, that they always came in the back and unhooked the cage before they pushed up the shutter.

Now, as Lily put it, the ball was rolling.

As she straightened, a taxi pulled around the corner and stopped in front of her, its headlights blazing. She pulled open the rear door, climbed into the back of the car and mentally ticked the first box in a long list.

*

The 5.16 from St Pancras to Luton Airport Parkway was busier than Vittoria had expected, although four people on the subterranean platform at St Pancras wasn't exactly a rush. Conscious of the CCTV in the station, Vittoria turned up the collar of Lily's coat to hide her face. She'd been watching Lily, noted how she walked, how she continually pushed her glasses up her nose. Body language was as important an identifier as someone's face.

As she settled into a carriage that she practically had to herself, Vittoria ran through the timing in her mind for the billionth time.

She was heading to Luton Airport, but not to catch a plane.

Right beside the train station was the Renew Motel and, inside it, the Sprint Hire budget-car-rental desk. It was just over a four-hour drive to Holyhead, all motorway. Vittoria had thought about taking a cab – there were lots of drivers who would do a trip like that for cash, off the record – but she couldn't afford any weak links in this chain. A woman travelling on her own to Holyhead from London in a taxi would be hard to forget and, whatever about fooling the CCTV cameras, sitting silently in the back of a car for that long gave the driver plenty of time to look at her, to wonder if the thick auburn hair hiding her face was perhaps a wig. And then if he saw the news and put two and two together?

Hiring the car was a bit more complicated but safer.

The Visa Debit card wasn't traceable to her, and she had a solid alibi worked out so there was no reason for anyone to link the car, and therefore the payment, to her. She intended to make absolutely sure that Aidan was safe.

Vittoria glanced at the time on her phone. She'd booked the 11.30 a.m. Irish Ferries swift ferry, which would dock at 13.19 in Dublin Port, just as Edward Croxley landed at Dublin Airport.

The beauty of the ferry was that they rarely checked your documents as thoroughly as they did in the airport. A woman travelling alone on an Irish passport would be waved through between the trucks.

If everything went to plan, she would have the car back in just over twenty-four hours. Vittoria was pretty sure that at 6 a.m. the staff were unlikely to be hugely alert, but she had all the required documentation.

Everything was worked out meticulously. There would be plenty of time this afternoon when she got to Dublin to make sure the circumstantial evidence was in place – her ferry back to Holyhead wasn't until 20.55.

But then would come the bit she was dreading – driving back through the night to drop the car off and repeat her train trip into central London. She knew she'd be exhausted, emotionally and physically. She'd factored in some time to rest – a vital hour when she'd force herself to sleep in a service stop on the way down from Holyhead to Luton. Falling asleep at the wheel and crashing the car would be pretty stupid after everything she'd put in place to get this far.

The train only took forty minutes to reach Luton and the dawn was beginning to break as they pulled in to the station. She stood for a moment waiting for the doors to open and then realised she needed to push the flashing green button to her right. Pulling up her collar again, holding the coat closed as if she was cold, Vittoria walked briskly along the platform to the stairs. A linking bridge connected all the platforms. She'd come in on Platform 4, knew she needed to cross to Platform 1 where she could exit the station through a small turnstile.

As she fed her ticket into the barrier she could see the back of the Renew Motel ahead of her. It was less than five minutes' walk from here, along a broad pedestrian walkway, the morning sun catching ripples on the artificial lake to her right as she hurried along.

In the hotel lobby the night receptionist looked at her enquiringly as she said, 'Car hire?'

The girl stifled a yawn and pointed wordlessly to her left. Vittoria followed her pointed finger.

'Good morning.' For six o'clock in the morning, the young girl sitting behind the reception desk looked surprisingly fresh, had a takeaway coffee on one side of her keyboard and her make-up bag on the other, and was applying blusher to her dark skin. She was wearing a thick padded coat, her black curly hair pulled back from her face revealing enviable bone structure.

'I've booked a car …'

Smiling, the girl looked over the desk at Vittoria. 'I have it all ready for you. If you can complete this form and give me two forms of ID?' The girl placed a pen and a photocopied form onto the counter in front of Vittoria as she took another look in her mirror and put the blusher brush back into her make-up bag, reaching for her mascara.

Vittoria smiled, unzipping her bag. 'Of course. My God, what time do you have to get up to start work? It's so early.'

The girl yawned, slapping her hand over her mouth. 'Christ, sorry! I got here at five – it's normally not that bad but I was out last night. That's the only problem with an early shift. I finish at two, though. Then I'm going back to bed.' Her accent was broad North London, her smile infectious.

Keeping her leather gloves on, Vittoria quickly filled out the form. The girl checked it and took her passport, copying it in a desktop copier. Vittoria unzipped her bag again and put the battered pink paper driver's licence on the counter. All the documents were in a completely new identity, one that wasn't linked to Lily or to herself.

'Oh, and here's my credit card. It's a Visa Debit.'

The girl glanced at it and smiled. 'Never seen one like that before, but once it goes through the machine, that's great. Do you need additional liability insurance?'

Her mouth dry, Vittoria forced herself to smile. She was about to explain the prepaid currency card but there was no need – it had a very healthy balance on it and would work perfectly. No point in drawing unnecessary attention to herself.

'Just give me everything you think I might need; I don't want to have any hold-ups today.'

'No problem. And will you be doing more than ninety-five miles a day while you have the car?'

Vittoria frowned as if she was thinking about it. 'Yes, I've got a long trip.'

'OK, just sign here. I need to charge you a bit extra for that.'

'No problem, just put it on the card. Maybe allow for a thousand miles? Might not be anything close to that, but just to be safe.'

A few moments later the girl was showing Vittoria to her car.

Chapter 47

As EDWARD CROXLEY walked out through the sliding doors into Dublin Airport, pulling his almost empty case behind him, he felt his mouth go dry. His instructions were very clear but until now it had all seemed like he was playing some sort of part in a TV drama. Now he was here, it was suddenly becoming very real. He'd had a couple of gin and tonics on the plane but it hadn't made him feel any better.

He just needed to keep telling himself that by this evening he'd be back in the air and he never needed to come to Dublin ever again.

It couldn't come soon enough.

The airport was busy. Vittoria had said he had to go out through the main doors and look for a taxi. She'd made him write the address down on the back of a bit of paper he'd had in his pocket, had slid a stiff envelope of cash across the marble-topped table in The Orlando Brasserie.

Sergei Andronov was one person Croxley didn't want to get on the wrong side of, and when he'd met him to give him the three amulets, he'd ramped up the charm, laced it with nonchalance, assuring Sergei that he'd have the last one by Monday. Sergei hadn't been impressed, but then Croxley'd asked him if Kaprizov had liked the painting and that had improved things a bit. One thing Croxley was sure of was that Kaprizov could see a sweet deal from a hundred miles away.

As the security doors slid closed behind him, Croxley walked into the arrivals hall and paused, getting his bearings. He knew he didn't have much time. She'd been so specific – it all needed to run like clockwork.

First he had to find the newsagent's and buy a razor blade. Then he needed to find the gents' loo.

There was a shop to his left, exactly as she'd said. A moment later he'd found the toiletries section and bought a packet of safety razors. Outside there were overhead signs guiding him to the toilets.

He walked in to find the row of stalls all occupied.

He fidgeted while he waited for one to become free. *He could just go home now, forget all about this. No crime had been committed. Yet.*

But he knew he couldn't. Sergei wanted the fourth amulet, and over the time Edward had known Igor Kaprizov, he'd heard enough to know that you just didn't mess with him.

He felt himself starting to sweat. Then a stall became free and he entered the cubicle. Closing the door, Croxley rested his head against the fake wood and took a deep breath. This was when it started getting real.

Flipping the seat down, Croxley sat on it and tore open the packet of razors, breaking the head off one of them to reveal the blade. His case on the floor, he focused on the bag containing his duty free. Inside, a bottle of Courvoisier VSOP was in an expensive gold and purple presentation box. Apparently Marcus had a thing for good brandy. He wouldn't be able to resist.

Croxley slid open the cardboard lid.

Vittoria Devine had done her homework well.

Inside was a bottle with a screw cap covered with a coated seal. This was the bit that might be risky but she'd explained how he needed to play it, how he needed to slice open the seal with the blade so it wasn't visible, then he just needed to make sure he was the one who opened the bottle. She'd drawn him a diagram of the kitchen, had explained exactly what her husband would do from the moment he buzzed at the electric gates.

Gingerly picking up the blade, he held the bottle between his knees and played the sharp edge along the lip of the cap. His face creased in concentration, tongue between his teeth, Croxley slid it along. The blade cut through the seal easily.

Croxley untwisted the top of the bottle. Vittoria had given him a plastic canister of crushed tablets. He had no idea what they were, but she'd said they would take effect quite quickly, during which time Marcus would get a bit woozy, and then they'd knock out a horse.

Popping the lid of the pill bottle open, Croxley tapped the contents carefully into the neck of the Courvoisier. Re-capping it, he turned the bottle upside down several times. She must have experimented with this, checking the powder would dissolve, that the dosage was right to be effective. She'd been very sure when she'd explained it.

Croxley held it up and looked into the bottle. The fine white powder appeared to have dissolved. He turned the brandy bottle upside down a few more times to be sure. She'd said he needed to drop the pill bottle in a bin in the airport, to put it in a paper bag or something. He wrapped it up with the rest of the razors in the paper bag from the newsagent's and slipped the bottle of brandy back inside its gold carton, tucking the flap of the lid back in. He put it back into the duty-free carrier bag.

She'd been sure that the new paintings would fit into his empty cabin case – he sure hoped so.

He ran through everything she had said again. It would be fine that his fingerprints were in the house – he was expected, after all. She'd say that she'd called Marcus to see how the meeting had gone and he'd told her that Croxley had left – he'd be recorded on the CCTV walking back down the drive. She'd explain that in a previous call Marcus had said he was exhausted after the stress of the last few days and she'd suggested taking some of her tablets to help him sleep. When he was asked, Croxley would say that Marcus had seemed a bit slow and sleepy, but he'd never met him before so he'd thought that was his normal demeanour. Croxley stood up and took a deep breath, trying to centre himself. Closing his eyes, he tried to shut out Vittoria's face, instead thinking of his little pug, Matilda. He'd be home tonight and this would all feel like a bad dream.

At least he had the security of knowing that Vittoria had to have planned this meticulously. Any suspicion about him would immediately go back to her and Croxley knew she couldn't allow that to happen. That was the whole genius of the plan. She was so far removed from the action that proving any involvement would be virtually impossible.

Croxley slid back the lock on the stall door and ventured out. There was no one else there. Thank God. He slipped the pill bottle and razors into the bin.

This was the first step.

Outside the main doors a road ran between the terminal building and what seemed to be the car parks. It was sunny, warmer than he'd expected, the sky pure blue, hardly a cloud. Croxley looked around and saw a row of waiting taxis. Striding down towards them, he focused on looking relaxed and confident. It was important if anyone reviewed the airport CCTV that he looked like he was going to a meeting, not that he was worried sick and his stomach was churning, his underarms feeling clammy and uncomfortable.

He needed to look innocent.

He *was* innocent. As far as everyone was concerned Marcus was going to have an unfortunate accident shortly after their meeting. Vittoria had explained that he just needed to remember to put his own glass in his case with the paintings before he left. Then, as he reached the drive, he needed to wave in the direction of the pool house as if he was saying goodbye. The security cameras would pick up everything. It would look like Marcus had followed her advice and taken some of her sleeping tablets, then had the brandy and the two had reacted badly, making him woozy and unsteady on his feet. With all the pressure he was under they might even think it was suicide. There was nothing to worry about. *The whole business with Arabella had been in the UK, and he hadn't ever been a suspect. There was no connection at all.* The only thing he needed to worry about was getting the last amulet to Sergei. And Vittoria had made it perfectly clear that that would all happen once he played his part today.

The taxi driver took the address and put it into his GPS. Croxley hoped to fuck he didn't get lost or that would mess up the timing totally. It was at times like this he fully appreciated London black-cab drivers and their training in the knowledge. From this guy's behaviour there didn't seem to be much going on upstairs, never mind knowledge.

'OK, mate, we're on the way.'

The driver pulled out and Croxley sat back, a bead of sweat running down between his shoulder blades. Thank God he hadn't brought his overcoat and was only wearing a tweed jacket over his crisp blue cotton shirt.

The way out of the airport seemed to involve a lot of lane switching and traffic lights. Then they were onto a motorway, heavy with traffic. Croxley pulled out his phone, not even looking at the screen as he flicked between Twitter and Facebook, anything to distract himself from the intense feeling of nausea growing in his stomach.

When the driver eventually pulled off the motorway, Croxley could see mountains against the skyline to his right.

'Nearly there now, mate.' The driver flashed a smile in the rear-view mirror, his teeth yellow.

Croxley glanced at his watch. 'Great. That's just great.'

The minutes were ticking on.

Chapter 48

HOLDING THE GOLD wire carefully, Lily leaned over and reached for her nylon jaw pliers. The tiny ruby she was about to mount into the tail of the jewel-studded bird of paradise she was making was lying on a velvet cloth in front of her. Around it, the surface of her work bench was scarred and pitted, so worn away from generations of jewellers sitting here crouched over their work that the whole of the front edge was curved, as if the bench itself was hugging her. And really, with everything going on today she needed a hug.

Lily glanced at her phone, her stomach fluttering with nerves. Vittoria had been so precise with her instructions that Lily knew she couldn't mess up. And the timing was crucial. Lily closed her eyes tight, willing the nerves to subside, grateful that she had the workshop to herself.

She'd found the padded envelope this morning when she'd helped Jack open up in Great Russell Street. He had been right behind her, balancing the coffees, as she'd slid up the shutter on the back door. Switching on the lights as she went, Lily had gone straight to open the front door to check for post. She didn't know what Vittoria was planning exactly, but something was definitely happening and it involved Edward Croxley.

While Jack was still getting the float out of the safe, she'd slipped the yellow envelope into her bag and left him to it.

She needed some peace and quiet to run through the plan in her head and make sure she had it exactly right.

It had worked perfectly so far.

Last night when she'd gone to the desk, the staff at The Hogarth Hotel had been talking about the eccentric American who had made such a fuss insisting on booking room 520, paid for it in advance and then cancelled – literally a moment before she'd walked up to the reception desk. Overhearing them, her voice had been full of relief.

'Is 520 available? Thank goodness – I've booked in down the road and it's absolutely awful. Could I take it for two nights? I was so worried you'd be booked out.' As Vittoria had predicted, they'd been delighted to welcome an Irish tourist happy to pay cash in advance.

She could hear Vittoria's voice in her head as she mentally ran through her instructions, visualising her sketch, the sounds of the fountain and children playing in Russell Square preventing anyone from hearing their conversation.

'In the envelope with my phone will be a Dublin telephone number. I need you to go through the connecting door from 520 into 521, and at 3.30 p.m. to call the number from my mobile. It will be answered, but don't say anything. The man who answers will think it's a bad line. After a few minutes, hang up.' Vittoria glanced at her to make sure she was following. 'Wait a few minutes and then ring the same number from the room phone in 521. The number will be engaged but hold on for a few minutes.'

'I understand: I use the mobile first then the landline.' She'd drawn a curly telephone cable down the side of the page.

'That's it. Then I need you to call Marcus's mobile number from my mobile phone. He won't answer, he has it switched off, but when the message minder starts recording, play the message that's on the USB key.'

'Won't the sound quality be terrible?'

'It doesn't matter. The mobile reception is very patchy at home, so if it sounds a bit fuzzy that's fine.'

Sitting at her work bench trying to concentrate, Lily ran through everything in her head. She had no idea what these calls could be part of, but obviously Vittoria had a plan. Lily smiled. Vittoria's plans so far had been rather incredible.

After she'd made the calls she had to stay in room 521 until around six and then call room service and say that she was feeling unwell, ask if they could deliver some chicken broth and toast and a glass of water. Vittoria had recorded an extra piece so Lily could listen to her accent and practise – if she held her nose she'd sound like she had a cold, which would help. She had to tell them that the 'do not disturb' sign would be on the door and she would probably be asleep, but that the waiter just needed to leave the tray in the room and not wake her. Then she had to get into the bed, pulling the duvet over her head. Once the food had arrived, she was to go back into her own room, through the connecting door, and leave from room 520. Lily just had to make doubly sure the 'do not disturb' sign was still on the door handle of 521 when she walked past on her way down the corridor, so that the staff didn't come in to turn down the bed.

It seemed a small price to pay for getting the shop back.

Whenever Lily thought about it, about holding the keys in her hand again, she felt such an enormous sense of relief that she teared up. And Jack hadn't stopped smiling since they'd got the shop back. The place would be a mess for a while yet – there was a lot to do upstairs – but he'd made a start and had got open again, and nothing seemed to have been damaged. Thank God.

Putting down the jewelled bird that she was working on, barely able to concentrate, Lily looked at the time again. The Hogarth Hotel was only fifteen minutes from Hatton Garden by tube from Farringdon, but she was going to get a taxi, had one booked to collect her. She was leaving with plenty of time – she knew she could wait in 520, but today of all days she couldn't afford for there to be an incident on the line or a train breakdown that held her up.

Vittoria had smiled when Lily had looked worried. 'There's absolutely no danger, honestly. Just do exactly what I've told you.'

'Right, got it. And what do I do with your phone when I'm done?'

'Leave it there in 521. I'll collect it.'

'And then I leave?'

'That's it. Easy. Come back Sunday morning and check out before twelve. I'll make sure your bed looks slept in.' Lily had nodded slowly, thinking it through, as Vittoria continued, 'It's very important that you don't try and contact me at all again, except as agreed. When you get to New York ask them to put my email on the invite list for the launch and I'll see you there. The shop is sorted now. Sergei will call in on Monday and ask for you. Give him the fourth amulet and the painting. You don't know anything about them.' Vittoria had paused. 'You've got absolutely nothing to worry about, really.' As if she'd detected Lily's nervousness, Vittoria had put her hand on Lily's arm and looked at her intently. 'Remember that, please. Whatever happens, you have nothing to worry about. I'll see you in New York at the launch.'

Lily had nodded and flipped over the cover of her sketch pad. She had been sure Vittoria wouldn't let her down and she hadn't. And she wouldn't let Vittoria down.

Lily glanced at the time on her phone again. Not long now.

Chapter 49

THE GATES TO Alcantara House were at the end of a long narrow lane overhung with tangled ivy and wild roses. Croxley had caught glimpses of the sea as they'd headed down the hill, amazed it was so close. The roads were narrow and winding, high old stone walls bordering stunning houses that overlooked a spectacular sweep of beach. Golden sand ran right around to what looked like a range of mountains, hazy in the distance. This place was truly paradise.

Eventually they reached a narrow lane, only wide enough for one car, the hedgerows high on both sides. At the end it opened out into a drive entrance, pillars and ornate wrought-iron gates towering above a paved apron that met the unmetalled road. Giving the taxi driver cash, Croxley got out and, as the taxi turned around, Croxley pressed the gate buzzer. A moment later the electric gates slid open.

Devine was expecting him.

The drive itself was gravel, sweeping into the trees, a fork heading towards the front of the house and the garages. Vittoria had said to stick to the left and walk around the back. As Croxley rounded the bend he found a sweep of lawn in front of him, the Spanish-style two-storey villa to his right, and at the end of the gardens he could see another big single-storey building. The pool house. It had a green tiled roof that matched the main house, was painted the same bright white. Croxley could see a path that ran across the lawn to it.

Beyond the pool house and high tangled hedgerow that ran along the perimeter of the property, the land seemed to drop away into the sea, sunshine sparkling on the water as far as he could see. The beach had to be close – he could hear waves breaking on the shore.

Swinging around to his right, he jumped – a man had come out of a set of French windows and was watching him from the patio that surrounded the house, a cup of coffee in his hand. He raised it when he saw Croxley looking his way.

Marcus Devine.

He looked just like the photograph in the paper, was wearing jeans and a white T-shirt. He didn't have a brunette escort with him this time, though. Vittoria had said he'd be on his own. Croxley fucking hoped he was or this could get very complicated.

'Good morning! Mr Devine?' Croxley raised his hand, smiling broadly.

'Marcus, please. Come on up.'

Croxley followed a path to steps leading up onto the slightly raised patio. 'Hope you don't mind me coming around the back. Your good lady wife assured me you didn't have a pack of Rottweilers.'

Marcus laughed, reaching out to shake his hand. 'Vittoria's the only Rottweiler around here. Come in. She said you're a bit of an art expert.'

'Well, I know my Renoir from my Rennie Mackintosh. Beautiful spot you've got here.'

'Thanks, my parents built the house. Vittoria built the pool house – she swims every day. That's where some of the paintings are, actually.'

Marcus moved as if he was going to go straight to the pool house. Panic fluttered inside Croxley for a moment. Vittoria had worked this out exactly. He needed to keep Marcus talking and have a brandy before they went to look at the paintings. She was going to call at 3.30 p.m. It was essential Marcus answered the phone.

As they'd sat at lunch in The Hogarth Hotel she'd drawn him a diagram of the pool house. The phone was at the back near the changing-room entrance. Croxley needed to make sure he was standing behind Marcus when he answered the phone – he could pretend he was taking a look into the changing rooms or something.

'She mentioned your father had a considerable collection. I'd love to take a look before we go down?'

'Of course, of course. Where are my manners? Come inside. Would you like a coffee?'

'I'd love one. And Vittoria mentioned you like a drop of brandy. I've been meaning to try this Courvoisier VSOP so I picked a bottle up in the airport – we might give the coffee a bit of a kick?'

Pushing open the sliding door, Marcus stepped into the kitchen, grinning over this shoulder. 'If you've a bottle of Courvoisier it seems a waste to mix it with coffee. Will I get some glasses and we can check it out first? Sun's well over the yardarm at this stage.'

'And it is Saturday …'

'Indeed.'

The kitchen was vast, black and white marble floor tiles covering the entire area from the huge white marble-topped island to a polished table that looked like it sat about twelve. Croxley wasn't counting chairs, though; he was watching Marcus lift two crystal brandy goblets from a cupboard.

Now this was the tricky bit.

Propping up his wheelie case, Croxley put the duty-free bag on the table and, opening it, flipped open the box, pulling out the bottle. He held it up to the light and quickly twisted the top off before Marcus could see that the seal had already been broken. Croxley wafted the neck of the bottle under his nose, sniffing it appreciatively.

'Have a snifter. It's rather good.'

He passed the bottle to Marcus, who looked at the label and poured the golden liquid out into two glasses, picking up his own to savour the aroma. He passed Croxley a glass and raised his for a toast. 'To business.'

Croxley clinked his glass against Devine's, the chink of crystal like the high note on a piano. 'Indeed. To business.'

Marcus took a mouthful. 'Goodness, as delicious as she smells.'

Croxley grinned and pretended to take a sip, but just as the glass reached his lips, he stopped. 'My goodness, is that a Yeats?' As if he had just noticed the small painting on the kitchen wall, he put the glass down and walked towards it.

'It is, my mother loved that painting. She often had friends call and they would all sit in here – she wanted it where the most people could enjoy it.'

Croxley turned to Marcus, grinning. 'She had very good taste. Is your collection mainly Irish?'

Marcus shook his head. 'No, mixed. A lot of European works.'

'Would you have time to show me quickly? I need to leave by four at the latest, but I'd love to see them.' Croxley glanced at the kitchen clock. 3.15 p.m. He had fifteen minutes to kill before the phone call. Vittoria had said to use the time looking around the house, but his palms were beginning to sweat.

What if he didn't get to the pool house on time? Perhaps they should go straight there now? Getting there would take a few minutes – it was a long walk across the huge lawn, and Croxley was sure he could keep Marcus talking once they were there

'Of course.' Marcus made to open the internal door into the hall.

Croxley shook his head. 'Actually, had we better look at the paintings Vittoria mentioned first? I know I'll get carried away and we'll run out of time.'

Marcus frowned, confused. 'Whatever you think. They're in the pool house. Vittoria was worried about someone breaking into the main house again.'

'Again? You make it sound like a regular occurrence.'

Marcus shrugged, obviously not happy. 'Twice recently. We lost several paintings the first time and the second time we almost lost Vittoria.'

'Good God, what happened?' Croxley said, pausing beside the patio doors.

'Don't forget your brandy – it's very good.'

'Oh, of course. Why don't you have a top up?' Croxley turned and picked up the bottle. Marcus grinned and held out his glass.

Putting the bottle down, trying to conceal the shake in his hand, Croxley grabbed his glass and the handle of his wheelie case, nodding towards the garden, a conspiratorial smile on his face. 'Lead the way.'

*

The pool house was exactly as Vittoria had described it, sliding glass doors on the southern side opening onto a sun terrace with cedar loungers. Double doors faced the house. Croxley had managed, he hoped, to conceal the glass in his hand on the walk across the lawn. As they reached the door, Marcus pulled a key chain from his pocket. It took him a moment to get the key in the lock.

'Vittoria was terrified these pictures might get stolen from the house – she made me hide them down here.' He rolled his eyes and took another swig of his brandy. 'This is really very good.'

Croxley nodded appreciatively, then frowned. 'It's really no harm to be cautious. From what she described and the images I saw, these could be quite valuable. And it's really best that not too many people know you've got them or you could get a claim from one of the original estates.'

'Don't worry, I'm keeping quiet. I just want to sell them.' Marcus pushed open the door. 'Here we are.'

Croxley followed him. It was hot inside, the smell of chlorine strong. The sunshine coming in through the glass wall played games with the water, reflecting moving shapes on the ceiling like quicksilver.

Croxley felt his heart rate increasing. Juggling with his glass, he looked at the clock on his phone.

'Tight for time?' Marcus glanced at him.

'No, just checking. I've a track history of missing planes.' It was Croxley's turn to roll his eyes. 'I get caught up in far more interesting things and time seems to slip away. This place is fabulous.'

'Vittoria designed it when we moved in – it made more sense than trying to convert part of the house. There's a dance studio and changing rooms at the end.' Marcus indicated with his head and, following his look, Croxley's eyes alighted on the phone on the wall.

'Impressive. Now, let's look at these paintings.'

Marcus swallowed the last mouthful of the VSOP and yawned. He shook his head as if trying to clear it. 'Sorry, of course. Must be the heat in here – I'm feeling quite woozy.'

'It's very warm. It needs to be warm when you're swimming, though. I can't bear the cold.'

Marcus shook his head again and ran his hand through his hair.

'Paintings?'

'Of course, this way. They're in the changing rooms.'

'Super, perhaps we can bring them out into the light?'

Marcus nodded and headed slightly unsteadily down the side of the pool towards the entrance to the changing room. Croxley could feel a bead of sweat rolling down his back. He followed Marcus, the wheels on his case rattling on the tiled floor.

'Won't be a minute, I'll get them.' Slurring his words slightly, Marcus put his glass down on a side table positioned beside a lounger and disappeared into the changing rooms. It took him a few minutes, but then he was back and carrying four canvases, all quite small.

At least they'd fit in his case.

Croxley put his glass down beside Marcus's.

Leaning the paintings against the wall of the changing room, side by side, Marcus took a step backwards.

'Goodness, I could do with some air.' He looked around vaguely. And shook his head again.

Just as the phone began to ring.

'Christ, that must be Vittoria.'

'Perhaps she's checking up on me.' Croxley grinned, his attention on the paintings.

Marcus looked like he was trying to grin but his face wasn't fully responding. 'That would be right.'

Moving towards the phone, he picked it up. 'Hello?' He paused. 'Hello?' He glanced at Croxley, his eyes slightly unfocused. 'Must be Vittoria. Her phone's probably on the blink or she's in a dead spot or something.'

As if he heard something at the other end, he paused.

And turned his back on Croxley.

It was the moment he needed.

Dashing towards him, Croxley shoved Marcus hard in the back. Caught off guard he fell forward, and Edward gave him another push, one that sent him into the pool.

The sound of the splash reverberated around the building.

Edward waited, paralysed, sick with fear. If Marcus swam to the surface now this would take a bit of explaining. When he'd said that to Vittoria, she said to pretend he'd tripped.

Easy for her to say.

He stood paralysed, waiting to see if Marcus swam to the surface. He wasn't moving. Perhaps he'd knocked his head on the way in, or perhaps the powerful sedative was doing its job.

Christ, he hoped so.

Vittoria had reassured him that she'd tell the authorities that she'd spoken to Marcus on the phone, that he'd seemed fine long after Croxley had left. It had sounded fool-proof. But now, looking at the dark shape of Marcus's body under the rippling blue water, Croxley wasn't so sure.

But he didn't have time to think about it.

As he straightened up, he saw a flash of black and felt the scratch of coarse lamb's wool on his face as someone put their forearm across his throat.

He barely felt the snap of his neck, was unconscious when he too hit the water.

Chapter 50

STANDING IN THE reception of The Hogarth Hotel, Vittoria stifled a yawn.

'How can we help, madam? I'm so sorry for the delay.'

'Not to worry, thank you. I need to check out when you're ready. Excuse my yawning – I've been a bit under the weather the last day or so.'

'I'm sorry to hear that, madam. Would you like us to call a doctor?'

Vittoria shook her head. 'I'm over the worst of it now. I think it was some sort of twenty-four-hour flu – I slept most of yesterday and I'm still tired. But a day in bed works wonders, and I'm so much better than I was yesterday morning. Maybe I was just exhausted, working too much. I just needed a break in your lovely hotel.'

Behind her an elegant older American couple arrived to check out. 'It is fabulous, isn't it? We've had the nicest stay.'

Vittoria smiled at the woman. 'I hope you've seen lots of London.'

Before the American could answer, the receptionist produced a printout of her bill and passed it across the counter. Vittoria pulled her business credit card out and handed it to her. The receptionist looked at it. 'That's lovely, Ms Devine – will we be seeing you again?'

'I certainly hope so. Can you call me a cab for 1 p.m., going to City Airport? I just need to make a call and I think I'll have a cup of tea while I wait.'

'Certainly. If you'd like to sit down, I'll take care of your luggage and I'll send someone to take your order immediately.'

*

At the far end of The Lighthouse Bar, Vittoria sat down on a corner sofa and pulled out her phone, looking for the number she needed.

'Aidan? It's me.' She put the phone to her ear and continued speaking a fraction too loudly. 'I'm still in London, just heading for the airport. I've been trying to get hold of Marcus for ages. I was in bed all day yesterday, some sort of flu thing …' She smiled at his response. 'Yes, I'm fine today, just exhausted. I tried to get up for some fresh air but it honestly wasn't worth it. I felt so terrible … I know. But he's not answering his mobile or the landline.'

Listening to Aidan's answer, she said, 'I thought I'd caught him yesterday – he answered the landline during the afternoon but the connection was terrible. All I heard was some splashing, so he must have been in the pool house. Were you with him?'

She tucked her hair behind her ear as he replied, then she frowned. 'You weren't? I wonder who it was. I arranged for him to meet an art consultant about some pictures he wanted to sell. But they would hardly have gone swimming. Perhaps he had some friends over.'

She paused again to listen his reply. 'I'm landing at 4.30. Could you call over to him? I did tell him he should turn off his phone in case the press started calling, but I'm starting to think he might have a visitor or two. I just hope there were no photographers watching the place.'

As Vittoria finished the call her favourite waiter appeared. 'Would you like to order, Ms Devine?'

Vittoria smiled. 'Thank you, Joel.'

She loved how everyone in this hotel knew who she was. When she called room service they greeted her by name. It was a very simple thing but made everything more personal. And Vittoria liked things to be personal.

Chapter 51

VITTORIA SWITCHED off her phone as the cab dropped her outside the expansive entrance of London City Airport. It was relatively quiet inside compared to normal. She usually travelled during the week, when it was packed with business travellers, but on a Sunday it was far less busy. This time she went straight through security with only her mascara arousing interest, a 'liquid' she'd left in her make-up bag.

The flight was half-empty and the seat beside her was vacant. The moment she fastened her seatbelt, Vittoria closed her eyes. She'd managed to get a few hours' sleep that morning but she knew she needed to cat-nap as much as possible so she would be alert later.

*

Vittoria felt much better when she landed to late afternoon sunshine in Dublin. It was milder here than in London and it had obviously been a warm day. The autumn could be beautiful in Ireland.

Her car was in the long term car park, only a short bus ride from the airport, and she was on the M50 when she remembered that her phone was still off after the flight.

Tempting as it was to turn it on, it was buried at the bottom of her handbag. She was sure it could wait. She remembered the phone again as she reached the lane that led down to the house, but ahead of her, the gates were standing wide open. Vittoria felt her heartbeat quicken.

Her tyres crunched on the gravel as she drove into the courtyard in front of the house. It was full, already occupied by Aidan's car, several garda patrol cars and an ambulance. She threw open the car door and jumped out just as Aidan appeared at the front door, his face pale and drawn. He was wearing jeans and his sailing jacket, as if he'd forgotten to take it off.

'Vittoria I've been trying to call—'

'I turned my phone off on the flight, I forgot to turn it back on. What on earth's happening?'

'You need to come inside. There's been an accident.'

'What?' Her tone shocked, Vittoria slammed her car door closed and ran up the steps to the front door.

Aidan caught her by her arm as she pushed past him into the house. 'You can't go into the kitchen – it's sealed. It's Marcus. And some guy we don't know. Something happened. They're in the pool.'

'What do you mean something happened? Marcus hates swimming – why's he in the pool?'

Aidan took a deep breath. 'He's dead, Vittoria. We don't know exactly what happened but they are both dead.' Behind him, Vittoria could see several men hovering in the doorway to the living room, all in plain clothes but with that unmistakable look of police officers.

*

Vittoria's hands shook as she cradled the whiskey Aidan had poured her from the decanter in the den. On the opposite side of the house from the kitchen and living room, it was Marcus's room but rarely used except in the winter. He kept it locked, had all his model planes and sailing pictures in here. This was the room he and Aidan crashed out in to plan their summer sailing when Vittoria was away or working late.

Now she sat on one of the red leather Chesterfield sofas, hunched forward, Aidan perching on the arm beside her. Opposite them, sitting on the matching sofa, two plainclothes detectives opened their notebooks. One was young, blond, very attractive in an all-American kind of way, the other older, greying, wearing a lilac golf jumper and matching argyle socks. If he hadn't been wearing a navy garda jacket she'd have thought he was one of Marcus's golfing partners. Perhaps he was.

Vittoria shook her head. 'My God, I still can't believe it.' Her voice wasn't much more than a whisper.

'We're sorry we need to ask questions at a time like this, but I'm sure you understand that in the case of a suspicious death we need to act quickly.'

'Of course, of course.' She smiled weakly, her eyes on the glass clutched in her hand.

'My name is DI Frank Gallagher and this is Detective Jamie Fanning. We're based at Dun Laoghaire Garda Station. You can call either of us at any time.' He passed Vittoria a white business card. She smiled weakly and reached for it, putting it down on the sofa beside her. 'We met after your first break-in. I was on leave when the second one happened, so you were dealing with a different team.'

Vittoria ran her hand over her face. 'I remember. I'm sorry I didn't recognise you – it's all a bit of a blur, to be honest. Do you think the break-ins are connected to this?'

'At this stage, everything is a possibility. But don't worry. It's not your job to remember us, it's our job to remember you. Now can you tell us when you last spoke to your husband, Mrs Devine?'

Vittoria cradled her glass in her hands as she answered. 'Friday. I think it was Friday evening. He'd had some trouble at work and he called me to tell me what was happening.'

'And where was he then?'

'On his way back to Dublin. I was in London.' Vittoria trailed off. 'It was all total nonsense. He didn't even know that woman. He'd never risk his career like that – it's all he's ever wanted to do.' She took a ragged breath. 'Sorry, there was this article in the newspaper … He had to fight it, but we needed money – I took a painting to London to see if we could find a buyer. The art dealer I met, Edward Croxley, liked the picture, so I arranged for Marcus to meet him here at the house yesterday. Marcus had some other paintings that he wanted to sell, but it needed to be incredibly discreet – we couldn't use a dealer here.'

As if the realisation had suddenly dawned on her, a look of horror crossed Vittoria's face. 'That's not him, is it? In the pool as well? Croxley? Oh my God.' Her hand shot to her mouth.

'It seems it might be, Mrs Devine. At least, the man we've found had a passport belonging to an Edward Croxley in his pocket. How did you meet him?'

Vittoria shrugged. 'I called Beaufort Fine Art. They work with him a lot, apparently – they introduced us by email.' The detective inspector nodded as she continued. 'I met Croxley at my hotel, The Hogarth on Great Russell Street. I'd found some paintings at the back of the attic – I was looking for a vase.' She took a ragged breath. 'I'm sorry – you don't need to know that. They were right at the back, these paintings. Marcus didn't even know they were there. So, anyway, I took one of them to London for Croxley to see. I didn't know if they were valuable. They were all so different from each other and the rest of the collection.' She paused. 'When I met Croxley, I showed him the painting. He was confident it was an original and authentic, so I showed him the photos I'd taken of the others. He was very surprised.' Vittoria drew another shaky breath. 'I should have done it before but I checked out the paintings on the Internet then.' Vittoria cleared her throat. 'They were all lost after the war, pictures that had been stolen by the Nazis.'

The detective inspector raised his eyebrows as she paused again, taking a sip of her whisky. 'Marcus's father was a friend of Eamon de Valera's. Apparently there was some Dutchman his father met through him who was an art collector. Marcus thought that's where they had come from. He was a war criminal, the Dutchman, Marcus said.'

Vittoria shook her head, her eyes filling with tears as she took another sip, the ice clinking in her glass. 'When I found out, I told him we had to give them back – we couldn't keep them. But Marcus said we'd had enough trouble with the press – he couldn't have anyone knowing about these pictures and he needed the money. Edward Croxley said he could sell them quietly, that he had Russian buyers who collected this type of stuff. I really had no idea when I met him that they'd had such a terrible past.'

'And why didn't you come back from London to introduce them?'

Vittoria shook her head like it was obvious. 'They're both adults. I had my flight booked for this afternoon, but I wasn't even sure if I was going to make it, to be honest. I was dying with the flu. I slept almost all day yesterday. I woke up about three and tried to get up to get some air, but I still felt terrible. I tried to call Marcus on the landline. He answered but he couldn't hear me – I called from my mobile so maybe there was a problem with the connection. I heard splashing so I guessed he was down at the pool. Then I tried from my hotel phone but the line was engaged, so I left a message on his mobile.'

Vittoria took another sip and looked up sharply. 'But what about the CCTV? I specifically asked the company to put a camera in the pool house, after the last time …' She shuddered. 'Marcus said they came last week. He was here – Thursday, was it? The company came to test the system and put in new cameras.'

'Unfortunately, it looks like someone has wiped the recordings from all the cameras on the property from about 2.30 p.m. yesterday afternoon.'

Vittoria's mouth fell open. 'But how—?'

The inspector continued, 'We've people going through them now. But the system seems to be missing approximately two hours of film.'

She sighed deeply, shaking her head. 'I can't believe this, after everything that happened before. The system is supposed to work! Do you think this has to do with the man who broke in before? Could Marcus have upset someone?'

'What makes you say that, Mrs Devine?'

Vittoria's lip trembled. 'Because he was supposed to be here that night. The night the man came into the bedroom. I only realised it later, but I told your colleagues. Something happened and he got held up in London, but we'd only spoken on the phone that afternoon and he'd said he was on his way.' She shook her head again. 'I don't know, it's all so confusing.' Vittoria put her hand over her face, biting her lip. A noise at the door distracted her. She looked up as a man in a full white forensic overall came in, his paper suit crinkling as he moved.

'Got something, Thirsty?' The inspector twisted in his seat.

The man in the forensic outfit was holding a large brown paper bag in his hand, the top rolled up, numbers scrawled on the outside in black marker. 'Just need Mrs Devine to tell us if she's seen this before?' Unrolling the top of the bag, he extracted a black V-neck lamb's-wool sweater, holding it up for Vittoria to see.

Vittoria stared at it for a moment, glancing quickly at Aidan sitting beside her. 'It looks like Marcus's. There's a hole in the sleeve …'

Thirsty turned the sweater so she could see the sleeve. 'I can't let you touch it, but there's a hole here.'

'Yes, that's his. I wear it around the house sometimes – I caught the sleeve in the French windows a few weeks ago and I haven't had time to get it fixed. Where did you find it?'

'It was thrown over a lounger beside the pool. It looks like someone had just taken it off. It's inside out.'

Vittoria frowned. 'Marcus must have been wearing it. I left it in the bedroom on my dressing-table chair so I'd remember to get it fixed when I got home from London.'

The forensics officer grimaced. 'We'll get it examined and then we'll have more idea who came into contact with it.'

The inspector turned back to her. 'We're going to need to take samples from you, if that's OK, for elimination purposes.'

'Of course.' Vittoria's voice was low. She stared into her glass. 'What on earth happened?'

'That's what we need to find out.'

Chapter 52

'WILL YOU have tea, Inspector?'

Vittoria picked up the heavy silver teapot and put the strainer over the top of the china cup in front of her. After talking to the guards yesterday she'd had to leave the house. It was a crime scene and they'd needed it for examination.

And she knew she was a suspect. Her husband had apparently been caught with another woman and publicly lambasted in the press. People had murdered for less.

As she'd driven out of the gate, a uniformed officer had started unrolling blue and white crime-scene tape behind her, sealing off the entire property. She hadn't even been able to get into her bedroom to get fresh clothes. Aidan had suggested she stay with him until she could get back home, but she wanted to stay close to the house, so she'd booked into Killiney Towers Hotel, a few minutes' drive up Killiney Hill.

The only room they'd had left was their largest suite – which was just as well, as this morning she seemed to have been playing host to half of Dun Laoghaire's gardaí, and chatting to them in the bedroom would definitely have been peculiar. The detective inspector she'd met yesterday and the young good-looking detective had arrived just after ten. Aidan had reorganised his surgeries and taken a few days off from the hospital, arriving shortly after them.

'I'm going to need you to come down to the station today to make a statement about your movements yesterday and on Saturday.'

'Of course. There's not much to tell. When I couldn't get through on Sunday morning I called Aidan.'

The detective inspector nodded. 'It was just as well he knew the code to your gates or …'

'It could have been me finding them.' Vittoria winced and sat back as the inspector helped himself to milk.

'Any sign of the paintings?' Aidan moved away from the French windows overlooking the narrow balcony. The morning sun was streaming in. He sat in one of the high-backed armchairs gathered around the glass-topped coffee table. The room was pure eighteenth century and utterly opulent, from the magnificent curtains to the enormous draped bed in the adjoining room.

The hotel had provided a fabulous spread of finger sandwiches and biscuits with the tea and coffee she'd ordered, although only the guards seemed to be hungry. Vittoria could feel the younger one watching her the whole time the detective inspector was speaking.

Aidan reached for the coffee-pot and topped up his cup as the inspector, Frank Gallagher – she'd remembered his name this morning – answered. 'I'm afraid not. We've had the pathologist's and early forensic reports, though. The pathologist's toxicology results won't be with us for a few days but there are traces of a powerful sedative in a glass of brandy that has your husband's fingerprints on it, Mrs Devine. It was on a table beside the pool.' DI Gallagher cleared his throat. 'We found a bottle of brandy on the kitchen table had been bought in London City Airport with Edward Croxley's credit card – the receipt was still in the bag – and the bottle was laced with it.'

'So you think he drugged Marcus deliberately? And then Marcus fell into the pool?'

DI Gallagher looked Vittoria in the eye. 'Or was pushed.'

Aidan let out a sharp breath. 'Christ.' He paused. 'But how did this Croxley end up in there too? Do you think they had a fight, or he was followed by someone?'

Gallagher shrugged. 'We've only got the facts to work with. But the post-mortem showed that Croxley's neck had been broken.'

Aidan leaned forward in his chair. 'Good God. But how? I mean how did he break his neck?' He glanced at her anxiously. 'Sorry, Vittoria – I'm a doctor, remember. The devil is always in the detail.'

Gallagher grimaced. 'The pathologist – Professor Saunders, you might know him?'

'Sure do.' Aidan raised his eyebrows and a look passed between them that Vittoria couldn't quite work out.

'The professor believes his neck had been twisted sharply. He likened it to a movement that's taught to special forces. Well, I'm not sure if it is any more – he was talking about the Second World War, but it's the same principle.'

Aidan frowned. 'It must have been someone fairly big then, to overpower him?'

'Apparently it's not just about strength, but you'd need to know what you were doing.'

'That's awful. He was such a nice man.' Vittoria rubbed the corner of her eye, catching a tear.

The inspector cleared his throat. 'I'm not entirely sure about that. We've been doing some digging and it appears Croxley was interviewed after the death of an Irish girl, Arabella Smyth, at a party near London some years ago. Coincidentally, she also died in a swimming pool.'

Vittoria raised her eyebrows. '*Mio Dio.*' She was quite sure the gardaí never saw anything as coincidental.

Gallagher continued, 'He was released without charge – the statements taken at the time were apparently conflicting – but there was a strong suspicion from our UK colleagues that he was, at the very least, a key witness who chose to keep quiet.'

Vittoria looked at him, shocked. 'My God, that's awful. I had no idea. Do you think he could have pushed Marcus?'

'It's a possibility. Perhaps he got away with it the first time and thought he'd try it again – who knows. But more interesting is the company he's been keeping in London. He's been closely associated with a Sergei Andronov who works for a Russian businessman called Kaprizov. Did he mention either name to you?'

Vittoria shook her head, her face blank.

'Both men have been under surveillance for some time by the National Crime Agency. They have links to serious organised crime.'

'Really?' Vittoria's hand shot to her mouth and she felt herself pale.

'My colleagues in the UK observed Croxley meeting you, Vittoria, in The Hogarth Hotel.'

'Yes, we met couple of times. I even had lunch with him. I didn't want to tell him about all the paintings straight away.'

Gallagher nodded, like he already knew. 'And then he was observed meeting this Sergei Andronov at a private club in Covent Garden. One of their team was in situ right beside Andronov and Croxley and heard them discussing your painting.'

'He said he had a Russian buyer.' Vittoria shook her head in disbelief. 'I left that first painting with him – with Croxley, I mean – so he could show him. My God, that was stupid, wasn't it?'

'Have you any idea what it's worth?'

Vittoria shrugged. 'Croxley said he'd had an offer of two million. But I've no real idea what any of them are worth. Bearing in mind where they came from, I'd imagine quite a bit. Honestly, with so much going on, once I'd realised their history I just wanted Marcus to get rid of them – I wouldn't want anything in the house with that sort of provenance.' She shrugged. 'And Marcus needed the money. Suing the *Inquirer* was a huge risk, but he was determined to clear his name.'

The Inspector frowned. 'We did a bit of research on the images you sent Croxley. The,' he checked his notebook, 'Pissarro is worth three to five million.'

'Jesus Christ.' Aidan leaned forward in his seat. 'And the others?'

'Something similar, nothing less than a million.'

Aidan sat back. 'Several million reasons to leave two blokes dead in a pool.' He glanced at her quickly. 'Sorry, Vittoria. But what about the CCTV, is there anything from earlier on Saturday or the previous day? Surely someone must have been scoping the place out? Vittoria made sure there were extra cameras installed.'

The young guard, who had been quiet until then, flipped open his notebook. 'I spoke to the security company. Mr Devine called on Thursday to ask them to do a rush job and their team came out Thursday afternoon. He made it worth their while.'

'That's Marcus all over – he leaves everything to the last minute and then throws money at it.' Vittoria smiled weakly and ran her hand through her hair.

Aidan leaned forward. 'So is it likely this Russian – Sergei, did you say? – followed Croxley, thinking he could get his hands on the paintings for free? Vittoria said she'd made it clear they needed to be sold very discreetly, that she didn't want any publicity. Perhaps he thought she wouldn't report it if they got stolen. Particularly bearing in mind their origins?'

Vittoria sighed. 'They weren't insured anyway – he must have worked that out. You'd need to be a museum to afford cover on anything that valuable. We've no way of even proving that they were here – or real, come to that – apart from the photos on my phone.'

'There is footage on your security cameras of Marcus taking what looks like a pile of paintings down to the pool house late on Friday evening. Do you have a safe down there?'

Vittoria shook her head. 'No, but he was worried about them being in the house in case there was another break-in.' Vittoria let out a sigh. 'He was very anxious about the paintings, about the lawsuit – about his job. I suggested he take them down to the pool house – no one would think to look for paintings there. He'd had terrible trouble sleeping – I told him to take some of my tablets – and I thought he'd be able to relax better with them out of the house.'

Gallagher nodded, his voice off hand as he said, 'What sort of tablets would those have been?'

'Sleeping tablets. I've got quite a cocktail between those and my painkillers.'

'And where do you keep them?'

'In my handbag, all over the house – some in the kitchen drawer. Some in the bedroom.' Vittoria stopped speaking, her eyes full of pain. 'I should never have told him to take them, but … oh God …'

Aidan leaned over and squeezed her arm, then turned to Gallagher: 'You think this Russian could have followed Croxley and wiped the tapes when he was finished?'

'It's possible he or an associate did. We're looking at the CCTV on surrounding properties to see if we can ascertain their point and time of entry to the property, assuming that's what happened. It's one possibility. Croxley's phone was in the water, but his call records show he sent two texts at 3.40 p.m., both about Andropov collecting a package at a shop in London on Monday. It seems likely he was attacked while he was distracted sending them, so we have a timeline of sorts.'

Vittoria shook her head. 'I've said to Marcus over and over again about that back hedge – the public footpath along the cliff is on the other side. That's why I wanted extra cameras. I should just have had it dug out and a wall built. Dear God, I still can't believe this has happened.'

Chapter 53

IN LONDON, Great Russell Street was humming with Monday morning traffic. Jack Power leaned over the shop counter, his sleeves rolled up, coffee cooling beside him, and looked out at the crowds passing the door. It was unseasonably warm today and he'd pinned the door open to let in the sunshine and the sounds of the street and perhaps tempt in some of the passers-by. There was always a constant flow of tourists to the British Museum and plenty of students going to and fro. Most of their business was from regular customers but in this part of London you never knew who might walk in.

He felt a surge of emotion. He was so relieved to be back here, so happy in this moment right now, with the sunshine falling in through the door and all the old books and prints around him, embracing him like old friends. There weren't even words to describe the feeling. He belonged here. The morning he'd woken up and realised what had happened at the card game had been the worst day of his entire life. His head had been pounding and it had taken him a while to surface, blearily wondering what he was doing passed out on a sofa in the library of a private club, but then it had hit him and he'd stumbled straight onto the landing to find the bathroom and vomited his guts out.

He'd literally wanted to kill Edward Croxley. Although he couldn't tell Lily that, couldn't tell her, as he'd dragged himself to her flat, of all the ways he'd genuinely considered to get rid of him. Like pushing him under a bus or a tube train or bashing him on the back of the head with something suitably heavy and then pulverising his brains.

But none of those would have got the shop back.

He'd felt so powerless, like everything was dark. And then he'd got to the bridge and— He cut the thought off. It had needed Lily's ingenuity and cool head to sort it all out. Perhaps that was why God had made women: to get men out of the huge fucking shit they got themselves into. She'd been so amazing, so unbelievably calm, when he'd told her. She'd said that she'd fix it as soon as she got back from New York. She'd change the ticket so she'd be back sooner.

And he didn't know how she'd done it, but she *had* sorted it all out.

He had the best sister on the planet.

Christ, he was going to miss her when she went to New York – he was dreading it really – but they had Skype and FaceTime and it was the job of a lifetime; she could hardly turn it down.

He nursed his coffee, deep in thought. He'd just have to get used to being on his own. Although, maybe he wouldn't be completely on his own. The new girl who had started working in the French restaurant next-door-but-one had been very chatty when he'd called in for his coffee earlier. She'd been taking her own coffee break, had been sitting at the back of the restaurant with her nose buried in a book. She'd jumped up when she'd heard his voice, had mentioned how much she loved Hitchcock, and there was that play on at the Dominion. Maybe he should ask her? She said she'd studied art history too and she had the most amazing French accent.

The key thing was that he needed to see Lily going to New York as an opportunity to develop what he was doing here. He had so many plans for the shop and the stock. He wanted to talk to people in the BBC props department, to meet developers and interior designers who needed original prints for renovations and conversions. There was so much accumulated stuff here that just needed dusting down and sorting out. And he was sure there were a few gems.

A sound at the door made Jack turn around.

A very tall, blocky blond guy had walked in and stopped to check out a print of the Baltic Sea. He was well dressed in sharply creased chinos and what looked distinctly like handmade shoes, looked like he could afford to drop a couple of grand on old maps. Which was exactly what Jack needed this morning after being closed for so long. Although, it had to be said, this guy looked more like a weightlifter or a Viking than a banker. He was thick set, with bright blue eyes set off by a pale blue shirt that strained across his chest and a dark blue blazer. No tie, but then his neck was so big Jack thought he'd have problems finding a tie long enough to fit.

Jack straightened up and smiled. 'Good morning. Nice out there today. We need a bit of sunshine.'

The man turned to him. 'It is.'

'Are you looking for maps? I've got more at the back of the shop.'

'Not really.' The man's accent was public-school but with an Eastern European or Russian inflection. As he spoke, Jack heard Lily's footsteps on the wooden stairs behind him. She came into the shop carrying a huge print of a bird of paradise in a golden cage, the ornate gold frame thick with dust.

'Look, I finally found it – see how strong the colours are? God knows how long it's been up there.' She glanced up and realised Jack wasn't alone in the shop. 'Oh, hello, lovely morning. Can we help you?' Lily leaned the print against the counter and wiped her hands down the front of her dungarees, smiling broadly at the man. She had her hair clipped up, a pencil stuck through her bun.

'Hello, you must be Lily? A friend of mine left something here for me. Edward Croxley? I think you know him?'

Jack looked at the man blankly for a moment. How did he know Lily's name?

Then what he'd actually said and the name Edward Croxley sank in, and he realised who the guy was. The text Croxley had sent. He was the Russian. Jack felt sweat break out down his back. Holy fuck, some days he could be really dense.

This was the Russian guy Lily's friend had said Croxley had been getting the amulets for. The amulets that had been smuggled into the UK along fuck-only-knew what route.

Jack forced himself to smile, said weakly, 'Oh yes …'

Lily interrupted him, her voice hard. She'd paled several shades but her eyes were blazing. 'I'll get it for you. How *is* Mr Croxley?'

'I've no idea. I received a text from him on Saturday afternoon saying I could collect it here.'

Lily's face was flushed as she turned to go into the back room.

As the door at the back of the shop fell closed behind her, the Russian began looking at another print on the wall. Jack shifted from foot to foot, his coffee forgotten. He felt he should say something to fill the awkward silence, but what? There was so much he wanted to say, but this guy was dangerous and he wasn't completely stupid.

He didn't need to worry; the Russian seemed very relaxed. His hands in his trouser pockets, he looked at various prints, at the first editions in the glass display cabinet.

Jack was so focused on the Russian that he almost didn't notice another two men come in. Then, catching their movement out of the corner of his eye, he turned. One was wearing a tweed sports jacket with navy chinos, the other more casual in a grey jacket. But more noticeably, one of them was holding a mobile phone, a wire running to the ear buds in his ears. Jack couldn't hear what they were saying but the one on the phone seemed to be listening intently to whoever was on the other end.

They seemed to be taking a great interest in the Baltic Sea as well.

Jack forced himself to sound relaxed. 'Morning, gentlemen – lovely one isn't it?'

One of the men turned to him and grinned, nodding. 'Certainly is.' He was pure London. Inside, Jack heaved a sigh of relief. He didn't think he could cope with any more members of the Russian mafia arriving this morning. And at least with two other people in the shop, the one they had was less likely to shoot him and Lily dead. Was that what they did? He froze. Maybe it *was* all nerve agents these days. Was this guy leaving some sort of invisible trail as he walked around the shop? *Jesus fucking Christ.*

Jack glanced at the Russian. He was looking at another print, had his broad back to him, his hands still in his pockets.

Behind him, Jack heard the door to the back room open and Lily appeared with a large bright-yellow carrier bag. The contents were bulky.

It took the Russian two steps to get to Lily. The guy had to be at least six seven. She handed him the bag. Jack could see she was fighting an expression of total disgust.

'I think you'll find everything is in there. There's a small jewellery box at the bottom.'

The Russian gave her a flirtatious grin that made Jack's stomach heave. 'Thank you, lovely lady. This is all I need.' Lily just stared at him like he was something on the bottom of her shoe. Something that smelled very, very bad.

He turned to leave but the two men in sports jackets had blocked the door.

'Excuse me …' He held the bag in front of him as if he was intending to pass between them.

'Not so fast there. Sergei Andronov? I'm arresting you on suspicion of—'

Jack hardly caught the rest of the sentence. The Russian moved fast, made to head out the door regardless of who was in his way, and at that exact moment there was a volley of shouts from outside and a swarm of black-uniformed, heavily armed police officers closed in around the door of the shop. Jack had no idea how many there were.

The two guys in the sports jackets had parted and now stood on either side of the Russian. Behind them, one of their colleagues filled the doorway. He was wearing a black crash helmet with the visor down, carrying an assault rifle, and stood poised with it pointed directly at the Russian's chest.

'Armed police, hands away from your body and lie on the floor.'

Holy fucking hell.

The command was shouted rather than said.

Jack glanced at Lily, who had dropped down behind the end of the counter. She glared at him and gestured for him to do the same. Jack had flattened himself against the wall and now slid down, praying they weren't going to open fire.

Just over the top of the counter, he watched as Andronov slowly put the bag on the ground and equally slowly, holding his hands out at his sides, knelt down. He was shaking his head and in the reflection of the open glass Jack could see he was smiling. A moment later Andronov's hands were being secured with plastic handcuffs. Outside the shop, through the window display, Jack could see a white police riot van had drawn up on the pavement, its blue lights flashing. With their weapons still trained on him, the squad indicated Andronov should stand, and then they manoeuvred him into the back of the van. He went easily, like it was all a big joke.

'Can we close up for a few minutes, do you think?' The sports jacket standing closest to the counter raised his eyebrows. He was mid-forties, his hair cropped short, the earbuds connected to his phone still in his ears. 'I'm DS Dave Thornton, this is DC Donal Connell.' He indicated the other guy who had come into the shop with him.

Standing up, steadying herself on the end of the counter, Lily flicked a weak smile at the detective sergeant and said in a small voice, 'Of course. Jack, just put the sign on the door.'

Jack reached for the shop keys from the hook under the till and came out from behind the counter. The van moved off as he pushed the main door closed, turning the key in the lock and flipping the 'gone to lunch, back in an hour' sign over.

Turning around, he looked in disbelief at the two men. 'What the fuck was that?'

DS Thornton smiled at him sympathetically. 'I'm sorry to launch this on you with no warning. We've been watching Sergei Andronov and his boss, Igor Kaprizov, for some time. We know about their smuggling operation, about the amulets and Edward Croxley's involvement. We heard Croxley was trying to sell Andronov a painting. A text was sent telling him to collect it here this morning. What can you tell us about that?'

Lily shrugged and put her hands on each side of her face, as if holding it helped her focus. 'Amulets?' She looked confused. 'What amulets?' Then, as if she'd realised he'd asked a question, 'I'm sorry, I've no idea what Croxley was doing. He's a total toe-rag – he swindled Jack out of our shop in a card game. I've no idea if it would stand up in court – I mean, it *was* a thing when people duelled at dawn – but we didn't have the money to go to solicitors.' Lily took a deep breath and leaned against the counter. 'I'm sorry, I just need a minute.' She closed her eyes tightly as if she was trying to calm down to focus on explaining. When she opened them again she said, 'We had no idea why or what Croxley wanted with the shop, but then he put the keys though my front door on Friday. I came home and there they were on the mat.' She shook her head in disbelief.

'When we came in, it looked like the place had been searched. Then Jack got a text from Croxley on Saturday to say he was to give the man that called in today the bag with the painting in it.' Lily took a ragged breath. 'We didn't look in it. I was too frightened to, to be honest. I'd no idea what he was up to. I just was so grateful to get the shop back.'

'So you didn't look in the parcel you just handed over at all?'

Lily shook her head, a look of panic crossing her face. 'Was that very stupid? It wasn't drugs, was it?'

DS Thornton shook his head. 'Nothing quite like that. Do you sell many original paintings here?'

Lily shook her head. 'None at all – we do antique prints and books. There are lots of bigger shops doing paintings. That's not us. You need know-how and experience to be able to identify proper art.'

'Have you arrested Croxley?' Jack had been keeping quiet until now; he knew it was always better to let Lily do the talking in these types of situations.

DS Thornton turned to look at Jack. 'Unfortunately, he was found dead yesterday just outside Dublin.'

'He fucking deserved that.'

'Jack!' Lily looked at him hard. 'You can't say that.'

'I can. He was a total con man and a thief. You said it yourself. Good riddance, I say. I hope it was long and painful.'

The detective sergeant looked at him, his face unreadable. 'He drowned, actually, under suspicious circumstances.' He paused. 'Who else knew about him getting hold of the shop?'

Lily looked at Jack expectantly. He felt himself blush. 'The other guys in the card game did. I was in school with a couple of them. One guy I didn't know. It was at a club, though – I'm sure they have CCTV.'

'We'll need these men's names.'

'Of course.' Jack nodded.

'So is Croxley really dead?' There was disbelief in Lily's voice.

'I'm afraid so. It's looking a lot like someone killed him and another man on Saturday afternoon.'

'Saturday?' Lily's voice caught. 'Who was the other man?'

'A bloke called Marcus Devine, a pilot. It was his pool Croxley ended up in. We reckon these Russians were involved. We've been watching them for a while.'

'But … are we in any danger? I mean he was arrested here …' Lily's voice trembled.

Jack felt like he was going to be physically sick. He couldn't take much more of this.

'We'll need to question you formally, but you seem to have got caught up in a scam that Croxley was involved in – importing goods illegally into the UK. I believe you bought a box from an auction in Hertfordshire?'

Jack frowned, his face confused. 'What's that got to do with it? It was all old books.'

'Croxley and Andronov have been under surveillance for some time. Croxley has been to auctions all over the home counties, and Andronov seems to be his contact for the goods purchased. Apparently the box you bought contained some valuable antiquities that Croxley was supposed to buy. Sumerian gold amulets. They're almost pure gold and very rare – and very small. I'd guess that's why he needed to get into the shop, to find them.'

'Do you think he found them – that's why he gave the keys back?' Lily shook her head, her eyes wide, then before anyone could answer said, 'But how do you know we're not involved? Are you going to arrest us?' Lily looked at him, fear written all over her face.

'Don't worry, love, we've been after Sergei Andronov and his associates for a long time. We know from their conversations that you aren't involved.'

'Well, thank God for that.'

'It seems Croxley was using your shop as a base briefly for another scam. He was in the process of swindling Marcus Devine and his wife out of a couple of million pounds.'

Lily shook her head in disbelief. Trying to hide her emotion from the police, her mind raced to Vittoria – was she OK? But as worried as she was, she couldn't get rid of a niggling feeling – a feeling that Vittoria must have had something to do with this ...

Chapter 54

STEPHANIE CARSON found the remote control and switched on the evening news. She was exhausted. She'd been cleaning all day, had suddenly realised that the windows were filthy and the skirting boards ... She didn't understand how she hadn't seen the build-up of dust before. And she couldn't wait for the window cleaner or Sally, her own cleaner, to come on Friday – she'd just needed to get it all done now. She shifted uncomfortably on the sofa, the buttons on the top of her elasticated jeans digging into her side.

She'd been so busy that she'd only realised that she hadn't heard from Lily Power, or more importantly Marcus, as she sat down a few moments ago. Marcus usually rang or texted to say goodnight but the last two nights her phone had been silent. And there had been no message all day. It wasn't like him, but she knew he had a lot to do this weekend, that he was seeing his lawyers today. She glanced across the oatmeal sofa at her phone, looking to see if a text had arrived without her hearing it.

Still nothing.

But he'd said he'd be over tonight when he got everything sorted out.

Stephanie wrinkled her face in a scowl, trying to concentrate. She couldn't remember anything these days – what did they say about baby brain? She hoped to God it went away or how would she be able to remember her lines? She pushed her hair out of her face. The last time she'd heard from Marcus had been Saturday morning, hadn't it? Or maybe later, around lunch-time? She couldn't remember a time when he'd left it longer than twenty-four hours without being in touch. Unless he was flying, but even then he'd text to say he'd landed safely.

Stephanie sighed to herself. He knew she worried about him pretty much constantly. About whether he was safe in whatever country he'd landed in, about whether he was eating properly and getting enough sleep. Perhaps it was the insecurity she felt in their relationship, but she did need him to reassure her everything was OK.

Vittoria was very attractive and successful. Very successful. She ran her own business and looked after major stars like that ballerina who was all over the papers. Stephanie couldn't remember her name. Vittoria was everything Marcus needed in a wife – who was to say he wouldn't get fed up with her, Stephanie, and decide it was simpler to make things work at home? Maybe he had days when he regretted their relationship.

Stephanie felt the baby kick and knew she was being paranoid. But perhaps that just came with the territory? She was his mistress and she had constant competition: it was vital she always looked her best when she saw him, that he enjoyed every minute of being with her, because if he didn't, what if he changed his mind?

The baby moved again, like he was reminding her she had it all wrong. Marcus had been shocked at first but then he'd been so overjoyed that she was pregnant, and then, when he'd come to the scan with her and found out their baby was a boy, he'd been absolutely over the moon. He'd bought her jewellery and a new car, they'd gone out together to choose everything for the nursery and he'd organised a decorator. It was all so perfect. Obviously, it would be a whole lot more perfect if Vittoria wasn't in the picture but that would come, Stephanie was sure. He said she was beautiful, that he loved being with her. She was the mother of his son.

And Stephanie knew Vittoria could be very difficult.

Stephanie's attention was suddenly brought back to the screen, to someone's mobile-phone footage of an arrest in Great Russell Street – she'd filmed there as part of a drama series, beside the British Museum and across the road at Senate House. It had been a period thing … She tuned into what the newsreader was saying.

'In what police describe as a major operation, members of a suspected Russian organised crime gang were apprehended this morning in central London. Armed police raided a premises on Great Russell Street in order to apprehend Sergei Andronov, previously an Olympic gold medallist …' A picture flashed onto the screen of an extremely attractive blond man in full ice-hockey gear holding his stick above his head. Stephanie felt her eyebrows lift.

'Andronov's arrest has been linked to a double murder just outside the Irish capital, Dublin, in which British art dealer Edward Croxley and TransGlobal Airways pilot Marcus Devine were found dead in Devine's pool.' The voiceover continued, 'Currently suspended from his job as a senior pilot at the airline over allegations of misconduct, Devine was recently photographed with reality TV star Bellissima Serata at a London nightclub.'

She felt the room swim, nausea rising spontaneously. Marcus was dead? He couldn't be – they had it wrong … How did she not know?

But who would call her? Who would know to tell her?

And Marcus had a pool, and he'd mentioned that name, Croxley – and selling the paintings. That was the whole reason he'd gone back to Dublin.

Stephanie suddenly felt her chest tighten; she was finding it hard to catch her breath, stars dancing in front of her eyes. Then she felt the most enormous pain across her stomach, like someone was ripping her apart. She couldn't focus. *Had they said Marcus was dead, murdered? Had they—?* Another pain split her in two. It was too early for the baby but something was happening. She started to breathe. In through her mouth, out through her nose, just like they'd taught her at antenatal classes. She focused totally on breathing and counting and the tension in her body began to reduce a fraction as she took control. It was too early.

The doorbell cut through her thoughts. Marcus, it had to be Marcus. Heaving herself up, her hand under her bump, supporting the weight, Stephanie headed for the front door. Another wave began to build and she stopped, leaning on the doorframe, bending forward, focused on her breathing, counting. It was all going to be OK. They'd got it wrong, Marcus was here and …

She got the front door open to find two uniformed police officers standing on her doorstep and her knees buckled.

Chapter 55

'WHEN DO YOU think I'll be able to get back into the house?'

The cry of a seagull almost drowned out Vittoria's voice. She'd needed to get out of the hotel, and for the moment couldn't face the office, so she'd driven down to the pier in Dun Laoghaire. Parking outside the National Yacht Club, she'd pulled a bright-red waterproof Helly Hansen jacket that Aidan had lent her out of the back of the car and set off for a walk and a think. She'd just passed the Victorian bandstand when her phone had started to ring in the depths of her pocket.

Detective Inspector Frank Gallagher's name had flashed onto the screen.

In the background she could hear the sounds of a busy office. It sounded like he was walking through it as he answered her question. 'Hopefully in a couple of days. We just need to finish the forensic examination and then we can let you back in.'

Vittoria wondered if that was a stock answer just to keep her happy. But she liked Detective Inspector Gallagher – he was a very straight, very genuine man, and she was sure he wouldn't lie to her. She was pretty sure that he knew she was a no-bullshit type too, and she liked nothing better than a clear answer. The one thing Marcus had never learned was that it was pointless lying to her because she had an incredible memory for detail, not just what he said but the way he said things, and if he'd made an excuse and then forgotten what he'd said, it was asking for trouble. Still, she'd learned a long time ago not to take it to heart. Marcus's failings hadn't been about her: they were all about him.

Vittoria cleared her throat. 'Is there any news?'

The inspector had apparently walked into an office. She heard a door closing and the background noise vanish. The wind had dropped for a moment on the pier and she went to sit down on the granite ledge that ran along the staunch protective wall. It shielded her from the weather and she could hear him better now.

'Some. Where are you?'

'On the pier, why?'

'Can you come up to the station?' He hesitated. 'No, actually, can you stay there for a few minutes? I'll come down to you.'

'Of course. I'll wait for you; I can finish my walk.'

'Great, there are some things we need to talk about.'

*

Vittoria easily spotted Frank Gallagher striding down the pier towards her. He was alone this time, his good-looking sidekick obviously otherwise engaged. She'd been down to the end and lingered for a few moments, looking at the circling seagulls, their cries shrill, at the twin red-and-white-striped chimneys at the entrance to Dublin Port, before turning back to walk along the pier towards land. She could see him now ahead of her, wrapped up in an army-green waterproof jacket, zipped against the wind, the new library building towering above him in the distance like an ocean liner.

'Vittoria, thank you for waiting.'

Vittoria smiled. 'Thank you for coming down to me. I find going into the police station a bit grim, to be honest.'

He smiled ruefully. 'You wouldn't be the only one who thinks that. Do you walk here a lot?'

Vittoria shrugged. 'Sometimes. When Marcus and Aidan are out racing it's fun to watch them. *Danny Boy* has a bright red hull so they're easy to spot.'

Gallagher frowned. 'Terrible tragedy that, Aidan's little brother Danny. He was only in first year. I remember it like it was yesterday.'

Vittoria looked at him, surprised. 'You were in school with them?'

'A few years ahead. I was on the landing behind him when it happened.'

'Marcus told me he tripped and fell?'

Detective Inspector Frank Gallagher's face went hard. 'That's what they all claimed, but I reckon he was pushed. I could hear them goading him from further down the corridor – they were at him like a pack of jackals. I just couldn't get there fast enough.'

'*Mio Dio*, that's awful.' Vittoria felt herself pale. 'I didn't realise.'

Gallagher shook his head, his face sad. Vittoria could see his regret, as if keeping Danny Kelly safe had been his responsibility. His voice caught as he spoke: 'It was a steep flight. He broke his neck.'

Vittoria felt her heart break again. She'd never forget Aidan telling her about it, the crack in his voice, his eyes glistening with tears. 'Aidan said that's why he became a doctor. That Danny died in his arms.'

Gallagher cleared his throat. 'And it's why I joined the guards if I'm honest. I think he blamed Marcus for not intervening and protecting Danny – Marcus was there, at the top of the stairs. They'd been best friends until then, but I remember him crossing the corridor to avoid him afterwards. They must have sorted themselves out, though. Naming the boat after him was a lovely gesture.'

Vittoria kept her mouth shut, remembering Marcus's face as they'd toasted buying the thirty-four-foot yacht and Aidan had proposed renaming it. There was so much unsaid. So much she hadn't understood until now.

'Will we sit?' he asked.

Following Frank Gallagher over to the ledge that ran the full length of the pier, Vittoria put her hands in the pockets of her jacket and sat down. 'Marcus didn't tell me he was there when it happened.'

Gallagher scowled. 'Well, he sure was.'

She cleared her throat. 'But you have news for me?'

'Of sorts. We're working closely with our colleagues in the UK on this case. They've arrested a Sergei Andronov – he's the chief bottle-washer for a Russian multi-millionaire, Igor Kaprizov.' Vittoria frowned, the name sounded vaguely familiar. *Had she read it in the newspaper?* She wasn't sure. Unaware of her thoughts, Frank continued, 'The art world is increasingly becoming a place to launder large sums of cash. Some paintings are bought legitimately and sold on; others are stolen to order and sold on for huge sums. Our colleagues in the UK have been watching Kaprizov since he arrived in London. He's involved in just about everything you can think of – drugs, arms but mainly art. They've been monitoring the movement of antiquities out of the Middle East and keep coming back to him.' He continued, explaining,

'Selling artefacts is a way to raise money for all shades of criminal activity, and with willing buyers it's a busy trade. Anywhere there's a war is vulnerable. At the moment that's Syria. It seems Igor Kaprizov has been receiving and selling art and artefacts for years. He's a clever guy, has all sorts of scams in place to legitimise the stolen stuff. That's where Croxley came in.'

'Do you think these Russians wanted to steal Marcus's paintings?'

'It's a possibility. Had your husband mentioned meeting anyone like this to discuss the collection before?'

'No, not at all.' Vittoria sighed. 'I've been so busy, particularly in the last few months, that actually we've hardly seen each other.'

The inspector didn't answer for a moment, allowing her regret to sit there between them in dignified silence. When he spoke again, he sounded serious. 'Are you on your own today?'

Vittoria frowned. 'Yes, who would I be with? I needed to get out of the hotel and get some air.'

'Perhaps we should go up to your hotel?' He looked unsure.

'If you need to tell me something, just tell me. Here's as good a place as any – there's hardly anyone about.' She grimaced. 'It can't be worse than my husband being murdered in our home, really, can it?'

The inspector cleared his throat. 'You've been through a lot, but I'm afraid there's more. I think we should go back to the hotel.'

'Please just tell me – let's get it over with. Ever since that newspaper article appeared in the *Inquirer*, every day has been a minefield. I'm lucky I haven't ended up in a pool too.'

'OK.' He cleared his throat again. 'You know we have to look at everything in an investigation like this?'

She interrupted him. 'I hope so, and I hope you're investigating me with as much vigour as everything else.'

Inspector Gallagher didn't comment, instead said, 'So I was saying we have to check everything ... Well, we've been looking at Marcus's bank accounts and a very large sum of money was transferred on Thursday of last week to a lady called Stephanie Carson, who lives in London.' He stopped for a moment.

'Go on, Inspector.' Vittoria put her hand on her forehead, running her fingers into her hair. He sounded so concerned. Part of Vittoria wanted to tell him that she already knew, that there had been many Stephanie Carsons ... *But the money was new. What had he done?*

'Our UK colleagues called around to her to have a chat, to find out what her connection was to Marcus, and, well, there's no easy way to put this ... She was heavily pregnant. It must have been the shock, but she went into labour. It was a bit fraught but the UK lads have gathered that the baby is Marcus's and that's why he was transferring money to her. Everyone's fine now but she'll be in hospital for a few days.' Gallagher cleared his throat again. 'Obviously there will have to be a paternity test ...'

'In case she was blackmailing him? Honestly, Inspector, I don't know much about childbirth but I think when you're in labour it's quite hard to keep a fraudulent story going. It all sort of goes out of the window as you hit level-nine pain. Or so my clients tell me.'

'We have to explore all the possibilities.'

'I know, but, Inspector,' Vittoria softened her voice, appreciative of his concern but letting him know that she was under no illusions as to her husband's fidelity, 'my husband was away from home a lot. He liked going out and he was a very attractive man. I have to say I'm not entirely surprised. I'd guess if you checked his phone, you'd have found her name, and you'd have seen that he'd been in touch with her and the tone of any texts.'

Vittoria sighed deeply. In front of her a seal's head bobbed out of the churning waters. He regarded her with inquisitive brown eyes like she was a vaguely interesting exhibit in the zoo. She would love to slip into the water and swim with him. Swimming had always been a vital part of her training and had become even more vital in her rehabilitation. She was weightless and pain free in the water, could dive effortlessly. That was how she wanted to be now. Free of everything. Of the angst and the pain, of the not knowing what was going to happen next. As she watched, the seal vanished beneath the grey water. The wind was coming up, the yachts anchored off the pier wall straining at their chains. *Danny Boy* was over on the marina, safe from autumn storms. She pulled the jacket more closely around her, zipping up the high neck right to her chin.

'How can you tell me all this, Inspector? Shouldn't I be your prime suspect if my husband was having an affair?'

The wind whipped Vittoria's dark hair across her face as she let out a sigh. 'Or perhaps several affairs. Aren't most murders crimes of passion?'

Sitting next to her on the harbour wall, Gallagher turned to look at her. 'Everyone is a suspect in a murder investigation. But we've looked at your mobile-phone records – they tally location, and time-wise, with what you told us. The staff at the hotel remember you – we've taken their statements. You couldn't be in two places at once.' Gallagher rubbed his hand over his chin. 'And everyone we've spoken to has mentioned your insistence on improving the security at the house, and particularly in the pool building. That tends not to be the action of someone about to commit an offence in the same location.' He hesitated. 'And Croxley's neck was broken. He wasn't a big man but unless you grew six inches overnight and are into weight training ...' He trailed off at Vittoria's sharp intake of breath.

'Poor Edward, it's so horrible.'

'I don't think he felt anything. It would have been very quick.'

'And then whoever it was pushed him into the pool to finish the job?'

'So it seems. But what's interesting is that Croxley's DNA is on the sleeve of the jumper you identified as belonging to your husband.'

'Good God, you think Marcus killed him?' She turned to look at him but he was looking out to sea.

He turned back to her. 'We really can't say just yet. It's clear that the same tablets you were prescribed were used to lace the brandy – perhaps Marcus had left them out and Croxley found them when he arrived, or perhaps Croxley researched your history and worked out what you might be taking.'

'I don't think there's any painkiller or sleeping tablet I *haven't* been prescribed.'

Gallagher grimaced. 'The thing is – I think I mentioned it before – Croxley was involved in a previous suspicious death in a swimming pool where drugs were a factor. It was a good few years ago, but our UK colleagues are going to re-examine the case in light of recent events. DNA analysis has come a long way.' He stopped speaking for a moment, as if there was more that he couldn't tell her. The wind began to pick up again as he continued, 'It's a bit of a conundrum. Looking at the times of the phone calls and the time Croxley sent his texts, it seems he was still alive at 3.40, but your phone records show that you called at 3.30.'

'It might not have been Croxley sending the texts.'

'Very true. Perhaps Marcus did kill him first and then sent the texts himself. There's no sign of his fingerprints on Croxley's phone but it ended up in the water somehow.'

Vittoria shook her head. 'It all sounds so crazy, really.'

'I know. Forgive me for saying this – Marcus was a bit of a bollocks, even when we were in school, but he didn't deserve to die like that.'

'You're right. Although, I have to confess I'm having a few difficulties with everything I'm finding out now. It's like he was living two lives.' She sighed. 'There's still no sign of the paintings?'

'None at all, but we'll keep looking.'

'Thank you for telling me, Inspector. I'd rather know – about everything. I don't want to find out what was happening in my husband's life from the press again. Once is enough. And thank you, I know you're working twenty-four seven on this.' She stopped for a moment, biting her lip. 'But what about Aidan? I asked him to check on Marcus and he found them. Does that make him a suspect too? Especially given their past?'

'Aidan Kelly was in the middle of Dublin Bay all day with a crew of five other people who can say categorically that he was with them until late evening. There are about a hundred others who can corroborate that. He didn't even go to the jacks on his own.' Gallagher said it with a degree of relief in his voice. 'It's looking increasingly likely that this Andronov character is involved. With the type of money and influence backing him, we think that he travelled to Dublin on Saturday. His tail lost him in East London that morning somewhere near Bethnal Green. He could easily have been heading to an airport.'

'But City Airport has massive security, CCTV – surely someone would have seen him?'

'It might not have been City. My British colleagues think it's more likely he used a small plane or helicopter and landed at a private airport here. They're checking flight records, but private pilots don't have to file their passenger manifests, just a flight plan. They're supposed to declare the number of passengers they're carrying but then it's up to immigration at our end to follow up.' He scowled. 'The biggest problem right now is that both Andronov and Kaprizov have suddenly acquired diplomatic immunity – Christ knows how. The embassy got in touch with the National Crime Agency after they arrested them.' He shook his head, 'You have to give it to the Russians – they look after their own.'

Vittoria sighed heavily. 'That's a bit of a brick wall, isn't it?'

'Yep, for us and for our UK colleagues, but look it, the investigation is heading in the right direction. There have to be other links in this chain who don't have the benefit of being friends with Putin. And we'll see what this Stephanie Carson has to say about things.' Vittoria pursed her lips, but didn't respond, as he continued, 'There is something else, though. It might make you feel better about the provenance of those paintings – well, at least the one you took to London.'

Vittoria sighed and rubbed her hand across her eyes. She knew Inspector Gallagher had seen the horror on her face when she'd explained where they had come from. 'Go on, tell me.'

'It was a forgery. Well, the Pissarro that you gave Croxley was. The team in London got Sotheby's to look at it. They've had some big problems with fakes and have their own forensic guy, an American who works with the FBI, apparently.' He paused. 'So they said the painting was extremely good, the paint was even cracking in the right direction – apparently paint from different periods and parts of the world cracks differently, and that's something these forgers can do – but it contained traces of some suspect pigments.' He paused again and pulled a notebook from the pocket of his jacket. He flipped it open, checking his facts. 'They said Hansa and arylide yellows were only available after 1910. So Pissarro would have had some problems finding it in 1897 when he was supposed to have painted your picture.'

'My God, do you think Croxley guessed when he saw the others, and that's why Marcus killed him?'

'Whoever was involved, that's a possibility. Your husband needed to sell them and he couldn't risk their real origins being revealed. Or perhaps he realised he'd been drugged and thought Croxley intended to steal them. Either way, Marcus had them commissioned. Apparently someone in Sotheby's was having a gossip with a woman who they recommend to museums and collectors, and it looks like she did all of them. She's based in Scotland but the art world is incredibly small. It's quite normal to get copies done for display – she does them for museums and private collectors, and she thought that's what Marcus wanted them for so she used the wrong yellow. He omitted to mention to her that he was planning to sell them as originals.'

Chapter 56

No. 42'S FLAGSHIP STORE on Fifth Avenue was closing to the public when Lily emerged from her meeting with Marianne Omotoso in the conference room on the tenth floor, the October evening sun slanting into the upper windows. Downstairs, the staff were preparing for the invitation-only evening, a celebration of the Freedom line with the announcement of their new bespoke designs that would be reflected in limited-edition suites available to retail.

Bespoke designs that Lily was creating.

Lily's mouth was dry with nerves but Marianne had been full of praise for her sketches and prototypes, insisted, even though she'd only just started, that she say a few words to open their event this evening. They'd been going through Marianne's presentation for most of the afternoon, ensuring it ran perfectly. Tonight was the pinnacle of some incredible marketing activity that included – Lily could still hardly believe that this idea had become part of it all – the release of a flock of white homing pigeons from the Statue of Liberty to fly back to the store. And Oli Lennon himself would be arriving in his signature silver Rolls-Royce to charm his very best customers. Lily had had several Skype chats with him, had been surprised at how friendly and normal he seemed. She hadn't known what to expect but had been completely wowed by the story of the little boy who had grown up beside the Kimberly diamond mine on the Northern Cape and gone on to build one of the most prestigious brands in the world.

Lily felt her stomach turn with a potent blend of anxiety and anticipation as she waited for the lift. Quite apart from the excitement of Oli Lennon actually being there, and all the A-listers arriving downstairs, her drawings would be projected onto a huge screen at the end of the first floor as Marianne made each of the announcements about the new ranges. It was a total cliché but working for No. 42 was literally a dream come true. The hours were incredibly long, the senior staff demanding and tempestuous, but she'd settled in fast and she was loving every minute of it.

But it wasn't just the excitement of the presentation making her nervous. Tonight Lily knew she'd see Vittoria for the first time since Sergei Andronov had been arrested in the shop and they'd discovered that Edward Croxley, the man she'd once wished to die, had literally met the deep end in Vittoria's swimming pool.

With her husband Marcus.

Lily felt fear prickle down her spine. She didn't know how involved Vittoria may or may not have been, and she didn't want to know. The moment she'd heard about the double tragedy, Lily had closed her ears *and* her mind. She'd made a point of not reading the papers or watching the news, had kept off social media.

Some things she really didn't need to know.

The Irish police and the British officers who had arrested Andronov were sure he was involved and they were the experts.

But whatever had happened that day, Lily needed to thank Vittoria. They had the shop back because of her, and Jack had already come up with some clever ideas to entice more casual customers in, as well as developing their specialist business. Almost losing it had made him appreciate how much he loved it. And with the shop to focus on, and the girl from the French restaurant next-door-but-one popping in every two minutes, her moving had been less of an issue. Lily still crossed her fingers whenever she thought about it, but he seemed to have come completely out of the depression that had taken him to Waterloo Bridge and the dark waters of the Thames.

Even George the one-eyed cat seemed happier. He'd never liked her flatmates' music, and when Jack had moved back into the apartment above the shop, George had gone back to his spot beside the till where he could spend most of the day curled up asleep – so still that many customers thought he was stuffed. At night he climbed out of the kitchen window at the very top of the building and vanished among the pitched roofs and chimney-pots of Great Russell Street to meet his feline friends and raid the bins behind La Lidoire, the French restaurant where the lovely Alessia, as Jack called her, worked.

Knowing Jack was happy was just so important to Lily that she couldn't explain it. It meant that she was able to relax and enjoy every waking minute here without any worries. She had to kick herself every time she got out of bed – and she still felt like she was on holiday every day, the sounds and the scents of the city strange and wonderful. She felt alive in New York, as if she was poised on the edge of something exciting. And at No. 42 they were constantly innovating – it was the perfect place for her to develop her skills and really make her mark.

As the lift – *elevator*, Lily corrected herself – arrived, she glanced in its mirrored wall and poked a loose strand of red hair back into her lucky silver filigree clip; with her hair up she looked *very* corporate. She was wearing a black crêpe pencil dress and wedge sling-backs that made her feel almost grown up – and about ten years older – but tonight she needed to look the part. The black fabric showed off the prototype diamond birdcage brooch pinned to her shoulder, the door open, a jewelled bird of paradise rising from its prison. It was the key piece in the collection that Marianne would be revealing later. The fashion magazines and New York press were all there, as well as some of No. 42's most valued clients. Tonight was all about making the right impression.

As the elevator doors opened on the second floor, Lily could hear the chatter rising from below, blending with the sounds of classical music from the string quartet located at the base of the stairs. She could have come out on the ground floor but she wanted a chance to see who had arrived already, and the best place to do that was from the top of the Art Deco staircase that swept down to the main sales floor.

Lily's shoes were silent on the soft carpet as she reached the top of the stairs and looked down. Uniformed staff were passing around glasses of champagne balanced on silver salvers, guests mingling and chatting. The store was certainly impressive, glittering display cases reflecting the equally glittering accessories of women who looked like they had just stepped off the red carpet at the Oscars. Many of them probably had. Around them men in dark suits filled the gaps.

Biting her lip, unable to resist a grin, Lily took in the crowd. In a few minutes they would be listening to her speak, talking about her caged-bird range, inspired by the old-world prints she loved so much. It was a metaphor for so many elements of modern life that connected with No. 42's long-term goals. Marianne would be going on to detail No. 42's campaign for using ethically sourced stones and for sustainability; they were proactively reducing the company's global environmental impact in ways that made Lily feel proud to be associated with the brand. It wasn't just about luxury: it was about taking real corporate responsibility, and Lily had been made to feel like an important cog in that machine from the moment she'd arrived.

Leaning over the balustrade, Lily scanned the crowd below her, one eye on the flow of guests filtering through the ring of security around the front door. She recognised so many faces from film and TV, but then she saw another face she recognised.

Lily's heart jumped as she saw Vittoria walk in, dressed in a figure-hugging navy silk dress with flowing sleeves, a good-looking man close beside her, his hand loosely on her waist. Lily watched as she accepted a glass of champagne and scanned the room. The man with her whispered something in her ear, smiling. Now, who was he? Puzzled, Lily watched them cross the room, taking in the crowd and the projected displays. Their body language was casual but intimate.

As if she could feel Lily's gaze on her, Vittoria turned and looked up the staircase. Her smile was broad and warm as their eyes met. Vittoria casually weaved through the crowd, crossing to the bottom of the stairs, apparently listening to the string quartet. Lily began to head down.

'It's so lovely to see you.' Lily air-kissed her on each cheek.

Vittoria smiled. 'You look amazing, very … professional.' They both laughed. The last time they had met on the park bench in Russell Square, Lily had been wearing denim overalls and Doc Martens.

'Thank you, I had to step up my game a bit.'

'It suits you – oh, this is Aidan.'

Vittoria blushed slightly and half-turned to introduce her friend. Lily held out her hand. His handshake was warm and genuine.

'Great to meet you. Vittoria told me about your wonderful job. Congratulations.'

Lily smiled. His accent was Irish. He was older than Vittoria and *very* attractive.

'Thank you so much. Do you work together?'

Aidan shook his head. 'No, I'm a bone man, backs and necks mainly, lots of whiplash. I fix the outside; she fixes the inside.' He grinned. 'Why don't I let you ladies catch up while I do some shopping? I'd love to have a chat with you before I go, though, Lily – I'm very interested in diamonds.' He picked up a glass of champagne from a platter and wandered off towards a case of men's watches, attracting glances from several of the women he passed.

Lily tuned to Vittoria, her eyebrows raised. 'He's rather lovely. Those blue eyes. Is he available?'

'I'm afraid not. He's got his hands full at the moment.' Vittoria smiled. 'But tell me, how are you getting on? All settled?' Vittoria took a sip of her champagne, her dark hair gleaming in the light from the chandelier above them.

Lily kept her voice low, shaking her head as if she still didn't believe it herself. 'It's been amazing. I haven't had a second to stop. They found me somewhere to live and I'm loving the design work. I'm working on a whole new range of little birdcages.' She reached up to touch her brooch.

'It's absolutely beautiful.'

Lily smiled. 'You'll see more in the presentation later.'

Vittoria's eyes were warm. 'I'm so pleased. Really. And how's Jack?'

Lily's eyes met Vittoria's for a moment and she felt them fill with tears. Lily caught them on the back of her finger. She couldn't get emotional now – she had to talk to at least a hundred of New York's elite in a few moments. 'He's back living above the shop, and he's doing great. He was going to come tonight but we decided Christmas would be better. I really—'

Vittoria held up her hand. 'Don't say it. That was the deal. You helped me and I helped you.'

Lily faltered, then keeping her voice low said, 'But your husband? What happened?'

Vittoria put her hand soothingly on Lily's arm. 'We don't know exactly what happened, the investigation is only getting going, really, but it looks like he was trying to double cross Croxley. He might have got in too deep with the wrong people. Really, trust me, it's not something you need to think about for one moment.'

Lily bit her lip. She didn't know if she'd ever get a chance to tell Vittoria the dramas that had unfolded at their end, about Sergei Andronov getting arrested and them all having to give statements. One thing was sure, Edward Croxley had definitely got in with the wrong people.

'Vittoria! How lovely, what are you doing here?'

Lily looked up sharply to see who had recognised Vittoria, relaxing a moment later as Vittoria turned and, smiling, embraced a beautiful blonde woman, her hair long and loose around her shoulders. She was even tinier than Vittoria; she looked so delicate she might break.

'Yana, what on earth are you doing here? I thought you were still in London?'

The woman called Yana gave Vittoria another hug – they obviously knew each other well. Turning to Lily, Vittoria introduced them. 'This is Yana. She's the prima ballerina with the Russian National Ballet, who is *supposed* to be working hard in Covent Garden at the moment.' Vittoria tried to look stern.

'Tsk, all work and no play. I've only come for two days. I love No. 42. Some invitations you *cannot* resist.' Yana turned to Lily. 'Vittoria saved my life. She is very quiet but without her I would be dust. *Poof.*' Vittoria blushed as she continued, 'She is the reason I am still dancing.' She turned to look behind her. 'Now, you must meet my uncle, Vittoria, he's been asking so much about you. One moment.'

Yana slipped through the crowd to a man in his sixties who was leaning over one of the glass display cases, apparently discussing a purchase with the sales assistant. He had some sort of earpiece wired to the inside of his jacket and seemed to be talking to someone through it at the same time. Distinctly overweight and balding, he was wearing a pale grey suit and appeared to be negotiating hard. As she slipped her arm through his, he turned to Yana immediately, his dark bushy eyebrows raised. He pointed to the display case but Yana shook her head and gestured for him to follow her. Shrugging to the assistant, he headed their way.

'Vittoria Devine, this is my wonderful Uncle Igor.'

As he held out a meaty hand, Lily saw Vittoria pale slightly, but she took it in a firm handshake.

'I've been hearing a lot about you, Ms Devine.' His English was heavily accented, but he bowed slightly as he spoke. 'I have heard you are a very talented lady with interesting skills. You have been busy recently, I know. But you have done wonderful things for my Yana, and for that I am forever indebted to you.'

Vittoria smiled. 'Yana did it all herself – she's incredibly talented: she just need a little direction.'

'You are too modest, Ms Devine. It is good that we meet tonight, though. I wanted to discuss a matter with you.' He didn't wait for her to reply. 'I would like you to join my organisation. I think a lady of your capabilities would be very welcome. You must join us, I think?' Then, as if by way of explanation, 'I have a clinic in Harley Street. I want you to lead the team that operates from there.'

Vittoria opened her mouth to speak. But at the front of the room Marianne Omotoso had appeared.

Lily felt her nerves surge. Oli Lennon was due to arrive in time for their presentation: he must be on his way. 'I'm so sorry, I need to leave you for a moment. Lovely to meet you Yana and Mr—?'

'Kaprizov ... Igor Kaprizov.'

Chapter 57

A T THE TOP of the room, Marianne Omotoso tapped the mic, drawing the guests' attention. Behind her, the No. 42 logo filled the entire wall.

But Vittoria wasn't focusing on the presentation. The moment Yana's uncle had introduced himself, Vittoria had felt her head spin. A smile fixed on her face, it was taking her a moment to centre herself. She glanced quickly at Lily; had his name registered with her too?

Had the police mentioned it to her? Vittoria knew Sergei Andronov had been arrested in Lily and Jack's shop, but how much did she know of his associates and their activities?

But Lily didn't seem to have heard their exchange. She was looking over his shoulder to the end of the showroom, her mind obviously fully on her presentation. Vittoria would have crossed herself if she'd been religious.

Igor Kaprizov, the man Detective Inspector Frank Gallagher had told her was Sergei Andronov's boss, the man Croxley had been going to sell her pictures to, *was Yana's uncle*. How had she not known about Yana's family connections?

Vittoria mentally shook her head. They had different surnames, so how could she? Yet Kaprizov had sounded vaguely familiar when DI Gallagher had mentioned him – Yana must have spoken of him in one of their early sessions.

But more importantly, how long had Kaprizov known about her? Had Croxley told him the name of the owner of the painting and explained why the sale needed to be private? Had he immediately made the connection with his niece? Her name had been all over the paper, for Christ's sake: she was the woman who had saved Yana from anorexia. And that story had been right across the page from Marcus's midnight activities in The Velvet Club. Kaprizov was a clever man, a clever and ruthless man. He hadn't got to be a billionaire by accident.

Lily interrupted Vittoria's tumbling thoughts. 'Please excuse me – I'll see you afterwards, I hope?' Not giving them time to answer, smiling, Lily slipped off into the crowd.

'So, Vittoria …' Kaprizov turned to her, his dark eyes penetrating, his smile fixed. And in that moment Vittoria knew for sure that he knew.

Her stomach lurched but Vittoria focused on keeping her face impassive. She raised her eyebrows and smiled. 'Igor—'

Before she could continue, her phone began to ring in her handbag.

'Oh, excuse me.' Pulling it out, Vittoria looked at the number: unknown. Right now, it didn't matter who it was – it could be an insurance salesman for all she cared – she just needed a few minutes to think. Whoever was calling her had just become her number-one priority. 'I'm so sorry – I'm on call. It must be a client. I'd better take it.'

Smiling deliberately ruefully, she turned her back on the crowd and, answering, headed towards a quiet corner at the back of the showroom. She'd get rid of the caller and pretend to be engrossed in a conversation on the phone. It would give her a few valuable moments to figure out what the hell she was going to do.

'Hello, Vittoria, how is New York?' The man's voice was unfamiliar, his Northern Irish accent strong. How did he know she was in New York? Had the office told him? Ruby hadn't texted to say anyone would be calling her.

'Lovely, thank you. How can I help you?'

'We were very sorry to hear about your recent tragedy.' The way he said it made the hairs on Vittoria's neck stand up.

And in that moment, she knew exactly who she was talking to.

'Thank you, that's very kind.' She needed to play for time, to shake off the shock and get her mind working. *It was all happening too fast.* A black hole opened up in her stomach. *Merda.* Glancing up, she could see Igor looking around at her. He smiled. *Holy Christ.*

'We believe you've come into some money recently?'

'And what has that got to do with you exactly?'

'I hope you're not spending it all in No. 42, Vittoria. You owe us. You put one of our men in an extremely awkward position.'

Vittoria felt her blood chill. 'I settled with you in full. And I gave him plenty of time to get out of the house. I texted to cancel everything. Why didn't he pick up the message? Why did he come when the job was off?'

'You pushed the alarm button, Vittoria. You could have let him go and wiped the tapes. It would have been our little secret.'

Her mind flashed back. The man had been so angry that Marcus wasn't there, that the plan had changed and he hadn't been told. She'd been terrified he was going to attack her. She kept her voice low. 'I had *cancelled* the job. I yelled at him to get out, and I gave him a head start.'

'He doesn't like running. It's not his style.'

It wasn't hers either.

'Are you threatening me?'

'We don't threaten, Vittoria. Let's just say we need to increase your bill to compensate our man for his distress.'

Distress? *She could tell him all about distress.*

'And it'll end there, will it?' Vittoria's tone was full of contempt. *Like hell it would.* If she paid, this would be just the start. She knew how these people worked. Her home town was run by the mafia. The mayor ate in her father's restaurant. She knew exactly how they operated.

She glanced again at Igor, thinking fast.

How would Aidan feel about working in London? Could she persuade him, say she needed to get away from the house, from everything associated with Marcus, make a new start? Vittoria could hear her heart beating hard, drowning out the sounds of the room. It would mean Aidan leaving his boat, the memory of his brother – unless he could move it to somewhere close to London? There had to be people who lived in London who sailed – the River Thames ran through the city. *Maybe they could keep Alcantara as a holiday house?*

She took a deep breath, her voice hard. 'You don't know what you're dealing with.'

'Oh, I think we do, Vittoria. We've been keeping our eye on you.'

'Really? So you'll know all about my close association with Igor Kaprizov then?' There was a pause. She filled it. 'I'd look him up before you go any further.'

'But we've got the paintings, Vittoria—'

Perhaps Kaprizov's name didn't mean anything to him. Yet. She cut him off. 'So sell them. They were stolen by whoever murdered my husband and Edward Croxley.' *How had they found the paintings? Had they been watching the house the whole time?*

Vittoria didn't wait for his reply. He'd know as soon as he checked out Kaprizov that he needed to back off. She ended the call.

Her back to the room, she closed her eyes and took a deep breath, thinking fast. Vital to her next move was that Kaprizov would never find out that the pictures were forgeries. She couldn't imagine he'd be very impressed that Croxley, and, by association, she, was trying to sell him fakes.

Vittoria's heart began to speed up, but she deliberately tried to calm herself. *There was no reason why he should find out.* The only people who knew were law enforcement, and she couldn't imagine that he'd be in conversation with the likes of DI Frank Gallagher anytime soon. It would all be fine. Eileen the copyist had thought Marcus had commissioned the paintings. She, Vittoria, had known nothing of their origins. *It would all be fine.* She needed to calm down and focus.

She had no idea what Kaprizov had in mind for her, was quite sure his Harley Street Clinic was a front for something, but she had to give it a try. She had no choice, and if the man who she'd hired to kill Marcus under the auspices of a break-in was planning to blackmail her, then she needed protection. Protection at a level that only someone of Kaprizov's stature could offer.

This was all Marcus's fault. His affair with Stephanie Carson had been the last straw, and that was even before Vittoria had found out Stephanie was pregnant. The first, genuine, break-in had given her the idea to organise a second, more violent one, and then Marcus hadn't come home and it had all gone wrong. Vittoria closed her eyes, pushing away the memory of the door opening, of the gun. She'd genuinely feared for her life. Getting the paintings commissioned and 'finding' them accidentally to invalidate the prenup had seemed *so* much easier after that, and had the added benefit of Marcus having to explain their origins to the press.

But then she'd met Lily and realised she could put the paintings to a much more practical use …

Poor Aidan, would he come to London? He'd loved her since the night their eyes had met at that party. He'd looked across the room at her and she'd just known. She could still hear Marcus's voice in her ear as they'd arrived. They'd literally walked in the front door and Aidan had appeared from the kitchen, two glasses in his hand. *'Jesus, why did nobody tell me bloody Kelly was going to be here. Don't go near him. He's full of bullshit lies. I was nowhere near his brother when he had that accident.'*

Aidan had been everywhere she'd looked after that, every time she turned she caught him looking at her out of the corner of her eye. She'd had to get out, had seen Marcus flirting with some girl and told him she wanted to go home, making even more of it in the car, like it was his fault they were leaving. And then he'd taken that bend too fast …

She should have left him then, as soon as she'd recovered, but Aidan had been engaged to be married the following year, and by the time she was able to think straight, Marcus had proposed. She'd needed some sort of security; her whole life was upside down. And how was she to know that Aidan would break it off with his fiancée? Christ what a mess.

Vittoria pushed her hair behind her ear, still only half-aware of the room. Putting her phone in her bag, she turned and realised Lily's part of the presentation was about to begin. She scanned the room, searching for Aidan. He was looking for her too, smiled at her as their eyes met.

He loved her.

She knew he loved her.

He'd do anything for her. He'd move to London if she wanted him to, if she needed him to. And she did. She needed Igor Kaprizov now.

Vittoria headed back towards Yana and her uncle as Lily stepped up beside the elegant woman on the stage and a round of applause erupted across the room.

Kaprizov turned to her. 'Everything OK, Vittoria?'

'Of course. Everything's fine.'

'Good. And there's no need to be concerned. I, too, am keeping my eyes on you.'

THE END

Acknowledgements

No book comes together without an army behind it and I'm absolutely thrilled to now be working with Corvus, Atlantic and their award-winning team. This book is a step in a new direction – Cat Connolly's busy training with the ERU, so I'm giving her some time to get into her new role, which gives you a chance to meet some of the other characters in her world.

Huge thanks to Sara O'Keeffe and Poppy Mostyn-Owen, my editors at Corvus, plus the PR and marketing team in the UK, and the Gill Hess team in Ireland, for all their support enthusiasm and excitement about Vittoria and Lily's story. Without Simon Trewin, my awesome multi-talented agent, there would be no books, and I wouldn't be able to do what I love the most – to write. Thank you, Simon, for everything.

When I stay in London, my absolute favourite hotel is The Bloomsbury, part of the fabulous Irish owned Doyle Collection (together with the wonderful River Lee Hotel, where I stay whenever I visit Cork, and the glorious Westbury in Dublin). Everything about the staff, the service and the ambiance is perfect, I cannot recommend it highly enough, but obviously The Bloomsbury are very select in their clientele and wouldn't ever have guests like Vittoria – which is why she's staying at The Hogarth Hotel, where anything can happen...

Last but biggest thanks go to you, my reader – thank you for getting this far, I hope you've enjoyed the ride and are as excited as I am about where we might go next. But that's for book five...

Read on for an extract from

THE

DARK

ROOM

Prologue

ALFIE'S HAND SHOOK as he slipped the letter into the mouth of the postbox, his bitten nails black against the cream of the envelope. He hesitated, holding it on the cold cast-iron lip, glancing behind him, checking the road again. The traffic was almost stationary, lights dazzling. He looked in the opposite direction, to the column of blazing red tail-lights.

Safe.

For now.

Above him, the ornate clock on the station tower clicked on another minute.

The letter was thick, his spidery handwriting spread over many more sheets than he'd expected. Once he'd made up his mind and he'd begun, the whole story had come out with detail he'd thought he'd forgotten. The smell of the car, the heat of the sun as they'd driven down from Dublin. The laughter. The roads had been so bad, winding and narrow, the tarmac potholed and loose. And no signposts; he didn't know how tourists found their way around the country at all.

It was important to get the story right. Exactly right. This could be his only chance. Things would spiral as soon as it was received. And everything would change.

He'd ended up writing the last page in cramped letters, the ink beginning to fade as he squeezed his initials into the corner.

A. B.

Alfie Bows.

It wasn't his name, but that's what they called him on the streets, and it had become part of him. Like the violin he was named after, held firmly now under his arm.

Still holding the letter poised to drop, he lifted his other hand, the carrier bag handle looped securely around his wrist, and shook back the tattered sleeve of his tweed overcoat. He looked at the illuminated dial of his watch, at the minutes flicking past. He didn't know when the letter would arrive – Frank in the hostel had only had a second-class stamp and he'd missed the post today – but it would get there eventually.

And when it did, they'd know the whole story.

They'd know what had happened.

Would they believe him? He wasn't sure. He was invisible now, his voice silent, like a whisper in the night. Not like before, when he was younger. He'd been someone then, had been loud and popular and laughing with the others; he'd partied hard but aced his degree, had had a glittering career ahead of him. That's what they'd been celebrating. A weekend away after the results, their last summer of freedom before the real work started and life began.

And then ...

In that one moment, everything had changed.

It was trying to get it all out of his head that had always been the problem, to switch off his imagination. Getting away, becoming someone else, had been the only way he could cope. But it was still there, every day. Like the dull incessant ticking of a clock in the background of his life. He didn't think he'd ever be free.

It had all come roaring back that night, all the alarms ringing together, like white water, filling his ears, choking, drowning him in the memories, suffocating him.

It had only been a week ago, but it felt like a lifetime. Longer than a lifetime. Before, he'd looked forward to what life offered; afterwards he'd lived day by day. Now it was hour by hour.

He'd had always thought of it as 'his' car park; he was the oldest one who camped there, had been there the longest. He didn't know why he kept going back. There were better places, but Alfie knew he liked the isolation, liked the fact that there were no security cameras, that he was usually alone. He was like a rat, he had familiar runs. Even if they weren't ideal, he knew them – what did they say, 'better the devil you know'?

He wasn't sure about that one.

Alfie had been shocked when he'd seen him swinging out of the cab of the lorry, his face illuminated by the interior lights. The devil himself. He'd had a heavy torch in his hand, and perhaps sensing movement in the darkness beside the bins, had swung the beam around on Alfie just as he'd started to pull his head back into his tent.

His muttered 'What the fuck ...?' had told Alfie he'd been recognised too.

Perhaps he hadn't changed that much.

His hand still on the edge of the postbox, Alfie smiled sadly to himself; normally the long hair and the dirt, the odd assortment of clothes, was a disguise. But not now. Maybe the recent graduate with his rugby jersey, the stiff white collar turned up, hadn't really changed that much, despite what life had thrown at him.

The torch had clicked off as another truck pulled into the yard, Nemo Freight emblazoned on its side. Alfie had a good idea what was going on, why they were here, but he didn't want to know any details. Crawling back inside his tent, he'd pulled his violin to him, buried himself into the furthest corner so he could feel the wall against his back. Shrinking down into all his layers – the sleeping bags with the broken zips, the torn tweed coat he wore now – he had rocked silently, sick with fear.

He'd been seen.

He'd got so used to not being seen – even when he was playing outside a Tube station people heard him, but they didn't *see* him. Now he'd been seen – and worse, recognised. And not by just anybody. By the one person who had every reason to want him to stay quiet, to silence him. He'd been quiet; he'd slipped into obscurity, getting by, not talking to anyone, keeping his story to himself. Until he'd met Hunter, and then it had started to change. He hadn't planned to tell anyone anything – ever – but Hunter was interested. He wanted to know what life was like on the streets, whether Alfie had people out there somewhere. He'd looked out for him, bought him the watch.

But why. Always why.

That was the question he wouldn't answer. Why.

And then Hunter's TV crew had arrived with their cameras and mics and questions in the car park. Alfie cringed again at the timing of it all. Why had it had to happen like that? As they were unloading their equipment, another Nemo Freight truck had pulled into the car park, this time turning and pulling out again just as quickly.

And Alfie had known he was in danger.

The driver had cleared out so fast he knew a message would

go back. It wasn't how it looked, but would he have time to explain?

Maybe he'd got paranoid living on the streets but this time he didn't think he was being alarmist.

He'd been found, and he'd been seen speaking to the documentary crew. Something was going to happen. He could see it in the shadows, feel it in the air. And whatever happened next, Hunter had been good to him, he owed him the truth.

The rain was getting heavier now, falling like a gossamer curtain illuminated by the street lights. Alfie took another look at the envelope and caught his breath as he dropped it into the box.

His violin under his arm, he pulled the carrier bag to himself protectively. He shivered. He'd got a new woolly hat when he'd called in to see if they had a stamp at the hostel, and a pair of fingerless gloves. They helped a bit, but Alfie knew he wouldn't feel warm again until it all came out. He'd been cold with fear from the moment that torch beam had fallen on him, like a spotlight centre stage.

But he wanted his voice heard – whatever happened, he wanted them to know the truth. It wasn't pretty. It was dark and dirty and had changed the entire course of his life – Christ, the number of times he'd wished he'd gone home that weekend instead of chasing a high. But there had been the promise of booze, of lines, of a country house by the sea and a long hot weekend. They'd had everything.

And then they'd had nothing.

In the road beside him, the traffic began to roll forward again. Alfie looked over his shoulder. He was sure he'd been followed before, but he'd been careful this time.

It had taken him all day to write the letter. But it was done now. All of it. And whatever happened they'd know; they'd have to hear him now.